Praise for HOTEL HONOLULU

"As always, Mr. Theroux writes with both energy and grace . . . His stylistic brilliance, his knack for absurdist, targeted entertainment, and his extraordinary ear for a brimming basket of idioms make him one of the most impressive living American writers . . . Theroux's cleverness is inexhaustible."
—Richard Bernstein, *New York Times*

"Compelling reading . . . an intriguing and rewarding expedition into the mind, method, and motives of a seasoned storyteller."
—Gregory Lindenberg, *Chicago Sun-Times*

"Highly entertaining . . . a colorful assortment of good short yarns set in an exotic locale, [by] one of America's most ingenious and prolific writers." **—Judith Wynn, *Boston Herald***

"Good, racy entertainment." **—Michael Harris, *Los Angeles Tim***

"A brilliantly written book, beautifully imagined . . . by turns grisly, and hilarious." **—Eve Zibart, *Book Page***

"Funny, ramshackle . . . Like Hawaii itself, the book pulls u its slightly goofy allure — it's one of Theroux's sunniest w
—John Powers, *1*

"Few capture the essence of a setting as sensitively as Paul [He] is not only a trenchant observer of humankind blessed with limitless imagination and a powerful sense
**—Gail Cooke, *Arizona* **

"An adroitly crafted work of vigorous description, complex pathos, and ironic humor." **—*Booklist*, starred review**

"Seedy, venal, mesmerising—and that's just the hotel owner. Paul Theroux builds a multi-layered portrait of modern America in *Hotel Honolulu* . . . So do yourself a favour: check in."
—Robert MacFarlane, *Observer* (London)

"*Hotel Honolulu* is part *Decameron*, part *Ship of Fools*, and perhaps also part *Satyricon*." **—Sven Birkerts, *New York Times Book Review***

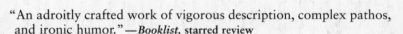

HOTEL HONOLULU

Paul Theroux

A MARINER BOOK
HOUGHTON MIFFLIN COMPANY
BOSTON · NEW YORK

FIRST MARINER BOOKS EDITION 2002

Copyright © 2001 by Paul Theroux
All rights reserved

Visit our Web site: www.houghtonmifflinbooks.com.

Library of Congress Cataloging-in-Publication Data
Theroux, Paul.
Hotel Honolulu / Paul Theroux.
p.   cm.
ISBN 0-618-09501-2
ISBN 0-618-21915-3 (pbk.)
1. Waikiki (Honolulu, Hawaii)—Fiction.
2. Hotelkeepers—Fiction. 3. Hotels—Fiction.
I. Title.
PS3570.H4 H68 2001
813'.54—dc21   00-054125

Printed in the United States of America

Book design by Robert Overholtzer

QUM 10 9 8 7

HOTEL
HONOLULU

1

Paradise Lost

NOTHING TO ME is so erotic as a hotel room, and therefore so penetrated with life and death. Buddy Hamstra offered me a hotel job in Honolulu and laughed at my accepting it so quickly. I had been trying to begin a new life, as people do when they flee to distant places. Hawaii was paradise with heavy traffic. I met Sweetie in the hotel, where she was also working. One day when we were alone on the fourth floor I asked, "Do you want to make love?" and she said, "Part of me does." Why smile? At last we did it, then often, and always in the same vacant guest room, 409. Sweetie got pregnant, our daughter was born. So, within a year of arriving, I had my new life, and as the writer said after the crack-up, I found new things to care about. I was resident manager of the Hotel Honolulu, eighty rooms nibbled by rats.

Buddy, the hotel's owner, said, "We're multistory."

I liked the word and the way he made it *multi-eye*.

The rooms were small, the elevator was narrow, the lobby was tiny, the bar was just a nook.

"Not small," Buddy said. "Yerpeen."

I had gotten to these green mute islands, humbled and broke again, my brain blocked, feeling superfluous, out of the writing business, and trying to start all over at the age of forty-nine. A friend of mine recommended me to Buddy Hamstra. I applied for this job. It wasn't for material; it was the money. I needed work.

"My manager's a typical local howlie — a reetard," Buddy said. "Fondles the help. Always cockroaching booze. Sniffs around the guest rooms."

"That's not good," I said.

"And this week he stepped on his dick."

"Not good at all."

"He needs therrpy," Buddy said. "He's got lots of baggage."

"Maybe that's what he likes about the hotel — that he has a place to put it."

Buddy sucked his teeth and said, "That's kind of funny."

The idea of rented bedrooms attracted me. Shared by so many dreaming strangers, every room was vibrant with their secrets, like furious dust in a sunbeam, their night sweats, the stammering echoes of their voices and horizontal fantasies; and certain ambiguous odors, the left-behind atoms and the residue of all the people who had ever stayed in it. The hotel bedroom is more than a symbol of intimacy; it is intimacy's very shrine, scattered with the essential paraphernalia and familiar fetish objects of its rituals. Assigning people to such rooms, I believed I was able to influence their lives.

Buddy Hamstra was a big, blaspheming, doggy-eyed man in drooping shorts, a wheezy smoker and heavy drinker. His nickname was "Tuna." He was most people's nightmare, a reckless millionaire with the values of a delinquent and a barklike laugh. He liked saying, "I'm a crude sumbitch." He was from the mainland — Sweetwater, Nevada. But he pretended to be worse than he was. He had the sort of devilish gaze that showed a mind in motion.

"What's yours, drink or weed?"

We had met in his hotel bar. He had a cocktail in one hand and a cigarette in the other.

"I got some killer buds," he said.

"Beer for me."

We talked idly — about his tattoos, a forthcoming eclipse of the sun, the price of gas, and the source of the weed he was smoking — before he got down to business, and he asked suddenly, "Any hotel experience?"

"I've stayed in a lot of hotels."

He laughed in his barking way. And then, out of breath from the laughter, he went slack-jawed and gasped blue smoke. Finally he recovered and said, "Hey, I've known a lot of assholes, but that doesn't make me a proctologist."

I admitted that I had no experience running a hotel, that I was a writer — had been a writer. Every enterprise I had run, I had run in my head. I hated telling him that. I mentioned some of my books, because he asked, but nothing registered. That pleased me. I did not want to have a past.

"You're probably great at thinking up names," he said. "Being as you're a writer."

"That's part of the job."

"Part of the hotel business, too. Naming your restaurants, your lounges, your function rooms. Naming the bar."

His mention of the bar made me look up and see that we were sitting in Momi's Paradise Lounge.

Buddy drank, held the booze in his mouth, frowned, then swallowed and said, "The manager here is a complete bozo. Dangerous, too."

"In what way dangerous?"

"Has an argument with a guest, right? The guest storms out. When he comes back he finds that the manager has bricked up his doorway, sealed the whole room off. What he was saying was, it's the guest's room but it's our doorway."

I tried to imagine a guest opening the door and seeing fresh bricks where there should have been an opening.

"Another guest — a real pain, granted — this manager put some goldfish in his toilet so he couldn't use it, but the guest flushed it, and so the manager filled the whole bathroom with industrial foam." Buddy sipped his drink, looking thoughtful. "Someone asked him, 'What's your problem?' The manager says, 'Masturbation takes points off your IQ each time. Hey, I could have been a genius.'"

At that moment Buddy's mobile phone rang. He answered it and handed me his business card and whispered for me to visit him the next day at his house on the North Shore. Then he exploded into the phone. Hearing him hollering at someone else, I realized how polite he had been with me.

Buddy was watching an inaudible television when I found him the next day. Because he was supine and less animated, he looked more debauched. He lay in a hammock on a porch of his house, a large square building with porches like pulled-out bureau drawers, standing among rattling palm trees at the edge of Sunset Beach and the toppling, sliding waves. The sound of surf overwhelmed the sound of the television program he was watching. The women in bathing suits on the TV were not half as attractive as the ones on the beach below where he lay.

"This *lolo* manager," he said, rolling his eyes, continuing where we had left off. "I'll give you another example. He sees a very pretty guest and introduces himself. He accompanies her to her room, they admire the view from her lanai, and he says, 'Excuse me.' He goes into her john and takes a big loud leak." Buddy shook his head with disapproval. "The woman is so spooked she moves out."

As I listened, I watched a rat moving smoothly along the baseboard of Buddy's big house like a blown leaf.

"He's got a professional massage table in one room. He offers massages to women. Now and then he goes a little too far. Some like it, others don't. There are complaints."

"He's a qualified masseur?"

"He's a three-balled tomcat. Like I said, he stepped on his dick."

I laughed in spite of myself, and Buddy joined me, barking. This second time I saw Buddy, he seemed more devilish. Watching him swinging in his hammock, like a big fish in a net, I was reminded of his nickname. Holding a glass of vodka on the dome of his belly, Buddy listed the manager's lapses. The man drank and disgraced himself. The man dipped into the cash register. The man insulted guests, sometimes using abusive language. He had been discovered sleeping in his office. He had a weakness for giving deals to guests who had done him favors, which was why the hotel had several long-term residents who could not be dislodged. He took pleasure in misleading people, and rubbed his hands when they went astray.

"This week he got into a world of shit," Buddy said. "He had a little flirtation with one of the guests. She's a fox but she's married — she's on vacation here with her husband. After this dipshit manager made love to her she passed out, and he shaved off her pubic hair. She had to explain that to her old man!" Buddy clucked, looked closely at me, and said, "What do you think?"

I laughed so hard at this weird outrage I could not reply. But I was also embarrassed. In the world I had left, people didn't do those things.

Buddy said, "A person's laugh says an awful lot."

That made me self-conscious, so I said, "He sounds pretty colorful. But I don't know whether I'd want him to run my business."

"You said writers are good at thinking up names," Buddy said. "We need a new name for the bar."

"'Momi's Paradise Lounge' isn't bad."

"Except that Momi is my ex-wife. She used to tend bar. We just got divorced. My new *wahine,* Stella, hates the name. So?"

He raised himself up in the hammock to face me. And I tried to think through all these distractions — the TV, the dumping waves, the women in bikinis lying on the beach, the scuttling rat.

"What about calling it 'Paradise Lost'?"

Buddy said nothing. He became very still, but his mind was in motion. I was aware of a straining sound, like the grunt of a laboring motor. Later I grew to recognize this as his way of thinking hard, his brain whirring like an old machine, cocked with a mainspring and the murmuring movement of its works coming out of his mouth. At last, in a whisper, he said, "It's the name of . . . what? Some song? Some story?"

"Poem."

"Poem. I like it."

And he relaxed. I stopped hearing the mechanism of slipping belts and uncoiling springs and meshing cogs from his damp forehead.

"You'll do fine."

So I had the job. Was it because I was a writer? Buddy didn't read, which made the printed word seem like magic to him and perhaps gave him an exaggerated respect for writers. He was a gambler, and I was one of his gambles. He was one of the last of a dying breed, a rascal in the Pacific. His hiring me was another example of the sort of audacious risk he boasted about.

"The staff is great," he said. "They'll do your job for you, and the rest is oh-jay-tee. But I need someone who looks like he knows what he's doing."

"I'll try."

"It's not rocket surgery," Buddy said. "And you've got the basic qualification."

"What's that?"

"Reason being, you're a mainland howlie." He laughed and hitched himself tighter in his hammock and sent me on my way.

The word "mainland," spoken in Hawaii, sounded to me like "Planet Earth."

2

Castaways

WHENEVER I felt superfluous, which was an old intimation, I reminded myself that I was running a multistory hotel. People in Hawaii asked me what I did for a living. I never said, "I'm a writer" — they would not have known my books — but rather, "I run the Hotel Honolulu." That gave me a life and, among the rascals, a certain status.

After thirty years of moving around the world, and thirty years of books, I was hired because I was a white man, a *haole*. I had made and lost several — not fortunes but livings; lost houses, lost land, lost family, lost friends; goodbye to cars, to my library. Other people were now sitting in lovely chairs I had bought and looking at paintings I used to own, hung on walls I had paid for.

I had never had a backup plan. My idea was to keep moving. Hawaii seemed a good place for starting over. This hotel was ideal. Buddy understood. He looked to be the sort of man who had also lost a lot in his life — wives, houses, money, land; not books. I needed a rest from everything imaginary, and I felt that in settling in Hawaii, and not writing, I was returning to the world.

We were not on the beach. We were the last small, old hotel in Honolulu. "It's kind of a bowteek hotel," Buddy said. He had won the place on a bet in the early sixties, when the jets had begun to replace the cruise ships. The hotel was a relic even then. What with the rising price of land in Waikiki, we were sure to be bought as a tear-down and replaced by a big ugly building, one of the chains. When I considered our certain doom, my memory was sharpened. I remembered what I saw and heard, every fugitive detail, and became a man on whom nothing was wasted.

There were residents, and some people who stayed for the winter, but most of the guests were strangers. By the time they checked out, I knew them as well as I wanted to, and in some cases I knew them very well.

"This the winner!" Keola, the janitor, said on my first day, welcoming me to the hotel. *Dees da weena!* But there was not much for me to do. Buddy had been right about the staff's running the place. Peewee was the chef, Lester Chen my number two. Tran and Trey were barmen. Tran was a Vietnamese immigrant. Trey, a surfer from Maui, also had a rock band, called Sub-Dude, formerly known as Meat Jelly, until all the band members found Jesus. "Jesus was the first surfer, man. He walked on water," Trey told me, more than once. "I surf for Christ." Charlie Wilnice and Ben Fishlow were our seasonal waiters. Keola and Kawika did the grunt work. I liked them for being incurious. Sweetie was for a time head of Housekeeping. She had been raised in the hotel, by her mother, Puamana, another of Buddy's gambles.

"In a small hotel you see people at their best and at their worst," Peewee said. "As for this one, we're in the islands, right, but this is where America stays. And some people come here to die."

We were too cheap for Japan, too expensive for Australia, too far for Europe, had little to offer the New Zealander, and didn't cater to backpackers. The business traveler avoided us, except when he was with a prostitute. Now and then we got Canadians. They were courteous and tried not to boast. They were budget-conscious. Another characteristic of frugal people: no jokes, or else bad jokes. Canadian guests despised us for not knowing their geography, while at the same time being embarrassed about their huge empty spaces that had funny place names. In conversation, Canadians were also the first to point out that they were different, usually by saying, "Well, I wouldn't know, I'm a Canadian." We had a Mexican family once. We couldn't be called child-friendly, but Peewee was correct: America walked through our doors.

People talked. I listened. I observed. I read a little. My guests were naked. I sometimes trespassed, and it became my life — the whole of my life, a new life in which I learned things I had never known before.

"I had plaque cleared from my carotid artery," Clarence Greer told me. A hotel manager in Hawaii hears lots of medical reports, as well as weather reports from back home. The Scheesers were from International Falls, where the temperature that day was minus-twenty. Jirleen Cofield explained to me the making of a po-boy sandwich. I got Wanda Privett's recipe for meatloaf, and other recipes, and learned that many of them, being from middle America, involved adding a can of soup. It worried me to see a man wearing a toupee. I trusted people who lisped. Your diabetic needs to be careful of infections in his feet. I was overprotective of African Americans, always saw them as having among the oldest American pedigrees. I tried to understand the sadness of soldiers, the melancholy of the military. Was it the uniform? Was it the haircut? I heard so many stories that I abandoned any thought of writing them; their very number gave me writer's block and made me patient. Now and then, on the day he was to leave, a guest might walk the two blocks to the beach and sob in the sunshine.

I liked Hawaii because it was a void. There was no power here apart from landowning, no society worth the name, just a pecking order. There was a social ladder but it wasn't climbable, and the higher on it people stood, the sillier they looked, because everyone knew their secrets. On such small islands there was hardly any privacy, because people constantly bumped into each other.

Hawaii is hot and cold volcanoes, clear skies, and open ocean. Like most Pacific islands it is all edge, no center, very shallow, very narrow, a set of green bowls turned upside down in the sea, the lips of the coastline surrounding the bulges of porous mountains. This crockery is draped in a thickness of green so folded it is hidden and softened. Above the blazing beaches were the gorgeous green pleats of the mountains.

The place was once empty and unchanging, as lush as paradise, a peaceful balance of animals and plants. It was then visited by humans. At about the time Chaucer wrote *The Canterbury Tales*, the second and largest wave of Polynesians were climbing out of double-hulled canoes, chanting in relief at having found land. They claimed it as theirs, but they were no more than castaways. They imposed a society of kings and commoners. People were eaten. They venerated the gods of fire and water they had brought with them. The first iron in Hawaii was stolen from the ships of Captain Cook — so many nails yanked out of the timbers that the ships lost much of their seaworthiness. With the iron the islanders began to carve more subtly in wood. After the arrival of the first canoes the islands changed. The voyagers had brought dogs and pigs. The first whites brought guns and gonorrhea. Everything began at once, and in that beginning was decay. Now, half the people could not even swim, and an unspecific paragraph of inaccurate history like this one was all they knew.

And there was the sun. The sun in Hawaii was so dazzling, so misleading, yet we regarded sunlight as our fortune. We quietly believed, "We are blessed because the sun shines every day. This is a good place for its sunlight. These islands are pure because of the sun. The sun has made us virtuous."

As the TV weathermen on the mainland took personal responsibility for the weather, each of us in Hawaii took credit for the sunshine here, as though we had discovered it and it was ours to dispense. "Stranger, be grateful to me for this sunny day" was our attitude toward visitors. The sun had been bestowed on us and we were sharing it with these alien refugees from dark cloudy places. The sun was our wealth and our goodness. The Hawaiian heresy, which we thought but never said, was "We are good because of the sun. We are better than our visitors. We are sunnier."

This conceit made us sloppy and careless. Never mind the palmy setting, the people here were as cruel and violent and crafty as people anywhere, but they were slower and so seemed mild. Close up, the islands were disorderly, fragile, and sensationally littered, with brittle cliffs and too many feral cats and beaches that were sucked and splashed by big waves to vanish in the sea. Our secret was that we hated hot weather and stayed out of the sun. The visitors ended up with pink noses, peeling shoulders, freckle clusters, sunstroke, and melanoma, while we kept in the shadows.

"They say the Hawaii state motto is *Hele I Loko, Haole 'Ino, Aka Ha'awi Mai Kala* — Go Home, You Mainland Scum, but Leave Your Money Behind," Buddy said. "The real motto is even funnier. *Ua Mau Ke Ea O Ka Aina I Ka Pono* — The Life of the Land Is Perpetuated in Righteousness. The fuck it is!"

*   *   *

The week I was hired, Buddy stopped coming to the hotel. I was glad. Buddy always introduced me by saying, "Hey, he wrote a book!"

I hated that. And I needed to learn the job. He was the wrong person to teach me. He was usually drunk and had the drunk's idiocy, mood swings, and facetiousness; he repeated himself; drink made him deaf.

To please me he tried to be funny, but that could be tedious, especially the formulaic jokes he told in order to define himself, or just to shock. I knew all the punch lines. The man at the bar who says, "I used to think I was a cowboy, but, golly, I guess I'm a lesbian." Buddy saying, in his terrible Mexican accent, "If God hadn't meant us to eat it, then why did he make it look like a taco?" The elephant telling the naked man, "How do you manage to breathe through a little thing like that?" Or Buddy's croaky utterance that amounted almost to a war cry: "Nine inches!" A boss's comedy is always an employee's hardship.

A few days after I started at the hotel, Buddy invited me to his house to introduce me to his new woman, Stella, whom I had not yet met. She was from California, she said.

"She's a tool of my lust," Buddy said, and handed me a platter of brownies. "Stella made them. There's weed baked into them."

I took one and nibbled it while Buddy praised them in a wheezy voice, claiming they'd saved his lungs.

"You ever swim?" I asked.

"Bad current," he said, pronouncing it *kernt*.

"I'm surprised Buddy didn't make you manager of the hotel," I said to Stella. "You're a great cook and you have the basic qualification. You're a mainland howlie."

"But you also had the other important qualification," Buddy said, poking me in the chest. "Reason being, you understood me."

I smiled at him, to show I didn't understand.

"That dipshit manager I was telling you about?" he said.

I remembered the aggression, the massage table, the blunders, the drunkenness, the practical jokes. Larger than life. Three-balled tomcat.

"That was me!"

He needed me to congratulate him for fooling me, and I did.

But I had guessed it, and people had whispered at the hotel. What surprised me was that he felt I could do a better job. "A man who doesn't make mistakes ain't doing nothing." But there were more surprises for me, and they taught me to be watchful. I had asked for a new life, but I saw that this meant many lives — wife, child, the world of these islands, and my misapprehensions.

3

Birdsong

NOT LONG after I nailed the janitor, Keola, as incurious, I saw him emptying trash barrels into a dumpster in the alley beside the hotel. Some papers flew out. He stooped and snatched at them with big blunt fingers, but instead of throwing them away, he looked at them. He began to read them, holding the flapping sheets to his face and smiling. That shocked me. He glanced back at me and gave me what the locals called stink-eye.

Later, when I summoned the courage to ask him why he had read the discarded papers, he denied it. If he sometimes seemed to be doing something crazy like reading, he said, it was because he suffered from "nonselective blackouts." He said he didn't even know what I was talking about.

"My short-term memory more worse, boss. Get real common in the islands. Real falustrating."

A week or so later I was in my office and heard, coming from outside the window, the voices of Keola and Kawika, who were weeding the flower bed by the swimming pool.

"Eh, where you was yesterday?"

"Eh, was working."

"I call you up talfone."

"I never hear."

"Eh, you never dere already."

"Assa madda you, brah?"

Fascinated, I cocked my head to listen. It was like hearing birds squawking.

"Figure us go Makaha. Catch some wave."

"I was lawnmowa da frikken grass. Weed Eater was buss."

"How was buss?"

"Da shaff."

"Eh, I get no more nothing to do."

"Was frikken choke grass. I just stay sweating. My pants all broke. Later I wen cuttin da tchrees."

Two birds on a branch, squawking together, squawks I was trying to remember and understand. A few days later, they were squawking again.

"Was one udda bugga. Was rob."

"Who da bugga?"

"One howlie guy."

"Who da steala-rubba?"

"Udda howlie guy."

"Frikken howlies."

"It da djrugs."

"Yah."

"They in depf."

"Yah. Hey, how he go do it?"

"Hide in one tchree."

"Up the tchree?"

"Back fo the tchree. See a waheeny with one bag. He say, 'That mines!' He cuckaroach the bag, and the waheeny she ampin like hell."

"They all on djrugs."

"Take da cash. Buy batu."

"Batu. Ice. Pakalolo."

"Pakalolo one soff djrug. Batu is more worse."

Squawk, squawk. I sat at the window, pretending to work. And another day:

"Eh, but da bugga."

"What bugga?"

"Da one new bugga."

"Da howlie, yah. He more betta."

"Eh, he look *akamai*."

"But talk hybolic."

"Yah. But everybody speak him too good."

"The waheeny she frecklish."

"She Housekeeping."

"She not Housekeeping. She Guess Services."

"But Tuna, he too much rascal."

"Man, numba-one *pilau* luna."

"And how come all da time he look us and then he laughing?"

"Bull liar. He job easy."

"Yah."

"Yah."

"Too much hard though my job."

"Stay sucking up beer. Talk story."

"And us stay sweating."

"Yah."

"Yah."

"Man, he got one big book, howlie bugga."

"I never wen see no book."

"In he office."

"Bugga office?"

"Yah. Howlie bugga office. Big book. Hybolical book."

"Eh, no easy fo read, yah."

"Too much easy for howlie."

"Yah."

"Yah. Bymbye, da howlie bugga be rascal."

"Frikken big rascal."

Squawk, squawk. There was more, and all in the dopiest apo-copes, but by then I had realized they were talking about me, and my Tolstoy.

4

Rose

HISTORY HAPPENS to other people. The rest of us just live and die, watch the news, listen to the guff, and remember the names. No one remembers us, though sometimes we are brushed by those bigger events or public figures. My boss, Buddy Hamstra, was a celebrity, because he knew many of the famous people who had visited Hawaii. He talked about them as though to prove that these little islands were part of the world and he was part of history. Babe Ruth had stayed in this hotel in 1927, before the renovation, when it was the height of a coconut tree. So had Will Rogers. Buddy had played golf with another rascal, Francis H. I'i Brown, who was part Hawaiian. Francis Brown had known Bob Hope. Hope was a regular in the islands.

"Zachary Scott — cowboy actor — I knew him," Buddy said. "He used to come here a lot."

I said, "His ex-wife ran off with John Steinbeck." But that didn't impress Buddy, for he had never heard of Steinbeck.

Buddy had found Zachary Scott an island girlfriend. "They did the horizontal hula." He could manage such an introduction in a friendly, uncomplicated way that took the curse off it and made him seem a matchmaker rather than a pimp.

A significant request of this sort was made early in 1962 when Sparky Lemmo asked whether Buddy could find him "an island girl" — and the implication was that she would be young and pretty and willing. Buddy asked for more details. She was needed, Sparky said, to spend an evening with a visiting dignitary who was staying the night with his official entourage at the Kahala

Hilton. The man's visit was secret, and he was so powerful he had not landed at Honolulu Airport but at one of the other airports — there were thirteen on the island of Oahu, including the military fields. The man had been brought to the Kahala in a limo with blacked-out windows.

"Howard Hughes?" Buddy asked.

It was the sort of thing Hughes was doing in those years, with his flunkies and his millions and his private jet. Sparky gave no details; a hesitation in his manner, when the name came up, suggested to Buddy that the man in question might have been Howard Hughes.

Yet he could have been anyone. Famous people came to Hawaii and famous people lived here. Doris Duke lived on Black Point, Clare Boothe Luce on Diamond Head, Lindbergh was in Maui, Jimmy Stewart had a ranch above Kona, Elvis visited Hawaii all the time. Famous people had famous friends.

"Bing Crosby?" Buddy asked. Crosby played golf in Hawaii.

Sparky just ignored that. He repeated that the man wanted a local girl, an island beauty.

"Ha!" Buddy Hamstra was triumphant. "So they can't find a *wahine* at the Kahala. They have to come to the Hotel Honolulu!"

He was pleased to be in demand, because even then his hotel's reputation had slipped. The Tahitian dancing on the lanai — his Pretty Polynesia show — only convinced people that Buddy was a rascal. And he was, which gave him some insight into how weak some men could be. He would say, "I never had to pay for it" — one of those men — but he was acquainted with the single-minded nature of desire.

"Tell me who the guy is," Buddy said.

Sparky indicated by tightening his face that he wanted to tell but couldn't. He said, "This man is very important. The idea is to find a girl who won't recognize him."

"Would I recognize him?" Buddy said.

"Listen, this is urgent. And not a hooker. Just someone who's friendly. A little coconut princess."

There was just such a girl, Puamana Wilson, who hung around the hotel saying that she was looking for work. Buddy had sized her up as a runaway and was protective of her. She had been educated in a convent on the mainland but had run away, and was still hiding from her family in Hilo. He gave her casual jobs in the kitchen, to keep her out of the bar and under the protection of Peewee. He put her up in a back room so he could keep his eye on her. If she stayed out of trouble, he might marry her when she got a little older. She was still a girl, twenty or so, immature for her age because of the convent, freckled, funny, but experienced, as Buddy knew. She was sweet, not very bright, alluring in the pouty island way, half surf bunny and half shrew. She was simple and she was willing. But Buddy said, "I want her back."

Puamana was summoned from the kitchen. Even damp-faced, in her apron, she looked pretty.

"You're needed across town," Buddy said.

"What I have to do?"

"Just be nice."

She understood this and knew what to do without being told.

While she washed and dressed, Sparky offered Buddy a tip, which Buddy waved away, offended by the imputation that he was part of the deal or that it was a commercial arrangement at all. This was something between friends, he said.

With a flower behind her ear and wearing a pareu, Puamana left for the Kahala with Sparky Lemmo. Buddy was asleep when she returned. Later that day he saw her in the kitchen — in a T-shirt and apron and rubber sandals once more — and asked her how it had gone.

"Beautiful room," Puamana said. "Was a suite."

How like Puamana to comment on the room and say nothing about the man or the money. So Buddy asked about him.

"He was stoked."

She said nothing else. And she grew quiet, staying in her room as though hatching an egg. Six weeks later, Puamana told Buddy she was pregnant. When the little girl was born, Puamana said, "She's *hapa*" — half islander, half *haole*. Puamana called her Ku'uipo, "Sweetheart," and with the birth she became a serious mother. She stopped flirting, saved her money, and devoted herself to her daughter, a lovely child who, before she was a year old, could totter across the hotel lobby and do hula moves without falling down.

That same year, President Kennedy was assassinated. Sparky stopped by the hotel and found Buddy Hamstra drunk and weeping. "I fought in the Pacific with that guy!" It wasn't true.

"He's the one that Pua cheered up at the Kahala Hilton," Sparky said.

Buddy said, "I don't believe it."

This sort of memory seemed wrong on a day when a nation mourned a man whose coffin was draped with Old Glory and pulled by six white horses on a gray caisson.

Buddy said, "Anyway, we'll never know the truth."

A short time after that, Buddy asked Puamana if the man at the Kahala could have been Sweetie's father.

"I never sleep with no one else that month," she said.

Buddy had watched her closely. The child had made her moralistic. He said, "You know anything about him?"

"That howlie guy," Puamana said. She smiled as she thought of the man who had made love to her that night. "From the mainland."

"That's all you remember?"

There was a look of reminiscence like a particular memory in her smile of concentration.

"He had one beautiful bed," she said, and laughed a little. "But he wouldn't do it in the bed. He did it in the bathtub — warm water, just him laying there, me on top. And after that, standing up, his back against the wall."

"You never told me that."

"It was too crazy." She remembered something else. "He say he have a bad back."

That one detail, the so-called "White House position," everyone knew about Kennedy, if you knew about Kennedy at all. Though Puamana was innocent in an island way when she met him, and was an attentive mother, that one-night stand seemed to corrupt her. When she drifted into prostitution, Buddy took a greater interest in the little girl, Sweetie, and for a time she became his *hanai* daughter under the loose adoption system of the islands.

Buddy told me this story nearly thirty years later, after I had fallen in love with Sweetie and we'd had a child of our own. Sweetie wanted to call her Taylor, Brittany, or Logan. *Logan?* But I suggested Rose, and Sweetie agreed, though she didn't know it was the name of the child's paternal great-grandmother.

5

Baptism

THE BOOK OF MINE the Hawaiian staff called "hybolic" for its pretentious size — all them big words — was the Penguin edition of *Anna Karenina*, which I kept near me my first months at the Hotel Honolulu so I could stick my nose in its pages for oxygen. Hawaii was a sunny, lovely place, but for an alien like me it was no more than an empty blaze of sunburn until I found love.

The problem with my plump Penguin was its unconcealable bulk, and it was much plumper for having swelled up in the damp air. All books fatten by the sea.

I sat and studied those big kindly waves rolling toward Waikiki, slowly rising from the smooth sea, dividing themselves into ranks, gathering shape near the shore to whiten in peaks before sloping and softening, just spilling and dying, declining in a falling off of bubble soup and draining into the drenched sand. It was as though the whole event of each separate wave had started when a great unseen hand far from shore had cuffed the ocean, shoving the water into motion, creating waves, a study of beautiful endings.

My Tolstoy was regarded as a handicap and an obvious nuisance crying out for bantering mockery. "What you gonna do with that thing?" "That gonna keep you real busy." "More bigger than the Bible," Keola said one day before setting down a lawn sprinkler so casually that its spray slashed the walls of my office and wet me through the window. The book, too, was doused, and swelled some more, and with acute curvature of the spine stayed fatter even after its pages had dried.

I said to Keola, who was watering the clusters of torch ginger by the pool wall, "A man goes to the doctor for a verdict about his illness. 'How sick am I?' he asks. The doctor says, 'Let me put it this way. Don't start any long books.'"

In grinning querying confusion and saying "Eh?" Keola turned to face me, playing the hose, wetting me and my book. He was a simple soul who sometimes yanked the hooked stinger out of a centipede's tail, and with the centipede in his mouth, he would smile at a stranger, parting his lips to allow the centipede to slip out and creep along his dusky cheek. "Dis what the devil look like." Keola had found Jesus.

The hot days passed in Waikiki and already I was sick of hearing "Pearly Shells" and "Tiny Bubbles" and "Lovely Hula Hands." I was still single and celibate in those early days, and still believed that I was starting anew, at an age when nothing seemed new. I was Rimbaud, clerking and sweating in Abyssinia. I had rejected the writing life. Writers who had abandoned writing to busy themselves in other affairs were my patron saints: Melville, Rimbaud, T. E. Lawrence, Salinger, Tolstoy himself. Now and then, Buddy showed up to discuss a hotel matter. One day it was to find a way of getting the old TV actor Jack Lord into the hotel once a week ("free food and beverage") so that Madam Ma, our resident journalist, could mention this fact in her newspaper column. People might visit just to be in the same room with the former star of *Hawaii Five-O*. But Lord, a reclusive sort, refused to show. Buddy said, "Tom Selleck has an interest in the Black Orchid, but George Harrison lives on Maui. That's a dynamite column item. 'Beatle Dines at Hotel Honolulu.'"

"What have we got to offer him?"

We were eating purple gluey poi and fatty kalua pig and scoops of cold macaroni. Buddy was chewing and smiling. Like Vronsky, he had a tightly packed row of white teeth, but he had Oblonsky's problems.

"I was thinking of an all-you-can-eat buffet," Buddy said, licking poi from his fingers, and without taking a breath added, "Don't you get a headache reading books like that?"

"I'd get a headache if I didn't."

At that time, in the early days, I was still lusting for Sweetie, waiting for an opportunity to take her on a date — I did not want to be obvious and felt awkward wooing an employee. To be oblique I asked Buddy about her mother.

"Puamana is the original 'Ukelele Lady,'" he said. "She started out as a coconut princess."

"I take it she's not too bright."

"You sound like you think that's a bad thing."

"She's probably illiterate."

"Books aren't everything. She's got *mana,* like her name. Spiritual energy." Buddy sniffed and said, "The longer you live here in Whyee, the more you'll see that a woman's low IQ can be part of her beauty."

"But your wife is smart."

"Stella's not my wife, she's my *wahine.* My fuck-buddy. In fact, I got woman trouble. Stella's going to kill me. I still think she's an amazing woman."

I wanted to tell him how he was a version of Oblonsky, just to see what he would say. But after lunch, walking from the dining room to the lobby, Buddy said, "Come here for a minute. I want you to look at something." He knelt by the pool and so did I, beside him. He said, "Do you see that dark thing on the bottom, near the drain?"

I leaned over and looked, and seeing nothing, leaned over more. As I did so, overbalancing, Buddy pushed me into the pool.

"You walked straight into that one!" Buddy said as I surfaced, thrashing in my heavy sodden clothes.

"Joker man," Lester Chen said as I passed by Reception, dripping wet.

After that, whenever Buddy saw me he seemed to recall this incident at the pool. The memory was a wistful glaze in his eyes, and I could not help noticing *a certain peculiarity of expression, a sort of suppressed radiance on his face and in his whole person.* That was Oblonsky in *Anna,* when he was at lunch with Levin, eating oysters and talking about love and marriage and not divulging his woman trouble, the fact that he was having an affair with the French governess.

Around this time Keola said, "Jesus is Lord. I woulda been in big *pilikia* without Jesus." I read Levin's expression of faith: *What should I have been and how should I have lived my life had*

I not had those beliefs, had I not known that one had to live for God and not for the satisfaction of one's needs. I should have robbed, lied and murdered.

Like Levin, Keola had found Jesus, and I was so moved by his faith that one day, checking his repair of the water fountain near the restrooms, I found myself inquiring into the nature of his belief and wondering at his passion.

"Jesus same like food. If you no eat, you go die," Keola said, giving the chrome nut on the fountain one last twist. "Marry for men and women. In Whyee we no want gay marry. Hey, I no mind gays. I forgive them, if they repent. Some people so stupid. Like, it one child, not one choice. It one human, not one monkey. I no tell these school what for teach. But that bull lie that we come from monkeys just another way of getting God out for you life. Try drink, boss."

I did, and the fountain's stream splashed my face and went up my nose.

"That so good for you," Keola said.

Was I saved? Keola wanted to know. I said I had been baptized. Wasn't that enough?

He just laughed the mirthless pitying laughter of the born-again Christian. "You never save! You one sinner! Just reading book all the day, wicked book like that one."

"The man who wrote this book thought the same thing, funnily enough."

"Howlie guy."

"I think you could say Tolstoy was a howlie. Anyway, he found Jesus, like you."

"It more better if you born again. Get baptize, like this." He flicked water on my face. "Take da plunge."

Seeing Kawika passing by with a five-gallon bucket of sticky rice in each hand, Keola winked and flexed his arms body-builder fashion and called out, "Hey, Rambo!"

When Rimbaud was in Harar, he wrote home: *I'm weary and bored . . . Isn't it wretched this life I lead, without family, without friends, without intellectual companionship, lost in the midst of these people whose lot one would like to improve, and who try, for their part, only to exploit me . . . Obliged to chatter their gibberish, to eat their filthy messes, to endure their treachery and stupidity! But that isn't the worst. The worst is my fear of becoming a slob myself, isolated as I am, and cut off from any intellectual companionship.*

But I liked Keola's euphemism for baptism — da plunge.

Trey the bartender said, "You think Samoans are tough? Only when they're in a gang. One on one, Solies are cowards. They're big but they're not tough. Remember that."

He squirted soda water from the bar dispenser into my drink and it soaked my chin.

Peewee the chef said, "*Popolos* sink in the pool," using the local word for black. "Ask any lifeguard. Something about *popolos* — they don't float."

"Brothers don't surf," Trey said.

Such talk made me wonder why I had picked this job, and it sent me back to my novel and a denser, subtler world: Vronsky contemplating, in a poignant and painful moment, Anna's jealousy. *He looked at her as a man might look at a faded flower he had picked, in which he found it difficult to discover the beauty that made him pick and destroy it. And yet he felt that though when his love was stronger, he could, had he wanted it badly, have torn the love out of his heart, now when, as at this moment, it seemed to her that he felt no love for her, he knew that the bond between them could not be broken.*

"That hybolic book keeping you real busy," Keola said.

I needed the novel as sustenance. Such paradoxes as I was reading calmed me here, especially when Buddy was restless and needed company. He would demand that we go to his favorite strip club, the Rat Room, where he sat drinking rum at the edge of the mirrored stage and encouraged women to squat in front of us. He slipped five-dollar bills into their garters and gaped between their legs, nudging me.

"Look. Abe Lincoln without his teeth."

Back in my room I read Levin's reflection: *If goodness has a cause, it is no longer goodness; if it has consequences, or reward, it is not goodness either.*

The novel continued to be my oxygen, and while I worked up the courage to make love to Sweetie, I usually fled to the beach, where I could hide in a folding chair, reading in the sunshine as waves broke on the sand, feeling I was fulfilling Lytton Strachey's dream of reading between the paws of the Sphinx. Now and then I would look up and see the brown bums of beach sleepers turned upward, the women — but only the skinny ones — forever tugging and adjusting their bathing suits, smoothing lotion onto their arms, sitting cross-legged or walking with that odd climbing gait in the sand and looking duck-butted. The waves laving the shore, the sparkle of sun in the distance, a whole sea surface of glitter. On the beach everyone is a body, no more or less than flesh, indistinguishable one from another, like a great pale tribe of hairless monkeys. I found myself staring at the small tidy panel between the women's legs, staring in fact at nothing but space, for there was nothing to see, nothing specific, just a wrinkle, a labial smile in the smoothness, for a bikini bottom was both a vortex and a vanishing point.

Sometimes, staring this way, I found myself yearning for love. And yearning, I dozed. I lay sleeping on the hot sand, snoring on my back. Bliss.

I always woke drooling and sweating, my back coated with sand grains, like a castaway, someone actually washed up on the beach, feeling distant. Yet I was more rested and alert than if I had been in bed: the heat was like a cure. The world was far away. I was a new man here in this simple, incomplete place, just an old green volcano in the middle of the sea. I was trying to make a life, but there was something so melancholy and unreal about solitude in the sunshine that it made me feel fictional.

There are no conditions to which a man cannot get accustomed, especially if he sees that everyone around him lives in the same way. Levin would not have believed it possible three months earlier that he could go quietly to sleep in the circumstances he now found himself.

Thus Levin, rusticated on his farm.

I was on the beach reading *Anna Karenina* one day and heard singing, a vigorous hymn, and I looked up and saw a procession making its way among the Japanese sunning themselves, and the children playing, and the men selling ice cream. Keola led the procession, singing loudly, with a woman in a white dress wearing a lei and flowers in her hair. Others followed, some people I knew from the hotel: Puamana, Sweetie, Kawika, Peewee, Trey and the rest of Sub-Dude, Marlene and Pacita from Housekeeping, Wilnice and Fishlow from the dining room, and Amo Ferretti, who did the flowers. There were others I did not yet know — Godbolt the painter from the Big Island, Madam Ma holding hands with her son, Chip, and Buddy's grown kids, Bula and Melveen — each of them recording this event in his own way.

Keola walked into the surf, taking the woman in the white dress by the arm, and he bent her backward and immersed her, all the while shouting a prayer. The woman was soaked and joyful, spouting water and raising her arms.

I watched, transfixed. This baptism gave the whole island a meaning. Now it seemed like a real place, a natural font in the middle of the ocean, built for baptisms. Although I did not in the least believe in any feature of this ritual, I was moved, because they believed. I beheld a powerful expression of faith. I walked nearer, my forefinger in my book, marking my place. A sudden muscular wave knocked me down hard and battered me, snatched my book, and rolled me into the surf. I struggled for air, tried to right myself, plunged in after Tolstoy, but I was tipped unsparingly again by a new wave, was rolled again, and my power to save myself was taken from me. More waves moved my whole body up and down before pushing me onto the sand. All this happened in the seconds it took to baptize that woman. My plump ruined book, more buoyant than me, danced in the foam of the shore break.

6

The Lovers Upstairs

IN THE BEGINNING, when I had asked Sweetie, "Do you want to make love?" and she had said, "Part of me does," I took this for delicacy, not humor. I was patient until all of her wanted it. Later I would beckon her to room 409, and we would make love with the sexual suddenness she gaspingly called a hurricane fuck. She had a beautiful laugh, full of desire and willingness. That we might be caught in the act was part of the excitement for her, and her excitement took hold of me. We did have neighbors, for the hotel's compartments were dense and busy.

The faded green plantation-style bungalow the height of a coconut tree that you saw from the street, with a sign saying *Hotel Honolulu,* was an optical illusion. The original building that Babe Ruth had stayed in he would still recognize. But Buddy Hamstra had built a squat eighty-room tower above and behind it. So what looked like a charming island inn with a swinging sign and a monkeypod tree in front was in fact a fairly ugly thirty-five-year-old hotel, twelve stories high, with a roof garden (potted palms, patio furniture, cork tiles) where guests seldom went, because it was the thirteenth floor. You understood the Hotel Honolulu only when you got inside.

Narrow and deep, like a tall book on a low shelf, the hotel was one of three on our side street — the Waikiki Pearl on our right, the Kodama on our left. Our lobby, at street level, was conveniently small. I could see everyone who entered, so I could distinguish the guests from the gate crashers, and I was within eavesdropping range. Being the manager here was like existing within an unpredictable jumble of episodes and characters to which I alone knew the narrative line.

Paradise Lost bar was unusual in Waikiki for being popular with locals, especially when Buddy was introducing his favorite shows on the poolside lanai: Tahitian dancers, topless hula, or the enormous Samoan in a muumuu who husked coconuts with his teeth. The lanai doubled as the Island Coffee Shop (thatched roof, scowling constipated-looking tikis, glass net-floats). Just inside, sharing Peewee's kitchen, was the Terrace dining room, unofficially known as Buddy's.

The hotel pool was picturesque but dangerous, from the loose tiles and slippery edges to the rusty ladder and the poor drainage. The water itself was either algal and germ-laden or else so strongly chlorinated as to seem toxic. Fortunately, most guests used the beach, two streets away.

The Executive Office — my cubbyhole — opened onto the lobby, where Lester Chen sat at Reception, his hands braced on the counter as though steering it. Everyone got a plumeria lei at check-in, a kiss from Marlene, and a coupon for a free Happy Hour drink at Paradise Lost.

The man arranging the centerpiece of torch ginger in the big lobby vase was Amo Ferretti, our flower man; the young man saying "Stop fussing, pumpkin!" his lover, Chip. The Hawaiian with the mop and bucket was Keola, and the cat taking up most of the lobby sofa, Popoki, belonged to my mother-in-law, Puamana. Slack-key guitar music, mainly Gabby Pahinui tapes, was played all day. Most of the décor belonged to Buddy: cruise ship posters, framed feather leis, fish traps that had been converted into lamps, bric-a-brac such as the gaily painted signs saying, *Duke Kahanamoku's* and *Boat Day,* and the small bubbling aquarium of island fish.

The woman entering the lobby on Rollerblades was my wife, Sweetie, and the reason she did not ever hear you was that she was wearing a Walkman and listening to a Stephen King audio book. The odors in the lobby: Peewee's fresh bread, Amo Ferretti's homegrown gardenias, and the guests' pungent sunblock. The laughter from Paradise Lost was that of Buddy and his friends Sam Sandford, Sparky Lemmo, Earl Willis, and the chef, Peewee Moffat.

The elevator was so unreliable we routinely put guests on the lower floors, in case they had to use the fire stairs. Older Americans, being fire-conscious, preferred this arrangement anyway.

A plaque screwed to the lobby wall boasted that the hotel stood on the site of the beach hut where Robert Louis Stevenson stayed in 1889, writing *The Master of Ballantrae,* when Waikiki was swampland.

Some guests I hardly saw — they were just slammed doors or ambiguous sounds — but the people right upstairs, in 509, were not ambiguous at all. They made the most explicit noises I had ever heard, and I became aware of them my first night in the hotel.

It was more than sound. It was physical motion, the walls spoke, the room was jolted. I was well acquainted with these noises. Once, in college, I had lived off campus, downstairs from a newly married couple — young woman, middle-aged man — and for one whole year I learned the rhythm and progress of such sounds: the repetitive rising voices, the clinking glasses and laughter, the rumbling floorboards and popping corks, the shrill teasing woman, the throatier man, a sort of dissolving chaos — footsteps representing whole bodies, silences standing for signals, and a shift from human murmurs to snorts of strained furniture fittings, the squawk of seat springs, the jingle of bed springs, the seesaw of the bed itself, the frenzy of caged parrots in a pet shop.

To these sounds I added the man and woman. It all appealed to my imagination. He was a grunting lover, she was a pleader — whimpering, shifting, her cries not quite smothered by the creaking bedstead. The lonely cries of the young woman were like a table saw slicing through splintering plywood.

I had a girlfriend then. Unable to endure this sexual fury upstairs, I would wake and startle her with my desire. She would laugh softly, lean back, make a cradle of her legs, and rock me until our bed was a squawking workshop too.

Sweetie and I had met on my first day on the job. And that room, 409, was one of the first she showed me. I heard the urgent murmurs, the yearning voices, the odd honks of the man, and the sudden sawing of the bed in which the lovers upstairs were rocking.

Sweetie pretended not to hear, but when I touched her at the window — she was showing me how to adjust the louvers — she did not resist my hot hands.

I said, "Buddy would kill me if he knew what I was doing."

"Buddy would get a charge out of it," she said.

I stared at her.

"I don't mean to be facetious," she said.

I stared at that funny word, still damp on her lips, and said, "Or your mother might kill me."

Puamana lived on the third floor near the back, so her customers could come and go without passing through the lobby. Sweetie had been raised in the hotel, and Buddy was the friendly uncle in this arrangement.

Sweetie said, "My mother says you're a good conversationalist."

Since her mother's contacts with men were confined to half-hour encounters in bed, it did not take much to be regarded as a great raconteur by Puamana.

As it was my first time in the islands, I could not gauge the impression I made. The islanders seemed pleasant, but they were giggly and inarticulate. They could sit for hours and say nothing. My talk exhausted them. My questions silenced them and sometimes made them suspicious.

Talk made Sweetie anxious, so I brought her presents — she loved flowers and trinkets. I took her car to the Samoan car wash. These to her were expressions of love. Her notion of intellectual activity was Rollerblading with the joggers on the promenade at Ala Moana Beach while listening to a Stephen King horror.

But I realized that it was fatal for me to linger in room 409 with those provocative sounds rippling through the ceiling. In my first moments in the room I had been stirred, and, inspired by the sensual polyphony from upstairs, nudged by the agreeable persuasion, I had touched Sweetie for the first time.

I said, "If we don't leave here this minute you're going to be in trouble."

She just laughed. She didn't push me away. The very fact of being in a hotel room aroused me, but I was with a twenty-seven-year-old girl and the people in the room above were groaning in the act of love.

She shrugged and smiled and said nothing. That was enough encouragement to give me patience. I looked for another chance. Buddy had said that I should be watchful. I had an office, Peewee was in the kitchen, Lester Chen at Reception, Sweetie in Housekeeping, Tran at the bar, Keola in Maintenance, Kawika in the garden; the poolside lanai, the narrow lobby — Amo Ferretti arranging the flowers; the potted palms, the monkeypod tree out front, the slack-key Hawaiian music. It was September.

"Shoulder season," Buddy had warned me, the quiet time.

It seemed to me that I was risking a great deal by making a move on Sweetie, so I delicately raised the subject with Buddy one payday when he stopped by to distribute checks.

I said, "She's very pretty."

"She's not interested in me. Maybe you'll do better. She seems to like you."

"I wouldn't want to jeopardize my job by taking advantage of the staff."

Buddy laughed in a jeering way. "Sweetie does what she wants. If I was in your shoes, I'd just pray for sex. Anyway, if she gave you a piece, I would obviously think more of you."

After that I looked for an opportunity, and room 409 became the symbol of my desire.

One hot afternoon I went to the room alone. The sounds from upstairs roused me. With numb fingers I dialed Housekeeping. Sweetie knew why I was calling, and though she seemed to linger a little, she knocked some minutes later.

She did not seem to hear the sounds from upstairs, but she heard me. I could hardly speak. What was there to say? It was apparent that I wanted her. I kissed her; that was the way I implored her. She let me undress her. I said, "I'll make you love me."

We fitted our bodies together and rocked until our bed moved in rhythm with the one upstairs. After that, I found an excuse for making love to her every day, always in that room. All that time I kept the room for us, never assigning it to anyone else.

When Sweetie told me she was pregnant, I was glad. This was the new life I needed, the better because I had not sought it. The baby was a surprise and a pleasure. I was still of an age to raise a child, and to see the child through college — that was the important thing. Puamana was pleased, too; she liked me, and that was significant. She knew men.

She said, "It will be a girl."

Buddy said, "Having such a young kid at your age is like having a thirty-year mortgage."

After Rose was born, Buddy told me about Puamana's night at

the Hilton with President Kennedy, and how only he could have been Sweetie's father, though for Puamana he was just a *haole* from the mainland with a bad back. Sweetie didn't know. The man who had arranged it, Sparky Lemmo, hadn't made the connection. Only Buddy and I knew.

I said to Buddy, "None of this would have happened if the people in 509 weren't so loud when they made love."

"There's no people in 509," Buddy said. "It's a bastard named Roland Miranda. He's a woodworker. That's his carpentry shop. And he refuses to leave."

7

Miranda the Carpenter

ROLAND MIRANDA murmured at his workbench, his sanding like sighing, his sawing like the rocking of a bedstead. He lived and worked in room 509 and hardly ever left. He had been a secret, another of Buddy's gambles, but one Buddy had lost. Old Miranda had done some work for Buddy, who had been in one of his playful moods: the prospect of debt made him creative. The renovation work that Miranda had done was considerable. He had put four men on the job for half a year, the bill had increased dramatically, Buddy just stalled, and when the day of reckoning came, Buddy said, "I've got a proposition for you." Miranda could choose to be paid immediately or else have a room for life.

Miranda accepted without hesitation. Buddy didn't mind — he thought the deal had worked in his own favor: Miranda was elderly and settled and so busy he would hardly use the room. But Miranda sold his house and business, and he moved into the Hotel Honolulu with his tools. The alternative for someone his age would have been the retirement home near Punahou School called Arcadia, which was ripe with old folks, and in its hushed air were the mingled smells of meatloaf, Jell-O, and mortality. Miranda, who was friendless, sent out for food. No one was admitted to his room. He was a forgotten tenant, just a set of alluring noises.

Miranda at his workbench I had taken to be an amorous couple. On the same evidence, others took those noises to be restless children left by selfish parents for their day in Waikiki, or a deaf man repeatedly yanking bureau drawers. The people who knew Miranda assumed he was making improvements to his room, and they said, "Do you think he'll ever finish?" After a while it was clear that Buddy had had the worst of the bargain; Miranda had lasted longer than most of the older employees. Buddy didn't want to hear Miranda's name. In the notes of the guest ledger beside 509 I read *Occupied* and *Resident* and *Do not service*. Housekeeping stayed away from the room.

Four years after he moved in, Miranda was still making carpentry noises in 509. Other guests complained, but he never hammered past six or six-thirty P.M., so I could do nothing. Yet what was all the hammering?

I had taken it to be foreplay and passion — how wrong I was — but that was a better guess than many ("He's fixing something," "He's angry," "It's kids"), and it had the effect of drawing me closer to Sweetie.

I asked, "Doesn't anyone ever go into his room?"

"He won't let them in," Buddy said. And then, resentfully, "I never thought he'd last this long."

Several years before, Buddy had proposed to buy him out. He offered him the same amount of money he had owed him, the hundred thousand for the work Miranda had done. The answer was no. Miranda would not even consider it. And when he talked about this stubborn resident — which was seldom, because the subject was so unwelcome — Buddy always ended by saying darkly, "If only I could get rid of him."

It was the noise, Buddy said. It was bad for business. "Not that it's loud — it's a strange scraping. I know it's probably him sanding, but it sounds like someone scratching dry skin."

"Or making love in a creaking bed."

"You got quite an imagination."

I realized that I had told him too much. I said, "I'm sure he's making something."

"Of course he's making something. It's covered by a cloth. I've seen the cloth — peeked at it anyway. He keeps the blinds drawn. Kawika, back when he was the window cleaner, used to think he was making a canoe. This was right in the beginning. Maybe he's been working on the same thing for years."

"How could it take so long?"

Buddy said, "I hate it when people ask me the same questions that I ask myself."

But something had been accomplished. In the room on the floor below Miranda's, under the spell of his seductive sounds, Sweetie and I had made love, and a child was conceived, and we were now living together in the hotel with our little girl, Rose. I had begun again from scratch: the shelf of books, the bank account, the credit card, a car, a Hawaii driver's license — another life, a narrower circle, different hopes. "Are you the child's grandfather?" the nurse had asked at Queen's Medical Center when I took Rose for a vaccination.

To be the manager of a hotel in which one of the guests was invisible was not so strange, Buddy said. He had known many reclusive guests over the years. There was an old Canadian woman in 1110, Melva Jean McHorn, who arrived from Calgary just before Christmas and stayed until March, who was so seldom seen that I stopped her in the lobby one day and pointedly asked if I could help her, not realizing that she had been a guest for months. "Seasonal affective disorder," she said. Other guests only went out at night. Buddy had said, "Get used to it."

Roland Miranda was a lot less odd than some, Buddy said. It was possible that one of these resolute old men who crossed the lobby without looking left or right was Miranda. I stopped asking.

And the *toc-toc-toc* of a mallet tapping wood still struck me as the possible prodding of an attentive lover. From this sound alone, the physicality of it, I knew it was old-fashioned work — no power tools, no harsh noises, just the rocking and squeaking that, when I heard it from below, still had the power to excite me.

"It's some kind of Whyan chest," the new window cleaner said when I asked. I could not contain my curiosity. I kept asking for details. "It's on two sawhorses."

"In his room?"

"What's wrong with that?"

The staff were annoyed that I should question Miranda's activities. They felt he had a right to do whatever he wanted, and they took a certain satisfaction in the thought that Miranda the local man had outsmarted Buddy and the mainland *haole* — outsmarted everyone.

I could deal with Miranda only by staying out of the room downstairs, 409, and by not listening, not caring. When I assigned the room, the guests either complained of the noise or smiled significantly, saying nothing, having found the sounds as inspirational to passion as I had. Miranda had outsmarted me, too. There was nothing to be done. The only remedy was to leave him to his privacy and regard him as another character in the Hotel Honolulu. Though it also occurred to me that Miranda had taken a lover and that the noises were exactly what they seemed — two people making love, a young woman jump-starting Miranda's engine.

One day, a new guest said, "The honeymooners are at it again."

This was Ed Figland from Sunnyvale, California, who had occupied 409 for two weeks with his wife, Lorraine. His very weary wife: Lorraine had become the object of Ed's unexpectedly frequent advances. It was reassuring to know that I was not the only susceptible one.

I said, "Do you want to be moved?"

He said no, and laughed, but the next day he reported that the lovers had stopped. I knew this was the first time in the years I had worked there that Miranda had ceased his daytime carpentry that I associated with afternoon delight.

After the Figlands left I went to the room and listened. Nothing. I gave it a few more days, then I knocked at Miranda's. No answer.

I used my passkey and entered. I found him lying in the most elaborately carved coffin I had ever seen, with all the chips and sawdust around it, masses of shavings. He was alone, and *hownah,* as Pidgin had it — reeking. He had at last finished making his coffin, and so it was his moment to climb in and expire.

8

Child's Play

THE CALIFORNIA GUEST said to Rose, "I have to make a telephone call." He picked up a banana, held it to the side of his head, and began talking into it in a serious voice, saying, "Look, this is Ed Figland, and it's important that you bring the toys to the hotel right away, because there's a pretty little girl here who wants them."

Rose frowned at him. She said, "That's not a telephone."

"It's a cellular phone."

Another guest, Mrs. Charmaine Becker, hearing this exchange, laughed hard into her newspaper, rattling the pages.

"It's a banana," Rose said.

"But what about the toys?" Figland said, and the note of pleading in his voice seemed authentic, like the symptom of an illness.

"If it's not a telephone, how can there be toys?" Rose said, almost tearful in exasperation.

Figland, struggling to recover but still holding the banana like a phone, said to Mrs. Becker, "I guess when she sees the toys she'll believe that this thing works."

"What kind of toys?" Rose asked.

"Nice ones. Little dolls that talk."

"They don't really talk. They have a machine inside that makes a voice."

"How do you know it's not a real voice?"

"Because it's a machine and because it says the same thing over and over," Rose said in a quaky voice. She was fighting the urge to scream at the man.

"But you can pretend it's real," Figland said.

And then she did scream. "It's not real!"

Speaking into the banana, Figland said, "What kind of little girl doesn't like dolls?"

"I like these," Rose said, showing her GI Joe in his combat fatigues, "but I know they're not real."

Looking up from her newspaper, Mrs. Becker, who also tried to play with Rose from time to time, said, "That's a doll, kiddo."

"It's an action figure," Rose said.

"Who said they were real?" Figland asked.

"You did. You said they talked."

"I didn't mean they really talked."

"What did you mean?" Rose was staring at Figland, who was stammering. Mrs. Becker moved her lips, encouraging him. There was both anger and pity in Rose's eyes, as though this sad ignorant man was trying to mislead her. She said, "Can I have that?"

"Want to make a call?"

"No. I want to eat it."

On another occasion, late one night when Rose was down with a cold but still feeling well enough to trail after me while I set the burglar alarm in the lobby, another guest, Harriet Najeeby, just arriving at the front desk, saw Rose and with wide eyes said, "I just made it! If I hadn't've hurried, that car would have turned into a pumpkin."

With feverish eyes, Rose looked at this white-haired woman and said, "It's a taxi."

"But it changes into a pumpkin at midnight."

"No it doesn't."

"How do you know?"

"Because it's a taxi," Rose said in a croaky voice. "A pumpkin is something you make into pies."

"And you pay 'taxis' to the government."

"Taxes," Rose said.

"What if I told you that taxi was pulled by twenty white mice, right under the hood?"

Her face crumpling, Rose turned away from Harriet Najeeby and said, "Daddy!"

Smart kid, these guests said, but I knew they didn't believe it. To them Rose seemed obstinate and flat-footed. No imagination. One guest who had failed with Rose said to me, "Kids are supposed to dream," and Figland seemed to hate her after his encounter, though he did not give up. Because my daughter was the issue, I began to watch Figland closely. He scratched dogs' ears, picked up stray cats and stroked them, bantered with waitresses, pinched the leaves off potted plants, engaged other children in conversation — all of that, I assumed, to draw attention to himself. But I saw that he was not malicious; he could be genuinely playful. His wife saw me watching him and said, "He's a kid at heart."

So I didn't intervene. Anyway, Rose could look after herself. She was not a child at heart. She was thoughtful, intense, a listener, a watcher, a rememberer, trying to make sense of the world from her child's vantage point, three feet off the ground.

Mrs. Becker and Mrs. Najeeby said Rose was cute. Figland said, "Great-looking kid." I suppose they were trying to reassure me, because she was of mixed race, a Hawaiian *hapa*. Get used to this, I told myself.

But Sweetie was head of Housekeeping, and Puamana kept odd hours and, except for exercise and her idiosyncratic work, stayed in her room on the third floor with her cat, Popoki. I did not tell anyone that Rose's grandfather was John F. Kennedy, but I could see the features of the late president in her, the Irishness as well as the islands in her face, something about the mouth and the bright eyes. I often looked after Rose, and I did not object to her playing in the lobby. Other children fooled there, though not many. The Hotel Honolulu was better known for its scandals than its children's programs (Buddy, who liked the scandals, told me, "No hula lessons, unless they're horizontal"), and so like most visitors to Hawaii, Mrs. Becker and the Figlands left their children at home, if they had any.

"That man's silly," Rose said. "And that woman is a *lolo*."

Figland said, "This is a magic wand."

"It's a fishing rod."

"The fact that it looks like a fishing rod doesn't mean it can't be a magic wand," Figland said. "Why can't it be both?"

"Because there's no such thing as a magic wand," Rose said.

Keeping himself in check — I could see his shoulders rise toward his neck — Figland grasped the fishing rod like a horsewhip.

"So it's a fishing rod," Rose said.

But Ed Figland, seeking friendship, persevered, and on another day, when there was thunder, he said to Rose, "My mother used to tell me that thunder was the sound of the angels' bowling balls."

"Why are you joking me?" Rose said in a demanding tone, not so that he would reply but so that he would stop.

"It made me less afraid," Figland said.

He was a tall man who had to crouch in order to hold this conversation.

"What were you afraid of?" Rose wrinkled her nose and looked up at the bent-over man.

"The noise."

"Are you afraid now?"

"A little bit," Figland said, hesitating.

"Thunder won't hurt you," Rose said in the childish singsong that suits the childishness of pedantry, "but lightning can. It's electricity. Electricity can kill you. Never put your finger in the wall socket or you'll get a shock."

"So you're afraid too," Figland said, pleased with himself.

Rose faced him, narrowing her eyes in mistrust as though he had unfairly cornered her; and then she raised her head and with the breathy haughtiness that only a child can bring off, said to Figland, "I'm afraid of scabby people in dirty clothes who scream bad words and fight in the street."

Mrs. Becker tried too. She showed Rose a potted orchid and said, "This is a happy little plant."

"Plants don't have brains," Rose said.

"A plant can still be happy."

"You mean healthy."

Instead of intervening I simply listened and awaited Sweetie's approach, her scooping up Rose in the early evening and saying, "Time for your bath, Rosebud," and my stern, literal-minded daughter was transformed into a picture of smiling placidity.

"Say good night, Rosebud."

"Good night."

Mrs. Becker was smiling at the mother and daughter. In a little far-off hotel among palm trees and volcanoes, these visitors liked being reminded of the most humdrum rituals of domesticity, even more than being reminded of the palm trees and volcanoes.

"Time for swimming," Mrs. Becker said.

"Not swimming," Rose said. She glared at Mrs. Becker. "A bath."

Ed Figland, on his way through the lobby with a towel over his arm, heard the exchange and said, "When I was little I used to be afraid that I'd go straight down the drain when my mother pulled the plug at night."

While Mrs. Becker laughed softly and touched Figland's arm in appreciation, as though he had awakened in her a memory of infancy, Rose said, "No one is little enough to go down the drain."

Upstairs, in the bathtub, she became exasperated again at the mere mention of Figland's name and said she didn't want to see him or talk to him. She did not use the words; she did not need to; but it was clear that she regarded Ed Figland and Mrs. Becker as irrational, shallow, and easily frightened, a skittishness that caused them to be unreliable, provocative, and unfunny.

Rose said, "I don't like them."

After that, these people kept away from Rose. Figland was much happier when his wife showed up and accompanied him. They went everywhere, in matching aloha patterns.

"That's the little girl I was telling you about," he said one day.

Mrs. Figland looked at Rose with disapproval, saying nothing. She had heard the whole story.

"Aren't you glad we never had any children?" she said, and soon after that the Figlands became friendly with Mrs. Becker and Mrs. Najeeby. I often heard their giggling at mealtimes and their shrieks as they splashed in the pool.

9

The Limping Waiters

P EOPLE THINKING it was remarkable whispered that two of our waiters, who were friends, had the same distinctive disability, each a foreshortened leg — Wilnice's left, Fishlow's right. They wobbled and bobbed, bumping shoulders, but it was no coincidence. They had met in a hospital ward where there were many others like them, and been roommates there in the hip unit, and become friends in rehab. Their common disability helped their friendship and formed a crude basis for mutual understanding, like a colorful ethnic trait. But that was not their bond. No one except I knew their bond was much odder, a disability of a profounder kind.

They were "seasonal hires." Our busy months at the hotel, November to March, and the Japanese frenzy of Golden Week, in late April and early May, meant we had to add more wait staff. Each year, from their home in Texas, where the slack season was winter, I hired these two men. They were in their forties, Charlie Wilnice and Ben Fishlow, who arrived as a pair rather than a couple. They came pedaling and pumping at you. They were through with the Waikiki Pearl, our neighbor hotel, and said they would tell me why, providing I never asked for references. I understood this to mean that the explanation itself would define them, as sometimes when someone wishing to express something forceful says, "Let me tell you a story."

Wilnice had been waiting on a young Japanese woman. You noticed their big floppy hats, which, with their skinny stemlike bodies, gave them the aspect of decorative flowers. This one had said, shyly but formally, like a sentence she had practiced, "Please you can deliver this to my room," and handed over a small purse. Wilnice did so after work, and she met him at the door. He was surprised to see her — what was the point of the delivery? — then he knew everything. She was dressed — undressed, rather — wearing a robe, a happi coat, which was undone, loose at the front, unbuttoned. No, the buttons were her nipples; this young woman was naked. "Like one of those pillow pictures," Wilnice said. Certain small, precise erotic Japanese prints, called *shunga,* depict egg-faced women improbably exposing themselves while observing the conventional horror of body hair, the love of crushed printed fabric and submission, the proper woman made wanton, the rape fantasies of Hokusai subjects incised in woodblocks. This young woman mimicked a courtesan, tempting Wilnice by seeming meek.

"Please you come in." And yet she cowered. Her bad grammar made her seem more innocent and helpless.

Wilnice stepped backward, bobbing on his bad leg, and went away, stride-hop, stride-hop.

Telling Fishlow about it later, seeing his friend smile, Wilnice had no idea that his shock, his puritanical disapproval, had made him remember every detail of the fleeting encounter — the button business, her slightly bowed legs, the pale hollows of her inner thighs, her red thick-soled clogs, her black-painted nails and black lipstick. And he repeated it, answered questions ("It was a junior suite . . . Yes, she was alone"), believing Fishlow was also shocked.

The next day, Fishlow sought out the young woman, went out of his way to serve her. She seemed to notice his leg, the way he walked, how he surged toward her, bumping people as he passed them.

She asked for tea. Fishlow brought it solemnly to her table. She offered him the purse that Wilnice had described and repeated the formula: "Please you can deliver this to my room."

Attempting a bow, Japanese fashion, Fishlow bent himself crookedly, lifting his arms for balance. At four, when he knocked off work, he went up in the service elevator to the woman's room. She answered the door. It was all as Wilnice had described, like a promise kept: the loose happi coat, the nakedness, skin like silk, hairless, smooth, without a mark, pigeon-toed in the red clogs. She invited him inside.

"You sit here?" she said tentatively, patting the sofa next to her.

Fishlow obliged. Without any preliminaries — Wilnice had supplied those — he kissed her. She clung to him, groped him through his clothes, but thoughtfully, as if she were squeezing a fruit, testing it for ripeness. Her small, almost pressureless chafing gestures roused him.

She suddenly got up, went to the window, and peered through the blinds, turning her back on him. If she heard the drawer open and shut she did not show it.

Holding the Gideons Bible, Fishlow came bobbing and swaying behind her, hiked up her happi coat, moved her feet wider apart, and as she canted forward to receive him, Fishlow chucked the Bible to the floor, placed his foot on it to brace his short leg, and thus braced, he entered, lifting her. Then she reacted, as though lifted onto a peg.

"No! No!" she cried out, which terrified him. He stopped, fearing that her plea might carry even through the closed window. But in a softer voice she implored him to continue. All the while, she remained turned away from him, said nothing more, did not appear to see him balancing on one leg to hoist his pants before pedaling out of the room, stride-hop, stride-hop.

Recklessly, against all hotel rules, he met her again. He could not help himself. It was a feature of their lovemaking that Fishlow never saw her face, that somehow she always contrived to hide it; and they were always upright, so the Gideons Bible was another feature. And "No! No!" And her reaching behind and clawing him like a cat. Like lovers on Sundays who sleepwalk through museums as a break from bed, they went to a movie and once to a sushi bar — perfunctory, almost meaningless, she had practically no English. But her body spoke. Her body said: For the sake of my modesty, I must pretend that it is rape, but don't be fooled — look closely and you will see it is rapture.

"Rapture?" Wilnice asked, and looked so wounded Fishlow said nothing more.

Still they worked, waiting on tables. Fishlow's intensity bordered on obsession. He had no words to describe it; he was possessed. What he wanted to say was insane: I understand cannibalism. What was that supposed to mean? Then, six days from the day he had met her, the woman left, her holiday at an end, Golden Week over.

Sneaking her name from the hotel register, Fishlow wrote to her. Her address was a whole incomprehensible paragraph of short words and long numbers. There was no reply. Fishlow called her telephone number. Now he could not remember whether she had ever spoken to him in English. He got someone shrieking in Japanese, a sexless squawk box, in answer to his pleading questions.

Wilnice did not know what to do with Fishlow during his crying jags. He wasn't sure how the doll woman had swept over his friend, nearly destroying him. Fishlow had been so happy, so hungry. She had made him into a willing dog, and now she was gone and he was still a dog, but a desperate whimpering mutt with his scummy tongue hanging out. That was the worst of love.

His only solution was to seek help from his limping friend Wilnice, who had seen the woman first. So he told him one day when they were out walking — bobbing and bumping, as usual.

Fishlow was so sorrowful that his story had the precision of regret, of guilt and blame, every incriminating detail noted: the back of her head and her neck as she turned away, the manner in which he had snatched the Bible and thrown it down, his mounting her from behind, her body full of chicken bones, the way she had pretended to resist. He was specific and self-mocking because he was wounded.

"What do you mean 'at the window'?" Wilnice asked, his mouth agape.

Guessing that he could have been the man she wanted, that the young Japanese woman could not tell them apart — how their staggering and limping made them equal in her eyes — Wilnice was envious, and the envy soured his guts, making him sick with sorrow for having retreated from the woman's door. He took a ghastly delight in Fishlow's descriptions of the woman's hunger. Like a cat! From behind! Like squeezing a fruit! Tottering on her clogs! Wilnice moaned to himself, I have always lacked conviction.

But Fishlow envied Wilnice's self-possession, the way in which Wilnice had simply backed off from the woman, this woman who burdened Fishlow's memory — more than that, infected him with regret, a humiliation, a casual demon. As Wilnice could not rid his mind of the details Fishlow had related, Fishlow continually saw Wilnice in their little apartment, taking his shoes off, one shoe thicker-soled than the other, microwaving some chili and eating it with a plastic spoon, all this innocent economy, sitting like a child in front of the television set, while he stood lopsided in spite of the Bible, his pants around his ankles, naked in the naked woman's room, the woman crying out "No! No!" and averting her face. Fishlow envied him and thought, I have always been too impulsive — it will shorten my life. And Wilnice thinking, I am afraid. I don't know how to live.

Each man was consumed by regret, the one from having rejected the woman, the other from having made love to her. Each man believed he had failed, and the way they walked was like emphasis, as though trying to trample on the memory of the woman.

10

A Game of Dice

LEAVING OUR Paradise Lost bar, shouldering his way through the hotel lobby, the young man caught my eye and said, "Now I've heard everything!" in a provocative way, too loudly, to get my attention. I was hoping my silence and my bland smile would calm him.

"Can I help you?" I said. "I'm the manager."

In his early thirties and handsome — all that springy hair — he wore a dark shirt that set off his pink impatient face. Breathless and a bit flustered, he looked like someone who had just been disarmed by an insult. The way a man looks when he's slapped by a woman.

"See that guy? He's out of his mind!"

He was gone before I could tell him that the man he had pointed out, Eddie Alfanta, was a regular at the bar, always came with his wife, Cheryl, whom he adored, and was a well-known accountant downtown — overserious but successful, with an office on Bishop Street. What I liked most about him was his passion for gambling. Eddie was not the first accountant I had known who gambled, though the risks of the crap table and the solemnity of the ledger made him seem paradoxical and confident. His wagers were modest. He usually won. He said he had a system.

So intent was Eddie on peering around the bar that he did not see me. Where was his wife? Cheryl was a small woman, elfin almost — short hair, delicate bones, tiny hands and feet, very tidy, always neatly dressed, and pale, especially in contrast to big, dark

Eddie Alfanta, who boasted of his hairiness. That Eddie was also proud of Cheryl, his *haole* trophy, was plain to see, and he had the slightly fussy henpecked demeanor that characterized the ethnic partner in many Hawaiian interracial marriages. He was self-conscious, eager to do the right thing but not sure what the right thing was, and had the uneasy notion that people were watching. And they were.

The next time I checked the bar, I saw Eddie with the dice cup in his hand, shaking it, making it chuckle. Buddy Hamstra had brought the leather cup and the pair of dice from Bangkok, where men in bars tossed dice to determine who would pay for the next round of drinks. I often studied the fixed attentive faces and bared teeth of the men going at it and thought how we are at our most aggressive and competitive, most animalistic, in our games.

What I noticed tonight was not the game but Eddie's opponent. We seldom saw surfers in Paradise Lost. The better class of surfer, one of Trey's buddies, out for a week of catching waves, yes, but never a local full-season hard-core dude like this one — barefoot, broad-shouldered, bandy-legged, tattoos on the small of his back and another between his shoulder blades, with the name CODY, all the tattoos visible through his torn shirt. His cap on backward, his long hair was sunned, the color and texture of straw, his eyes pale and vacant, his skin burned, his masses of freckles, big and small, adding to his look of recklessness. He was young, probably not more than twenty-two or -three. Eddie Alfanta was over forty, so it looked funny, the two of them struggling with the dice cup: the swarthy accountant with his shirt tucked in and two pens in his breast pocket, the youth in ragged shirt and shorts — Stüssy cap, Quiksilver shorts, Local Motion shirt. He had dirty feet, bruised toes.

"A water rat," Trey said.

The two men hovered over the tumbled dice on the bar, and I also thought how sad games are for their rules and rituals, for making us absurdly hopeful, for being predictable, for their pathetic purpose, which was to divert us for the length of time it took to play them. All players looked to me like desperate losers; games were the pastimes of people — always men — who could not bear to be alone, who did not read. There was a brutal pathos in the game of dice, the little chuckle, the toss, the click, the overwhelming significance of the dots.

Or was it just harmless fun that defied interpretation? There was something wrong in my caring about it, or even noticing it, so I turned away and concentrated on what was much more obvious: for the first time Eddie's wife was not with him in the bar. His laughter made that emphatic, and he crowded the surfer, maneuvering the dice cup, making the dice chatter, his mouth open a bit too wide, his laughter a bit too shrill, touching the surfer's arm when he won. Eddie was dark and baked, the boy fair and burned — I sensed attraction. But I was glad they were laughing there; I liked thinking of my hotel as a refuge.

Back at the desk, fishing for information, I mentioned to Chen that Eddie Alfanta was alone in the bar.

"His wife's upstairs," Chen said. "I gave them 802. They checked in a few hours ago. One night."

That was unusual, the Honolulu couple staying in a Honolulu hotel for one night. Maybe it meant that their house was being tented and fumigated, but if so, they would have had the work done on a weekend or else spent the time on a neighbor island.

"These flowers just came for Mrs. Alfanta."

The bouquet was on the desktop. The greeting card read, *Happy birthday, my darling. All my love, Eddie.*

A romantic birthday interlude — it explained everything. I went through the month's occupancy record in my office, and afterward, in search of a drink, I saw Eddie alone in the bar, nursing a beer, looking reflective. There was no sign of the surfer, and I remembered what the fleeing man had said about Eddie earlier in the evening: He's out of his mind.

But Eddie was the picture of serenity. Somewhat quieter than usual, perhaps; alone but content. Had the gambling made him thoughtful? Anyway, the game was at an end.

Had he been rebuffed by the water rat? The last time I had seen him, he was pushing against the young man as the dice clattered onto the bar, shouting for drinks, tapping the young man's tattooed arm. I resisted drawing any conclusions, but it had certainly seemed to me a playful courtship, the two men jostling at the rail in a rough mating dance, laughing over the game of dice.

I said, "Who's winning?" because Eddie was still absentmindedly shaking the cup.

"We're spending the night," he said, and his chuckle was like the sound of the dice.

"So I see," I said, and to test him, because I already knew, I asked, "A celebration?"

"Cheryl's birthday." He tossed the dice, frowned at the combination, and gathered them quickly. "This is a big one. Her fortieth. Last year we went to Vegas. Cheryl's lucky. She won five hundred dollars at the crap table. Guy came up to her and humped her for luck. 'You're on a roll,' they said. You should have seen it."

He stopped and saw the half-smile of concentration on my face. I was thinking, Humped her for luck? He understood the unspoken question in my mind.

"I loved it," he said.

Small, pale Cheryl in her tiny shoes surrounded by big, hopeful gamblers, and Eddie gloating like the winner in a dog show.

"Birthday before that, we spent the weekend learning to scuba-dive. Getting certified. I was terrible. I figured it was a gamble. I almost panicked and drowned. The guys on the course were amazed that Cheryl had picked it up so quickly. They were all over her. You should have seen her — what a knockout in a wetsuit. Skintight."

Pleased with the recollection, he touched his thighs as though tracing a wetsuit, and he gathered the dice again. Another chuckle and toss.

"For her thirty-fifth we had a real blast. My buddy and I took her to Disneyland. She was like a kid." He smiled, remembering, and wheezed with satisfaction. "She wore him out!"

Wagging the dice cup, he rolled again.

"Where is she now?"

"I got her a surfer. They're upstairs." He looked happy. He was still rolling the dice.

"Who won?"

"Who do you think?"

The young man in the torn shirt entering the room, his bruised toes on the carpet, the lamp low, Cheryl in her birthday lingerie, no bigger than a tall child but game for this, and the whole business more or less wordless — this was how I imagined it. The pair of them tossing on the bed with Eddie downstairs. And at the end of it all a certain apprehension, because no one knew what would happen when it was over. That was the sadness of games.

"I have no idea," I said.

Eddie just smiled. He had forgotten the question.

I sent Keola and Kawika up to monitor the corridor near the Alfantas' room in case of trouble. Later, they told me how they had seen the surfer leaving, "looking futless," and heard Cheryl sternly saying, "Don't kiss me." Still later, I saw Cheryl and Eddie very lovey-dovey in the lounge, Eddie still tossing the dice. Perhaps he was the only one who had gotten what he wanted.

11

Love Letters in the Pending File

MY CAREER as a writer had not trained me for anything practical. I thought of describing this in a despairing book of exile I would title *Who I Was*. Writing had made me unemployable, had isolated me and given me the absurd delusion that I could perform tasks that were beyond me. Even my typing was poor, so I wrote with a pencil, but in this scribble I had put up buildings, designed cities, fixed cars, robbed banks, settled arguments, wooed beautiful women, given eloquent speeches, managed businesses, committed perfect crimes. And I had always had the last word. I had even run hotels, and in one book ran a highly successful brothel in Singapore. All this while ardently fantasizing at a little table in an upstairs room.

I had no marketable skills. I had done nothing except try to turn words into deeds: just dreams. I was useless at managing money. I had never had any employees, not even a secretary. I could not imagine being able to deal with workers' moods and temperaments. So, as a hotel manager in Hawaii — the job was a gift — I was grateful to my employees for their work. They ran the hotel and they knew it, knew they were in charge of the place, and of me. I understood fantasy — it was what writing had taught me.

Still new to the job, I spent hours in my office, the one Buddy had vacated when he made me manager. I was looking for clues as to how to run the hotel properly. I found unpaid bills and faded Polaroids of blurred bodies. I found foreign coins, postage stamps, plastic bags of "killer buds," scraps of paper with women's names and telephone numbers scrawled on them in Buddy's writing, and cartoons torn from the newspaper that Buddy must have thought funny. I found, neatly typed, a description of Buddy's death, which was unexpected, because he was alive, enjoying his early retirement on the North Shore. *Buddy Hunter Hamstra, Rest in Peace.* It was Buddy's obituary, but who had written it? It looked genuine, two typed sheets, the letters pounded into the paper, most of the punctuation punched right through to show daylight, in the manner of big old typewriters. This had been written some time ago.

"From the outside [it began] he seemed a clown, a fool, an incompetent, but deep down he was very serious, often weeping on the inside. He was proud of his ability to fix anything that was broken. He was proudest of being able to mend a broken heart. In his youth he had been handsome and women had fallen for him. He was unable to resist, but he was gallant and they never forgot him, and he never forgot them. He served his country in the field of military intelligence, finding his way in secret from one Pacific Island to another, befriending the natives, who praised him in song and story. It is said that he left many a token of love behind on those islands and on his return he was greeted with cries of 'Darling!' and 'Daddy!' which brought a smile to his lips. 'I will pass this way but once,' he used to say . . ."

I read on. The grammar faltered, the spelling was childish ("risist," "gallent," "milatery"), but it was earnest. I did not recognize this deceased person until I got to the end, where the paragraph about friendship and what it meant to him was described.

"Friendship was everything to him. He never turned away a friend. He was generous to a fault . . . the ultimate in kindness. No one was a stranger to him, which was why his name was so apt: Buddy."

The sensitive, sweet-natured man in this obituary was unknown to me. Buddy was a rascal, he was explosive, and he took pleasure in tricking his friends. And he was alive.

Yet I was fascinated. Whether this obituary represented the man he believed himself to be, or the one he wished he were, did not matter. What mattered was that in the peak of health he had sat down in his office at the Hotel Honolulu and composed this obituary, and got someone to type it. The last line read, "No flowers. Aloha attire."

It inspired me. A person had to be bold to write his own obituary, and even if it was a joke, it was a good joke. I thought I would do the same, as a parody, writing the obituary I feared I would get, with wrong dates, erroneous inclusions, deliberate omissions, just an illiterate's version of my life.

In my head I began to envision my own inaccurate obituary. I was the grumpy traveler in a book that had been a bestseller in the 1970s. I had lived overseas. Movies had been made of some of my books — the movie stars' names were given. I had abandoned my family and run off. Of the thirty-odd books I had written, two were mentioned by name, and one of my worst reviews was quoted, along with the bitter remarks of one of my enemies who claimed to be my friend. A woman who had stalked me for years accused me of having taken advantage of her: "He groped me." I had come and gone. I had vanished in the Pacific where, in total obscurity, written out and written off, I had been running a small hotel.

This balance sheet made me so melancholy I spent a day writing more versions of my obituary, then tearing them up, writing epitaphs (*Here lies . . .*) and destroying them. Sweetie interrupted me while I was writing and asked me what I meant in a room report when I wrote, "feety smell . . . cheesy sheets," and what was I doing?

"Nothing," I said. "By the way, when I die just scatter my ashes off the North Shore."

"Then can I find another husband?"

"Of course."

"You reading Buddy's stuff," she said, peering over my shoulder.

What I had been doing was more intrusive even than Sweetie imagined, for bundled with the obituary was a stack of love letters, written over a long period to Momi, Buddy's ex-wife, the earliest a few years ago, the most recent ones dated just before Buddy hired me. They were passionate appeals, they were descriptions of daily activity, much of it improbable, they were requests for help and advice, they were promises, and they were also the most tender declarations of love I had ever read, the more so for their heartfelt artlessness, all of them handwritten in Buddy's imploring blue scribble. The more clumsy a piece of writing, the greater its capacity to move, and these love letters of

Buddy's in the Pending file seemed to prove what the poet said, that imperfection is the language of art.

"Does Momi ever come to the hotel?" I asked.

Sweetie said, "She *mucky.*"

Dead, for ten years, which explained why Buddy had never sent the letters, why they had accumulated in the Pending file.

Buddy had seemed to me to be borderline literate. I was wrong. He had no gift, but he had a complex motive. In his heartache he had discovered the impulses that lay behind all good writing: ignoring everything that had ever been written, taking control of time, and most of all, inventing the truth.

Writing his own obituary was a wonderful conceit, even if the writing itself was cliché-ridden and mawkish. The love letters were classics, the better and more convincing for their crudeness. Buddy already knew what it had taken me years to discover — that fiction can be an epistle to the living, but more often the things we write, believing they matter, are letters to the dead.

12

Sex, Thirdhand

SNEAKING LOOKS at other people's mail, I told myself, was part of my job, my exploratory life as a writer. Yet after I abandoned writing in Hawaii I felt an even greater need to poke into people's mail. There were treasures in my boss's files — his own mendacious obituary, and years after his first wife had died, he still wrote love letters to her. Was he just lonely, or was this a bizarre form of atonement? The only qualm I had — it was my perennial qualm — was that I would be found out in my snooping and seen living my life thirdhand, the writer's maddening distance from the real world.

So as not to embarrass him, or myself, I took Buddy's entire filing cabinet, containing the personal papers I had read and the business documents I had shuffled, and hand delivered it to him at his house on the North Shore. I was directed by his bulky son, Bula, to the lanai.

Buddy lay face down, regal, on a massage table and was being scrubbed with what looked like fine white gravel by an island girl wearing a wet bikini and dripping mittens. She walked barefoot, on tiptoe, in decorous silence, and even the tiny bows on her bikini looked delicate to me, asking to be tugged. Buddy looked baked and iced, like an enormous sugar-coated pastry.

"This is Mariko. She's half Japanese and half *popolo*," Buddy said. "Every seventh of December she has an uncontrollable urge to bomb Pearl Bailey."

"Not true," said Mariko in the squeaky, grinning voice of local girls that still set my teeth on edge.

"Salt scrub," he explained. "She's another tool of my lust."

She just laughed and went on coating him with salt.

"Recognize this table? It sure has seen plenty of action."

He showed no interest in the papers I had brought.

"If I cared about that stuff, would I have left it at the hotel for everyone to read?"

This seemed to be his way of saying that he knew what I had done. Now I was sorry I had not read the whole lot and studied it for its fantasy and invention.

"Just toss it."

Had he forgotten the self-serving fictions he had placed in the Pending file? Only a writer like me could be so concerned, and I was perhaps the more obsessive for being unable to write myself. So I had become a more intense listener and snooper — *niele,* as the Hawaiians said. Nosy.

Now the girl stood aside and a young man hosed off the clinging salt slush, spraying it from Buddy's skin. Sludge and coarse salt and water splashed to the blue-tiled floor of the lanai.

"That's the old me," Buddy said, sitting up, looking pink and peeled. "I'm exfoliated."

"Finish," the girl said. "Time for massage."

"This is the part I like best," Buddy said. "Hula hands."

At that moment I had a vivid glimpse of a man his age in a soaked raincoat hurrying in wet shoes down the Strand on a winter-dark afternoon to join a mass of sodden people jamming themselves into the entrance of a tube station smelling of damp newspapers to begin the stifling trip back to a clammy house. Then the vision passed. It made me more attentive to Buddy, who had tucked his towel together like a pareu and was entering his house, followed by the pretty girl.

The young man with the hose said, "Buddy mentioned the hotel. You connected with the Hotel Honolulu?" He smiled. Something was happening behind his eyes, a memory surfacing and glazing them.

Most of the people I knew at the hotel, both locals and visitors, were essentially undomesticated. They hated questions, because a question required an answer that forced them to think; usually the process of thought convulsed them and produced nothing more than a grunt. I became used to silences as replies, or talk so slow as to have no meaning. This man surprised me by saying something more.

"Because I hear some amazing things about that place, man."

"I work there." I didn't want to encourage him by seeming too interested, though I was struck by his using the word "amazing." "But nothing ever happens at the Hotel Honolulu."

Glancing around, the instinctive head-swivel of a cautious bird just before it pecks, he said, "Want to burn a fat one?"

"I'll pass."

Dropping the sprayer he had used to wash the salt off Buddy, he approached me and lit a chubby joint. He sucked and gasped and said, "That place rocks."

I smiled again. *Amazing? Rocks?* I wondered what he knew of the old seedy hotel on the back street in Waikiki where I worked. The doubt on my face must have been obvious. It made him energetic.

"There's this surfer, Cody, a real gnarly dude. He rides the big waves out at Waimea, came eighth in the Eddie Aikau. Like, he was drinking at the bar, the Paradise Bar —"

"Paradise Lost."

"Whatever." He had the blinking, stammering delivery of someone whose brain had been fried by chemical substances — overstimulated and fused circuits that made him smile or tune out for no obvious reason. "He's in the bar and a woman offers him a grand to go upstairs and hose her."

"Let me get this straight," I said, because one element in the story sounded familiar. "This surfer guy was offered money to sleep with a woman at the hotel?"

"Yeah," he said eagerly, reminded of what he had just said. "He's hanging out, drinking at the bar, and a woman comes up to him and buys him a drink. She's some tourist chick from the mainland, right? With a killer body. It's her birthday. She tells him that she's alone and wants a really nice birthday present. 'Like what?' Cody asks. 'Like you.'"

In a halting way, blurring his mimicry, attempting the two voices, pausing too long, sucking on the joint, he conveyed the information that Cody had demanded a thousand dollars, that the woman had laughed and said, "Follow me."

She had been wearing a light raincoat, buttoned to the neck, which was not odd, as a drizzle had been falling on Waikiki. When Cody had hesitated, the young woman unbuttoned a few buttons and showed that she was wearing lingerie underneath, nothing more. This glimpse gave Cody traction.

"It was like this incredible honeymoon suite at the hotel, with a huge mirror on the ceiling."

I nodded, because there was no such suite.

"The woman takes off the raincoat and she's just wearing this Victoria's Secret stuff. She hands him a Polaroid camera and says, 'You be the photographer.'"

"What was the point of the Polaroids?"

"Chicks like that love them. They collect them. But Cody was still sort of smiling. So she puts a porno on the VCR, to get him going."

I did not want to spoil a good story by telling him there were no VCRs in the rooms.

"The babe in the porno is wearing a dog collar and playing doggy. So this one with Cody does the same thing, puts on a dog collar and gives Cody a leash to hold. She shows him the stud in her tongue and goes down on him."

"What happened to the Polaroids?"

Camera, leash, collar, porno, mirror, stud — specific details, but the arrangement was vague. He didn't hear me.

"She's like, 'I'm your doggy. I'm your slave.'"

I said, "What kind of birthday present is this?"

"A skeevy one," he said, licking his teeth. "They order room service. They're in the Jacuzzi. When the food comes, they're like 'Hey, get in with us' to the Room Service babe."

No Jacuzzi either, and the Room Service waiter, our only one at night, would have been the limping middle-aged seasonal hires, either Charlie Wilnice or Ben Fishlow.

"She gets in with them! They do a few joints and pretty soon the two chicks are scarfing each other on the floor while Cody is standing over them choking his bone."

He thought he had impressed me, I laughed so hard, but I was laughing at the language. My laughter was a goad, so he laughed too, and went on.

"The husband comes in. He sees what's going down and there's a huge fight. Cody punches him out. The husband's covered in blood. He's just lying there. The women are so excited by the fight that they want more action. They both go down on Cody and he comes all over them. They love it. They're licking each other's faces and snapping Polaroids. Cody walks out with a thousand bucks."

Now he took a long, squeaking pull on the joint and sucked his teeth as he filled his lungs with smoke.

"Cody told you this?"

"He told TJ. TJ's a friend of Dean. Dean told me."

"What happened to the husband? the Room Service girl?"

"I don't know. They probably just grooved on it."

"What about all the blood?"

"Don't ask me. Hey, you're the one who works there."

For all its inventions and falsifications and outright lies, his story seemed truer than the one I had witnessed, for nothing was truer than fantasy. A little cry from inside the house signaled that Buddy's own fantasy had ended.

13

The Prevision of Hobart Flail

ONE OF THE happiest aspects for me of hotelkeeping in Honolulu was that we secretly assigned names to our guests — but only the odd, the impossible, the most colorful ones. "Chewy," "Dilbert," "Pac-Man," "Samurai," and one whose nose was always running, "Hana Bata." It made them easier to remember. I supplied "Mr. Prufrock," "Bunbury," "Mrs. Alfred Uruguay," and "Pinfold." I saw that my staff could be observant and imaginative and witty; I felt I had succeeded with them when one of my names was accepted. Naming these people satisfied my need to fictionalize what I was seeing in this new world of mine. They never lost their names. "Crazy Al's coming back next week," someone would say, and we knew what we were in for. One guest who was always making dire predictions was awarded the name Hobart Flail.

The most apparently helpful, complaisant people are often the nosiest, the most intrusive and manipulative. Hobart Flail, here for his annual two weeks, was one of those, and more. He was a large, dark, horse-faced man who always looked uncomfortable — too many clothes, too hot, needed a shave, hair matted and tangled. Seeing Rose for the first time, he said to me, "Be very careful. A child like that is always in danger. This is a world that devours its young."

He seemed to represent the modern tendency in public utterance toward prediction. Much of the day's news fell into the category of the prophetic — the direction of the economy, the eventual fate of a well-known figure, the outlook for a team, the prospects for a country, a yet-to-be-revealed trend. Was there anything more maddening than these overcertain and uncheckable pronouncements? There are news hounds who write about what has happened, but nothing is newer than a forecast of what is going to happen — the ultimate news is prophecy. Hobart Flail, who implied that he had the gift of prevision, was always making such forecasts, but in a sadistic manner, as though thrashing us. And he alone had the word. "What most people don't realize," he would begin, and he always finished with, "Very few people know this." It was always bad news — prophecy is often pessimistic, a kind of hostile gloating misery. He often said, "We live in wolfish times."

Flail had insulted me by predicting misfortune for Rose. He said he was doing me a favor. Usually he concentrated on larger issues. He surprised me one day by saying, "The whole Pacific is overfished. Fish stocks are at dangerously low levels. People don't realize that there is nothing for the sharks to eat. It's obvious they'll start feeding on swimmers."

If he had smiled even slightly, you would have taken this for black comedy. But no, he was serious.

"It's also the graywater runoff," he said. "Golf course pesticides are leaching into the aquifer. Very few people know that the low rainfall is already creating drought conditions and threatening the ecosystem. Bad water. Rationing. Toxic spillages are killing the reefs. Nick your shin on a reef and it's certain death."

Ozone depletion, ciguatera in sashimi, leptospirosis from rat urine in the Ala Wai Canal, projected drownings, fetal alcohol syndrome, the symptoms of lupus and osteoporosis and lymphoma, the frequency of cruise ships' tipping raw sewage offshore — he knew it all. And he knew medical terms. One guest announced at the bar in Paradise Lost that he had just peed red. He had eaten beets for dinner, but Hobart Flail said, "Renal carcinoma."

A guest who stayed with us to scuba-dive — "Scooby-Doo," from St. Louis — cut his leg on some coral.

"Even if you have that seen to, it's as good as infected. You're going to lose the leg."

Scooby stared at him and then cursed and limp-hopped away, favoring the leg.

"Algal blooms," Flail said. That was another thing. He used

oddly poetic terms in this dire news. "A cocktail of poisons," "a salad of rotting vegetation," "a plume of effluent." Another was "strange fruit."

And still his refrain was "We live in wolfish times."

It distressed me when he concentrated his attention on Rose. I wanted to shove him aside. I didn't mind his gabbling at me, but something diabolical darkened his eyes when he looked at my daughter, and I could see that she felt it too, the darkness like a bad smell.

"What is that man *for?*" she screeched, then clamped her mouth shut.

He winced at the remark; he was unused to anyone challenging him. Rose's small size seemed to enrage him. He was never more furious or animated than when he was among weak or simple people, because he was a bully. Hobart Flail was an enemy of the underdog. If he saw a football team struggling to win on TV he said, "They'll lose." He loved world news for all the disasters that were reported. Earthquakes. Cyclones. Fires. Massacres. Plagues. He was well acquainted with the horrors of Rwanda and Ethiopia and Chernobyl. He knew the death tolls.

"I predicted all that."

Years before, he had called attention to the logging that had caused rivers to be silted up and the terrible floods that had resulted. People's stupidity had brought them diseases and war. He had previewed it all; few people had listened.

The world's major religions were corrupt, he said. "The Vatican has the largest collection of pornography in the world."

Tunnels linked convents with monasteries; the cellars of nunneries were used for orgies. Some of his stories predicted the disinterring of thousands of strangled fetuses that had been buried alongside convents. Politicians were cheats, the police were crooks, sales clerks were thieves, waiters spat in your soup before they served it, waitresses were whores, the unions were run by the Mob, the Mob was run by the Vatican, the Vatican by the Freemasons — assassins all of them, funded by the drug trade. All of this would be revealed in the near future.

"We live in wolfish times."

If you were incautious enough to say, "Lovely day," he became agitated and would flail and reply, "You think so?"

"Ever been to Michigan?" he said. "There's some real funny

smells in Michigan. Chevron had a spill they admitted to, but there are other smells. No one knows what they are, and I know they're bad."

He spoke, even in Hawaii, of dust particles in the air, of tainted water, adulterated food, carcinogens in peanut butter, mouse droppings in the Happy Meals he saw me bringing home to Rose.

After my first encounter with him, I asked Buddy Hamstra who he was. Buddy said, "He's one brick short of a load," and just laughed. "Don't listen!" The man was harmless. He stayed at the Hotel Honolulu for two weeks every winter. He had been born somewhere in the Midwest to elderly parents and had polio as a child. He had not been expected to live. His recovery had been slow, and, bedridden, he had received his education at home, from those old, fretful people. For his first seventeen years he had not left the house. His parents died while he was still house-bound. He was diagnosed with clinical depression. He refused all medication. "Side effects!" Even so, he was afflicted by severe weight loss, liver damage, migraines.

None of this stopped him from prophesying a catastrophic future to anyone who would listen — arson and mayhem and decay. "Wolfish times." Understandably, no one listened. I first named him "Doctor Wolfpits" and then "Hobart Flail."

Nothing would induce him to take his medication. Rose was afraid of him, and Sweetie just laughed uneasily and walked the other way. Unless a guest was a public nuisance, you tolerated his eccentricity. I could not eject him for his ridiculous predictions, nor the way he dressed, though both made me uncomfortable. He wore dark long-sleeved shirts, heavy wool trousers, and fuzzy socks with his sandals. He was rumpled; he sweated. Why did he come to Hawaii?

"While it lasts," Hobart Flail said. "A little more global warming and one bad storm and the whole of Whyee is history."

We laughed and at last he went away. But that man Scooby-Doo, who nicked his shin on the reef? He lost his leg.

14

The Key Chain

THOSE PLOW-SHAPED metal detectors that old men on beaches use to find lost jewelry and money in the sand — the kind you wish you had, which looks so simple and profitable, "like an advanced form of agriculture," said Hobart Flail, who told me this story — the man in question had one. He was making his way down Ala Moana Beach, where the water is calm because of the reef. This was Glen Cornelius, from St. Louis, a shoe salesman, on his second day in Hawaii. He was the scuba diver we called Scooby-Doo.

"I dropped my key chain in the water," a small boy said, approaching him.

Glen glanced down at the squinting sun-struck boy, who was about the same age as his own son, Brett, a nine-year-old.

"This thing doesn't work in the water," Glen said, the metal detector in his hand.

"You've got a mask and flippers."

The kid was observant: the mask and flippers were in Glen's scuba diver's backpack, which, constructed of strong mesh so they would drip dry, made them visible but not obvious in the bulgy netting.

"It's a red key chain," the small boy said.

Glen had found the usual junk with his metal detector — buttons, foreign coins, rusty nails — but he hoped for more. He had brought the metal detector from St. Louis. It was new and worked perfectly, emitting a whistle when buried metal was nearby. You could strike gold. Alice, his wife, had taken Brett to a movie —

that dinosaur one. He had the afternoon free, for treasure hunting and maybe a swim later.

"I was out swimming," the boy said, "and reached into my pocket for my earplugs and pulled out my key chain and dropped it."

Glen wanted to think that if Brett had asked a stranger to help him, the stranger would oblige, especially if it was as serious as a bunch of keys. So he told the boy to mind his metal detector and earphones, and he put on his mask and flippers and swam out to the reef where one hunk jutted like a shark's fin, which the boy had indicated.

The seawater sloshing across the reef was soupy with suspended sand flecks, which blunted and twisted the light. The flat-topped reef itself, now skeletal, like dead pitted rock, was coated with the mouse fur of accumulated algae. Glen dived deep three times and saw nothing, not even the bottom. Some yellow antlers of coral drew him onward, for their shape alone, nothing to do with the keys, but when he got close he saw the silly thing under that cluster of antlers. He dived down — the key chain was lodged within the prickly prongs — and after a few tries he plucked them from among the antlers. Short of breath now, he thrashed to get to the surface, pushed his arms, kicked his legs, and with one of the kicks felt a sudden pinch against his shin. Swimming back to the beach, he saw that he had nicked himself, but he was smirking at something else. There were no keys on the key chain.

"I said it was a key chain — I didn't say it had keys." The boy spoke in a pedantic monotone, a bored indignation, as though he had been unfairly contradicted by this simple-minded adult.

"Where's my metal detector?"

"Your brother took it."

"What? I don't have a brother," Glen said, and then howled an obscenity.

He was still furious, muttering swears, when he met Alice later, but she reassured him, telling him he had done the right thing. He had volunteered to help the boy. It was not the boy's fault that some sneak had stolen his metal detector. The police had listened sympathetically but had not held out much hope for the recovery of his stolen goods. They repeated what Alice had said: It could have been worse. And instead of challenging them, Glen saw the logic of this. Yes, it could have been worse.

"The stupid key chain was just like Brett's, one of those McDonald's dinosaurs."

"It's a velociraptor, Dad!" Brett said. Another pedantic juvenile.

Within a few days, the nick on Glen's shin became infected. But it didn't hurt. "It just feels a little tingly." He used the Neosporin he had brought from home. That was another thing about Hawaii. The same tube of Neosporin would have cost him almost twice as much here. Within a week his wound looked like decayed fruit and he was running a fever. The fever subsided after he dosed himself with aspirin, but his lower leg was badly swollen.

"I'm not covered by my medical plan here," he told his wife when she said he should see a doctor.

His leg grew worse. He could hardly walk. His temperature rose again. He reluctantly went to the hospital, dreading the expense, and was asked whether he was allergic to any antibiotics. He said no and was given large doses of an antibiotic that brought on nausea and dizziness and made his flesh creep with a kind of skin disease that gave him large welts all over his body. Various other treatments were applied — heavily sedated, he was scarcely aware of them; Alice was in charge now — but the leg infection worsened, and his foot was purple with gangrene. He lay in the hospital bed as though in a trap, observing a succession of sudden decisions. "We'll have to operate." The leg was amputated just above the knee. "You're lucky to be alive."

A month later — a two-week vacation had become six weeks — he was on his way back to St. Louis. He was one of those wheelchair passengers who boarded the plane first and got off last and often blocked the aisle. On the plane he noticed that Brett no longer had the dinosaur key chain on his belt loop. Glen could not bear to ask his son if he had lost the thing and whether he cared.

His boss at the shoe store was sympathetic: "It's just plain bad luck." And, seeming to console Glen, he stated the obvious — that a shoe salesman was always on his feet or kneeling when fitting the shoes. Glen was forty. He had a young child. The boss went on to say that he could take a leave of absence but that he would not be paid. "Maybe you could apply for workers' comp."

Glen said he would be getting a prosthesis, virtually a new leg. Now the boss reminded Glen that the store sold mostly sports shoes. "A wooden leg would send the wrong message."

The man quickly apologized when Glen turned on him, raging, but at home the expression "wooden leg" kept invading his thoughts, taunting him. And the new leg was not wooden at all, but metal and plastic. It even flexed, and there was a new shoe on the end. He tried it out using crutches.

"Here comes Long John Silver!" his friends said. "Get yourself a parrot! 'Arrrgh, Jim, me lad!'"

Glen knew they didn't mean to hurt him with their mockery. They were being hearty. They told him every wooden-leg joke imaginable. They believed that if they made crass jokes about his disability, he would be encouraged to do the same. But Glen went home and wept. He didn't go back to work. Even Alice failed to lift his spirits, but she was hearty too. Seeing his tears, she said, "You're just feeling sorry for yourself," which was true, but so what? No one else seemed to care. Why was it that everyone seemed to think that brutal mockery was a cure for such a loss?

"I'm too old to learn how to walk," Glen said in defiance.

"Well, at least I'm not a cripple," Alice said, wounding him again. She returned to her old job as a legal secretary, the job she had left to raise Brett. Now Glen, who was home, could look after him.

Brett complained to his mother that Glen hit him. Glen admitted it. Brett was selfish and frivolous and ungrateful, like that horrible little boy in Honolulu who had demanded that Glen risk his life to find his key chain.

Seeming to fear Glen for his depression and futility, Alice stayed away from him for most of the day, calling only to speak to Brett. "Mummy's stuck at work again, honey." She developed another life outside the house, not just her work at the law firm, where she was liked, but her small investments in the stock market that were appreciating; the man who was giving her investment advice, a young paralegal, became her lover.

Glen was possessed by the delusion that the plastic and metal leg strapped to his stump was the only part of his body that worked; the rest of him was faulty. He was very angry, and the loss of his leg was also the loss of his potency. His head ached, his stump gave him pain, and he could not shop. He wanted to hit his wife, but his child would do — that would hurt her. One day he succeeded in injuring Brett — gave him a nosebleed — and that night Alice moved out, "for Brett's sake," and took out a temporary restraining order on him. It happened so quickly that Glen was impressed by the way Alice had organized it. But then he discovered she was living with Milton, the paralegal, and he despised her. She told him what she had done.

There was no worse, no more demoralizing taunt than someone telling you the truth. Glen Cornelius wondered whether he should kill himself. He drank instead and his drinking helped, but he knew his life was over in this wolfish world.

"This sort of thing happens a lot," Hobart Flail said. "Most people don't know that."

15

Madam Ma

MA *ma ma ma ma ma ma ma ma ma,* the Chinese stammeringly say, and if the pitch and tone of each *ma* are right, the meaning of the apparent repetition is, "Does Mother scold the horses, or will the horses scold Mother?"

This sentence often murmured through my mind when I saw Madam Ma, who scolded the horses and everyone else. She objected to Rose's being around, and so I was more familiar with Madam Ma than I wanted to be. The woman was a resident of the hotel, and the residents were mostly pests, like members of an unhappy household, contributing nothing but conflict, always claiming privileges, and forever blaming the family.

I did not need this woman to tell me my daughter was a monkey. I loved Rose for her antics. I knew she was a monkey in the way she hooked her fingers on a chair and swung herself into the seat, where she knelt instead of sat. Reaching for a candle, she would snatch the flame with a fat-fingered monkey pinch. But she was not only a monkey. Once she said, "Why does the fire of a candle always go up and never down?" and she waited for the answer.

"Don't play with that!" Madam Ma said on the day of the candle question, and the old woman startled Rose with her wicked white mask and twisted scolding lips. Her face was like a formal portrait of Edith Sitwell, but when I mentioned this my staff just stared at me. Rose stumbled and fell to the floor, the result of being scared by Madam Ma, who said, "Serves you right," in a harsh gloating voice as my little daughter sobbed.

Madam Ma was the worst of Rose's critics, and the slightest sound from the child had the older woman going expressively silent and rigid. Finding the child with her disapproving face, her eyes like dark bulbs, Madam Ma gave a theatrical, haughty snort. She was a *haole;* she had been married to a Chinese man named Ma; she had a column in the *Honolulu Advertiser.*

"She *pupule,* but she a guest," Sweetie said. Never mind that the guest was crazy, my wife knew the protocol: Madam Ma had been a resident of room 504 for a number of years, from long before my time. The Chinese man Ma had long since left her. She had a *hapa* son, Chip, whom she adored and mentioned often in her three-dot column, which was full of plugs and boasts and practical advice and mentions of restaurant openings and celebrity sightings. She wrote endlessly of food but could not cook. She went to every party, she knew everyone's name, she was a repository of postwar island history, and the history was mainly scandalous.

Madam Ma's photograph at the top of her column depicted an attractive, even glamorous woman in her forties, though she was really in her sixties. In the column itself she was a woman whose feet were firmly planted on the ground, guided by the folk wisdom of her Irish grandmother, a *kama'aina,* who was a font of old-country good sense. Chip could always be counted on for a smart remark. He was a lovable kid, eternally fifteen years old in the column, but I knew for a fact that he was forty-one and lazy, and pretty sad from drinking, and that his lover was Amo Ferretti, an older man who made a living as a florist. Ferretti was Portuguese and had a wife and children in Kailua. Often Madam Ma had her son and his lover over to the hotel for Sunday brunch. It was at one of these brunches that she snorted with pleasure at seeing Rose topple over.

"I would never have a daughter," she said to Chip. "How could I do that to you, my darling."

She was one of those people who, instead of turning away, take a visceral delight in preoccupying themselves with something troublesome, for the joy of creating greater fuss and adding to the confusion with a louder complaint. Her intention was a wicked wish to prove how much happier and more orderly her own life was. At the Hotel Honolulu I noticed how odd people sought out even odder people as companions, to show by contrast how normal they were.

I wanted to say to Madam Ma: Never mind! Leave her alone!

"Look at her," Madam Ma said. "Isn't she awful?"

Why did she care? She was being queenly, with Chip on her right and Amo Ferretti on her left, both men strenuously flirting with her while she pretended not to notice. Trey, meanwhile, ran back and forth with a chilled bottle of chardonnay, refilling her glass.

Rose had not stopped screaming from her fall. Sweetie picked her up and comforted her. A little while later, Rose was sitting a few tables away, eating with her fingers and, having locked her toes around the chair legs, tipping her chair backward.

Madam Ma gave Rose an ugly superior smile and said, "Her hands are forever dirty. Feet too. She never wears shoes."

Rose pinched her sooty fingertips and parroted my explanation. "Because the rising air makes the flame rise by feeding it oxygen. Oxygen is a gas."

"Look, she's bleeding," Madam Ma said.

Rose laughed. "Taco Bell hot sauce!"

"She's combatative and mischeevious," Madam Ma said, unmindful of her malapropisms. "She's rotten spoiled. Just looking for attention. And look at her horrid little pet."

Rose clutched her grandmother's cat and pouted.

The heavy makeup on Madam Ma's face gave her the cracked and broken mask of a decaying empress. Perhaps fascinated by the woman's leer, Rose said, "What are people made of?"

"How should I know?" Madam Ma said, making her voice screech, and she winked at Chip to show that she thought the question absurd. "But little girls are made of rats and snails and puppy dogs' tails."

"That's little boys," Rose said.

"She's right," Chip said.

"Stop playing along with her. You're doing just what she wants you to do," Madam Ma said to Chip, and to Amo, who shrugged, she said, "He's flirting!"

"Why do you have hairs sticking out of your nose?" Rose said to Amo.

After the meal, Madam Ma made a point of showily detouring around Rose, who was playing on the floor. Chip smiled in what seemed like sympathy. Amo had not let go of Madam Ma's arm; his was crooked in hers, like a formal couple in a procession.

"We are mostly water, with some carbon and specific minerals," Rose said, scrupulously quoting me.

The old woman screeched again, but Rose continued talking.

"Hyenas eat the whole animal they kill, and that's why when they poo the bones it looks calcified."

"What does?"

"The scat, which is the poo," Rose said. "You didn't finish your ice cream."

"That is none of your business," Madam Ma said, and hooked Chip onto her free arm.

"And he's your horrid little pet."

I was watching all this from the maitre d's lectern, so attentive to the absurdity that I wanted it to play itself out to the last exchange. Rose made for the left-behind ice cream melting in the bowl.

On other occasions, Madam Ma seemed to seek Rose out, looking for trouble, as though to provoke the child and challenge her. If Rose was playing at the far end of the lanai, that was where Madam Ma sat, to go on glowering. Rose had lunch after she got home from nursery school, always at one; Madam Ma never failed to eat at the same time, sitting nearby. Once Madam Ma's newspaper column was finished, she was free the rest of the day. So she sat sipping a drink, usually with Chip, often with Amo, who did the flowers in our lobby in return for bar credit — a Buddy Hamstra arrangement, like Madam Ma's room.

"My mother used to say, 'I don't care what you do in life — just be fabulous,'" Madam Ma said.

"And every year you get better," Amo said.

"But every year seems shorter," Rose said. She had been listening. "Why does this year seem shorter than last year?"

"It's that horrible little child calling attention to herself again," Madam Ma said.

"Give her a break," Chip said.

"You always stick up for her. You need to process that."

Flexing her monkey fingers, Rose said in a lisping way, "Because as you get older, each year is a smaller proportion of your life. How old are you?"

"Forty-seven," Amo said.

"Why encourage her?" Madam Ma said.

"Next year will be one forty-eighth of your total age, and the year after that will be one forty-ninth." Rose pursed her lips at Madam Ma, who, to show her indifference, had picked up Puamana's cat. "Each year is even less for her."

"This cat's paws are wet."

"Because there's a puddle where I did shee-shee on the floor," Rose said.

"Rat shit!" the old woman said.

"You said a bad word," Rose said. "But there's a rat in my room."

"Not true," I said, and gathered Rose into my arms, holding her like an infant, a heavy infant. I carried her away as she protested. I began to understand that in the way Madam Ma sought her out, Rose did not object, and even seemed to enjoy doing battle with the woman: two coquettes vying for attention, with Rose usually having the last word.

She would ambush Madam Ma only when either Chip or Amo was around, sensing perhaps that she was protected by their more benign presence. One day in the lobby, seeing the three of them walking abreast, Rose tagged along behind, and as they entered Paradise Lost, Rose said, "Why is the past so sad?"

"There is something seriously wrong with your daughter," Madam Ma said as I blocked Rose from entering the bar. "Probably a chemical imbalance."

"Because it is only when we look back that we see how weak we were," Rose said. "The sun is actually a star. And Moby-Dick is a white whale. And rat shee-shee can make you sick. There's a rat in my room."

All this in her parroty singsong as Madam Ma sighed. "There she goes again. God, she's never at the beach."

"UV rays are bad for you. They cause melanoma on your skin," Rose said.

One night Rose crept downstairs to where Madam Ma sat with Amo and Chip, silently drinking, each man holding one of her hands.

"What thing succeeds?" Rose said.

"I pity the man who marries her," said Madam Ma.

"The thing that makes us less lonely."

When Sweetie coaxed Rose away and apologized, saying,

"She's afraid of the dark," Rose squawked and said, "No! It's the rat in my room!"

Rose loved ice cream and fruit smoothies and flavored shave ice, and though Housekeeping swore there were no rats, we put a sticky trap in Rose's room to humor her. The next morning she found a brown rat struggling in it.

16

Chip

IN HER THREE-DOT column in the *Advertiser,* Madam Ma
wrote in the hollow bonhomie of press-release prose about
restaurant openings and celebrity sightings and parties at
which she always seemed to be guest of honor. She claimed to
know Hawaii's elite, had jogged with Willie Nelson on Maui,
sung a duet with Bette Midler, clinked glasses with Tom Selleck at
the Black Orchid, had years before made a cameo appearance as
herself in an episode of *Hawaii Five-O.* "Jack Lord is a very private person," she told me when I said he seemed an oddball — he
wore makeup whenever he left his house. "Jack's an old friend."
The widow of Boris Karloff, another local resident, was a dear
friend. I mocked the column by reading it aloud until Sweetie objected, saying she liked it. For Sweetie, Madam Ma was sophisti-
cated. "She went go to the mainland all the time! Was regular in
Vegas! Was up to Yerp! Was one class act!"

I was familiar with hack work, but this sort of journalism, an
adjunct of the public relations industry, was new to me. Madam
Ma was always on the receiving end of free concert tickets and
merchandise, wonderful meals, press junkets, complimentary hotel weekends, and neighbor-island hospitality. What looked like
freeloading was standard practice for the newspaper, which did
not reimburse her for expenses. She received more invitations
than she could possibly accept and was deluged with T-shirts and
baseball caps from resort logo shops, bottles of wine, crates of avocados. Baskets of fruit were always arriving at Reception and
being sent up to her room. She was a welcome guest wherever she
went, because she was so profligate in her mentions.

Buddy Hamstra said we were lucky to have Madam Ma as a resident: "The Hilton would have killed to get her." Her column appeared in the *Advertiser* every day. It had once been headed "Around Town," and then "My Islands." Now, under a dim passport-sized photo of her, which, however flattering, I knew to be a bad likeness, it was just "Madam Ma."

Neighbor Island Getaway . . . I leave my cozy nest at the Hotel Honolulu for the fabulous opening of the Maui Lodge and Ranch with its view of Lahaina and environs . . . Scrumptious dinner with Chip studying the extensive wine list (he opted for the Mondavi Fumé Blanc, 1987), served by Chef Erik on aptly named Sunset Deck . . . Rising Son crows, "We lucked out again, Mom!" and as the chef (trained on the mainland) makes his signature dish, crêpes suzette . . . Glimpses of Don Ho and Jim Nabors at Honolulu eateries . . . Wonder what they're hatching? . . . Rumor Mill: Sly Stallone said to be putting his Kauai mansion on the market, a bargain at $7 million, probably inspired by the sale of Jimmy Stewart's ranch on the Big Island . . . Chip: "Go for it, Mom!" so I bought a ticket in the 'Frisco lottery. Wouldn't you? . . . Memory Lane: The Niketown Building now occupies the spot where we used to get plate lunches at Auntie Anna's . . . Also staying over for the Maui opening were the Russell Wongs and the Ray Taniguchis . . . Memo from Chip: Don't forget the Punahou Carnival comes earlier than usual this year . . . Chip will scream, "Mother, your waistline!" as I chow down on a plate of mochi and Spam musubi . . . After luxuriating at headquarters, Chez HH, back to Maui on Aloha Airlines Friday with the kid again, sampling Chef Hans's caviar pupu platter while waiting for the charity fashion show — to benefit At-Risk Teens — at the Grand Hyatt . . . Chip says, "Get me one of those, Mom!" . . . No, not the elegant Lynette Sadaki fashions, he was pointing to the ethereal models from Poetry in Motion modeling agency, Maui's own . . . "Down boy," I sez . . . But I couldn't blame him . . . Swimsuits to die for . . . This is Lynette's Spring Collection . . . You will recall that Lynette and hubby Rob did the costumes for the Honolulu Opera Theater's production of *Tosca,* the Rising Son's favorite opera, unless you count *Annie* . . .

And so on. You could not miss the grace note of Chip's name and Chip's boyish witticisms. In fact, delete Chip's name from the column and there was hardly anything of substance in it. In the crudest way, Madam Ma was doing what fiction writers did all the time: she assigned her sayings to him; he spoke for her. Chip was the clever one and Madam Ma was merely recording what he said. He accompanied her wherever she went and always had a bright remark.

In the column Chip was a high-spirited kid, full of beans, a bit of a rebel, something of a traveler, impatient, exuberant, with a sweet tooth and a big appetite. Irrepressible himself, he would reprimand Mom in an admiring way for being a fuddy-duddy. He dared her to go for swims, jump into Jacuzzis, try new drinks or a new dance. "My dance partner!" Madam Ma sometimes wrote. Chip famously played the guitar and surfed on the North Shore. He knew a thing or two about wines.

Chip was harum-scarum (an expression Madam Ma often used) but he was lovable, not always punctual but someone you could rely on. It was Chip who recognized the celebrities' names that Madam Ma dropped in her column, and Chip who knew the source of quotations: "'Sound and fury' — I thought it was Faulkner but Chip tells me it's Shakespeare. *King Lear?* What do I know? How about *Queen Lear?* Now there's a challenge for the girls at Manoa Valley Theater . . ." Chip was a snappy dresser. Chip loved fast cars, though it was impossible to know whether he owned one, or whether he was even old enough to have a driver's license.

Chip's age was a mystery. From most of his remarks you would have taken him to be a pubescent teenager. He was forever drooling over pretty girls ("At the Hooters opening at Aloha Tower Marketplace I had to caution Chip not to step on his tongue . . ."). He gobbled ice cream ("devours Chunky Monkey at Ben & Jerry's") and liked nothing better than "chomping a thick juicy steak, preferably Ruth's Chris Steakhouse, Restaurant Row — reservations suggested." Chip could dance, he knew how to juggle, he had been a Punahou School cheerleader. He was "the kid," or "the eligible bachelor," or "the man about town," or "my *hapa* son" — a reference to Madam Ma's husband, Harry Ma. He was often "the Rising Son" or just Chip, as familiar to the reader as a close relative.

Chip quoted poetry. Chip could sing. Madam Ma mentioned how he might be on the mainland "auditioning for a part in *Phantom*" or a revival of *South Pacific*. Madam Ma mentioned how spruce Chip looked in a sailor suit, and his personal traits: his late nights, his hatred of getting up in the morning, his love for Starbuck's coffee and Mauna Loa chocolate-covered macadamias ("Chocolate Chip") and Sunday brunch on the poolside lanai of Hotel Honolulu, "which is prospering under the new general manager from the mainland" — that was the sort of plug that she thought would have me eating out of her hand.

When Michael Jackson gave a concert in Honolulu, Chip had a seat in the celebrity box with Quincy Jones — "and Mr. Jones remembered Chip's singing ability and suggested he look him up next time the Chipper is in LA . . . 'Will do!' said the kid . . ."

Chip was the vitality of the column, the guiding spirit, the spark of life, all sunshine.

Which was odd, because I got to know Chip well and pitied him as a quarrelsome, sometimes violent alcoholic who had lost his driver's license in a tragic DUI case and was even more foul-mouthed than his mother; who had made himself unemployable and had not finished school; who boasted and lied and went on crying jags; and who was in an abusive relationship with a middle-aged florist, Amo Ferretti, who was himself married and a compulsive drinker.

17

Rose's Rival

ROSE WAS "NEEDY," Madam Ma said. "Korean adoptees from abusive orphanage situations sometimes show the same traits. It could be her trampy grandmother, or post-traumatic stress disorder." The old woman would go on and on, wincing when Rose sang nursery rhymes, as though it were a sign of lunacy, frowning when Rose, popping her pretty lips, said, "Penal colony."

As the girl's father, I was an "enabler." Sweetie was "in denial." We were "co-dependent." It was clear that my daughter had "attachment disorder." The way she ate ice cream indicated "an addictive personality." Her continually climbing on chairs and kicking off her shoes were indications of OCD, which Madam Ma spelled out for me: obsessive-compulsive disorder. Or ADHD, attention-deficit hyperactivity disorder, as well as symptoms of autism. She didn't understand "limits."

"That's all true," I said. "She's five years old."

Chip had never been that way. He had been "centered." He had made "choices." He understood "limits" and "options."

"Daddy, why is Mrs. Ma's head slanty?"

"I have a frozen shoulder," Madam Ma said, and jerked her head and groaned to show the ailment. "She might be autistic — she has no empathy. I pity your poor wife. That little girl dominates her something rotten. She just stands there making faces."

"She's an exceptional child," I said. "And she's mine."

"'Faces' sounds like 'feces,'" Rose said, and gave a throaty laugh. "I'm not making feces!"

"Dysfunctional kids like that have a terrible time at school."

This irritated me, but because Madam Ma was a long-time resident, I was obligated to defend her right to free speech in my hotel. I didn't mind when journalists pontificated in the daily paper; it was a newspaper's role to be a theater of the absurd, where morality was a masquerade, a pretense, just shtick. But when such views were solemnly repeated to my face, as if I were obligated to listen and accept them, I found the whole business too laughable to be insulting. What I wanted to tell Madam Ma was that even in her banal column of trashy and insignificant news items, the only true flavor was of moral squalor.

"Didn't you ever teach her about boundaries?" Madam Ma said.

True, when we were shopping Rose would slip items into the grocery cart — gum, cookies, Froot Loops, a frog-shaped potholder. Her doing so delighted me. She was a lovely little girl, precocious but obviously bright. She asked all those unprompted questions, offered so many insightful answers, or quoted me as a way of pleasing me — as, I suspected, another child might be sulky and unresponsive in order to punish the neglectful parents. Rose's vivid talking and word-perfect quotation were joyous and generous.

"She is so infantile," Madam Ma said one day at lunch. "She is just seeking attention."

Madam Ma was at her usual table on the lanai, facing the entryway so she could see and be seen; she was smiling at a person entering, someone who recognized her, as she spoke to me. My back was turned to her in my hurry to clear a table for the next diner — Trey's job, but he was at the chiropractor's for the knee he'd twisted while surfing. Bent over, harassed, and surrounded by the impatient lunch crowd, I had a glimpse of myself alone at a desk and thought, I used to be a writer.

"Did you hear me? She simply wants attention," Madam Ma said. "You're just like her. You never listen."

The bland submissiveness and tact that were necessary to the smooth running of a hotel were qualities I had never possessed and found difficult to acquire. But there were rewards for being patient. At this stage of my life, on these distant islands, where everything was new to me and books did not exist, I was learning unexpected skills. I was middle-aged and more attentive. I could not be an uncompromising writer here, or a writer at all. I had to be social, one of the bunch; I had to be a good monkey.

"I agree with you. That's why I didn't say anything, Madam Ma," I said, balancing an armload of dirty plates.

"Your daughter is watching me eat. I can't stand that."

Rose had crept onto the lanai, and with her head cocked to one side seemed to be mimicking Madam Ma's frozen shoulder, as though re-creating the posture might reveal what the ailment felt like.

"She wants to see whether I will finish my ice cream."

Without relaxing her neck, keeping one shoulder rigid, Rose denied this with a jerk of her head and a serious face.

"But you see, there will be none for her."

Madam Ma finished the bowl of ice cream, ostentatiously licked the spoon with her gummy tongue, and glanced in triumph at Rose, who straightened her head again, looking cheated.

Though she had a large head — my Panama hat nearly fitted her — Rose was small, even for a five-year-old. Most of the guests took no notice of her. And I resented Madam Ma's unkind attention, yet I would not have understood Madam Ma if it weren't for Rose. She threw the older woman into relief, like a known object placed next to a weird artifact.

People tell you about your child and conceitedly think they are saying something that you have never heard before. Some guests stated that Rose ate too fast, or not enough, or preferred cereal to vegetables, or went barefoot when she should have been wearing shoes, or that she interrupted adult conversations. But I knew this. I knew much more: she remembered everything, she was impressionable and wished to be older, she was brighter than her mother, and raged at her as a result. "But why do chickens have scaly legs!" she shouted, grasping Sweetie's face to get her to listen. Afterward she lectured everyone with the answer I had supplied: "It's because they were once reptiles, like scaly snakes."

I wondered why Madam Ma's mealtime so fascinated Rose. Why did this small girl stand and gape? Rose told me in confidence: "Her teeth aren't real." Rose stared at the woman's mouth; she enjoyed watching her laboriously masticate. It was the pleasure of seeing an old machine clumsily operating, for the possibility of witnessing the mechanism falter; at some point those false teeth would fail or fall out of her mouth. That Madam

Ma was a sourpuss made the failure not only more likely, but all the more welcome.

"I'm going to be naughty," Madam Ma said, holding the dessert menu. She was sitting with Chip and Amo.

Chip clucked, as though at a child, and Amo said, "You know what happens to bad little girls?"

"I'm going to be sinful," Madam Ma said.

"They get spanked," Amo said. He was a broad-shouldered man with a neatly trimmed mustache and close-cropped hair. A gold chain around his neck held a locket. I wondered whose picture it contained.

"As if I care," Chip said, and just then realized that Rose was staring. He made a horrible face at her, monkey cheeks and wicked eyes.

Madam Ma was fumbling with the glass beads of her necklace, holding them against her neck. She was vain about her breasts, vain about her legs, vain about her body generally. "Not bad for an old girl," she'd say. Playing with her beads was a way of covering her scrawny neck and calling attention to her legs. Her dresses were shorter than they should have been, her necklines so deep they showed her sun-freckled cleavage. She put the menu down, let go of her beads, and as she took Amo's hand in her right and Chip's in her left she gave a girlish sigh.

"I'm going to have a chocolate mousie," she said.

Hearing her, Rose said, "It's not 'chocolate mousie,' it's chocolate moose."

Sweetie had crept up behind Rose with the intention of tugging her out of the dining area, but holding Sweetie's hand seemed to give Rose more conviction.

"Isn't it, Mummy? It's 'moose.'"

Lifting her son's hand, and Amo's — like a playground gesture — Madam Ma said, "What is that child doing here? Isn't there a house rule about that?"

"Just playing," Sweetie said.

"Go play with your doll."

"It's not a doll," Rose said. "It's an action figure."

Chip said, "Oh, Ma, give it a rest. She's just being a brat."

"She upset your mother," Amo said.

"Oh, we're going to make a scene, are we?" Chip said.

"He said 'mudda,'" Rose said.

"You see, Amo? Chip doesn't care if I'm insulted," said Madam Ma. "Children are fundamentally intrusive."

"Thunder mentally," Rose said.

"Take that kid out of here," Amo said.

"A kid is a little goat," Rose said.

"Hey, listen up."

"Hay is for horses," Rose said.

"I'll smack your ass."

"That man said a bad word!" Rose cried out, pretending to be shocked. He said 'ass'!"

She scuffed her feet on the rush matting as Sweetie coaxed her to leave. But Rose's eyes were on Madam Ma, who had narrowed her own eyes at the child.

"I brought you something," Amo said to Madam Ma. "It's a surprise."

"I love surprises."

Madam Ma's eyes teased Rose as Amo handed over the gaily wrapped box. Madam Ma plucked at the silver ribbon, peeled off the tape, and removed the bright paper slowly so as to torment Rose. She fondled the red velvet box for a while, holding it up to admire while glancing at Rose from time to time with gloating eyes.

"Is it a necklace? What adorable beads," she said, popping the lid of the box. "Are they jade? I love them! I want to put them on right now."

Her words, each of them, seemed directed at Rose, who watched mournfully as Amo fumbled with the clasp while Chip simply stared.

"I want beads, Mummy," Rose said, watching the necklace being fastened on Madam Ma. "Daddy will get them for me."

She began to cry, and as she was led out, kicking the floor, Madam Ma screeched, "How did you know it was exactly what I wanted?" and clutched her neck.

"Look, darling," Madam Ma called out to Rose.

"I'd rather sit in the dark alone than look at a butt-head like you," Rose said.

After all that, it seemed strange the next day that Chip should take me aside and say, "Mother wants to go grocery shopping. Will you give her a ride? I don't trust her with that creep Amo."

Wasn't Amo supposed to be his friend? Anyway, I took Madam Ma to Holiday Mart. "You push," she said, shoving a shopping cart in my direction. Chip had said "grocery shopping," but Madam Ma kept slipping other items into the cart — chocolates, sherry, macadamia nuts, cognac — saying, "I'm a bad girl. I am very naughty."

Perhaps Rose was no different, with her chair, her table, her storybook, her special soup spoon, her binkie, her demands. "Daddy! Mummy! Wake up! I'm hungry. My bear is hungry. I have a cold shoulder. I want someone to watch television with me!"

"There's no ice in this drink!"

Who was that? It might have been Rose, but it was Madam Ma, demanding her special glass and her own table — the one with the view of people entering the lanai. She refused to read a newspaper that had been handled by anyone else. "Get me a fresh one!" With a little-girl pursing of lips, she complained about Chip — poor Chip, who, it seemed, could do nothing right.

But after Chip murdered his lover, Madam Ma stopped complaining about my daughter's indiscretions.

18

The Return of Amo Ferretti

T FIRST I FOUND it sad that visitors to Hawaii snapped pictures with cheap cameras of each other smiling, or of things I saw every day: the palms on Magic Island, the big banyan in the park, the rack of surfboards at the beach, and sometimes the battered monkeypod tree at our entrance. Sometimes it wasn't pictures but old, soft white people from the mainland walking sorrowfully with their heads down and stooping to pick up broken shells and junk coral. But in time they ceased to be sad. Those white old folks weren't sorrowful; they were a lesson to me to look harder.

What I noticed had nothing to do with Hawaii. It was my daughter and her tetchy moods. Whenever something was going wrong, she seemed to sense it beforehand. Her little friends got screechy too, in the same way, when they were with her at tense times in the hotel. Bright, high-strung children seemed to me keenly receptive to whispers of trouble, which reached them as a whine of gossip that traveled at a frequency different from broader and more vulgar murmurs and gave them a kind of clairvoyance. So new to the earth, Rose lived close to the ground.

She had been very cranky lately. What had she heard?

"Nothing!" she said, and was so exasperated by my question she began to cry.

"I can't do anything with her," Sweetie said. "She's wired."

Wired was the precise word. Madam Ma had been in and out looking haunted, and Rose, who often followed her, staring at her powdered face and smiling so as to get the woman to show her false teeth, now avoided her. Madam Ma, who had made a habit of complaining about Rose, now ignored her and just seemed numb and clumsily furtive. What had she done? What had she seen? Where was Chip? I suspected something serious. I had seen Madam Ma's tantrums, I had listened to her rants. But this was the first I had known of her silence, and it terrified me. I would not have seen it without Rose's detecting it first.

Guilt shows clearest on the faces of older people, whose skin is so full of detail. There is a certain face that an aged woman has when she is stricken and heavily made up. Intending to look like a doll, she ends up looking like a corpse — the lipless cheese-white face, rouge splotches on the sunken cheeks, bony teeth, blank eyes, sparse hair, the sort of mask you see propped up in coffins. From across the room Madam Ma turned this face on Rose, and Rose was out the door. It was a face with guilt showing in all its contours.

There was also a twang of truth, a dying vibration in the air that only little Rose sensed. Her instinct was not to give me information but to protect me. She said she didn't want me to be Madam Ma's friend anymore, which was odd, because when the news got out, it was Chip who had the problem, not his mother.

"Chip's in big trouble," Sweetie said. She had heard the gossip in the kitchen, where it had been gathered in the Paradise Lost bar. "You know his Portugee friend . . . ?"

"Amo Ferretti."

"He wen *mucky*."

In times of the most solemn emotion, Hawaiians slipped into Pidgin English, gabbling sententiously, and though they found this lingo more neighborly — more tragic for its realism — it just made me smile and say, Oh, cut it out. But Sweetie found bad news more bearable in Pidgin.

Soon after, in Paradise Lost, I saw Captain Yuji of the Honolulu Police Department and got the story from him.

"This Chip business is the strangest case I ever handled so far. More worse than the Hotel Street pickup."

"What was that all about?"

"Woman cruising Hotel Street looking for a lesbian goes into a bar and picks up this woman. Only it's her husband, dressed up in women's clothes. Their car is stopped on suspicion and it gets into the newspaper. The man is a state rep. Big disgrace. They went to the mainland."

As always, the word "mainland" sounded to me like "Planet Earth."

"Maybe that's what Chip should do."

Captain Yuji looked serious and said, "Chip's in jail." I must have reacted sharply to this, because he grew stern again and added, "It's real bad. One of these gay things. They never know when to stop. It's okay maybe when some gay guy is decorating your house or doing your wife's nails, but when a gay guy commits murder it's a mess."

This perhaps explained Rose's mood, and it certainly explained the hollow-eyed somnambulism of Madam Ma.

"How did they solve the crime?"

"That's the interesting part."

The argument between Chip and his lover had begun at the hotel, apparently, and continued at Chip's apartment in Harbor Tower. Amo had fled when Chip got violent. Chip searched for him in the gay bars in Waikiki and then found him in Kailua, where he was hiding in his bungalow with his wife and two children. Amo's life had been complicated, but until that night it had worked. He had not lived steadily with Chip, but as Chip's lover he had shuttled back and forth between Harbor Tower and his own place in Kailua.

"Amo is my time-share lover," Chip used to say.

Madam Ma had encouraged them. They joined her at Sunday brunch on the lanai, cadaverous Ma, hairy Amo, smooth Chip, a comic threesome always somewhat overdressed for the heat — the men in plantation hats, long-sleeved shirts, white shoes, and kukui-nut leis. Buddy Hamstra loved them for the atmosphere he said they gave the hotel, especially when they were drinking, and sloshed — which was often — and "Lush Life" was being played in the lounge, Hawaiianized by Trey and his band, Sub-Dude.

The night of the attack, Amo had cowered with his wife, but Chip confronted him, screaming. Perhaps (so Captain Yuji conjectured) not wishing for his secret — what secret? — to be divulged, Amo hurried out the back door. Chip heard his lover drive away and gave chase.

On this small island the only continuous road was on the coast, so the only escape for Amo was to drive west in a circle along the shore, Kamehameha Highway. It was eleven at night, very few cars were on the road, and as the road was narrow and curving, it was easy for Chip to shadow him. For five miles or so he kept Amo's red taillights in view, but passing the Crouching Lion Inn, Amo's car grazed the guardrail on the cliff side and sped up and out of sight as it approached Kahana Bay.

Chip drove into darkness as he slipped around the bay, but passing the beach park and seeing no cars ahead, he reasoned that Amo must have swung off the road and killed his lights. Chip swerved, and seeing Amo's car, he braked hard and blocked the entrance to the beach park with his own car. Amo was trapped. He stumbled from his car and tried to run, but Chip was faster, and he caught Amo and pounced. Impatience and pent-up anger from the car chase burst forth as an unstoppable fury. In a violent parody of lovemaking, Chip seized Amo from behind in a strangling embrace, then punched him to his knees. Still clinging, and kneeling himself, using one hand for balance, he grasped a lump of lava rock that just fitted his fist and smashed it into Amo's face and head, tearing his lover's scalp. Amo was stunned, went down heavily, and seemed to snore.

Chip, calmed by the violence but out of breath from the shudder that had run through him, got to his feet. He rocked back and forth, sucking air, not noticing that Amo was stirring. The injured man revived, thrashed around, made the mistake of going for Chip. He hugged Chip's legs and began biting. This provoked Chip to rage again. He had not let go of the chunk of lava rock. This time, standing, less like a rapist than a man fighting off a rapist, he pounded at Amo's reaching arms and on Amo's skull — much too hard, far too many blows, any one of which could have been fatal.

Yet no sooner had the man slumped than Chip attempted to revive him. There was something especially awful about that blood, so black, so sticky in the darkness. Chip could not see it clearly but he could feel it. Everything he touched was wet with it and slippery and had that bad fish blood smell. It was the man's life leaking into the sand of the beach park this hot, moonless night.

Chip dragged Amo to his car and lifted him into the back seat. He thought of leaving him there in Amo's own car, but he knew the body would be found much too soon — it was illegal to park in the lot after sunset, and the Kahuku police patrolled the area. With Amo folded in half, Chip drove toward Punaluu with a sentence repeating in his head: The body was found in a cane field. It was a common statement on the nightly news. Corpses were dumped in cane fields because such fields were labyrinthine and dense with cane stalks. Bodies were not found for weeks, months even, until the cane was cut. Sometimes they were not found at all, for wild pigs with big tusks ate them, bones and all, leaving only rags and rubber sandals. The cane harvest was weeks away; Chip could be on the mainland by then, in hiding.

If he dumped Amo into the sea, off Kawela or Waimea, the body would turn up on some beach — everything washed ashore. Even bodies that were dumped from ships far from land found their way to the beach, with the torn nets and floats and plastic bottles.

A cane field was the right place, but the deepest fields were at Waialua, in the great expanse beyond the big rusty sugar mill. It was hardly midnight, a dim sliver of moon still rising, the occasional car on the road. Chip drove fast through Kahuku and up the hill to Pupukea, where he parked at the Boy Scout camp at the end of the road and waited, too tremulous to drive more. This was a good place to hide for a few hours but not a good place to leave a corpse.

He slept, he woke, he said aloud, "Yes?" He thought he heard muttering — more than muttering, distinct words whispered quickly. That odd voice startled him. What he took to be the lights behind the hill of Wahiawa was the first glow of daylight. Too late to hide the body! He got his beach blanket from the trunk and covered the body, then drove down the hill. He washed his face at Sharks Cove and bought a new T-shirt and a cup of coffee at Foodland Supermarket.

Driving in circles, he reminded himself that he would have to leave the islands that day if he was to be safe, fly to the mainland and lose himself there, not even tell his mother where he was. A cane field was no longer an option. He set his face toward the part of the road that was distorted and watery-looking with rising heat and spoke out loud.

"I have to think of something."

"Yes," came an answering voice from the back seat, though it sounded like *Yarsss*.

"Mo-Mo?"

The pet name for his lover was one he used when he wanted to console the man.

The *Yes* sound came again — mocking lips and the flatulent bubble-words trailing off like a deflating balloon, just air and ambiguous syllables.

"What did you say, Mo-Mo?"

The silence seemed calculated to annoy Chip, as Amo often fell silent when an answer was expected. But Chip had not gone half a mile before he heard Amo Ferretti's voice, jeering at him.

"Stop it!" Chip said. He was hot, perspiring. Even the air through the open windows scorched his face. "I said I was sorry."

That was a lie. He had never said he was sorry; he had only thought it. He was panicky — eager, too, for Amo wasn't dead and now instead of being relieved, his anger returned at the sound of Amo's contradictions. He wanted to pull over and smash Amo's face again. Or should he try to revive him? When he heard the voice again, much louder, he became unnerved and began to scream. He drove screaming around the northern part of the island as the dying man in the back seat mocked him in a foolish failing voice.

Chip was hysterical, calling out, "He's still alive! I didn't hurt him!" when he entered the station house in Wahiawa. He had chosen this small police post so as not to attract attention. He was still saying, "He's alive!" as he was led to a cell.

Captain Yuji said to me, "It's kind of funny. You know what happens to human remains in the heat. Like balloons. And the gas gets out any way it can, right?"

I had not said a word, yet that night when I put her to bed, Rose shrieked, "Don't tell me!"

19

Crime of Passion

T HE SIMPLIFIED news items in small-town papers are charming and untranslatable to outsiders, but wonderfully evocative to the small-town reader: the townie can decode anything local. Just the names are telling enough — family names are like a whole language of revelation. In such a place, everyone knows the background to the latest news, and the innuendo in the reporting itself. In this respect, the local news story is often like a concentrated tale by that subtle enchanter from Argentina, Jorge Luis Borges, much of whose work was just that — news from Buenos Aires. Graceful and graphic, such a story was a coiled clinging beauty, a tiny trailing narrative, the sort of vine that suited its name, vignette.

In the small town of Honolulu, the headline in the *Advertiser*, MAN HELD IN KAILUA DEATH, was understood to be intentionally circumspect, because Madam Ma was one of the paper's most popular columnists. The rival *Star-Bulletin* was more teasingly explicit: JOURNALIST'S SON ARRESTED IN FLORIST'S MURDER. Yet what had happened was obvious, and the facts in both stories were the same: a quarrel was mentioned, with a hint that it had been a lovers' quarrel; the men were said to have been friends; and Chip was identified as "a leader in the campaign advocating same-sex marriage in Hawaii." That said queer as "florist" said queer, and Madam Ma was well known for being a prima donna. It was colorful but no crime to be a *mahu*. Indeed, it was an old Polynesian custom. A shortage of daughters in the family meant one of the sons was raised as a girl.

For most newspaper readers, this seemed an open-and-shut

murder case. Two local homos got into a screaming match that became a catfight that turned physical; one bashed the other's head in. What tickled people's interest was that Amo was married and had young children. This was the single scandalous detail, the tiny fact of the family house in Kailua that spoke volumes to the local reader. The wife was quoted as a witness. She was not ashamed, she was sorrowful, and who could blame her? But some people held her accountable. Married to a *mahu,* she should have known better. She was an enabler, playing with fire, turning a blind eye. She was asking for trouble, and hey, what about her poor keeds?

A Portugee florist and a *hapa-haole* and all the journalistic shorthand for sexual orientation that was understood locally: "an aspiring *kumu hula,*" "active in the theater," "served a stint in the Honolulu ballet," "a protégé of Richard Sharpe" (Sharpe was a shimmering old queen who prided himself on being a hoofer), "male model," "chorister," every significant term except "faggot."

The most vocal public reaction in Honolulu was that of gloating Mormons and sanctimonious Christians. Mormons — polygamous until just the other day — claimed gay marriage to be immoral. Such people tended not to question the motive or the violence in a gay murder — being gay was motive enough, for gays were seen as jealous and excitable, as Gypsies once were; it was a catfight between men, and because men, even gay men, were strong, violence was expected. In the case of a man and woman, the woman was nearly always overpowered, but in a gay fight either party might win, since (being gay) the two men were equally matched. Therein lay the interest: the outcome — who was the victim?

There was perhaps also a factor that we understood to be common on the mainland — a certain pleasure taken by the public when a gay man murdered his partner, or did anything that placed him in the ranks of the unambiguous criminal. Theft, battery, destruction of property ("The weapon was a shod foot"), anything would do, because then the onlooker could gloat and decry without appearing to condemn the man for his homosexuality. Yet in such cases the queerness was the very thing that was being condemned, because it proved that, after all, they are even worse than the rest of us.

And there is always a shiver of satisfaction that the smugly voy-euristic public feels when marginal people kill each other, when a boxer dies from a lethal punch, or when the corpse of the unwel-come boat person is revealed by the ebbing tide. It is the rush of the spectator at a cockfight, for the faceless struggler has no char-acter beyond his struggle, no personality, and all anyone cares about is the outcome — the loser is indistinguishable from the winner. Mexican farm workers suffocating to death in a boxcar, prison inmates clawing each other to death, vengeful mobsters, furious gays — such murders arouse little emotion. You don't feel that their distress places you in any personal danger. They asked for it.

So when Chip murdered Amo Ferretti in Kahana Beach Park in Punaluu there was no scandal, nor any outrage. No one felt any of that retrospective horror that grips the public when a hideous suburban crime is reported — the instant identification of the fear that sounds like a boast. *I live right nearby! I use that road all the time! My best friend lives there! My kid went to school with that dead kid! That could have been me!*

But in the case of the gay or the mobster or the Mexican illegal, people think, *That could never have been me.*

Murder seemed a natural outcome of the quarrel between Chip and his lover. People said "Where?" and "How?" but not "Why?" But "Why?" would have elicited the most surprising answer.

The version that Buddy Hamstra heard — it was going the rounds of Waikiki — sounded perverse enough to be true. Sus-pecting that something was wrong — his mother had not called — Chip had visited the hotel unexpectedly one afternoon. I could vouch for that. I remembered the day. Chip's visit was not as ca-sual as it had seemed. Because it was deliberate it had all the ele-ments of calculation: suddenness, surprise, daylight. Being on duty, I was aware of movement at the back of the house, and I knew that Chip had entered the hotel by the rear door, moving quickly through the kitchen and then to the service elevator.

"These gay guys have very strong *manao*," Buddy said, using the Hawaiian word for gut feeling or intuition. Chip and his mother were on the same wavelength; he was like her in every way.

It was as though Chip had heard his mother calling from across the island, like the cry of some panicky jungle bird in bright plumage, that same helpless squawk. Chip had been at Salt Lake, out near Aloha Stadium, getting the oil changed in his car. Sensing trouble he called his mother, and Brenda, the hotel operator, said, "She's not answering." Not "She's not in," but "She's not answering." That made Chip suspicious.

As soon as the oil was changed, but not staying around for a new air filter, Chip raced back to Waikiki on Nimitz Highway. Instead of parking near the hotel, he used a meter on Kuhio and hurried around back. He was spotted by the kitchen staff, who told me how he had come and gone, all within a few minutes, "chasing his friend."

What Chip had seen — so the story went — had shocked him. He had not knocked. Using his own key, he had opened the locked door and heard muffled cries from the bedroom. There he had found his lover, Amo Ferretti, furiously assaulting his mother. The big naked man with the hairy back was violently raping the old woman, who, sallow and shrunken, looked defenseless. In this horrible glimpse, it seemed to Chip like the worst child abuse, like a brute assaulting a small girl, for his naked mother had a child's insubstantial body. The dark man was holding her legs apart and driving deep into her as she thrashed, gulping for breath. It was the rapist surprised in his crime, a son witnessing the violation of his own mother. And that same night the man was killed.

So, though it had all the conventional details of a gay crime — the bitchy quarrel, the car chase, the smashed skull — it only looked stereotypical. It wasn't a gay murder after all.

Chip's arrest and this explanation caused an outpouring of sympathy for the man in the orange jumpsuit in Oahu Community Correctional Center. He had the best motive on earth — the love for his mother. He had avenged his mother's honor by smashing the rapist's skull at the beach park. It was justified. Some people in Honolulu demanded Chip's release, but his mother was not among them.

If he had killed to defend her and had saved her life, why was his mother avoiding him? It was a question no one asked.

20

Rapture

BLOOD IS ADHESIVE. In a hotel it is like a curse. It is a taint that never goes away. For selfish reasons I was glad that the murder of Amo Ferretti was not committed in my hotel. Murders leave a sweetly poisonous smell that lingers, and any hotel unlucky enough to be the setting for a murder ceases to be a hotel and is known only as the scene of the crime, vicious and provocative, attracting all the wrong people, photographers and thrill seekers. The hotel never gets its reputation back, even after the charade of the most elaborate and noisy purification ceremonies, the howling monks, the gongs, the firecrackers, the tossing of salt, the prayers, the expensive and conceited exorcists. We were in the clear. Yet I still wondered why Chip had not killed Amo in the hotel, and why had he killed him at all.

"Chip in shock," Keola said. I loved hearing this dim, unlettered handyman use technical terms like "nonselective blackouts" and "short-term memory." At that moment he was cleaning the pool filter. I had approached him for the pleasure of hearing him say "I'm purging it," which meant nothing, the way "in shock" meant nothing.

Chip had committed the murder of Amo Ferretti on the windward side of the island, avenging his mother's honor. Public sympathy was with him, and Ferretti was seen as a villain. Chip was charged with murder, pleaded guilty to a reduced charge of aggravated manslaughter, was sentenced to twenty years with the possibility of parole. He could be out of Halawa Prison and back on his surfboard in five or six years if he behaved himself.

"Shock" did not explain why Chip, described as "furious," had not murdered Amo when he was naked, at his most helpless, his hairy back turned, in the act of rape. No one asked the question. Still, it seemed unusual for so much time to pass.

"They were arguing," Buddy said.

"The man raped his mother," I said. "What was there to argue about?"

Around this time I found Rose in my office looking at a dictionary. I asked her what word she was looking up.

She hesitated and then said, "Rapture."

Her innocent literal-mindedness made her a bad liar. Why had she concealed from me the real word she had searched for and found on that same page? The word "rape" was all over the hotel.

Trey, the assistant barman, told me that Amo and Madam Ma had had lunch and that Chip had not been present. The rape had occurred after lunch. Chip had surprised Amo in the act and then left the hotel the way he had come. In the earlier version of the story he had been chasing Amo, but the kitchen staff said he left alone and that Amo had left later. Why had they left separately, and why no chase? Our phone records showed that Madam Ma had reported the rape later that evening. She had also called Ferretti's wife, whom she knew, looking for Chip.

"There was a beef. They was fighting," the woman said. "Your kid went off on my husband. They left, I don't know where."

Instead of looking for her son, Madam Ma went to Honolulu Police headquarters and filed a complaint, reporting in detail that Amo Ferretti had raped her, that her son had stumbled upon the crime, and that Ferretti had threatened to kill him.

There were discrepancies in the exact times, but certain facts were not in dispute: Chip had been to the hotel, seen the rape, and left; Amo had been seen leaving later; Madam Ma had not reported the rape until after she had spoken to Mrs. Ferretti.

"I wanted to find out where he was so the police could arrest him," Madam Ma said, explaining why she had not reported the rape earlier.

But the complaint she filed late in the evening was explicit. The time of the incident was given as 2:25 P.M. She was taken to the hospital and examined. The report was made public — "evidence of bruising in the genital area," and "traces of semen were found," and more of equally grotesque clinical descriptions on page two of the family newspaper. What vindicated the publication of these unseemly facts was that justice had been served, and the murder charge had been reduced. Even so, there was general disapproval that a son had been given any jail time at all for killing his mother's rapist.

Talk about the case finally ceased, but Madam Ma was still on my mind. As a resident of the hotel, she was visible every day. I knew her movements. She said nothing. Chip was in jail, Amo was dead, she was her old antagonistic self, writing her insincere column. If she knew anything more about the case, she wasn't saying.

Of course, the hotel staff knew everything. The Honolulu police had interviewed them, yet shrewdly they answered only the questions they were asked. In the police station they did not volunteer any information; they were unspontaneous and monosyllabic. With me they were more forthcoming, however, especially when they saw that Madam Ma had begun to order them around. Sweetie, as head of Housekeeping, supplied me with informants.

"We saw the guy Ferretti all the time on the fifth floor, and in the room," Pacita said. And Marlene, her cleaning partner, said, "If you clean someone's room, you know all about them. The wastebasket is full of secrets. The bathroom too."

Amo regularly visited Madam Ma in her room. On the days he replaced the flowers in the lobby, Amo stayed for lunch — it was part of his contract — and Madam Ma joined him. Usually they drank on her lanai afterward, and Room Service had a record of those orders. Housekeeping did the rest — disposed of the bottles, picked up the glasses — and part of performing their job was to wander the corridors, tidying, vacuuming, trying doors and entering unoccupied rooms. On the days of Amo's visits, Madam Ma's door stayed locked, with the Do Not Disturb sign hung on the knob. Later, the Please Service This Room sign went up and the sheets were changed.

"If you make the bed, you know everything," Marlene said.

Madam Ma was one of the strongest women I had ever known. She looked birdlike but she was a bully. There was a reason for Marlene to confide in me. One day she had broken a glass in Madam Ma's bathroom. To punish her, Madam Ma insisted that Marlene pick up the bits of glass with her bare hands, and she stood over her, scolding. She hectored Rose, she nagged me, she bossed the staff. How was it possible that she had been overpowered by Amo?

Simply, she had not been. Amo was her lover. She had been in control the entire time. The staff knew every detail: how she was dressed on the afternoons when they were together, the pink negligee, the high-heeled slippers. "She looked beautiful those days." And they had games, fantasies that she scripted, that they acted out, that were audible in the adjoining rooms. After the drinking, she slipped into the bedroom to get ready, and Amo entered the bedroom from the lanai as Madam Ma admired herself in the mirror. She saw the man's menacing reflection. Hairy Amo slipped the negligee from her shoulders, pushed her to her knees, and took her from behind. Her greatest pleasure came later, when Amo was so frenzied he ignored her pleas. He took her roughly on the floor of the room, and that was rapture. And though their endearments could be heard afterward, on the day in question they were interrupted by Chip, who drew his own conclusions and saw the lovemaking as rape.

21

Insecticide

IN THE ANNALS of true crime there is no darker comedy than that of a murder gone horribly wrong — the blundering blood-smeared killer with sticky hands, frantic in the front seat, as the corpse in the back seat rises up bloated with gas and seems to come alive, protesting with assertive farts. That Hawaii story was plenty for most people and was macabre enough to satisfy them and make them tune out. But there were sequels. This story kept changing as time passed.

The principals, Chip and Amo, were gay. Amo, the older, soon-to-be-bludgeoned one, was known to boast, "He's my bitch." So it was a gay man killing his presumptuous lover, a crime not unknown in Hawaii, except in this case the dead and gaseous gay Amo had been married, with a wife and two kids in Kailua. People said, "I pity the kids." And "What kind of wife puts up with a husband like that?"

"A crime of passion," the papers reported when it was revealed that the dead man had been caught in the Hotel Honolulu raping the mother of the man who killed him. In the next version, I learned from Housekeeping that what looked like rape had been sex play: the gay man's gay lover was having a steamy affair with the gay man's divorced mother, the prominent Honolulu columnist Madam Ma.

And when I thought I had had enough of the affair of Chip and Amo and Madam Ma, there was more. Soon after the trial had ended and he was imprisoned in Honolulu, Chip sent a message through his lawyer that he did not wish to receive visits from his mother. Given the fact that what had looked like rape had in reality been rapture, and that he was being two-timed by his lover with the connivance of his mother, it seemed unexpected for Chip to keep the woman away. He did not have another friend in Hawaii, which was his whole world.

"He paranoid," Keola said. And, watering plants in Paradise Lost, Peewee agreed. I liked this, the pair of them in bare feet, discussing paranoia.

"What does 'paranoid' mean?" I asked.

"He freaking out," Keola said.

Madam Ma, still resident in the hotel, was not downcast by her son's refusal to see her. With the trial over, her newspaper column reappeared in the *Advertiser,* and the only difference was that her son, who had previously been a friendly feature in her writing, no longer appeared. There was nothing in her column except the trivial babble of restaurant openings, celebrity sightings, and the free weekends she spent as a guest of public relations. And repeated mention of the Hotel Honolulu, "Waikiki's multistory secret."

"I am getting on with my life," she said whenever I asked her how she was. As for Chip: "I feel great compassion for him." She also said, "I know where my son is every minute. That's a mother's prayer."

Was I imagining that this tone, which bordered on comedy, suggested that she was relieved by the outcome? She surely didn't seem like a woman whose lover had been murdered by her son, who was doing twenty years for the crime. There was a liberated look in Madam Ma's eyes, and even the way she walked and dressed showed definite confidence. This was not the demeanor of a woman whose son had been jailed unfairly.

I saw her every day, crossing the lobby, eating on the lanai, drinking in Paradise Lost. We fed her, we cleaned her room, we looked after her. No, I was not imagining it: Madam Ma was more relaxed, like someone for whom a problem has been solved, whose life has become simpler and less stressful.

My daughter reflected this change. Rose, too, was calmer. She no longer contradicted Madam Ma, or competed with her, or cried after they quarreled. There were no more quarrels. Instead of offering friendship, they made a wiser and more prudent offering: they gave each other space.

Though I doubted there was any such thing as closure, Madam Ma called it that. I didn't ask why. I was grateful for the peace that had descended on the hotel. But in that serenity I began to reflect on what had happened, and to wonder at the paradoxes — the death that had not been a death, the gay murder that had nothing to do with gayness, the rape that wasn't a rape, and now the imprisonment that seemed to satisfy everyone, even the prisoner's mother.

Madam Ma was such an enigma, so calculating and insincere, I knew she would not tell me anything truthful. There was nothing new in her column, but there was news from prison. As the months passed, another story came out, for Chip had a succession of cellmates, and Halawa Prison was a revolving door for villains, and the whispers reached the Hotel Honolulu. A sense of grievance makes a person talkative, and Chip was aggrieved. The kitchen staff were the first to hear it, for the lower a person was on the payroll, the closer they were to the ground, and the more they heard. At the lowest level — Keola manhandling the dumpster — such people had access to the most detailed information. Smoke was just smoke to me, but my workers knew whether it was a fire set by rivals or Teamster arson, and they could whisper every turn of the plot. They knew the truth about Chip.

"What is it?" I asked.

Keola said, "Insecticide."

What a dark and beautiful way of summing it up.

From an early age, Madam Ma had dressed Chip as a girl. Her husband, Harry Ma, had objected — it was one of the reasons for their divorce, but of course it was just what Madam Ma had wanted. Chip was born in the sixties, and long hair was in fashion. Madam Ma put him in sundresses. She brushed his hair and used cosmetics on his face. Chip was her dolly.

This is what Chip told his cellmates, pleading for understanding.

Early on, the Ma family had an apartment in Makiki, but Madam Ma could not cook and would not clean. She hired people, but she was too demanding. They never stayed, and because she frightened them with her bullying they left abruptly, without giving notice, meaning to be stealthy and also causing the greatest inconvenience. When Madam Ma became established on the *Ad-*

vertiser, she made a deal with Buddy and got a cheap rate for room 504. In return she would mention the hotel in her column whenever possible and entertain travel writers from the mainland in our bar and dining room.

Chip was still in school when they lived in the squalid seclusion of the apartment in Makiki. At night, Madam Ma had dressed her son as a little girl — overdressed him, that is, for cross-dressing is never subtle or understated. There was no man in the house — Harry Ma was a Filipino Chinese for whom Hawaii was a steppingstone. He was now in Las Vegas. In Makiki, in bed, chain-smoking and sipping her vodka tonic, Madam Ma had made little Chip practice curtseying and asking nicely for his food. The plate of food, his dinner, lay on Madam Ma's lap.

All the repulsive details had the ring of truth: food in the bedroom, Madam Ma in bed, cigarette ash on the pillow, smoke in the air, crumbs and stains on the sheets, Madam Ma's bare thighs propping up the dinner plate, the little boy dressed as a girl having to ask for his meal in a certain way, using a specific formula. This lasted years. For periods Chip stopped eating altogether, or was bulimic, sticking a finger down his throat and barfing in the toilet.

They moved into the hotel. The androgyny of the late sixties and early seventies still served them — unconventional son, hippie mother. Buddy Hamstra teased the boy but loved him. He seemed to understand the boy was damaged. At the age of fifteen, when he was in Punahou School, he was still sleeping with his mother — actually sleeping. Buddy knew that from Housekeeping. In the Hotel Honolulu we knocked and turned the knob at the same time, and Madam Ma was as careless about locking the door as she was about keeping the room tidy. Because Madam Ma and Chip had so accepted their oddness, they did little to hide it. Many times the staff glimpsed them together, just snuggling.

The rest of it — that his mother dressed him in panties and put a ribbon around his neck and made a ponytail of his long hair and told him to massage her feet and paint her toenails — all that came out in prison. In that role he was aroused. "What are we going to do with that?" Madam Ma said, slipping on a pair of silk gloves. "I can't leave you that way." In the beginning Chip was just confused and looked away, but later Madam Ma learned to say, "I know what you want," and Chip went to her for relief. It had never stopped, even after he had taken a lover, even —

though he didn't know it — after his mother had taken a lover. So Chip told his cellmates. He was not complaining. What he could not understand, and what infuriated him, was that Amo Ferretti had taken his place.

Madam Ma was forbidden to visit the prison, but on Family Day he was sometimes visited by Ferretti's widow. Had Chip also been conducting an affair with her all along? If so, it explained everything.

The coconut wireless dispersed these details to the island at large, and soon Madam Ma's column was canceled. I did not have the heart to kick her out of the hotel. What interested me was that she stopped writing just as (you would have thought) she had something to write about. I saw her in Paradise Lost, sipping a pisco sour, and I thought: Who will tell her story? And how? And, Is there more?

22

Nevermann the Searcher

"IT'S LIKE THAT delightful evening you spend with your best friend and his wife in their cozy house, eating a home-cooked meal, and you think, Isn't it great to have a marriage like this!" Benno Nevermann, a visitor from Naples, Florida, said to me. "And then your friend, whom you took to be a wise old man, takes you aside and starts whispering about a girl he has fallen in love with."

I said, "And you're disillusioned and you think, What a fool."

"You're a fool and he's a bigger fool, and the whole bottomless world seems absurd and disloyal."

Nevermann was a good listener, which made him a more interesting talker. He had the irony of a true cynic, and a humorous way of expressing it. He traveled alone. He was a reader who usually took a book to the beach. Never a novel — he liked reading history, "delving into the past." But when I inquired, he said he was not a war buff, and all he said of Pearl Harbor was "We trusted the Japanese!" and that he had no intention of visiting the *Arizona* Memorial: "It's too sad."

Nevermann's candor made me forthcoming. I said, "My version of your marriage story is that at the end of my visit, when I'm thinking, What a happy couple, the wife tells me pointedly how long it's been since her husband made love to her."

"I've been there," Nevermann said. "I was the husband."

In the tennis match of male conversation, such is the growing momentum of the serve-and-volley that I found I was telling Nevermann things I had not told my wife — not secrets but confidences of a sort. Nevermann's seriousness was persuasive, but also he seemed wise, someone I might learn to trust. Also, in that same tennis match, we serve confidences to people who we hope will lob their own secrets back to us. But after knowing him a while I saw Nevermann didn't need much encouragement. He had something on his mind; he was candid without requiring me to bare my soul.

Almost at the outset he explained to me that he had been very poor. He had grown up in a suburb of Chicago with his divorced mother. His father had remarried but within two years had been financially ruined and soon had committed suicide. After leaving high school, with no money for college ("But so what, college never gives you any useful job skills"), Nevermann got work in a factory. The factory made rust-proof garden furniture — Nevermann ran the vinyl-coating machine. He labored in stinking heat among vats of noxious polymers.

Intelligent and ambitious, Nevermann found ways of improving the machine so it was no longer necessary to dip the product. Instead a fitted sleeve was made for it. "A kind of extruded vinyl," Nevermann explained. He patented this so-called Nevermann Sleeve and, applying the technology to other products in his basement, came up with a way of vinyl-coating window frames with the sleeve. He patented that process too, and registered the name Wadsworth's Weatherproof Windows. There was no Wadsworth, but Nevermann was a funny name, and anyway he needed some memorable alliteration. At last, here was a vinyl-coated window — tested in Chicago winters — that did not rust, chip, warp, or leak, nor ever needed to be painted.

He had no start-up money, did not trust investors or partners, so he became a salesman. For three or four years he drove all over the Midwest, taking orders and building up his business. He sometimes went abroad, to India and China. "I outsourced some of the machine-tooling."

"Outsourced" was an even better word than "extruded." Nevermann, who had moved from his basement to his garage to a small factory, now had a rapidly growing business. To keep costs down he relocated to Tennessee, where, during the building boom of the eighties, he sold the company for a large amount of money. He moved to Naples, Florida. He still made money on the patents he had taken out. He was then forty-five years old. He traveled and read. He recognized my name. He knew my books. This familiarity seemed to make him talkative, even confessional. Books and travel were not enough, he said.

"It's a secret, but I'll tell you what I really do," he said. "I look people up. I search them out and see what time has done to them."

"That's your hobby?"

"It's my passion," Nevermann said. "I'm a searcher."

"Give me an example."

Nevermann said, "When I was in high school I had a job in a supermarket. I was a terrible student, had no time to study, and we had so little money that I gave my whole salary to my mother. I envied the popular kids in the school — the jocks, the brainy kids, the beautiful girls, the rich ones who had new cars. One drove a Thunderbird."

That was in Des Plains, Illinois: Des Plains High. Years later, with the sale of the vinyl-coated-window company and the move to Florida, Nevermann went back to his hometown and traced the big shots and achievers from his high school class. Some of them had gone on to greater things — had married well, started businesses, succeeded as professionals; but Nevermann was interested in the nuances. One of the most accomplished was also an alcoholic. One of the wealthiest, George Kunkle, had lost his fortune gambling. The pretty girls in high school had become plain and middle-aged. Nevermann charted their rise and fall. He collected pictures. In albums he created little histories. The detail in his work gave it depth, and it resembled natural history, as though Nevermann were describing the life cycle of a new species. And it was intentionally specific. The high school friend Kunkle had insulted him one cold day when Nevermann was working at the supermarket. Kunkle approached him in the deli department and said, "Where can I get a hat like that?" Just a joke, but Kunkle's girlfriend was with him. Twenty-five years later Nevermann found Kunkle — broke, living in a welfare hotel in San Francisco. He was wearing an old hat that said *Go 'Niners*. Nevermann said, "Where can I get a hat like that?" and told him who he was.

"Not revenge, but justice — and revelation," Nevermann told me. It wasn't personal, and much of it was more complex than this. It made him a time traveler. His frugality as a salesman had forced him to stay in inexpensive motels and eat in cheap diners. He killed time in cocktail lounges, listening to music. He had written everything down — kept logs, diaries, journals — his struggle.

Decades later he looked up Florence Bestwick, who had served him breakfast in a diner outside St. Louis; Sylvia Shaw, who had sung "When You Wish Upon a Star" at the Four O'Clock Lounge in Columbus, Ohio; Fred Casey, who had fixed his car in Davenport, Iowa, when he had been on the road; Ronald Markham, a hotel clerk who had been rude to him in the Highlands Motel in Highlands Bluff, Missouri; Leda Hemperly, whom he had desired, who had gone to the senior prom with George Kunkle.

The oddest names, the deepest searches, were the most satisfying. Florence Bestwick was a widow and ran a catering service from home. Sylvia Shaw lived in a trailer park in Englewood, Florida, and was now the mother of a singer. Fred Casey had had a stroke. Nevermann gave them each a check for five hundred dollars. Ronald Markham, he had learned, had serviced swimming pools in Cape Girardeau, Missouri, after leaving the hotel and was now dead. He took Leda Hemperly out for a drink. He did not desire her. It was she who suggested staying the night, but Nevermann said, "Maybe some other time. Maybe never."

Old girlfriends, old enemies, old bosses, competitors from the past — they necessitated his groping in the wonderful tunnel of time, searching for clues. Why had so few people succeeded? Why had so many failed? But for most of them nothing at all had happened except that time had passed and they had grown older: he found them living in the same town, on the same street, in the same house. Leda was one of those.

Nevermann had no wish to feel vindictive, nor any desire to gloat over anyone's disgrace. He wanted only pitiless excavation and discovery, and he undertook many of the searches because of the sheer difficulty they presented. Why else go to India? In October 1973 in New Delhi, on one of his outsourcing trips, he had heard a lovely young Indian woman sing a Carpenters song, "It's Yesterday Once More," in a hotel lounge.

The search took almost a month, but he found that woman. She was married to a businessman in Bombay. She was still lovely. She had a daughter in Chicago. "I used to live in Chicago!" Nevermann said. But that was not the point. In the process of finding the Indian woman he had learned to penetrate India.

Nevermann was not the eccentric millionaire people claimed he was when he found them and revealed himself. He had turned his excavation of the past into a quest, something almost existential, and it had given him a way of living, a mode of discovery, something purposeful.

"On the way I have found out so much about the world and met such amazing people," he said to me. "I would not have met you otherwise."

His searches gave the past meaning. They illustrated the passage of time. They made him kinder, he said: you saw how frail and fallible people were. He liked the surprises.

"I am a detective," he said, though he was soft-spoken, circumspect, and had the manner of an old priest. "But of course there is no crime, only existence."

"What's the point?"

"Time is pitiless, time is awful," he said. "Just to allow people to live is the greatest justice of all. It is not a reprieve — for most people it is punishment. I need to see it."

"What are you doing in Honolulu?" I asked.

"I came here to see Madam Ma, the journalist."

The mask-faced woman, mother of a murderer, who had seduced her own son. But I didn't say so.

"She was my mother," Nevermann said.

23

Infidel

"WHILE I WAS making my fortune I was very happy," Nevermann said. "I was alone. It was like being in the wilderness." He said that nothing in his life had compared with the long period of frantic solitude in which he had invented the vinyl-coating process that made him rich. I had complimented Nevermann on his tenacity in searching the past. "It's just a hobby," he said. "But there is very little I don't know about lamination and polymers."

He liked to reminisce about his solitary struggle: the late nights, the shortage of money, the patenting process, the building of his business, Wadsworth's Weatherproof Windows — a long period of reflection and work.

"Probably like writing a novel," he said.

"Inventing the perfect window?" I said. "Yes. A writer once said that the house of fiction has a million windows, and writers are looking out, watching the same show but seeing different things. One sees black where another sees white, one sees big where another sees small. Paradise out one window looks like the human comedy out another window."

"Henry James, *Portrait of a Lady,* the introduction," Nevermann said. "Surprised I know that? She gave me lessons in Henry James."

Yes, I was surprised. "Who gave you lessons?"

"Tell you later," he said. "The window that made the most money was the cellophane window on the envelope, invented by Joseph Regenstein," Nevermann said. "I know that, as a Chicagoan. Regenstein made a fortune and gave it to the University of Chicago."

I was reflecting on the envelope window as Nevermann told me the inventions he wished he had thought of, the simple breakthroughs: the snap-on lid of the Tupperware container, the notion of Velcro, the science behind Gore-Tex and Teflon.

"I envy the man who first thought of the snap-up opener on soda cans. I knew the tear-off loop was environmentally unfriendly." He liked the snap-up opener because it was nondetachable: the perfect solution, no waste. "It was probably too idealistic of me to want to make edible packaging, but soluble plastic is within our grasp. I like simplicity. One of your Hawaii residents invented the supermarket shopping cart."

"Goldman," I said, a name spoken in Honolulu in a whisper, for it was associated with drugs, bad luck, and suicide. "His fortune was the ruination of the family."

"I wanted to avoid that," Nevermann said. "All the time I was struggling I didn't have a woman."

Nevermann was so preoccupied with making his fortune that he remained single and celibate. His work made him happy. This combination of solitude and happiness gave him an aura of innocence, and when he became wealthy he was pursued by women, sought out not only for his money but also for the serenity that had become part of his character. Yet Nevermann had become almost monastic. He did not need a woman, he hardly needed companionship; he needed nothing. He had everything. But he knew he had neglected the cultural side of his life. He had little formal education, no time for books. He was musically illiterate. He wanted to catch up. This was after he moved to Florida. He found a college professor in Fort Myers who agreed to design a reading list of great books. It was important for a man of his wealth to know the classics and to understand the expensive objects that he had bought. "*Avoir sans savoir est impardonable*," the French-speaking professor had told him, and translated it for him.

The professor's name was Vera Shihab — Lebanese father, Irish mother. She was thirty-five, unmarried, specialized in women's studies, but had a Ph.D. in comparative literature, which she always called comp. lit. She made the list for Nevermann: some Greek drama, Shakespeare's "problem plays" including *Hamlet* and *Pericles, Don Quixote,* Turgenev and Chekhov rather than Dostoyevsky. *Anna Karenina. Great Expectations.* Flaubert. *Diary of a Nobody.* Mark Twain. *Portrait of a Lady. Death in Venice. Heart of Darkness.* Stephen Crane's *The Monster.* Also Zora Neale Hurston, Edith Walters Olgivie, and more. Racism and oppression were themes on the list, and consequently so was liberation. Nevermann was impressed by the list, its reach and its seriousness. Vera was like someone with a vocation; she had that intensity.

Small, blond, talkative, she was pale and rather thin, all nerves and alertness — he guessed from her working hard. Her physical type appealed to Nevermann much more than if she had been the embodiment of big buttocky health, which he would have found intimidating for being too hearty. Vera's eyes were vivid green: contact lenses, but oddly attractive and catlike. She lived alone and hardly ate. She had had, she said, two or three lovers. "Sex partners" was her term. A previous marriage had ended swiftly: "I'm sure he was gay, but I don't think he knew it."

"I love your smile," she said to Nevermann. She also said she was fascinated by his name, Benno.

"It's German, you know."

Seminars — their informal discussions of the books — at her small, untidy apartment often ended late, Nevermann feeling pleasurably stimulated by the talk. One night Vera excused herself for about ten minutes and then reentered the room in a beautiful silk kimono, carrying a bottle of champagne, and said, "Do you think you could open this for me?" Nevermann did so, and they clinked glasses, but his thirst remained and made him attentive. As he drank, Vera said, "I want you in my mouth," and knelt before him. She did something to his body that he had sometimes fantasized about, and she murmured hungrily, holding him in her mouth. He lost control, he cried out, he sat down, he fell asleep, and then he stirred. She was not through. She said, "Turn over, darling." He slept again, and woke up bewitched.

They were married a few months later. Time seemed to mean everything, and then it meant nothing. He became unhappy. It was a new feeling. He had never been unhappy that way before. Uncertain, yes, and anxious, but not unhappy. With her next to him, he felt intensely lonely.

Vera had told Nevermann how her husband and those lovers

had become cold and remote with her, and hypercritical; how they simply disliked being with her. They had begun reading bad novels. They watched television. They took vacations on their own. They lost their temper with her, shouted at her, cheated on her.

As though assuming the lead role in the sort of melodrama he hated, Nevermann saw that he had taken on the characteristics of his wife's ex-husband and former lovers. He, who had hardly ever raised his voice, began shouting at her. "Keith used to read by the pool, to ignore me," she had told him. Nevermann started doing that! He avoided her, because the closer he came, the greater the chance of conflict. She had changed him, but she was fundamentally the same, except that she was no longer the coquette. No champagne. No "Turn over, darling." No books either.

She had what she wanted. In a weary, self-righteous, persistent way she was a nag. He knew the marriage was a mistake, that she was wrong for him. Yet she looked the same as when she had fascinated him with "*Avoir sans savoir est impardonable*" and the startling "I want you in my mouth."

People said to him, "You've changed."

Nevermann, who had been happy alone and had never needed anyone, now was deeply unhappy and sought the companionship of prostitutes. He told them what he wanted: it was what Vera had once offered him. He talked to people in bars, anyone who complimented him on his work. He was an easy mark for praise, and became needy, hated being alone. He had lost the solitude that had stimulated his imagination. He had never been lonely then. He had merely been alone. He badly missed his old single problem-solving self.

There seemed no solution to his dilemma. Looking into the future, he saw images of himself as a sorry middle-aged man. He gave people money! Handed it to them on trips he took!

In this fearful mood of low spirits he could not invent or create. He was dissolving inside. But the fear Vera had induced in him prevented him from leaving her. Castration was a terrible word, but that was the plainest way of saying what she had done to him, and she had managed it without touching him. So he stayed married to Vera. All that was required for him to stay married to her was for him to ask nothing of her.

He needed strength. He found it in the past, because he had no future. He found it in other people, because he himself was dying. It was, he admitted, partly sexual. There was nothing better than to find a woman he had once known and to discover that he desired her. And sex was easy — everything that followed it was impossible.

Yet his real passion lay in looking people up, everyone he had known or seen in his past, great and small, teachers, schoolmates, janitors, hotel workers, people who were memorable for having been kind, or rude — simply to see what had become of them. All were older, of course; most were sadder, fatter, sorrier, less secretive, facing death. Some were sick, many were dead. Nevermann did not feel superior. He said, "I am now like them."

24

The Seductress

"MY FATHER, when he lived," Benno Nevermann said, "suffered for having made a terrible error."

His father, Bruno, had been a prosperous Chicago businessman. He had a loving family and an uncomplicated life — one child, a lovely house, no debts. Recklessness was unknown to him, and (so Nevermann said) perhaps that was the problem: he seemed to hold himself in check. He did not drink or smoke. "Maybe he should have had a beer now and then. Maybe he should have smoked the occasional cigar." But the old man's background had been very strict. His mother, Nevermann's grandmother, a German immigrant, always with a Bible, talked Scripture with strangers on buses and readily asked about the condition of their souls. Nevermann's grandfather was less intrusive but similar, a perpetual frown beneath his mustache.

Nevermann's father had not rebelled. He was a churchgoing man, but there was rigidity even in that: he went every Sunday without fail, yet never at any other time. He did not talk about religion, but his disapproval was like a bad smell whenever he saw something ungodly. His son came to understand his severity. After he had bought a television, Nevermann's father would leave the room if a woman appeared onscreen in a skimpy dress.

Though Bruno Nevermann did not drink alcohol, his firm supplied brewery equipment, a business his father — Benno's grandfather — had started by importing it from Germany. Later, it was manufactured locally, and he had expanded the business until he was considered wealthy, in a city where only the very wealthy were singled out. Bruno Nevermann could seem stern, but he was the kindest and most merciful of men: he hired people for their poverty — men for their bleak pasts, women for their plain features. Nevermann noticed that at his father's warehouses and factories each person seemed somewhat maimed — the woman with one eye or a hump, the man with a limp or a kinked hand or a terrible scar, the twitching messenger. This was the 1940s. Who else would have them? They were old and lame and they mumbled. Nevermann found the workers frightening and misshapen, especially when they clutched him and tried to be friendly or playful — holding him in their claws, fixing him with cloudy eyes. "This is your son!" they screeched to Nevermann's father. "Come over here!" Then the small boy felt all the breath go out of his body.

But one of the workers held Nevermann's attention for being attractive. She was younger than any of the others. Nevermann asked who she was. "Edith's daughter," the old man said. Edith had a foot that dragged and stiffened fingers on one hand. A stroke victim — the explanation meant nothing to Nevermann, but he was hardly listening, for the young girl was so fragrant as to be a distraction.

She was no more than eighteen. Nevermann was twelve and just able to understand that she was very pretty. He took an interest, went to the warehouse and stared, but his father warned him off. And at last Nevermann's father threatened him and told him to stay away.

Only later did Nevermann realize how his father was tormented, how whenever Edith's daughter showed up, her pretense of seeming submissive tempted the man. She had a way of walking that was an invitation, suggesting herself as an offering, of moving her arms as if to say, Hold me. She found a way of turning her back to the old man and peering over her shoulder and smiling, of appearing to be timid and encouraging him to calm her fears. All this without speaking a single word.

Comfort me, she seemed to say, and was all the more effective for not saying it. She needed to be rescued. She was so innocent. The old man took her aside and warned her of the wickedness of the world. She said she was shocked, and she was, but the description also excited her. The lurid warnings excited the old man, too. At last, when she was trembling with fear at what he said, when she was in his protective embrace — she was so warm and damp

— the old man found that his greatest consolation was his body across hers, and he found himself fumbling with her overalls.

After that he could not help himself anymore. He pitied her for being Edith's daughter, and he was sick with desire. Still married, well known in Chicago, and greatly respected, the old man persuaded Edith's daughter to become his lover. He was grateful to the girl for giving in, never suspecting that it had been her idea from the beginning. Her idea and Edith's too — Edith the badly injured woman whom the old man had admired for her struggle. She had hissed in her daughter's ear.

I remembered how Nevermann had once told me, "It's like that delightful evening you spend with your best friend and his wife in their cozy house, eating a home-cooked meal, and you think, Isn't it great to have a marriage like this! And then your friend, whom you took to be a wise old man, takes you aside and starts whispering about a girl he has fallen in love with."

He had been talking about his own father.

The old man's blurted confession made Nevermann's mother hysterical. The marriage ended messily, like a car crash, every passenger injured. Long afterward, Nevermann saw that the girl, Edith's daughter, had set out to seduce his father. His remarriage wrecked the family. Nevermann's mother got some money and promises from the man, but only a few years after the marriage, Edith's daughter said she wanted a divorce. She ended up getting the house and half the business, and she wrecked her half by spending the capital on herself, and that killed the whole of it. She so thoroughly got hold of the old man's money that he was destroyed, with pills and alcohol — he who had never had a drink! His suicide note was a love letter, to Edith's daughter.

Nevermann's mother was bereft, and her sobbing had scoured her of all emotion. She was skeletal, she trembled, she could hardly speak. No money remained of what was owed her. She was reduced to living in a rented room in Des Plains, with her schoolboy son, Benno, who worked in a supermarket most nights, and after high school got a job in a factory making garden furniture. Nevermann's aim was to give his mother some years of comfort, to return her to the prosperity she had known. But she died miserably before Nevermann made his fortune.

The girl, Edith's daughter? She married again, and again it was as though she were stalking prey. The man was wealthy. She left him. The next was a dentist, Filipino Chinese, who had invested wisely, Harry Ma. They had a child, Chip. She divorced Mr. Ma but remained Madam Ma — our Madam Ma. I told Nevermann how that had ended, and now all the rest of it: how the harmless-seeming columnist, friend of my friend Buddy and a hotel resident, mother of a murderer, had seduced her own son, and her son's lover, and created havoc here, did not seem to be a broken woman, but only enigmatic and empty. Pretty soon Nevermann, his search at an end, checked out, and at last so did she.

25

Hopecraft

FROM THE JERKY, hesitant steps the man took, the way he sized up my hotel, leaning forward to glance through the lobby, his head twisted sideways, the way birds peer at a speck to see whether it is edible — from all this it was clear to me that he was looking for someone who had not yet shown up. His dithering made me think it might be a person he did not know very well.

He wore a look of distinct anticipation, which did not alter, for he was taking shallow breaths, cautiously sipping the Waikiki air. He also blinked a lot. I could not improve on his real name, which was Charlie Hopecraft. He was pink, portly, friendless, a middle-aged man in the sort of lumpy clean sneakers that seemed to give him white hind paws. Putting him on the third floor across from Puamana turned out to be an inspired idea.

Normally in assigning rooms I separated the short-term guests, who were mostly on the upper floors, with a sea view, from the long-term residents, who were down below, no view but within easy reach of the lobby. This Golden Week we were so full that the only room I had for Charlie Hopecraft was on three. He said he liked being there. He had a nervous habit of giving me irrelevant information.

"My uncle was here during the war."

"This hotel?"

"No, Whyee. He was on Maui. Some air base."

Hopecraft was from Utah and was possibly a Mormon, but if so not a devout one. He drank. He complained that Provo, near where he lived — his hometown was in the mountains — was too noisy for him.

"But it's a real nice town — no hookers," he said, and looked around, not in curiosity but wincing, dodging slightly, as though expecting me to say something. Was he trying to remind me that Waikiki was full of hookers?

"I've never been out of the States before," he said.

"This is the States."

Hopecraft was one of those shy people, inarticulate men mostly, who become animated by the sight of someone's pet. They see some damp animal in a collar and begin slobbering. In this case it was Puamana's big cat, Popoki. Oblique people, who avoid eye contact with others, seem responsive to strangers' animals, as if the pet stands for the person. Just seeing the hairy beast, Hopecraft got on his hands and knees and stroked it, talked frankly and foolishly to it. Popoki was a fat, suspicious, wicked-faced cat with beautifully brushed fur, black with a few white hairs, the true coloration of its owner. As for its name, *popoki* meant cat in Hawaiian, an old corruption of "poor pussy." For some reason — pet lovers probably broadcast benign signals — the cat took to Hopecraft. That was enough for Puamana.

"His name is Popoki," Puamana said. "He hate strangers."

The cat bared his teeth as though he knew his personality was being discussed. Hopecraft took up the challenge.

"You are a big, sassy pussycat who likes his belly scratched, yes you do," Hopecraft said, hunkering down in the corridor.

Puamana watched this with a calculating gaze. I introduced them, but I did not explain that Puamana was my mother-in-law. The next question might concern grandchildren, and while Puamana loved Rose, she hated the notion that she was a granny. Who could blame her? She was in her late forties but looked younger. Puamana was blond this month. She still entertained men in her room. But she was choosy. She worked only when she needed money for clothes. She was small-boned and girl-sized, but healthy, even somewhat muscular. She exercised — jogged, lifted hand weights, did step aerobics on the hotel roof. One of the first things Sweetie had told me about her was "My mom has five vibrators. Different sizes!" She believed she was revealing a dark secret about her mother, but it was a secret that ex-plained nothing. Puamana seemed to me like someone on vaca-tion, her whole life a holiday, with the same painless ups and downs. Someone had always looked after her — first Buddy, then Sweetie, and now me.

Without appearing to take any notice of Puamana, Hopecraft obviously liked her — I could see that from the way he lavished attention on her cat. He also had a deeply preoccupied air, some-what troubled and urgent, always seeming on the verge of asking a question and then thinking better of it and shutting his mouth so hard he squashed his lips.

From the first day, Hopecraft followed the usual breakfast-beach-lunch-snooze routine of the mainland tourist. He walked around with a rolled-up beach mat and a hotel towel. From his posture and concentration, I could see he was looking for some-thing more. I kept thinking that he had an assignation that had not yet taken place.

Or was it the effect of Puamana? His attachment to Popoki made him an instant hit with the woman. He bought some cat treats and a ball for the creature to gnaw. In return, Puamana asked him about his job and family, and they stood on the roof and looked at the crags on the crater rim of Diamond Head or the lights of Waikiki or the sunset beyond Waianae, all the while tak-ing turns scratching Popoki. Unmarried, Hopecraft was in haul-age.

After a drink or two — budget-conscious Hopecraft mixed them on the roof with ingredients from his room — Puamana ex-cused herself and took her cat downstairs. Hopecraft was relieved by her going away, because that was when he went out and looked for a prostitute. This nighttime quest in an oversize aloha shirt and thick white sneakers on the sidewalks adjacent to the hotel was Hopecraft's solitary reason for visiting Hawaii.

Hookers were almost everywhere in Waikiki. Though they used the alley next to us as a shortcut to Kalakaua Avenue, they seldom loitered near the Hotel Honolulu. The streetwalkers had gotten the message — we were at the edge, we got too few Japa-nese, and any hookers would have been conspicuous if they had lingered in this area. There wasn't enough traffic. Farther down Kuhio and Kalakaua, where there were big concealing crowds, the young women stalked in high heels, that unmistakable hooker walk, not going anywhere, just moving in place, big-haired women on a treadmill.

But — was it the time of day? was it the time of year? — Hopecraft had a bad eye for such women. A country boy from a small Utah town for whom Provo was a noisy city, he could not tell a hooker from a socialite; both were beautifully dressed and businesslike. I sympathized with him, for the fact was neither could I, not in Honolulu, where you could easily mistake one for the other because, in many cases, one had *been* the other.

We discussed this, Hopecraft and I. "It's just so frustrating," he said. Being in Hawaii made him feel amorous. The hula moon, the lisping sea, the fragrant flowers, all of it. So he prowled, trying to tomcat, but he made no headway.

"Whyee's got everything," he said to me early on. "If I had a woman it would be perfect."

"What sort of woman?"

Making a face as he struggled to think of a euphemism for "whore" — all the alternatives were vulgar — he finally settled on "working girl." It was true that hookers made the whole arrangement easy. They were adept at simplification — they knew it was a waste of time to wait for an approach, so they usually initiated contact. But for johns they preferred Japanese men, who were polite and fast and paid more, were quickly intimidated and easily robbed.

Hopecraft said, "Honolulu has a wild reputation. I wish I knew how the place got it."

Because it was not any part of my job to help him in his hopeful quest, I remained a sympathetic listener and keen observer, who had unwittingly given him an advantage by assigning him a room across the hall from Puamana.

By his fourth night, Hopecraft was on the point of giving up. After his usual prowling he returned to the hotel looking flatfooted and went up to his room. Passing Puamana's door he knocked, hoping to play with the cat. Just as his knuckles hit the door, he thought he heard a woman's voice saying, "No, please!" and that so alarmed him that instead of calling out "Puamana," he said, "Hey, Popoki!" There was silence. He went to his room. The subsequent commotion in the hall kept him in his room. The next day Puamana was furious.

"Why you go bang on my room door at almost midnight, you *lolo!*"

"It was only eleven." Hopecraft was looking down at his big, lumpy hind paws. "I wanted a little time to play with Popoki."

Puamana squinted at him and said, "Bad timing. Is why you one loser."

The blunder upset him — Puamana was annoyed. A few days before, he had considered asking her, as a friend from out of town, pretending to joke, where the hookers were, and the famous red-light district, and what about those hula girls in grass skirts? He put that thought aside and shyly asked her if she would go out for a meal with him.

She said okay, if she could bring her cat. Hopecraft was secretly pleased she did so, and sat throughout the meal holding Popoki on his lap, feeding him fish scraps, scratching him behind the ears, listening to his bubbly purring. Puamana smiled; she had forgiven him. Hopecraft was happy. He had made a friend.

"How about coffee?"

"Sorry. Gotta run." Puamana lifted her hands and Hopecraft passed her the cat. Puamana said, "Don't ever bang on my door at night, okay? I hate disruption."

In his room later, consoling himself with the thought of the companionable meal but vowing that he would never come back to Honolulu, Hopecraft heard Puamana enter her room. He thought of going across the hall and thanking her for being a friend, but decided not to. And it was a good thing he did, because he would have disturbed Puamana, as before, turning a trick, pretending to be frightened, saying "No, please!" and submitting like a scared schoolgirl to the nervous Japanese man.

26

Puamana's Cat

SHE HAD KNOWN all along what the man across the hall, the stranger Charlie Hopecraft, had wanted: a woman just like her. He had been friendly and respectful. But he had too much time on his hands. He had limited money. He was lost in the Hotel Honolulu. Puamana said it wasn't worth losing a week's privacy for a hundred dollars. "I would never get rid of him."

At first I let her stay at the hotel because Buddy had told me to. He seemed to like having this loose woman somewhat in his debt. Or was it a favor he owed her? Buddy had told me her secret: that as a twenty-year-old in 1962 this coconut princess had made love to a VIP at the Kahala Hilton, and the child of that casual encounter was Ku'uipo, Sweetie, who became my wife. Puamana still did not know the deeper secret, that the VIP was President Kennedy. As Sweetie had grown older, Puamana ranged more widely. But I suspected that for many years she had been Buddy's mistress and that he still felt an obscure loyalty to her, in spite of the way she lived.

There was also something catlike about her. I imagined that certain dependent people served as pets for big patronizing hearties like Buddy, who liked them for their wildness as well as their domestication. When I married Sweetie I became the patron, and I sometimes wondered whether Puamana had contrived the whole plot to make herself my mother-in-law. Now and then, like Buddy, she would introduce me by saying, "He wrote a book!" and she laughed at the absurdity of such a thing.

"She's careful. She's clean," Buddy said. "She was born here, but her mother sent her away. She was educated in California."

Puamana was loving toward Rose. If someone is kind to your child, you can forgive a great deal in her. And Puamana's residence at the hotel meant that other hookers, the most territorial of souls, tended to stay away. She had a seat at Paradise Lost bar, but she averaged just a few men a week. It was not odd that she had not serviced Hopecraft; he was needy and not a spender. He seemed to be looking for a friend. Friendship took time and strength, and Puamana did not have enough of either. Other johns were richer and swifter. Puamana hated chitchat on the job, anything that wasted time. She liked the nervous types, the rabbits, the fumblers, the apologizers, the ones plagued with hair-trigger problems.

Untypically for an islander, Puamana was time-conscious. Punctuality made her seem prim. She was polite and somewhat fastidious in the way she dressed, which was why I had no objection to her sitting alone in the bar. Nor was she ever sitting alone for very long. Buddy said, "The hooker-as-a-librarian is much more of a sex magnet than the in-your-face bimbo." Puamana wore expensive eyeglasses some nights.

"Men are less threatened by me — they've kind of vouchsafed that," she said.

I stared, not at her but at the word.

She would sit meditatively but always alert, like a long-legged bird on a riverbank, one of those herons that is motionless until it swipes suddenly with its sharp beak when a fish swims by.

The clothes she wore in the evening were almost severe, hiding rather than revealing, and there were too many layers for such warm nights. You would not notice her unless you were looking for her, but she would see you first. Then she would empty her glass and look you in the eye and give you an opportunity to say, "Want another one?"

"That would be very nice," she said, improving her English but speaking sharply, to keep you in your place.

The rest of the moves were all hers.

"Shall we go out for a meal?" the stranger would say.

"A meal at any restaurant near here cost you a hundred dollars, a lot more with a bottle of wine. After that you'll want to do me. Why not give me the hundred and do me now?"

She could say that in such a reasonable tone of voice that the stranger was disarmed, too startled to laugh.

"You're worse than I am," the stranger would say.

Upstairs, all business, she took off her glasses and said, "No Greek. No oral. No pain. Use a condom. I don't kiss. I need the money up front."

If the man hesitated, she said, "You cross my palm with silver first, and then you get action."

Men in such circumstances were notoriously hoarse, or even mute. They needed guidance. They were shocked by the bareness of her room, a stark little cell dominated by a bed. Popoki took up most of the sofa.

"I hate that cat," Sweetie told me.

Popoki was a shapeless bag of fur with a flat face that was always scowling, a huge fussy appetite, and a bad temper. He seldom moved except to raise his head and hiss. He slept on the sofa, did little but sleep, hogging two cushions out of three, and he complained, yowling, if anyone used the third cushion.

The men sat compactly in the narrow armchair instead, watchful of the cat, fearing he might spring, paws splayed, claws out. I could just imagine a cat like that hooking its claws into a man's scalp, smothering his face and gagging him with its big rank body of fur-covered guts.

The cat was slovenly, Puamana excessively neat. She took endless showers. She was quiet — no music, no TV. She did not read, which was why "My son-in-law, he wrote a book!" sounded so absurd to her. When she was in her room she sat very still, in a yoga posture. She was a heavy smoker but only smoked on the lanai. "I heard of cats catching lung cancer from their owners' cigarettes."

Puamana was superstitious, solitary, vain about her looks, never late, indeed fanatical in matters of punctuality, a brisk walker, not a loiterer or a lingerer. Even sitting at the bar she was heron-still, yet she could seem busy, sometimes murmuring urgently into her cellular phone.

Up at eleven, breakfast at noon, exercise on the roof, and then she prepared for the evening. She never went to the beach. "Sunshine turns skin to leather." She ate carefully, never gossiped, seldom conversed, and when she did, it was about skin care products or health food. She could be boring on those subjects because, as she wasn't a reader, everything she said she had heard somewhere secondhand. She was a dieter, she was a self-denier, she was cheap, she hardly ever shopped.

When she was not exercising, or preparing for the evening ahead, or turning a trick, she was sleeping. For a while she saw a psychiatrist. That was after the incident with the priest. The priest had first come to me. "I am offering counseling." He knew Buddy. I said that was fine and told him to keep to the public areas and out of the guest rooms. Soon after, he burst into my office with a grievance and a story. Puamana had attacked him — scratched him and sent him away. But when I asked her, Puamana denied it. The priest had pushed her onto the sofa, pulled out his penis, stood over her, and said, "You know what to do." It wasn't the sex, though she hated that sort; it was that he refused to pay up front. There was a quarrel. Puamana protected herself with her cat, lifted the heavy creature like a weapon and let him rake the priest's face with his claws.

I said to the priest, "A cat did that. Anyone can tell a cat's scratch from a woman's. You'd better get a jab or you'll have a problem."

The priest vanished into Oahu for a while, but later I saw him again, "counseling" in Waikiki. He always looked as though, on the pretext of saving souls, he was prowling for women's bodies.

"I know the type," Puamana said. "You get those."

"He might be back."

"No," she said. "He was mortified."

It was another unexpected word, like "vouchsafed." That and the way she lived should have told me a lot, but she was my mother-in-law and I did not want to look too deeply, for fear of what I might find. Already I knew more than I wanted to. I knew, most of all, her melancholy.

"No one misses me," she said.

"Speaking as a man, I know that's not true."

"When I die, who will go to my funeral?"

"I will," I said.

That touched her. She said, "I want a Catholic funeral. A high mass, worthy of a bride of Christ."

The expression on her soulful face kept my smile from surfacing.

"I was going to be a nun."

27

Mortification

"THERE WAS this novice nun, Sister Anthony, in Holy Cross Convent in Eureka, California," Puamana said. She had gone there at the age of fourteen. "The age of consent in Whyee."

Her mother had sent the girl from Hilo, where they were then living, and had told the mother superior to communicate with her directly, not with anyone else in the family, and especially to avoid the girl's father, Wendell. Was he a tyrant? the mother superior asked. No, the woman said, far from it. Her husband was weak and cried easily. He couldn't bear to be alone, he hated the dark, and he looked for sympathy.

"He can't control himself," the woman said.

So the girl was admitted to the convent, and the secret was kept. It was not unusual in those days for someone even that young to prepare for a lifetime as a nun, renouncing the world. The mother superior knew of certain details and discerned others. Families could be monstrous, and for that reason the child would remain secure, under her protection and the protection of Jesus Christ, for the rest of her life. She would pass quickly from novice to nun.

Taking the name Sister Anthony, with a pale face and staring eyes that seemed a solemn expression of belief and understanding, for even fear could inspire a sort of faith, the girl said nothing more, and that silence seemed like prayer.

She was slim but strong from working on the family farm, outside Hilo on the Big Island. There were four boys and three girls.

Sister Anthony was the eldest girl and therefore responsible for the welfare of her younger sisters. She had quit school early and was hardly literate. She looked careworn, and at fourteen had the face of a woman, roughened by the weather and made serious by all her responsibilities.

The brutal fact was that when Sister Anthony's mother had been pregnant a year before, the father, Wendell, had begun sleeping with his daughter, demanding that she be silent and blaming his pregnant wife for his having to do this. "It's all her fault." Though she was frightened, the girl did not cry. "I don't know what to do," she whispered. Her father said, "Be like a rat. A rat will do anything to stay alive."

Discovering the father and daughter together, the mother howled at the half-naked man and hid the girl for as long as it took — about ten days — to send the girl to the convent on the mainland. She did not tell the police. She told the priest, who was roared at by Wendell when the priest visited and raised the subject. The woman was careful to keep the girl's whereabouts secret, though Wendell nagged her. He was demanding in a passionate way, not as a father searching for his daughter but as a man desperate to be reunited with his lover.

What would he have said if he knew that the novice Sister Anthony in her iron bed in her cell missed him — missed him more than any person she knew, more than she did her mother. She who had feared him was astonished by how badly she wanted him. She did not miss the dreary chores or the responsibility of looking after her little sisters, but she did miss the company of the little kids. Yet nothing and no one, not even the risen Christ, could fill the void left by her father, and she often imagined him, so sad, sitting alone — as she sat alone — thinking of her.

"Pray for your soul," the mother superior said, because she knew that Sister Anthony had been corrupted by her father, that she was in danger of becoming lost. "And pray for your father's soul."

Praying for her father summoned up the sight and smell of him and made her long for him. As a novice she was watched closely. She knelt for hours with her head bowed, murmuring prayers, and with every utterance she was roused to passionate reflection and memories of his hands and his mouth on her. Prayer made her lustful, and meditating upon her father, she saw him rising out of the darkness, becoming a flame, as with folded hands she clutched her bent-over body, warmed by his nearness. So she prayed willingly, knowing that in prayer she would feel the rapture of her father's body.

Even the expression on her face lost its solemnity and became rapturous as she was praying, for in this imploring posture her father had possessed her; kneeling, she had become his lover. So prayer became the sort of passion for her that she knew other nuns must have shared, looking so exhausted in the morning after a whole night of whipping themselves, thrashing their backs, between prayers.

Nothing could cure her of loneliness, though prayer — her lust-inspiring prayers — gave her a little relief. Her mother had visited twice, bringing Hawaiian food — mochi, saimin, pickled plums, crackseed, poki, lomi salmon. But now she was never visited except by priests. She learned to read, she sewed, she cleaned, sweeping and mopping the floors of the convent, or worked on the convent farm. Being a novice meant being a menial. She did not mind; it was all she had ever known.

In the confessional she spoke fearfully of her thoughts — she knew they were wrong. There were so many church words for what she felt, and even the crucifix and the death of Christ were like a sexual passion. The priests, her confessors, who visited Sister Anthony seemed eager to forgive her, but they also said they needed specific details before they could give her absolution. She did not name her father. She even said that she had reached the age of consent. She spoke of "a man" — sometimes he seemed like all men, even the priests, for as she spoke to the priests, she sometimes wanted them to ravish her.

The priests themselves, as though sniffing it, seemed to know and were afraid. One suggested mortification. She did not know the word. "Mortify your flesh."

In the convent barn one afternoon, pitching hay, she found a rat twitching in a crate — not cowering, rats never cowered. She clapped a lid on the crate and afterward coaxed the rat into a small box, which she sneaked into her cell.

From Hawaii, archipelago of rat life, she knew the small roof rat and the black wharf rat, but this was a naked rat, a kind she had never seen before. The thing was hairless and mottled pink, with freckly patches on its tight skin and an even pinker tail that looked chewed. It stank in a way that attracted her, for it was a man's stink, and it was always active. It did not seem to sleep at all. She remembered what her father had said about rats. This one gnawed its box, but when she fed it the rat was calmer in its twitchy way. She kept the rat in her room and gave it the food she was served in the refectory — bread crusts, bits of meat, a paste of beans or potato, anything she could hide in the folds of her robe.

Not eating very much made her weaker and thinner, and she sometimes felt faint with hunger. The other nuns saw how enfeebled this young novice had become, how mortification had made her look so sorrowful. They did not know that her starvation, feeding the rat, had become like a drug; how the fever brought on by her hunger gave her intense hallucinatory images of her father demanding that she kneel and then clawing her head and making her gag. Mortification was deeper than prayer. Prayer gave her imagery, but hunger made her retch with lust, and she clutched herself and moaned as though in the death throes of love.

Meanwhile, the naked rat grew fatter and sleeker. The rat was a friend. When she was not praying she was lonely, and the rat relieved her loneliness. The rat was her father and her lover. The rat was bold, and yet while he was fed, he was as content in his box as Sister Anthony was in her cell. She brought the creature food from every meal. But there was no end to a rat's hunger, and when it wanted more Sister Anthony extended her knuckles and let the rat gnaw them until they were raw. Then she folded her skinny bleeding hands and prayed.

Sister Anthony became a wraith, ghostly and pale, her trembling limbs sticklike under her thick robes. Hunger blinded her with migraines, but she endured it, believing that she was dying from love, and love was worth it. In this weakened state her fantasies were more intense.

The naked rat was monstrous and slow and fat now, almost too big for its box.

She returned from dinner one day to find the box clawed open, the lid under the bed, the rat dead, its belly torn open, bloodied like the human organ she had always taken it to be. Nor was it over, for the cat that had killed it was still biting it and playing with it — a wicked-faced cat that reminded her of herself.

Not long after, she left the convent and returned to Hawaii, Puamana said. She had to leave the cat, but would never be without a cat of her own.

28

Naked Strangers

ONE MORNING at first light, quite by chance, she entered the hotel's coffee shop in a tight tube dress that rode up her thighs from the heel-and-toe motion of her wicked shoes. But you did not see a dress, you saw a body. Like a lot of Honolulu newcomers, she made it a habit to stop in after the night, superstitiously feeling safe with a routine in this strange place. She could not have known about Puamana, or else she was defiant. She was unusual in another way. At this time of day they always had a pimp with them, and they never handled money. She carried cash, and there was no sign of a pimp except perhaps the tattooed name *Cobrah* set off by flowers between her breasts — her dress was that skimpy. The pimpish name could have been a hammerstroke to end a story. It was her three-year-old son.

"You a cop?" she asked when I first spoke to her.

It was my intrusive questions, my unconvincing smile, my noticing details, my impartiality and confidence. She was in the keeping-secrets business, and I was a collector of secrets.

She ate alone, picking at scrambled eggs bloodied with hot sauce, and then smoked, drank coffee, and around six went somewhere to bed. She got up for work as soon as darkness fell. She was black and always wore white and in this dazzling place hardly saw any daylight.

A full week passed before I had approached her, and I did so only because she seemed relaxed. As soon as I began speaking she got impatient, as though I were wasting her time and she had important things to do, like the lawyer in whose eyes you see thoughts of billable hours, and who, even at his idlest, becomes a clock watcher in conversation, talking in quarter-hour increments.

"Would a cop tell you the truth?"

She didn't smile. She saw the logic in it, but was impatient again, that fake-weary hurry-up sigh of a bad actress.

Her name was Jasmine, and she had come here from Las Vegas. "That's a real tourist town. I don't care what they say here." She was disappointed by Honolulu and said she probably wouldn't stay much longer. There was another tattoo on her thumb, a small stark symbol.

"I don't want to talk about it," she said.

She tapped her feet and fingers and gave me that sigh again that said, Look, I'm busy.

But she wasn't busy. She was pausing over breakfast, smoking a cigarette.

"You want to talk to me?"

I smiled in a helpless friendly way instead of answering.

"Then it costs money."

As a hooker, she was paid for everything she said or did. All contact with a man had a price. And so I signed for her breakfast, buying time, and said, "I'm the manager here."

That meant something to her; I could see it in the way she kept from showing that she was impressed. I had authority over this whole establishment — bedrooms, drinks, food, the guests themselves.

And strangely, as I signed her bill and looked at the total, I instinctively looked at her body, as though comparing what I had paid with how she looked. She was big, soft, loose-fleshed, not exercised. Her skin was coarse. She had nicks and small scars on her legs, and tiny scratches on her arms, and I felt that each mark represented a separate and much larger incident. She had shadows on her body that you see on overripe supermarket fruit. And was I imagining the thumbprints?

She was unlike Puamana, whom I never thought of without seeing her welcoming posture and her big made-for-men smile, as though saying, Come to Mummy.

"Get me another cup of coffee and a pack of More Lights," Jasmine said.

"More Lights," I said, in a croaky voice, for the absurd name, but she didn't smile or thank me for them. Any attempt at humor only made her suspicious for the way it seemed a time waster. She sneered, she challenged me, she gave little away, and when I tried to compliment her, she said, "Why shouldn't I be confident?"

I said, "How many men did you have last night?"

"I'm going," she said, and left, like that, not offended, just out of time. But the next morning she was back at five, as dawn broke, looking for breakfast and willing to talk again.

Her instinct was to find the man's weakness, whatever need he had, and to exploit it and make him pay. Her line on the street was "Want to spend a little time together?" If the man did not react, she moved on fast, no "Excuse me." If the man nodded, she offered a few seconds of friendliness, even sweet talk to him before the taxi pulled up. After that she went cold. It was just a matter of getting to the room, finishing the business, and hurrying back to the street. She was uninterested in anything else. "I'm not looking for a friend." She was indifferent about the men, hardly noticed what they were wearing. They were all the same to her; they hardly had faces; anyone with money would do. And yet I suspected that each man saw her in his own dramatic way.

The price quoted on the street was a hundred dollars, double that if you were Japanese. Once in the room, when the man was naked, as he had to be to show he wasn't a cop, more money was demanded.

"A guy yesterday made me walk three blocks to his car. I told him, 'Get a taxi!' but he wouldn't. So I made him give me an extra forty for all the walking."

The person who says "You are asking me to walk another hundred yards and therefore you will have to give me forty dollars" — that person has the hair-splitting, get-the-boss-over-a-barrel, union mentality, in which every detail of a job is a matter for negotiation.

"That's fair," I said.

"But you don't really think so," she said.

"In my janitors' contract there's a clause that says they can't be asked to climb higher than nine feet."

"They go higher, you pay them more. That's righteous."

She understood at once. She went on to say that when the man was in the room, she'd say, "If you want more, that's going to cost you more."

And of course a naked Japanese man with his dick in his hand fished out the money and handed it over.

"Don't touch me," she said when that same man reached for her breasts. And when he touched her tattoo she stiffened and said, "Ouch! That hurt! I just got that tattoo!" — although her tattoos were several years old — and the man backed off. Then she scolded him for going soft.

Time was everything to her. At just the moment when I was most eager for her to answer, she said she had to go. A whole day passed before I could resume.

She sat smoking in her ridiculous dress, in stiletto heels, her stiff, dry, dull-colored bunches of hair askew and sometimes spiked like a sea urchin. People sized her up as a hooker instantly — well, that was the whole point of the dress, subtlety being another time waster in this business. And she was impolite, not to say rude, but the fact was that every minute counted, for she was rude the way an air-traffic controller might be rude. Even the way she walked in long strides was tick-tock, tick-tock, marking time.

"What if they want to touch you?" I was thinking of the other day, the Japanese man reaching for her breasts.

"I don't care what they want. I'm in charge."

A local man had been arrested for using a stun gun on hookers, and soldiers beat them up, and now and then they were murdered — invariably knifed. Jasmine was too professional to talk about any of this; she knew it, so there was nothing to discuss. Two months after arriving in Honolulu she spoke enough Japanese, a dozen words perhaps, to spend half an hour alone in a room with a naked businessman from Osaka. A dozen words were plenty, and the men were relieved to go.

Hurry hurry was the opposite of erotic, impatience and fuss confounded desire, but it seemed that Jasmine did not even know this, or if she did, she ignored it in the interest of a quick buck.

On a really good night she had six or seven men, and though I had to pay her almost as much as any one of them had, she gave me the details for the previous night, the five men.

The evening had begun with one of those irritating ones who made her walk to his car. She could not remember whether he was a white guy or where he came from, only that he was worried about the police, losing his car, being seen. He kept going soft. She finally gave up, could not demand more money while he was soft, and he left, still soft.

A Japanese tourist, also nervous, was the second. When she said, "No, don't touch," he was startled, like a boy. She slipped the top of her dress down, exposing her breasts, sat beside him on the bed, and kept warning him to keep his hands off her. She manipulated him, and when he was finished he went out, trotting to the elevator, his shirt untucked.

It was midnight. She stood before a mirror fixing her makeup, then headed to the street again, very tall in her stylish heels.

Something about the way the third man answered her told her that he was drunk. Within seconds she knew he was uselessly so — loud and boastful when she selected him from his group of friends, but quiet in the taxi. He was so subdued and dozy in the room that he fumbled with his money and she got almost two hundred in the beginning. There was no end. He could not finish. She was only afraid of his falling asleep, this big unmovable man, so she pushed him and talked sharply. She hated him for trying to kiss her.

An experienced man who knew what he wanted was helpful, though first-timers were more easily intimidated. The fourth customer knew the moves but was too explicit. He said, "I want your ass." She said, "No one gets my ass." And when he sighed, seeing her tearing open the condom wrapper, she said, "I do nothing without a condom."

He paid the extra. She lay and parted her legs and looked away, and winced when he entered her, as if she were being vaccinated.

The man had spit strings in his mouth and his eyes were glazed. Jasmine shoved hard at his groping hands. A moment later, when he seemed to be enjoying himself and taking his time, she said, "Okay, that's all," and he had to hurry to finish. "Bitch," he said as he turned to go. She was so vicious in reply, the man stepped quickly through the door.

After that, two soldiers approached her in the street. They weren't in uniform, but she knew they were military from their haircuts and the position of their tattoos — they could be concealed by a T-shirt — and their shoes, which were too heavy, too shiny. They were insistent.

"One at a time," she said.

But they both wanted to go. One yanked up his shirt and pushed his belt down. She read on his lower belly, *Ball Till I Fall*.

They wouldn't go separately, so she turned them down. Two men were dangerous, needing each other more than they needed her. Anyway, it was weird and they were soldiers and she was wary of watchers.

The last john of the night, this one at around four A.M., was a man of about fifty who never said a word. Probably foreign, but he made a fuss about the money by sighing and grunting. He, too, tried to kiss her. She said, "I don't kiss," and "Don't touch me there," and "That hurts."

"This is a waste of time."

She was talking to me, trying to be tough again, the way fearful people pretend. She wanted more money to go on talking. I thought: People call what she did sex, but what she did was whatever was the opposite of sex, and beyond nakedness, something skeletal, just money in a hand so bony it looks like a claw.

No one knew who she was or where she was from, nor would she tell me, except to say it was on the mainland. No name, utterly anonymous, probably not more than twenty-something, yet she stood for whatever particular fantasy was in the grateful man's mind.

Jasmine wanted nothing more than money. When she asked for more from me she became unconvincingly flirtatious. But she had already told me too much. I said, "I've never paid for sex."

"Men don't pay me for sex," she said. "They pay me to go away."

29

The Widow Mrs. Bunny Arkle

O N O N E O F T H E last mornings the hooker Jasmine ate breakfast in the hotel's coffee shop — soon after that, I never saw her again — Buddy Hamstra said to me, "Look at that woman. She's outrageous." I glanced at Jasmine in her white slinky dress, and Buddy said, "No, her," and nodded at a slim, delicate-featured woman, about sixty or so, moving toward a table, looking graceful and patient. The new flower man, Palama, Amo Ferretti's replacement, was doing the lobby arrangement, sorting stalks of heliconia and bird of paradise.

"Mrs. Bunny Arkle." It sounded like one word to me, *Bunnyarkle*, and from then on I never thought of her without imagining both names. But this woman could have had many more names. She had been married four times.

She was not local. She was from California, no one knew where. She had come to Hawaii with her first husband, a stockbroker, and decided the place was for her. They bought a house on Black Point, even then an expensive address.

"She's having her place repainted, so she's going to be with us for a few weeks," Buddy said.

"Where's the stockbroker?"

"She ditched him years ago, pretty soon after she first got here."

What I had taken to be the whole story was merely the opening detail, of hardly any consequence, except that Mrs. Bunny Arkle, the woman from nowhere, was now resident in a big house on Black Point. When I pressed him, Buddy muttered that he had heard that Mrs. Bunny Arkle had been raised somewhere in the South by her ambitious but hard-up mother, who had introduced her to the stockbroker and told her how to please a man.

"She had a pretty torrid affair with one of the Coulter heirs — lots of land on the Big Island. Divorced the stockbroker. Huge settlement. Kept the house. She sort of worked out of there, you might say. Coulter's wife got wind of the business. Killed herself and cursed them in her suicide note."

"That sounds like the end of the affair."

"In a funny kind of way it was the beginning, and it made the whole affair serious. Coulter married her after that. When they divorced — the dead wife's curse had worked — Mrs. Bunny Arkle got a chunk of property. Later on, it was rezoned for mixed use, commercial and residential. A hotel developer bought it and built a resort. Part of Mrs. Bunny Arkle's payment was in shares. Beachfront. The woman was instantly wealthy."

Not needing a husband, and possessing the Coulter name, she was secure. Two husbands, especially wealthy ones, made her more than respectable, gave her a kind of invincibility — even she thought so. A famous photograph showed her playing polo at Mokuleia.

Boyfriends, "takers," came after the second divorce. But at the time she had not known they were parasites. One, an Australian, Keith, had seemed almost genteel. His Australian accent sounded British, he drank tea all the time, he said "grawss," "poss the catsup," "cawnt," and even when he swore he sounded delicate, words like "bawstid" and "betch." He also said "figgers," and "I reckon," and "strait" for street, as though he saw a world better than the one she knew. He moved in with her and one day was gone with most of her jewelry.

Another opportunist — how could she have been such a fool? — was ten years younger than she, had nice clothes and a sports car. He didn't move in but he begged to, and she almost allowed it. She was lonely. He said he loved her. He borrowed money — not much. And one day she went to see where he lived and found it to be a Samoan apartment block in Kalihi. Barefoot children surrounded her car. He was a fireman! Never again, she said, and hated the memory of pleasing him in bed, his howls.

The gossip gave her a reputation. She was lonely again. She was introduced to a widower, an old enemy of Coulter's, and smiling at him she thought, I am going to marry this man.

He called her a few days later, as if the same thought had occurred to him, too. They went to the opera. It was *La Bohème* at the Blaisdell Concert Hall. Mrs. Bunny Arkle wore her loveliest gown. He wore a tuxedo. That night, when he drove her home, she invited him in for a drink. She seemed prim, but her attention to him was full of oblique suggestions: the champagne, the cigar, the way she folded his dinner jacket, and the man was encouraged to be bold. They slept in the same bed that night, though he could hardly recall the steps to the bedroom. They were married within six months, their two fortunes combined. His name was George Gideon Wright, a descendant of the man who gave his name to Wright's Point.

"She had a knack," Buddy said. "The successful ones all do, forget what people say about brains. Wallis Simpson became Duchess of Windsor. Reason being, she could tighten her vaginal muscles. It gave her a grip on the Prince of Wales."

After seventeen years in England, I had to come to a small hotel in the Sandwich Islands to discover this secret that had profoundly affected the future of the British monarchy.

"Pamela Harriman had three rich husbands and lots of upscale lovers. Sure, she was glamorous, but hey, was the key to her success her savoir-faire? Try this. She was a demon in bed. She did 'tea bags' — the old testicle trick, make like they're marshmallows. Drove them wild. She checked out as U.S. ambassador in Paris." Buddy swigged his drink and added, "Jackie Kennedy looked like she had class, but she was a real negotiator. Her marriage contract with Onassis was all worked out. They would stay married for seven years, she wouldn't have to sleep with him, and when it was over she would get twenty-seven million bucks."

"And Mrs. Bunny Arkle?"

"Look at her." The woman, solitary, dignified, was sipping tea, her head upright. "Looks like a precious little bird lady with breakable bones." Buddy wheezed for emphasis and said, "But her secret is she's a slut."

I frowned at the insulting word, but Buddy just laughed.

"Men talk," he said, before I could ask. "Women do too. She was expert at rimming — that's what it was called in the cathouses of Nevada. Nowadays it's 'tossing his salad.' A tongue job. It's probably illegal in most states, but then all the fun things are. George Wright was a very happy man."

The teacup was back on the saucer, and Mrs. Bunny Arkle was unfolding the napkin in the muffin basket.

"When George Wright died there was a free-for-all over his fortune — his kids objected to this woman getting so much. Mrs. Bunny Arkle made a deal, settled out of court and ended up with assets of fifteen million. A mac nut farm. A horse ranch. Still had shares in the resort on the Big Island."

In her late fifties, she had become one of the wealthiest women in Hawaii. Men pursued her as she had once pursued them. One of Buddy's friends caught her in a weak moment and they had an affair. It lasted a month; she sent him away.

Arkle was the last. He owned a chain of movie theaters. He was Jewish, he had changed his name, he too was a widower. She converted. She wanted him because he was somehow real. Now she found it hard to be alone, and she was uncomfortable going out. She who was contemptuous of most men saw Arkle as practical, strong, and the easiest of friends. She wanted his protection.

This man in his seventies was sexually active, but you did not want to think of the details or even imagine him naked. Buddy made a face and said, "Can you imagine what it's like to be a proctologist?"

Arkle was delighted with her, but he also said, "Lose fifteen pounds and I'll marry you."

It took months, much longer than she had expected, and they were married in his mansion in Nuuanu, near the synagogue. When he died, half his art collection went to the Honolulu Academy of Arts, the Arkle Bequest, and she sold the other half, keeping only a Bonnard for its peculiar shade of blue.

Buddy said, "She probably slept with no more than ten men in her life."

"Some hookers do that in one night."

"But Mrs. Bunny Arkle put her heart into it. She gave better head than any hooker. Reason being, she was patient."

Still, the little old woman sat in the hotel coffee shop now buttering a muffin, her fingers extended, her rings catching the sunlight. Perhaps she was thinking, I wanted to leave those men I married, but they paid me to stay.

30

Local Color

IN THIS PICTURESQUE PLACE, one of the most stickily visual scenes I had ever witnessed occurred right next door, in the Kodama Hotel courtyard. It was nighttime. I heard chanting, sudden grunting, shouts and mutters, and then creeping toward the pool, peeking past the monkeypod and through the oleanders that hid the fence, I saw the torchlight, the gleaming bodies — Hawaiian men in loincloths and Hawaiian women in ti-leaf skirts slapping fat calabash gourds they called *ipo*. In counterpoint, like a heartbeat, I heard men thumping thick upright poles on the courtyard flagstones. The Kodama guests snapped pictures. Some of them tape-recorded the chanting. It proved that in the world of Waikiki, local color had not faded.

That was the first night. After that, the Hawaiians came in relays, wearing street clothes, shorts and aloha shirts, office wear, and some of them had briefcases. They brought food, they seemed businesslike, but still they chanted, some scattered ashes, and you would have thought for the ordinariness of the clothes they would have seemed unexceptional, but in fact they were more impressive standing and chanting that way, in scuffed sandals and faded shirts.

Amazing, all this traditional-seeming oddity at a fairly new Japanese hotel, where Buddy took his *wahine*, Stella, for sushi, to cheer her up when they were in town for her chemotherapy.

Stella said, "That music is so depressing. Do they think it's good for business?"

But the Kodama had not hired these Hawaiians, as some hotels did for torch-lighting ceremonies and hula dancing in cellophane skirts at sunset. The Kodama was trying without any success to get rid of them: the Hawaiians were not on their property but just behind it, and for some guests it provided an attraction.

The chanting was almost unearthly, filled with an urgent and solemn litany of growly sounds, a low-frequency pleading that was a repetition of sad groaning notes. The chant was made into a polyphonic dialogue between two contrasting groups. Dressed in working clothes, they attracted fewer tourists, and more and more they seemed just a nuisance, a pack of island eccentrics.

"I talked to the Kodama manager," Buddy said on one of his sushi days. "He has no idea what to do. I told him to hire them for his Happy Hour. He didn't like that."

The general manager was Japanese. He hardly spoke English. The deputy G.M., a local, spoke to the leader of the Hawaiians and reported back.

"They say this is their land," the deputy G.M. said. "This hotel stands on what was once a fishing *heiau*. Their ancestors have always met here and made offerings. It was a sacred shrine."

Kodama guests reading by the pool complained about the noise. No longer wearing their loincloths and ti-leaf skirts, the Hawaiians had ceased to be picturesque. The Kodama security team, three big, plump-faced, scowling Samoans, talked to them, urging them to leave, but they refused to budge.

This fuss became audible to the adjacent part of the Hotel Honolulu. "It's one of these access issues," Buddy said. But even when the Kodama security men persuaded the Hawaiians to move farther away, the chanting voices, directed at the Kodama with throbbing monotony, were still loud enough to be heard as a pulse inside the hotel. When they started wearing their loincloths again, and carrying torches, the complaints stopped.

Seeing that the accumulation of people had become a sort of vigil, I asked my hotel staff if they had any idea what was going on. Everyone speculated. Sweetie said, "They are *kanaka maoli*," meaning that in Hawaiian terms the people were the real McCoy. She could not elaborate. Trey said, "Maybe they're practicing for something," but he didn't know what. Keola the janitor suggested they were praying.

"What sort of prayer?"

He shrugged. Here in Hawaii, the land of long pauses, people might know the answer to one question, but never the answers to two.

"Whyan prayers not same like howlie ones," he said. "Not *pono* anyway."

What sort of prayers were not righteous? I went to the chanting people themselves, walked around to Kuhio Avenue and through the narrow space between the buildings. On the assumption that the fattest man slapping the biggest gourd was probably the leader, I put the question to him.

"Why do you come here every night?"

"Because we work during the day," he said.

That was logical. They had jobs. But the fat man would not say any more to me, and he would not speak to Keola. The oddest thing was that no one knew these people. If they were entertainers — and they seemed in some sense to be — they were not associated with any groups known in Waikiki. They were, as Keola had said, real Hawaiians, the big, fleshy, statuesque sort, who had been on the islands from the beginning. I did not need to be told that they were related. It was obvious from their faces and physiques that they were of the same *ohana,* or family. That affinity, and the way they were gathered, made them seem immovable.

"Stella thinks they're spooky," Buddy said.

I told him what Keola had said, about Hawaiian prayers not always being pious.

"Maybe they're trying to get even with someone," Buddy said. "They do these things better in Micronesia. In Tarawa, if someone wants to hurt you, he finds your shit and burns it. No matter where you are, you get boils on your ass."

Because the chanters were unintelligible, everyone invented a fanciful reason to explain their presence. They were mourning, they were praying, they were giving thanks, they were pronouncing a curse. They remained for many weeks, through Halloween and Veterans Day and Thanksgiving — perhaps there was a connection? Did it have something to do with the upcoming anniversary of the overthrow of the Hawaiian monarchy? It was a celebration, it was a blessing, it was a protest. Maybe it was about some people who had been laid off in Waikiki, or on the verge of it. Maybe it was the beginning of some serious wage negotiations — union trouble.

None of the bystanders had the slightest idea of what these Hawaiians were doing. When they were dressed in loincloths and ti-leaf skirts, people took pictures, but in office clothes they were scarcely visible, like those lost souls, their belongings stacked on luggage carts, who traipsed through Honolulu Airport all day, looking like every other traveler, but much grubbier, and who slept on the benches at night. In time, the Hawaiians became like another nighttime feature of Waikiki.

Something about their chanting and slapping calabashes kept the police at bay. Hawaii was not a place where anyone was ever arrested for singing. These Hawaiians did not fall into any recognizable category of offense. They could not be compared to people who played ball on the beach or had loud radios or noisy dogs. They had children, many of them, but the children sat solemnly and chanted with their elders; they were well behaved. Such responsible people set a good example. Anyone could see that this semicircle of sonorous voices, sitting cross-legged on the sand behind the Kodama, would stay there as long as they liked.

The chanting grew darker, though, becoming lower, deeper, like the wind, but in Hawaii, where there were one hundred and thirty words for wind, this was an especially black wind, mournful on a moonless night, that seemed to issue a warning.

Remembering what Keola had said, I looked up the word "prayer" in a Hawaiian dictionary and found the word for "sorcery." It seemed there were no other kinds. There was a Christian sort of prayer, of course, but all the Hawaiian prayers seemed related to black magic, curses, and casting spells. One specific prayer, 'ana'ana, was defined as "evil sorcery by means of prayer and incantation."

"You know what 'ana'ana is?" I asked Keola.

He didn't have a clue. That was the trouble with Hawaii: the language was so secret, known to so few people, it was like part of a cabalistic ritual, even when what was being said might be no more allusive than remarking on the weather.

After almost two months, in the early days of December, as the wind was rising, they reverted to their Hawaiian clothes that looked like costumes — loincloths, leaf skirts, leis of green leaves encircling their heads like the laurel crowns shown on Greek vases — and to the thumping poles, the slapped calabashes, the scattered ashes.

An urgency gathered in the dark chanting, and all this time

tourists promenaded in bathing suits and matching aloha shirts, kids ran around in baggy trousers and expensive caps worn backward or screamed in the surf at Dig Me Beach. There was traffic, too, and the wearying honk of car alarms, and the drone of planes overhead. So the chanting Hawaiians were not a single noticeable group, but rather one group out of many.

It ended one night with a scream — not theirs but someone at the Kodama, a female guest hysterical at seeing a man hurtling through the awning by the pool, tearing it and twisting the poles that held it. The man's body smacked the tiled apron near the diving board. "A jumper," Buddy said. He had fallen twelve floors.

The Hawaiians, who, it seemed, had driven him to destroy himself in expiation for the destruction of their fishing *heiau* — who had prayed him to death — packed their things and slipped away before the police sirens began.

31

Christmas Cards

HIDEO TAKAHASHI — he was a Waikiki hotel owner I knew somewhat — had so much to do, was feeling so weak and inattentive, felt so assailed by distractions, was so haggard, that he made a list, because Christmas mattered. There was so little time for all the parties, the golf games, the Happy Meals to be bought in bulk from McDonald's and distributed to the employees' children, the gift-wrapped bottles of whiskey, the Christmas cards that had to be signed personally, in two scripts, Japanese and English. And you could make such terrible mistakes — one year, the decorations had included a small smiling Santa Claus nailed to a cross and a Jesus doll in a plastic saucer surrounded by the Seven Dwarfs.

Takahashi had a sense of a door closing, not an ordinary hotel door, but the sort of heavy ceremonial one you might find in a traditional Japanese house, securing the treasure room, ironbound, carved with a chrysanthemum, a complex lock near the base — the sort of dense door that did not swing but rather slid on a track — and he was trying to squeeze through it before it shut with a bang. The door in Hideo Takahashi's mind was traveling in a silent slot, sideways into a narrowing gap.

He had read MARY CHRISTMAS on the label of the whiskey bottle, and while each word looked right on its own, joined together they looked wrong.

Calling the sales and marketing director, Takahashi said, "Come here." When the man arrived in his office, he began at once to complain that he was not happy.

"I've done the best I can with them locals."

Takahashi had no idea what the man was talking about.

"Them singers and that."

"It is Christmas," Takahashi said. Every inexplicable excess, every unreasonable demand, every ridiculous price, every unexpected shortage, he put down to Christmas, which was the high point of the business year. He had agreed to attend all the parties and to assume all the responsibilities.

"Is this correct?" Takahashi held the label in his small, clean palm.

"No. Should be 'merry.'"

"Please." Takahashi handed it over to the man. "It must be re-printed."

"I'll see to it."

A hundred and twenty labels, bearing the company logo and a scroll-enclosed window for a personal signature, had been misspelled.

"Some dumb secretary okayed this."

"Do it quickly."

Takahashi was far too busy to recriminate, and anyway, it was this director's responsibility. He should be fired — he should have been fired over the crucified Santa that had been written about last year in the newspaper — but the height of the season was not the time to fire someone. After this, when business slackened, the man would be given his notice. For now, the place was decorated, the tree had been put up in the lobby, the blow-molded plastic images of angels, Santa Claus, little furry bear cubs, Mickey Mouse, ducks in sailor suits, reindeer, rabbits, the Christmas menagerie, all had been hung.

It had been the director's own idea for Takahashi to sign each label and paste it to a bottle of Johnnie Walker Black Label and put it into a slender box, gift-wrap it, and make a present of it — one hundred and twenty of them.

There were many more Christmas cards, a thousand at least, to be signed, so many that Takahashi set himself the task of doing a certain amount a day. Fifty was the number, not just the signature in Japanese and English script but a personal message — the same message: "Holiday Greetings from Us All at Furabo Properties."

No sooner had the director left and Takahashi resumed his signing the Christmas cards — he had done about half of the day's allotment — than the phone rang: a golf game he had forgotten, the tee time had just passed.

"You are all right?" his friend Yumi asked.

"Fine, fine, fine, fine," Takahashi said, sounding disturbed, agreeing to eighteen holes. Before he set off, he signed ten more cards.

At their palest, the indoor Japanese are chalky, whiter than any *haole,* and Takahashi looked dusty and translucent — sleepless, skinny, fading to gray. It was almost Christmas. There was too much to do. The whole point, as Takahashi saw it, was to distinguish yourself with the gift by giving it a personal touch. Sign the labels, sign the cards, wrap the bottle's box with elegance, a silk ribbon, Takahashi's monogram, the company's logo — didn't anyone ever listen?

At best Takahashi was an amateurish golfer with an absurd handicap. Today his play would have been embarrassing had he been well enough to notice. He lost seven balls and just went through the motions of putting — once almost toppling forward. He hated climbing off the golf cart and having to hit a ball. He did a crazy thing: he picked up a ball and made as if to take a bite of it. Fortunately Yumi did not see him. Realizing that he almost put the golf ball in his mouth, he threw it away. This Yumi did see.

"There was a bite in it," Takahashi explained.

Yumi stared and mouthed, A bite?

Takahashi had agreed to play so as not to arouse anyone's suspicions. But the golf had given him away. He was behind in all the tasks he had set himself. Back at his room, he saw that there were three messages waiting for him from Chizuko, his *kumu* — his sweetheart. He called her.

"Don't call me," he said, very angry.

Chizuko said that she was worried about him, not having heard from him for a week. He accused her of being selfish. It was Christmas in Honolulu. What she was really suggesting was that she wanted to be taken to the parties and out to eat. She wanted to see the Christmas lights in Waikiki. And presents — she wanted presents. She collected Mickey Mouse dolls and Mickey Mouse accessories; anything with Mickey on it she wanted. And she wanted to marry Takahashi.

The thought of Chizuko's expectations filled him with rage. He shouted at her, "There is no time!" He would not let her speak, nor even allow her to squeal her apologies. She was so abject that beneath his shouting he heard her saying "Sorry" in English, to give it emphasis, and she repeated it, "Sorry," saying it softly and submissively like a scolded child.

Takahashi banged the phone down. He was still so angry that he didn't even tell Chizuko he was going to the governor's residence, Washington Place, for the annual Christmas party. The instruction on the invitation was "Please bring an unwrapped toy for a keiki."

Takahashi's deputy general manager put a large red fire truck, a wooden pull toy, into Takahashi's hand and said, "I could always drop it off, if that would be easier for you."

"This is the governor's Christmas party!" Takahashi said, his voice breaking.

The deputy G.M. nodded, trying not to look too deeply into his boss's sunken eyes, the slack dusty skin, the hollow cheeks and bony jaw. What made this collapsed and scrawny body especially horrible was the crisp Zegna suit that Takahashi wore, his neatly combed hair parted on his bony skull, the bumpy finger joints, the fever-bright eyes behind the stylish glasses.

Still in that shrill faltering voice, Takahashi said, "And the stamps for the envelopes are not Christmas stamps."

"The post office ran out."

"Get some."

What a pity he would have to wait before he could fire this man. After Christmas and all these sacrifices, he would get rid of them all. He had already begun to rehearse the expression: We will not need you anymore. But he was so far behind on the cards, he had stayed up most nights laboriously inscribing his signature and personal greeting, wishing health and prosperity to the recipient.

One of those nights Chizuko called him, she had tears in her voice, and he felt a pang of sorrow for her. When she hung up, he left a message with the Christmas Hot Line at the Disney store, ordering a charm for her charm bracelet, a tiny Christmas Mickey Mouse in gold, wearing a ski hat and red gloves.

The gift to his mistress brought his wife to mind, so he stopped to write a short letter of regret to her, asking forgiveness. And still he sat signing the cards, only dimly aware of the commotion outside when he lifted the window to clear the room of his cigarette smoke — chaotic Christmas noise, which sometimes resolved itself into a sort of syncopation, as when simple unmelodious people sang.

The day the cards were entirely inscribed, he put them on the bed in twenty piles. The forgiveness note to his wife, in a different envelope, he placed on a side table, with his watch, his fountain pen, and his ring. He kicked off his slippers.

His next moves, also sacrificial, he had pondered for a month, as he had gone through the motions of administering the Kodama, dying all that time. There was hardly any life left in him, just the insignificant scrap that fluttered like a rag within him as he hurled himself off the balcony.

32

Ms. Furman's Honeymoon

EVER SINCE GETTING OFF the plane, they had joked about the fact that, because they had been so busy, this was the first chance they'd had to take their honeymoon. They had been married one Sunday three months before, in Carmel-by-the-Sea, which they had chosen for its doll-town charm and also for its nearness to Dave's client in Monterey and to the high-tech company in Sunnyvale that Allison would be pitching the day after the wedding. The preparations for the wedding had been so strenuous — she had never come closer to calling it off — that it seemed more sensible to take the honeymoon when it was practical. This was perfect, a week in the Hotel Honolulu. I upgraded them to a junior suite and sent up a fruit basket. In thanking me, they gloated over their other success, how they had paid for the airfare. "We used miles."

"This is a funky place," Allison said of my hotel. Dave added that he hated the pretentious hotels on the beach. And, "This area has so much character."

All these backhanded compliments I took to mean that we were cheap. And wasn't "character" another word for nasty, or at least in need of fresh paint?

Instead of telling them how the owner of the Kodama, right next door, had jumped out the window at Christmas, in full view of the previous month's talkative guests in this hard-to-rent suite, I said, "People appreciate value these days."

"Luxury places are way overpriced," Dave said.

He was a handsome young man, about thirty-one or -two. I

guessed Allison to be older by a few years, something in the way she took charge and knew her own mind, a certain rigidity, the way she hated wasting time. And her facial downiness said something too. She had kept her own name, Furman; surely that was a sign she was single-minded and had prevailed. Dave's family name was Womack. The two different names created confusion in the hotel. They wanted to split the bill, using two credit cards, and had put two names on the register so they wouldn't miss any calls or faxes. "Just because it's a honeymoon doesn't mean we can't do a little business." My back was turned — either of them could have said this. Dave was with a large firm of San Francisco accountants. Allison was in computers, militantly so. She jeered at me for not having my own Web site.

Yet our low-tech approach appealed to her budget-mindedness. When Buddy Hamstra saw her hat, he said loudly, "Those are going to come back someday." Since she heard him, out of embarrassment I complimented her on it. "Catalogue," she said. Usually she wore the hat when sitting with Dave in Paradise Lost. "Friendly!" they said. They never missed our Happy Hour, some of the best pupus in Waikiki, and our barmen — the surfer, Trey, and the refugee, Tran — "poured heavy." They even played with Rose. She said, "Daddy, I made words on Allison's computer."

"I can't believe this kid's not online," Allison said.

"She's six," I said. "She reads."

"Computerwise, she's illiterate. Plus, schools get great deals on software."

After three days of honeymooning, Dave began receiving faxes, many of the documents too thick to stuff under the door. Something had come up. He was called to Seattle. He hurriedly left. Allison understood: "I knew I married someone who had a demanding job. If I had been called away, Dave would have said, Go for it."

Her habits did not change with Dave gone. Breakfast in the coffee shop, lunch at the beach, Happy Hour at Paradise Lost, and we didn't see much of her later on. Predictably, the night after Dave left, she was approached in the bar several times by single men, one of them the fascinated barman Trey, who was roughly Dave Womack's age. It was not my habit to issue warnings, but only to observe. Trey's band, Sub-Dude, was playing in the lounge. His girlfriend was on a neighbor island, visiting relatives. When Allison told him that her husband had been called away on urgent business, Trey said, "So I guess we're in the same boat."

"Not really. You could have gone with your wife."

"And you could have gone with your husband."

Allison laughed. "This whole week was prepaid. We'd have lost upwards of a grand!"

Seeing that Allison's reading matter was a mail-order catalogue, Trey said, "Those things drive me nuts," and explained that they were a waste of trees. Allison said that the only real retail bargains were in the catalogues. She listed the best catalogues for kitchen equipment and computers and home furnishings. She knew about camping catalogues: Dave and she had met in a campground, had driven cross-country in his old Lumina, kayaks on top, looking for white water.

"I do some paddling. Outrigger."

"We were in Class Five rapids."

"There are great deals here on the new Luminas," he said.

Hearing her saying, "There are six good reasons not to buy a new car," Trey looked at her pretty face and thought, I want to nail this woman.

"Want to go for a walk?"

She said yes, and on the way to the beach asked Trey about the health insurance and tax implications for small businesses and independent contractors in Hawaii. "Like I say, I'm part time at the bar and I've got the band," he said, wanting to kiss her. It was a lovely night, of mild air and moonlight. People filled the promenade, traffic jammed the main street, but the beach was empty. Trey was anxious that just behind them a man pissed against a palm, and another, wearing an overcoat, pushed a supermarket cart piled high with plastic bags. Allison appeared not to notice and was looking instead at the sea. It was vast and black far off, and nearer shore the surface was scaly with liquefied moonglow and the surf phosphorescent from hotel spotlights.

"Romantic," Trey said. "That surf line you see is Queen's Break. There's the Wall. Canoes. Poplars. Threes. Fours. Rock piles."

"Those homeless guys." So she had seen them after all. "Ugly people scare me."

Not knowing how to respond, Trey said, "It's a good thing we got out of the hotel. I wanted to take you up to your room and make love to you."

"Right," Allison said, and smiled at the man's presumption. "But I could never do that. This is my honeymoon."

Trey closed his eyes. He was too embarrassed to look at her. Finally he said, "I'm really sorry. Please forget what I said."

It seemed grotesque to him that so soon after this woman's wedding he was trying so bluntly to seduce her. He saw her in her wedding gown. He heard music, wedding bells, laughter. He saw a proud groom, happy relatives. He quickly realized that it was not Allison's wedding that he imagined but a joyous one he craved for himself.

"I'm a dumb water rat," Trey said to excuse himself, because he felt like a hairy demon who was trying to insinuate himself in this new marriage. And what was he offering?

Allison just smiled. She explained that the actual wedding had been three months before. "How long have you been married?"

Trey said, "Not married. Going with. Coupla-three years."

Allison nodded but did not say anything, and Trey sensed her scrutiny. He was so ashamed he forgot his ardor. And, strangely, without feeling the need to win her over, he talked more naturally to her, as a friend; teased her; listened to a story she told about seeing cans in the street, how recycling could be incredibly profitable. Somehow this led to her talking about giving used computers to schools for the tax deduction.

"I've read something about that," Trey kept saying, and made no arrangement to see her again. He walked her back to the hotel and warned her to be careful, and he sensed he was warning her against himself.

The evening before her honeymoon week was over, Trey and I happened to be in the lobby, talking about Sub-Dude — I should keep them on as the hotel band, like Don Ho's at the Hilton, Trey said.

Allison passed us on her way out of Paradise Lost, the end of Happy Hour, and smiled. Trey did not hesitate. He cut me off in the middle of a sentence and approached her. I heard Allison saying, ". . . drink" and ". . . in my room. Give me a few minutes."

Trey was transformed into a panting, tail-wagging dog with a wet twitching nose and slaver on his lips. His tongue was too thick for him to make any sense when he spoke to me. But the next day he told me that he had gone upstairs, that Allison had met him at the door wearing her honeymoon peignoir, and that they had made love on the sofa and on the floor and against the wall, at her insistence. Afterward, in the bed, she challenged him to guess why she had changed her mind. She laughed at having stumped him, and she explained in her practical way that in the past few days it had dawned on her that Dave would eventually be unfaithful, months or years from now.

"It's sad, really," she said. "But since it always happens — doesn't it? — I wanted to be first."

After describing her mood change in the room, how she went from being all business to crouching and calling him "Daddy," Trey clawed his long hair and said to me, "Hey, boss, would this be the wrong time to ask for a raise?"

The following year, Allison Furman and Dave Womack returned to the hotel. I said I would upgrade them again, putting them in the same suite, "for the memories." But they said they were just dropping in to say hello. They were staying in another place, down the beach. It had a kitchenette with a microwave and a small refrigerator, and it was, as they put it, "competitively priced."

33

Happy Funeral

THE ONLY DIFFERENCE between a Hawaiian wedding and a Hawaiian funeral, Buddy Hamstra said, was that there was one less person singing at the funeral. How could I laugh when he was telling me this at his own wife's funeral? Though he knew he had shocked me, he slugged me on the arm and said it again, much louder.

"Want to come to my wife's funeral?" he had asked me, then he howled, "Hey, that's a dynamite pickup line!"

Loudness was comedy to him, and his howl was whiffy with alcohol. He was so drunk that day he was staggering, but that was comedy too. All human frailty was funny to Buddy, especially his own, and death was just a practical joke. He demanded I take the day off to attend.

Stella's coffin was on the beach, so festooned with big bright edible-looking flowers it looked like a salad bar. The mourners, all hot-faced people in shorts, stood barefoot in the sand, singing and twitching their damp aloha shirts — Buddy's dusky children by his islander wives, his two grandchildren, surfers, strippers, illegal immigrants, Boogie-boarders and aunties, as well as Buddy's rascally pals and old business cronies, leathery fishermen and opihi pickers, and all Stella's family from the mainland. Their bare feet, as lumpy and expressive as faces, said everything about their lives. Buddy's children had a common characteristic: If they didn't understand something, they opened their mouths. Death was the sort of befuddlement that made them slack-jawed.

It was one of those brilliant orchidaceous days on the North

Shore of Oahu, under the towering palms. A silky breeze lisped through the needles of the ironwoods edging Sunset Beach. The cliffs behind us were as dark and leafy as spinach. Somewhere nearby a radio was playing, an insolent voice giving a weather report and then a sales jingle about fast food in Honolulu, but it was just more comedy for Buddy. Down at the beach, a man was casting into the surf, working his fishing rod like a coach whip. The breeze carried a scent of flowers. The greeny-blue Pacific, the dazzling sunlight, the new blossoms — it was all bright with life, and the tears on the cheeks of the dark fresh-faced people were like another aspect of their health.

Just offshore, the smooth-sided waves at Banzai Pipeline were rising and bursting toward us, collapsing loudly, dissolving in thick froth and fizz. While the rest of the mourners sang, the surfers kept glancing back.

"The Pipe's cranking," one said. He turned away from Stella's coffin.

"It was junk this morning," another said.

"I'm stoked," the first one said. "Look at Piggy in the tube."

A surfer in gleaming shorts, braced on his board, traveled under the curling lip of the large wave, arms outspread, his head washed by foam.

Then the singing stopped and Buddy tramped forward on the sand, looking unsteady. Several people snuffled. Melveen, his eldest daughter, blew her nose, a rat-a-tat that turned heads. Garlands of leis were piled to Buddy's ears, and he held a glass of vodka in one hand and simpered as though he were going to burst into song.

"Stella's not *mucky*. She's watching us, she's listening, and she's *huhu* because some of you are crying." Buddy said. "Stop crying over her wooden kimono. Put away the Kleenex — she's not *mucky!*"

He had the snorting stubbornness of a huge hairy animal, with an important belly, a raspy voice, and a Tahitian tattoo, a plump blue fish picked out on his arm, because of his nickname, Tuna.

"Funny thing happened on our honeymoon," he said, stepping close to his wife's coffin. The coffin tilted as he hooked his foot on one of the sinking sawhorses that propped it up. "This was in Moorea."

He told a story about his arrival at the hotel on the little island off Papeete, where he noticed that everyone was wearing the same T-shirt — the gatekeeper, the gardeners, the Tahitians Weedwacking the lawn, the women at Reception, the room boy, the bar help, the waiters. The image on the front of each T-shirt was indistinct, but exactly the same — perhaps a political figure? No, up close it was a furiously scowling Polynesian woman, a silk-screened portrait of Momi, the second Mrs. Buddy Hamstra.

"Thanks, needledick," he said, leaning over Stella's corpse to speak to one of the rascals, Earl Willis, who had sent two hundred Momi-face T-shirts all the way to Moorea. "That's when Stella realized she was marrying trouble. Big *pilikia!*"

"You cemented up my *lua* and stuck a stop sign in it," Willis said. "I couldn't shee-shee."

"Because you're a needledick," Buddy said. "Hey, people, lay off the crying!"

The singing resumed. The surfers distracted me, and looking out toward the ocean I saw a pod of whales, plumes rising from their blowholes, as they made their seasonal way to Kauai. I thought, I am happy. It seemed to me that this was what a funeral ought to be. On this beautiful day I saw continuity, an eternal return, only harmony. Nothing died.

After that song, Buddy said, "Anyone hungry? We got fresh opihi and Spam musubi and lots of good grinds in the house. Hey, let's eat!"

We were glad he was drunk. It dulled the pain. It set an example. Pretty soon everyone was drunk, and when I looked back and saw Stella's coffin, casting a black boxy shadow on the white sand, I remembered what Buddy had said, about there being only one person at a funeral who was not singing.

When the funeral turned into a party, I saw four goldfish swimming in every hopper in the house.

"Buddy always does that when people are drinking," a man said, seeing my puzzled face as I left the little room. To be helpful he added, "Everyone's using the mango tree."

He introduced himself as Royce Lionberg. He said he lived on the bluff behind the beach. There was something about him, his serenity perhaps, his gentle smile, his apparent health, his confident look of achievement, that made me envy him. He seemed very happy.

The music was loud and Buddy was dancing with one of Stella's old girlfriends. The dark woman had long hair and a corona of pretty flowers on her head. She performed a smiling, sinuous hula for Buddy, who looked terrible: slow, fat, breathless, his eyes glazed and heavy-lidded with alcohol. At the time, I put it down to bewilderment and suppressed grief. Then he saw me.

"Got a minute? Meet me upstairs. I want to show you something."

A little while later, I found him in his large bedroom, lying in his carved four-poster in front of a big-screen television set. He had a small, heart-shaped object in one hand and the remote-control switch in the other.

"Watch," he said, and worked the remote with his thumb.

Over the sound of romantic music came the title, *Great Expectations*.

"Is this by Charles Dickens?"

"The hell's that supposed to mean?" Buddy said. He had no idea.

On the screen, a young toothy Filipino woman, her shiny shoulders showing above her summer dress, was sitting in a large wicker chair.

My name is Isis Rubaga, but my friends call me Pinky. I like music, dancing, and reading. I love God and my family. Two sisters, four brothers. Mother. Father is passed on.

Offscreen, a whispery prompting voice said, *And what sort of man would you like to meet?*

A kind man. Age is not important. He can be thirty or even sixty, it does not matter. But a good heart, that is the most important thing.

The girl named Pinky smiled shyly as she talked, and she laughed each time she was asked a question. Though she was never at a loss for words, she was clearly nervous, but her nervousness and her laughter seemed to reveal a distinct innocence. She had big dark doe eyes, full lips, slightly protruding teeth, and rich black hair that tumbled onto her shoulders.

"Twenty-three years old," Buddy said. "She's a real coconut girl."

He was still in his big bed but had raised himself up a bit, and now he had a drink in his hand instead of the remote. Almost without an education, he preened himself on his ignorance the way others preened themselves on their erudition, believing that it licensed him in his recklessness. Without any knowledge of history, he was somehow able through his natural ruttishness to re-invent the complex and indulgent habits of an Eastern potentate, one of those Ottoman pashas, right down to holding court half-naked in his sumptuous bedroom.

"I'm seeing her in Manila," he said. "And Stella approves, don't you, Mama?"

With that, he shook the heart-shaped object in his left hand.

"Her ashes," he explained, smiling, seeming to respond to words of encouragement to which I was deaf. "Reason being, coffin's empty."

The videotape was still playing — other girls, in frilly dresses, interviewed in the same wicker chair. They all looked pretty, but none was as young or as winsome as Isis "Pinky" Rubaga.

A few days before he flew to Manila, Buddy called me and said, "I'm giving a party. I want to borrow Peewee. You come too. It's just guys."

Underlying Buddy's boisterous sense of occasion was his inno-cent superstition that a loud sendoff with great food was a guar-antee his trip would be a success. We closed the hotel kitchen early and I drove Peewee to the North Shore, where he set to work making Buddy's favorite meal: Peewee's signature Serious Flu Symptoms Chili, garlic bread, and Caesar salad. Dessert was haupia cake with fresh Big Island strawberries and hot fudge sun-daes. Buddy's cronies were there — Sam Sandford, Willis, Sparky Lemmo, Royce Lionberg, and some others. Peewee spent most of the time serving the meal, while Buddy, uncharacteristically, made himself useful with the pepper mill.

"Fresh-ground pepper? Fresh-ground pepper?"

He suggested pepper on the chili, pepper on the salad, and he said that nothing was better on fresh strawberries than ground pepper. To please him — and it seemed we were always trying to please Buddy — we accepted his offers of fresh-ground pepper.

"That pepper is special," he said at the end of the meal. "You all know what peppercorns look like." He screwed the cap off the pepper mill and tapped a gray dusty substance onto the table. "Go ahead, taste it."

Peewee wet his finger, poked it, and put it on his tongue. He said, "Ashes."

"It's Stella!" Buddy said, and laughing — his laughter proved he was drunk — he showed us the heart-shaped container that had held her ashes. Empty.

34

Courtship in Manila

A BADGE LETTERED *Trainee* was pinned to Pinky's dark green hotel uniform when she met Buddy for the interview in Manila. Interview? The idea was that she would spend a few days with him, including sleep with him. She was one of six possibles. If they hit it off, he would marry her and bring her back to Hawaii. "Pinky had the face of an angel," Buddy told me. "An angel."

"A friend of mine once said that your whole life is in your face," I had told him.

Looking at Buddy's face, you believed it. It was puffy and piratical, too big from food, lopsided with booze, blotchy with broken veins and grog blossoms, leathery from too much sun. He had wet, doggy eyes. His nose was a pickle. His joker's smile showed expensive crowns. He was only sixty-six but you knew when you saw him that he had gotten that face from overdoing it. He had tried everything. He had somehow survived the generation that drank and smoked too much. He had money and young friends. He was reckless enough to experiment with drugs, progressing from reefer to acid. For a while he took cocaine. But he was easily bored, even by drugs, and in the end he showed his age by overeating and drinking too much vodka. He was old at sixty, when I first met him. "I'm not going to last forever," he said, meaning he felt he had only a few more good years left.

He was still recovering from the death of Stella. He missed her so badly he could deal with the pain only by joking about her, telling himself she was still alive, writing letters to her, or, as at his sendoff dinner, pretending that he had put her ashes in the pepper mill.

"I liked hearing her call my name," he said. "I wouldn't reply. I would just listen to her calling, 'Buddy! Buddy!'"

Doubt and then alarm would enter her voice, which would falter when, getting no response, she realized that she was alone. Buddy would wait, in silence, then leave when he knew he was missed.

"Is that childish?" he asked.

"No, I don't think so." It was a lie, but it helped me understand the power he had over his friends. We wished him well, but also, knowing him was a spectator sport. What would he do next?

"I want to get married again," he said.

The video dating service had given him his first glimpse of Pinky. She was young. He feared older women. He mocked the idea of marrying a woman his own age, the way they walked, the way they looked. "Imagine me with a sixty-six-year-old woman!" Yet I felt such a woman would be just the sensible and kindly person he needed. But, "I want a doll," he said.

He wanted someone who had not yet begun to live, who had never left her island, much less left the Philippines. He wanted an entirely innocent girl, whom he intended to teach.

"All I want to do is fuck her and feed her fish heads."

Of the five other girls, he talked with three of them. Two were obviously unsuitable — they had children — and one was too old, at forty. The two remaining women he slept with. One said, "I am a nurse. I can help you." He was tempted by this, but she was rather plain. The other one bit him and scratched him when he made love to her. He objected. She said, "Men always like it." He wondered about her saying this and also thought she might be crazy.

Pinky showed up at his Manila hotel with her uncle and aunt. Uncle Tony ceremoniously unpinned her *Trainee* badge. "You won't need this, Pinky," he said. Auntie Mariel ostentatiously plumped Buddy's pillows. They said they would sleep on the floor of Buddy's hotel room, and after chatting for a while they actually bunked down, using sofa cushions. At midnight Pinky asked Buddy for some pesos. She gave her uncle and aunt the money.

"I tell them go buy Coca-Cola."

She made love shyly, but it was clear that she knew how to give pleasure. Afterward she said she'd had lovers before. But that was not so strange. Buddy did not expect miracles.

In the morning she sat up naked, so near him her nipples grazed his skin. She said, "When you are leaving Manila?"

"Thursday."

"Please marry me before you go, Buddy."

He brayed loudly at the recklessness of her bold demand. Then he watched this young naked girl get out of bed and go to the bathroom. He heard water music. She returned to bed, a small, thin sprite moving across the room like a bird flying to a nest, not going directly but at first obliquely, to a nearby branch, as though to distract attention, and only then flitting to the nest. She went to the window and looked out — daylight on her body. She had a bird's twitch and instincts, habit and caution. She moved sideways.

"Now I gotta go."

In the bathroom mirror Buddy examined his face and saw the whole of his life, a dog's life.

Back in bed he said, "Okay, it's a deal," and they kissed. She climbed on him and hugged him with all her bones, clinging like a little gecko on a big crumbling tree trunk.

When her uncle and aunt returned later that morning to resume chaperoning her, she gabbled in her own language, Visayan, and they hugged him, and laughed. Buddy knew he had done a good thing.

Pinky's aunt said that she could arrange everything, but because it was such short notice she would need some money, and she specified two thousand dollars.

"Let's see what one thousand will get us," Buddy said, squinting defiantly at the woman.

The wedding was held in the Hello Hospitality Suite on the fourth floor of the Hotel Rizal. The elevators were out of order. Exhausted by the stairs and half drunk, Buddy could scarcely speak. The ceremony was conducted by a little old man wearing judge's robes, except the robes were bright blue. Pinky wore a frilly white dress. Uncle Tony, in a crunchy Filipino shirt, gave her away. He sobbed, and so did Aunt Mariel. The fifty or so relatives and friends seemed shy until the food was served. Buddy just watched, thinking that it was like one of those dreams when you feel like a stranger. "Or else are hog-whimpering drunk."

35

Story Time

"**I** WANT TO READ you something I wrote," Buddy said when Pinky and Uncle Tony and Aunt Mariel were back in his room. "So you know who I am."

One day he had shown up at the Hotel Honolulu with an urgent request. He wanted to dictate a story to me. "You know what I mean — hey, you wrote a book!" Of course I agreed to write it down and do some light editing. He saw the story as a chapter of his autobiography, which he imagined would be a long, fascinating book about the colorful American he believed himself to be. Whenever he reflected on his life, the episode that came first to his mind, the most telling, was his experience with his neighbor's dog, Fritzie, the summer Buddy was twelve.

"It's a dog story," he said. "Filipinos like dogs, right? Yum yum!"

His new wife and her uncle and aunt sat stunned and damp after the wedding reception. They had been exuberant at the reception, but their bewilderment in Buddy's room made them anxious, and attentive in a fearful way. He was not dismayed that no one laughed. He took the papers out of his briefcase, opened a can of San Miguel beer, took a sip, and began.

"Growing up in Sweetwater, Nevada, in the late thirties and early forties was, at best, an enigma," he read, rattling the papers. "A high-desert town of some five thousand people, it sat at an altitude of fifty-one hundred feet and was surrounded by snow-capped mountains. Sweetwater was the last of the shit-stomping western cowboy towns. The final Indian war in the U.S. was fought but a few short miles from the city limits. Tumbleweed, jackrabbits, coyotes, rattlesnakes, and scorpions abounded, along with several legal whorehouses, plus some twenty-odd wide-open gambling casinos, whose crap, roulette, and card tables ran around the clock.

"We catered to a diverse group of profligates. We had Utah Mormons, who had absolutely no qualms about hauling their ashes in our infamous bawdyhouses and trying their luck on our crap tables. We had for-real cowboys, Basque sheepherders, hard-rock miners, Shoshoni and Paiute Indians, wild-game hunters from all over the world, various and sundry railroad workers, and tourists passing through on U.S. 40, the main highway bisecting the nation at that time.

"There was one theater. My grandfather owned it. This automatically put me in the driver's seat with my buddies, who were always trying to cockroach free tickets from me. For amusement, we had our weekend movies and, a couple of miles out of town, a natural hot springs swimming pool that was fed by a volcanic hot hole. Aside from swimming there, we also had our introductory lessons in the female anatomy via a few small holes drilled into the side of the building housing the girls' dressing rooms. It must have been an inspiring sight — us frantically fighting over who got the best hole and then three or four of us lined up, loping our mules.

"Some of my greatest childhood memories were of my family gathering around the radio and listening to *Jack Benny* and *The Great Gildersleeve*. The kids also got their shot at the airwaves with *Little Orphan Annie* and *The Lone Ranger*.

"When Orson Welles did his *War of the Worlds* our whole family sat riveted to the radio. My mother and grandmother were wringing their hands and having the 'vapors' while my grandfather was figuring what supplies we could throw into the car and escape with up into the Ruby Mountains. They were all so sure that the alien invaders were interested in Sweetwater, Nevada, that if anyone had rung our doorbell at that moment I'm sure the whole bunch of us would have shit our pants on the spot.

"I shouldn't forget the Humboldt River, the world's most crooked waterway, where a gang of us would play Tom Sawyer and Huckleberry Finn along its willow-covered banks on many a hot summer day. We were given .22-caliber rifles at a young age and turned loose in the desert that surrounded the town. I cringe today when I think of the wanton slaughter we shamelessly perpetrated on the desert wildlife. There was such a plethora of game, though, that the reckless abandon by the town's youths never seemed to dent it. No matter how many coyotes or jackrabbits we massacred, their numbers got bigger.

"It was on one of these Saturday forays that I learned one of life's most valuable lessons. Our hunting safari consisted of Stinky Davis, his poi dog Fritzie, Freddy Woods, my best buddy, and Jerry, my weird cousin. It was a calm, hot desert day with nary a breath of air blowing on the riverbanks. Our group stealthily moved among the willows that lined the Humboldt, looking for anything that moved so we could zap it with our trusty rifles.

"Fritzie, who was not pretty, was an intrepid dog. He had the unerring instinct to be able to detect anything with breath in it. He would flush anything that had legs, wings, or slithered, and the 'Death Squad' would automatically fire away, all the time trying to avoid shooting each other and Fritzie.

"Around noon, we flopped down under a willow patch and ate the sandwiches my grandmother had made for us that morning. Homemade bread, sliced rare roast beef, and fresh crisp lettuce along with homemade cookies. We were blissfully unaware of our good fortune to be raised in the nation's largest cattle and sheep county, where even at the height of the Depression we ate damned well. Meat, potatoes, and milk every day of the year!

"After lunch, we laid around in the shade and speculated about how great it would be when we'd be old enough to sneak into the whorehouses and lose our virginity, all for the princely sum of two bucks.

"As a reward for flushing our morning's game, Fritzie came over by me and flopped down on his back to have his belly scratched. I obliged him and in the process noticed a tick on his dick, which, being the good Samaritan that I was, I removed. Somehow, Fritzie mistook my intentions and immediately got a big red dog boner that could have won him a blue ribbon at the Westchester Dog Show. Being the perennial dipshit and showoff, I obliged him by giving his engorged tallywacker several good jerks, much to the delighted whoops and hollers of my perverted companions. After my little fling with Fritzie, we finished our lunch and forgot all about it as we resumed our afternoon carnage.

"That evening, after our mandatory Saturday bath, whether we needed it or not, I was sitting in Stinky's living room, talking to Stinky and his dad, when Fritzie came in, headed straight for me, and immediately started to hump my leg. I did my best to ignore this blatant attempt for canine romance when to my horror I felt and saw this raw, wet, bright red dog boner sliding all over my leg! Now, I don't know how it was in other areas of the country, but in Sweetwater, Nevada, in 1936, the most uncool thing a ten-year-old could do was to lose his nerve.

"The old axiom 'My life flashed before my eyes' was never truer. I panicked as all kinds of guilty mind-flashes started to ricochet around my brain: 'My God, his father knows that I jacked off his stupid dog! Look at that asshole Stinky, flopping around on the couch, turning purple and blowing large snot bubbles trying not to laugh. If he laughs, the jig is up. His old man is going to know for sure and he'll tell my grandfather! How will I explain that to the old folks? "Yeah, well, you see, Gramps, heh-heh, I was just laying there and, you know, this dog sort of liked me and . . ." Oh Shit. I'm dead!'

"His dad, in a moralistic Mormon rage, jumped up and kicked poor Fritzie across the room, all the time yelling, 'I don't know what got into that goddamn dog! He ain't never done that before!' Fritzie, totally undeterred and undaunted, snuck right back, boner and all, and proceeded to resume his romance with my leg again. This earned him another drop kick across the room and caused Stinky to bolt out of the house before he totally lost it. His old man sat there shaking his head and mumbling, 'That crazy fucking dog. Must be a bitch in heat around here somewhere.'

"Fritzie never forgot that moment's indiscretion on my part and made damn sure that I never did either. Forever after, whenever I got within humping range, I became a target for his misguided affections.

"At this stage of my life, I can now see where more than a few 'moments of indiscretion' in my relationships with the female gender should have taught me a lesson. That is, never tell a female you love her just to get into her knickers."

He straightened the typed pages of his story, smiling at them with satisfaction. And then he became aware of the silence.

"Get it? Never jack off a dog," Buddy said. " 'Cause they'll never leave you alone."

By his side, in her wedding dress, Pinky smiled. Uncle Tony and Aunt Mariel looked apprehensive, as though wondering whether there was more.

36

Another Death

"PINKY. She's coming in a few weeks, when she gets her American visa." What sounded like his chuckling was the ice in his drink.

At a family gathering to which I was invited that week — Bula, Melveen, all the rest of them — Buddy pulled a snapshot out of his wallet and held it up: Pinky smiling with her lips pressed together and the nail of one slender finger held against a dimple.

"Look at your new mother."

Buddy was drunk, in his thronelike chair, drinking while the others ate. He masticated the ice, his chewing giving him a crooked grin, and he shifted the noisy stuff to the side of his mouth like a dog with a bone in its bulging cheek.

Two days later I remembered Buddy's funny face with anguish. The eldest boy, Bula, called me and told me in a stuttering voice that his father had drowned in a fishing accident off the Big Island, near Earl Willis's place. It was something I had been both dreading and expecting from this reckless man.

"I think my dad would have wanted you to know first. Willis called from Puna to say that they picking opihi and my dad get hit by one wave and he wipe out." After this hesitant explanation Bula honked, "They never find him!"

"Missing or drowned?" I asked.

I heard the bugling sour notes of the boy blowing his nose.

"Missing mean drowned!"

"I am very sorry." Then I remembered. "What about that woman from the Philippines, the one he married?"

It was so hard to think of her as his wife, I could not use the word.

Bula said, "Man, we need you help wid dis incredulous thing."

I was put in mind of a cruel folktale or a myth. The new wife arrives in a far-off country only to discover that her husband has died and she, a total stranger, is the mistress of the house.

The moment I saw her at the airport, arriving in her cheap new traveling clothes and carrying her cheap old suitcase, after the nine-hour flight from Manila, I knew that I could not give her the tragic news. I recognized her from the video, though she was thinner, not smiling, watching nervously for Buddy.

"Pinky Rubaga?" I said, heading her off.

She looked wary and vulnerable, the way tired, rumpled passengers do just off a long flight, like people who have been interrupted while sleepwalking.

"Where is Buddy?" she said, stiffening with suspicion.

"This is his son Bula. He'll explain."

Bula was standing just behind me, breathing hard through what sounded like baffles in his nose. I could sense the damp heat radiating from him. He was big, his body a large, anxious parody of his father's.

When I looked again she had gone gray, her skin was ashen, and her face was dusty, as though decomposing with sorrow. She got into the back seat of my car and did not say a single word for forty miles.

"This the house," Bula said as I pulled into the driveway.

Pinky winced at the house and then, with an involuntary smirk of fear twisting her face, headed for the front door.

It was a two-million-dollar house on the beach, not pretty, even boxlike, a squarish, flat-roofed building. But big — three stories, with fluttering awnings, famous for its large size and the number of rooms, for the long dining table that could seat eighteen people, and for the wonderful view over the most dangerous surf breaks. She saw a castle with an entrance like a gaping mouth.

Pinky kept walking, through the open door, leaving her shoes at the bottom of the stairs with the jumble of sandals. She stepped back on the top landing and clutched her throat.

"What is that noise?"

It was the boom of surf, a long buffeting punch, traveling across the beach and through the house; when it subsided with a sigh, there was another, much louder. The winter swell had hit with its ceaseless cannonade. At the edge of the shore the breaking waves collapsed into a mass of foam that creamed the whole beach, sliding and bubbling to the foundations of the house, before percolating through the sand.

The family was waiting, though only the small children were active. Taunting, laughing, hogging the chairs, they seemed to be speaking for the others, who remained silent. Pinky timidly asked for a drink and was given guava juice.

She sniffed a flower. "Nice smell. Ylang-ylang."

It was a mistake to presume, and wrong, in that flower-loving household, to be so specific.

"Pak-lan," Melveen said, correcting her, and Pinky withered and went gray again.

Buddy's room had been locked and secured by Jimmerson, his Honolulu attorney, the day the news came of the disappearance. All Buddy's personal effects were there, with Stella's jewelry, and his photographs and curios, glass-ball net floats, fish traps made into lamps, potted plants, the big-screen TV, the four-poster on which he had held court, the filing cabinets, the locked safe.

Pinky was taken to the guest room on the second floor, where she remained with the door closed. Sometimes the splintery sound of her weeping could be heard. After two days, she came downstairs, gripping the banister tightly. She looked unsteady, fearful, and a bit feverish, not ailing but seasick, and she walked as though on the deck of a ship in a rising storm. Her makeup had turned her face green.

Pinky found the telephone in the kitchen and, with a scrap of paper in her hand, dialed a number.

Melveen stared at her. "You know some people here?"

"I meet one on the plane."

Melveen's eyes were blank, and so were Bula's, but when they met, they shared the disapproval and uncertainty that was in their hearts.

"Mrs. Pinky Hamstra," the woman was saying into the phone.

Everyone listened, everyone heard. Switching to her own language, there was a note of timid inquiry at first, and then a sudden screech of urgency, a sort of sobbing explanation, but her passion made it sound like a beseeching prayer spoken backward.

None of Buddy's eavesdropping children knew the foreign language they took to be Filipino. To them it was grief and a torrent of twanging talk and some sharp rejoinders that resembled warning barks.

This young woman was explaining her plight, one she felt was desperate, to a stranger who was quickly becoming her friend and confidante. They knew this without knowing the language.

When Pinky hung up and stared into space, her eyes glazed and vague with concern, Bula said, "You went invite this woman over the house?"

Somehow he knew that, too — that it was an older woman, that an invitation had been extended, that it was for a visit to the house, that the answer had been yes.

Perhaps it was deliberate on Pinky's part that she was playing with her wedding ring, twisting it against her small knuckle to make the stone sparkle. She was hesitating, as if working up the courage to speak. No one helped her, but after some moments of wringing her fingers she began to speak, asking for something, a keepsake, to remind her of her husband.

"Like a memory relic," she said. "Maybe a watch."

"He wearing it when he died," Melveen said. "Poor old *kolohe* bugga."

"This house his relic," Bula said. "You standing in one relic, sister."

It made them sad to think how much had changed since Buddy had died. On the beach, staring at the surf with salty eyes, they were not thinking of the sea but of their father, tossed in it, pocked with fish bites and swollen, his corpse bulging against his clothes. They had seen such corpses on the edge of the beach some mornings, staring blindly at them with dead eyes and big blue lips. They could not bear to think that he was being nipped by sharks.

The friend's name was Ronda Malanut. She simply appeared in the doorway one day, carrying a large handbag. She was dark and quite plump in a topheavy way — skinny legs, pot belly, large flat face losing its shape. A gold tooth showed when she laughed her hungry laugh, but not when she smiled her scheming smile.

"I am here to see Pinky."

The woman's bag was full of candles. That afternoon a shrine was set up on a table that faced the ocean: Buddy smiling in a framed picture inscribed, *Stick with me, Pinky, and you'll fart through silk,* and surrounded by twenty twinkling votive lights and some scattered flower petals.

Pinky Rubaga spent most of the day in her room, except when she was changing the candles on Buddy's shrine. She kept fresh flowers in the vases and a garland hooked on Buddy's picture. Bula noticed that Pinky also began picking the ripe mangoes from the tree at the side of the house. What did she do with them?

Ronda made herself inconspicuous by being helpful. Now she knew where everything belonged and could empty the dishwasher without asking where to put anything.

A strange boy was eating breakfast one morning at the long table.

"Tony Malanut," he said, keeping his elbows on the table, smiling as he chewed.

He was Ronda's son, and he went on moving food to his mouth with stubby fingers. A bracelet with his name on it clanked on his wrist. He was short and stocky, in his late twenties, with a wispy mustache, a big square head, and dark, deep-set eyes. A noisy bunch of keys hooked to his belt made him seem idle and self-important.

"That red pickup yours?" Bula asked.

Tony nodded, his mouth too full for him to speak. He swallowed and said, "Dodge Ram. Turbocharged. Loaded."

"Blocking the driveway," Bula said. "So move it."

The place was filling with strangers — Ronda mopping the floor, Pinky tending Buddy's shrine, now Tony tinkering with his pickup truck. Far from making them seem like menials, these chores gave them an air of authority. Each time Ronda polished or dusted something, she seemed to be taking possession of it.

"I miss Dad," Bula said.

"I miss him too," Pinky said.

"How you go miss someone you know for two-tree days?"

"Five days," Pinky said. "Also five nights."

Bula and Melveen, who had remained in the house, resented their father for choosing this woman. They hated him for dying. They were angry that his business affairs were in such a mess. The bedroom was kept locked, the bank accounts had been frozen until the will could be read and probated. The Hotel Honolulu was his main asset, so I was involved. But the will was an enigma. Melveen, the executor, would not discuss it, taking her cue from Buddy, who had been superstitious about mentioning it.

Unable to enter into the grief, I had stayed away from the house. But one Sunday after a picnic with Sweetie and Rose on the North Shore, I drove past and saw a young woman sitting at a wooden table by the roadside. The table was heaped with green fruit, and on a hand-lettered sign was the word *Mango's*. The misspelling caught my attention, and so did the woman, who was Buddy's widow, Pinky.

"She say she need money," Bula explained the next time I saw him.

The strangers ranged more freely in the house. Tony Malanut started sitting on the lanai to watch the surf, his feet braced on the rail. Bula hated the man's feet. And that was the very spot where Buddy used to sit and drink, with Stella's ashes in one hand and a drink in the other as he studied the sunset for a green flash.

Buddy's shrine remained, swelling with flowers and trinkets, though the photograph of the man was darkened and its frame scorched from all the candle flames.

Bula called Jimmerson, and in the middle of explaining his anxieties, he became inarticulate and, struggling to speak, was overcome by a fit of sobbing.

"I can hear the concern in your voice," Jimmerson said. "I've been meaning to call you. Her lawyer's been in touch with me about the will."

Bula stopped weeping, and now his mouth gaped over the receiver. "What do you mean, 'her lawyer'?"

The reading of the will was held in a large conference room at Jimmerson's office in downtown Honolulu. Buddy's children occupied the first row of chairs. Pinky, Ronda, and Tony sat at the rear with their lawyer, Pagal, a middle-aged Filipino man with a lined, anxious-looking face, who kept his worn briefcase on his lap.

"Jimmy, I got a question before we start," Melveen said. "I thought this just the *ohana*."

"That's up to you."

"So what these people are doing here?"

Pagal, the lawyer, said, "May I remind you that this is Mrs. Hamstra."

Then came a voice from a side door that was swinging open: "Did I hear someone say my name?"

It was a familiar voice, gravelly, rising to a howl. Pinky screamed. The children turned. The grandchildren cried, "Grandy!"

"I'm back!"

It was Buddy, in a T-shirt and shorts, looking rested, grinning, holding a cellular phone in his hand. Only Ronda and Tony stayed seated, wondering who this man might be. Tony reached for Pinky, but she slapped him away and began to tremble, looking ashen, as she had that first day at Honolulu Airport.

Before Buddy could say anything, his children began screaming at him. Bula snatched at his shirt and smacked him repeatedly on the shoulder. The others brayed at him and pummeled him, while the grandchildren yelled and clung to his legs. Buddy was looking across the room at Pinky, who, having stood up, still seemed to be rising, as though unwillingly levitating in apprehension.

"Don't go!" He was laughing, but his face was grubby with tears.

37

Joker Man

THAT SUDDEN reappearance became famous on the island, and Buddy's howl of "I'm back!" was soon a catch phrase among his cronies. It was shouted by those men who hung around him, who thought of themselves as rascals and basked in his reflected glory, borrowing money from him, eating his food, sleeping on his numerous sofas and hammocks, running up big bills at Paradise Lost. No one mentioned Buddy's tears.

The Buddy-back-from-the-dead story made the rounds. It was told hilariously by his friends, and it was muttered resentfully by his denigrators, the few who existed — people who owed him so much money that they avoided him and nervously tried to slander him, not realizing that the worst slander was like praise to him. When I expressed surprise, not to say shock, at his audacity, his friends said, "That's nothing," and recalled other, better, bolder practical jokes he had brought off.

Buddy and his family told me everything. "He wrote a book!" he had told his kids and his friends. None of them was a reader, so I was mysterious and magical, almost priestlike, treated with a respect I was unused to in my old indoor life among bitter writers and overfamiliar readers, the well-meaning bores of literacy.

This is who I am, Buddy seemed to be saying as he wheezily related something scandalous — the time he had sealed Willis's toilet with cement; the night at the hotel when a guest's wife passed out after Buddy seduced her and he shaved off all her pubic hair before sending her upstairs to her husband; the scoop of dog shit he jammed into Bula's hair dryer. Bula said, "I went turn it on and what a stink, yah?" Far from shocked, I felt privileged to share these confidences.

That the husband and wife still stayed at the hotel was testimony to Buddy's powers of persuasion or, I suppose, his genius for friendship. He had envious denigrators, but he had no serious enemies. Despite all the emotion, all the tears and grief, cruelly hoaxing his friends, his family, and his new wife by playing dead, he was forgiven. More than that, soon everyone was laughing about it, praising him for having fooled them.

"Buddy's amazing!" they said, and laughed. Mostly they were relieved to have him back.

Not for the first time, I thought, Buddy's a sadist, and I didn't laugh at all. Still, I was even more curious about the man. Before I expressed this curiosity, I was offered many other examples of Buddy's great stunts. Some were equally cruel, many were expensive and convoluted, all of them seemed gratuitous. A streak of childish brutality ran through them, but when I pointed out an especially painful aspect to my informants, they said, "That's the funniest part."

Sadism, which is an element in all practical jokes, perhaps the central element, was in the grain of Buddy's character. I witnessed him torturing his kids with jokes. But he could also be a gentle soul. "Horsing around," he called his style of joking, but sadism is horsing around too, just a wilder sort of horse. Buddy's gentleness was almost childlike, verging on the ridiculous — his doting on dogs and little children, the love letters he had written to his dead wife Momi, his devotion to Stella's ashes and the green flash at sunset, his assiduous attention to his flowers. He was sentimental as well as sadistic — not so unlikely a combination of traits, a natural pair in fact. I once asked him if he thought he was cruel.

"I am an American," he said whenever he was asked a question he could not answer, or sometimes he made a silly face and screamed, "Guilty!"

From what I heard, his life so far had been a series of practical jokes. Buddy had come from a long line of pioneers and bankers who had made so much money they had never had to pretend to be respectable and instead boasted of their crudeness. His ancestors had prospered at a time when America was huge and empty and hard up. Buddy followed their example, moving westward across the ocean. He had made his money in the postwar Pacific, a boom time of relative innocence. Buddy's forebears had headed west, inventing America en route. Buddy's great-grandfather had left Chicago in the late 1860s, driving a wagon into the prairie on a dare, to impress his father, who was a feed merchant. "I'll match any capital you make, if you come home," his father said. "If you get into debt, don't come home."

Perhaps jokes ran in Buddy's family. That man never came home to claim his prize. Instead, he put up a house, made improvements, started a farm, and ran a store. In doing so, he founded a settlement, the town of Sweetwater, where travelers stopped on their way to California to buy supplies and to take on water. Buddy's great-grandfather had discovered a spring. Water was the key: thus the name Sweetwater. The town still stands. I drove through it on the only road trip I have ever taken cross-country. I didn't stop — people don't anymore. But years ago it was famous for its spring water and its hospitality.

The family wealth allowed Buddy's grandfather to start a bank, just as useful an institution on the way west as the dry goods store and the blacksmith's shop and the water. The town prospered. Buddy's father broke with family tradition by investing in the new movie industry, and it gave Buddy a second home — homes, rather, for Ray Hamstra, an early backer of talkies, was married and divorced five times.

"Buddy had some famous stepmothers," Peewee the chef said. Buddy's own mother — his father's first wife — had been a well-known horsewoman in Sweetwater. Two others were actresses, one was a dancer, the last a famous singer. No one in Hawaii knew their names. Peewee said, "You'd recognize them if I could remember them."

Buddy was raised by his grandmother, the widow of the banker, but as a boy he visited his father at various addresses in southern California. Did all this shuttling around anger him and turn him into an obsessive prankster? The violence in practical jokes is undeniable, and all jokes need a victim. Buddy's friends said he laughed a lot. He was reckless. He had money, too. Perhaps he was spoiled. All these wild elements, yet he had a sense of power and did not lack confidence.

His earliest jokes were played against his father: putting Limburger cheese on the steering wheel of the old man's car was an early one, which he repeated in Hawaii against his own children when they began to drive. At the age of ten or eleven he stuck a sign saying *Smile if you want a blow job* under the hood of his current stepmother's car, to be seen by the next garage mechanic who checked the oil. He used that one in Hawaii later, too — such jokes had a timeless simplicity. And the fact that they often backfired (his father drove the car that day) only made them sweeter.

At the age of thirteen Buddy lost his virginity at Sunshine Saloon, Sweetwater's other useful institution, the brothel. The joke was that the woman who initiated him was his father's mistress. He stole a pair of the woman's lace underpants and sent them to his father on his birthday, with a card saying, *Love, Buddy.*

Around this time he created a scandal in Sweetwater — something to do with a neighbor's dog — but no one I spoke to knew the details, only that it was shocking. Eventually he told me the story, as part of a projected autobiography, and I wrote it down and typed it for him.

Preying on the passive is a standby for practical jokers, but Buddy liked preying on strong people by finding their hidden weakness. The toughest kid in his school confided to Buddy that he wanted to lose weight. Buddy said he had just the answer. He sold the big brute a worm and said, "It's a tapeworm. It works day and night. You'll never be fat again. All you have to do is eat it." The big fellow ate it, and Buddy laughed and spread the story — it was an earthworm.

During one of his father's rare visits to Sweetwater from California, Buddy filled his father's car with sand. It was another practical joke he repeated as he grew older, substituting sand with cat litter, cow manure, and potting soil, and at last expanding industrial foam, which hardened like cement. Technology is the prankster's friend, but so are traditional skills and peasant cunning. Buddy was expert at obtaining smears and swipes of bitches in heat — I did not ask how — and applying these to the clothes of schoolteachers who punished him. His revenge was seeing them besieged by packs of amorous dogs.

Sabotage can be simple. The exploding toilet seat. The potato jammed in the exhaust pipe. Sugar in the gas tank. The collapsing chair leg. Phantom voices on the phone. The dismantled lawnmower. The reusable cockroach. Mail-order madness: a pileup of

Sears, Roebuck deliveries. The believable turd. The reversed road sign. The ambiguous classified ad, inviting breathy phone calls. These were practical jokes for the cash-strapped schoolboy. Buddy was soon expelled from school.

He was hired at the family bank and with a little income was able to conduct his first experiments in turning the staff toilet into an aquarium — first eels, then goldfish, then the tropical fish that belonged to the manager, dipping and diving in the hopper. At the very moment he was being berated for this offense, he contrived to slip some glue on his tormentor's chair. Before he could be fired, he was able to smuggle a live pig into the walk-in vault, leaving it to be discovered, dung-smeared and skidding, in the morning.

In themselves, none of these practical jokes were unusual, but their simultaneity gave them force and made them memorable. He was fired from the bank by a man who, later that same day, found another pig in his car. Live pigs were to play a prominent part in many of Buddy's jokes.

Now seventeen, Buddy was sent to live with his father and a new stepmother, who were soon contemplating the significance of an enormous torpedo in their bed when they retired one night. Perhaps a bizarre form of salutation? They knew the perpetrator, of course, but weren't able to discover the means by which he had shunted the half ton of metal. Had they known, they would have rid themselves of it more quickly. The expensive removal took days.

"I think your son is insane," the new wife said.

Putting his finger in his mouth, clownishly playing dumb, Buddy said he knew nothing about it. I was wondering what a psychiatrist would make of the symbolism of the torpedo in the marital bed when I heard of his next embellishment. Buddy insinuated himself in the bed one night when his father was delayed by a ruse Buddy himself had rigged. Buddy was welcomed in the darkness by his stepmother, who took his bulk for her husband's, and it was only after they were engaged in strenuous foreplay that Buddy revealed himself — by braying like a donkey. The woman was too ashamed and humiliated to report him, but before long Buddy was evicted.

Hobbling his friends and family with large, immovable objects was a recurring motif in these jokes of his late teens, as though the object in question stood for Buddy himself: the gigantic safe sinking into the rain-softened lawn, the anvil in the bathtub, the motorcycle on the roof, the porch swing in the swimming pool. As he grew heavier, Buddy himself became harder to remove. On his twenty-first birthday he was six feet three and weighed 220 pounds.

Incidentally, he was working at a film studio owned by his father, but what seemed like relentless aggression was too much for the man, and Buddy was soon on his own. He was never to return home, and though he looked after his mother for a while in Hawaii when she was senile and near death, he did not see his father again.

At the age of twenty-two he got a job on a merchant ship out of San Francisco, his first joyous taste of the Pacific. But the work was hard, he was a fractious seaman, so he was punished. His revenge: stinky cheese on the hatch handle, the ship's horn blown in the wee hours outside the first officer's cabin, his signature turds in the desk drawers of senior officers.

He knew what was coming; he welcomed it. The Pacific ports, battered by the war and thoroughly corrupted and deranged, were an invitation to Buddy. Put ashore in Noumea for insubordination, Buddy laughed and learned French. In New Caledonia he discovered firsthand France's designs in Indochina — it was 1952 and the French were recruiting soldiers locally. Buddy tended bar and kept a mistress. He was hired as an informant by the CIA, and he thrived.

To Tahiti. He made himself popular with bootleg whiskey and married a sixteen-year-old. The CIA found him and demanded their money back. Buddy gladly gave it to them, two thousand dollars — in pennies.

Buddy's practical jokes, essentially vindictive, became for a time inseparable from pure revenge. He was a card player, an irrational and usually successful gambler. He won the Hotel Honolulu in a card game. He made the hotel popular by bringing the first Tahitian dancers to Hawaii, putting on a show on the hotel's poolside lanai. His envious friends, led by Lemmo, intending to deflate him, sealed up his office — bricked in the doorway and painted it.

Buddy broke through. And laughed. He liked the extravagance of it. He declared war, and lodged a telephone pole through the length of Lemmo's house, skewering the whole dwelling through its windows.

Once, returning from Tahiti with some black pearls Buddy had ordered, Peewee was taken in for questioning by the airport police. Buddy had called Honolulu customs and tipped them off that Peewee was an international jewel thief. And often, in an excess of sentiment, he installed live pigs in offices overnight and got fat men to eat "tapeworms" he had dug up in his garden.

The magazine he started, *Teen Hawaii*, put him in touch with as many pretty girls as his Tahiti show had done, but the magazine failed. For a time his hotel was a meeting place, crackling with Buddy's diabolical energy, but before long other, bigger hotels were built, and his was shoved to the edge of Waikiki.

Claiming at his sendoff dinner that Stella's ashes had been in the pepper mill was a great joke, Buddy thought, but the best by far was his coming back from the dead. Many of his friends said they had guessed the outcome all along, but it put the fear of God into Pinky and made her a compliant wife.

38

Trainee

"THIS IS MY FRIEND," Buddy said to Pinky, nodding at me. "He wrote a book! Go on, angel, give him a kiss."

She was too shy to kiss me. Looking at her unmarked face, I saw someone who seemed to be entering the world for the first time, and uninterested in it, perhaps even repelled by it. I saw what Buddy meant by "angel": inexperienced, childlike, innocent, just beginning to learn the coarse language of life.

Her posture, the way she hunched her shoulders, was like that of a trapped bird, one captured in the wild and still fluttering with fear, her heart pounding like mad. Her smallness made her seem even younger than twenty-three. She wore a T-shirt, and her blue jeans showed her narrow hips and spindly legs. If a woman is a woman for the alluring way she stands, the opposite of a coquette is an adolescent boy. Wearing a baseball cap, she looked like a Little Leaguer.

"Funny thing," Buddy told me. "She was in the dining room alone this morning. She bumped into the table and the flower vase shook a little. I was in the downstairs john. I heard her say 'Sorry.' To an empty room. Is that beautiful or what?"

Her face told nothing except her age. Her smile was trusting. She was glad to be married. She held Buddy's hand the way one of his children might have, staying in his shadow like a triumphant pet, as an angel sometimes seems to be.

"Isn't she a sweetheart?"

I knew nothing about her at the time. I wanted to know everything. I did not succeed at that, but in time I learned enough. It was a lesson in faces.

*   *   *

Uncle Tony, her mother's brother, the man who had brought her to the hotel room and, in front of Buddy, said, "You won't need this, Pinky," as he unpinned her Trainee badge, had been her protector. Her father was a factory worker in Manila. Pinky lived with her mother and Uncle Tony and a brother and sister in a small hut on a crowded slope of huts, San Antonio, outside Cebu City. Uncle Tony was her first lover.

She had been twelve at the time. She was relieved when she saw it was her uncle kneeling next to her that night. She had feared it might be a stranger. "It's Uncle Tony," he whispered. Her mother was away, working at one of the tourist hotels. He did not wake the others. He kissed her, putting his sour tongue in her mouth. He slipped his hand between her legs and poked his finger into her. She lay bewildered, counting, to calm herself, wanting him to stop.

A pair of shoes in white tissue paper was propped on the table the next day.

Her mother had just returned from her shift. She said, "Say thank you. Give Uncle Tony a kiss. It's a lovely present."

She kissed Uncle Tony. The next time was two weeks later, on her mother's night-shift week. He had given her a pair of pink panties when he came home from the bar. He told her to wear them. That night when the children were asleep he turned the lights out and said, "Take them off." When she hesitated, he said crossly, "Who gave them to you?"

In the darkness he put his mouth on her and used his finger again. The rawness there reminded her of the pain she had felt the first time, which she had never felt before.

"Now you can put them on. They were a present, you know."

After that, whenever her mother was working the night shift, Uncle Tony came to her mat on the floor.

"Hold this," he said.

She could hardly get her fingers around the warm thickening thing that reminded her of her small brother's arm.

"Tighter."

His smothering mouth was on hers, his tongue tasting of adobo and beer. Her mind went blank. She was counting again, not to any particular number. She knew that in a few minutes it would be over and he would leave her. Yet it never ended when she wanted it to.

Nearly always there were presents — underwear, once a blouse, another time a dress, but candy was the usual thing.

"Give Uncle Tony a kiss," her mother said.

"She don't like her Uncle Tony," Uncle Tony said.

"I love you, Uncle Tony," Pinky said.

She was afraid until she understood that when she kissed him, he would not harm her.

At school the envious girls teased her whenever she wore something new. Seeing her new shoes, the girls were cruel. That year some of them came to school holding a Walkman, with earphones. She waited until the night-shift week and told Uncle Tony she wanted one. He seemed glad to be asked. He came to her mat the next night and knelt and said, "Open your mouth." And she did, almost choking as he said, "Make noises." She had her Walkman.

The old man Bong-Bong in the hut next door watched her all the time. She had turned thirteen. Bong-Bong was a landlord. The way he eyed her convinced her that he knew her secret and made her afraid.

"Come here, Pinky."

She did not move.

"If you don't come here I'll tell your mother."

Tell her what? There was so much to tell. She went into Bong-Bong's feeling tiny, because his hut was so much bigger than her mother's, and it had different smells. Bong-Bong took her on his lap. He arranged her hands, placing them where Uncle Tony had placed them, as though he had seen everything.

"You know all about this. Kneel down."

Her fear had been that he would hurt her. But not at all, and she was glad and grateful, and he was quicker than Uncle Tony. He gave her money and made her promise that she would visit him again.

In time, Bong-Bong's presents added up to a thickness of pesos, which she saved and hid. How could she explain where the money had come from?

She dropped out of school. "I want to work." She said she had a job, but each day she went into Cebu City, where she met other girls, who looked like schoolgirls. They were thirteen and fourteen and some were older. They used a particular shaded portico one of the girls had found. The girls had friends who were men like Uncle Tony and Bong-Bong — no worse. Pinky went with the men.

The secret lay in saying yes. If a man threatened her, she did not run or hide, but instead went closer to the man. There was even a smell she recognized. And when she touched the men she was safe; they would not hurt her after that. They held her tightly, defended her, sometimes gave her money. This was in cars and in the rooms of the abandoned building beyond the portico. The closer you went, the safer you were. She felt confident enough now to spend the money on clothes. She bought a pair of orange vinyl hot pants and high heels.

Pinky's mother was now with her father in Manila. Pinky looked after her little brother and sister. Uncle Tony still touched her in the dark now and then. He lay on top of her, too, as the other men did. She wondered why she was not pregnant, and then one month she knew she was. One of the girls gave her the name of a man who said he was a doctor. He locked his door and lay on top of her and said, "Sometimes this works." Then he opened her legs and put them in a clamp and used a piece of glittering metal that might have been a knife. It hurt. She bled.

"That will be five hundred pesos."

She did not have the money, and she was angry with herself for having spent the money on clothes. The doctor said that he knew where she could earn the money, as a dancer.

"I can't dance," Pinky said.

"They will teach you."

He took her to a club in Cebu City and said, "This is Mama." Mama gave her a room and food. "This is worth two thousand pesos," Mama said. "But you will earn it very fast."

Mama was kind. Pinky danced naked, wearing a dog collar and platform shoes, and afterward she sat with the men in darkened booths. She knew all the rest. The men were Koreans, Japanese, Chinese, even Americans.

"You can't dance, but they like you," Mama said.

At noon when the girls woke up, they had a meal together, like a family, at one table, Mama at the head of it. "What is this adobo?" Pinky asked. It was made from a cat. Even on her hungriest days at San Antonio she had not eaten a cat.

One night a Japanese man sat with her in a booth. He did not touch her. He said, "Put this on." It was a blouse, which she slipped over her sequined bra. The man raised a camera and blinded her for a second with his flash.

Some days later, preparing to dance, she saw Mama beckon to her. The same Japanese man was sitting with Mama in a booth. He had a suitcase. He said, "Open it."

"They are all yours," Mama said. The suitcase was full of folded clothes. "You are going on a trip with Mr. Nishiwara."

"Call me Tony," the Japanese man said. Another Tony. He gave her a passport, *Republic of the Philippines*. It was her face in the little picture, but beside it was the name Tina Cojugo, four years older than Pinky and with a different address.

That night she flew with Tony the Japanese man to Guam, and was driven in the rain to a small house crowded with Filipinas. Seeing Pinky crying, a woman hugged her and comforted her. This woman, Rosa, was a manager of the club, which was called Club Night Life, near the beach at Agana.

At Club Night Life the customers were mostly Japanese. Pinky danced. She sat with them in the booths. Now and then they bought her for the night by giving Rosa five hundred dollars. In their hotel rooms the Japanese men took pictures of her naked. They watched her on the toilet. Often they did not touch her, only took pictures. But one man tied her to a chair and blindfolded her and splashed on her. He returned another night, but Pinky refused to go with him.

To punish her, Rosa locked Pinky in a dark room in the house. Though she had no idea how long she had been in the room, when she was released into the light Pinky fell to her knees and hugged first Rosa's legs, then Tony's.

In the month before Christmas, Japanese Tony brought her to Honolulu to work in another club, the Rat Room, dancing on a stage that was a mirror and sitting with men, mostly Americans, some Japanese. Tony still sometimes brought her to his room in Honolulu, where he pulled her hair and bit her until she cried. She reminded herself that she was in America, but it seemed no different from Guam. One night in the Rat Room, a man at the edge of the stage shouted "Watch this!" to his friends. He waved a five-dollar bill at Pinky, she spread her legs for him, and he stared intently between her legs like a man absorbed in contemplating a small shy animal. He tucked the money between the animal's pink lips. His friends cheered, "Tuna!"

It was Buddy. He never saw Pinky's face, nor did Pinky see his, but when he did that, she wanted to cry. Though the thought did not come to her in an arrangement of words, she felt humiliation and fear and hatred, like a sickness that would never leave her body. But she was smiling. When she went to another man, Buddy hurried away.

39

Truck Whore

IN PINKY'S SHORT TIME in Honolulu, with her different name, many things happened very quickly. An American man in the Rat Room said he had bought her for the night. He took her to his hotel room and showed her his tattoos, but he hardly touched her. His name was Skip. He was angry when she told him how she got the bite marks on her. He helped her get away with her false passport. He said, "I want to marry you, Tina."

"Please call me Pinky," she said. She loved him, she said, but they could only get married when she was safe. She told Skip she was afraid of the Japanese man Tony.

"You've got real good people skills," Skip said.

Skip flew with her to California, where he had a motorcycle. He bought Pinky new clothes and said he wanted to introduce her to his mother, who was ninety-four and living in Pennsylvania. He began calling her Christy, the name of his dead wife. Going through Ohio, they stopped at a motel truck stop. It was raining. He said, "Stand over there," and left on his motorcycle to buy beer. At midnight he had not returned. She went to the clerk at the motel desk and said she was afraid.

"There's been an accident — a biker on the interstate. What was your friend's name?"

"Skip."

"Skip isn't a name," the clerk said. He showed her to a room and told her he would make inquiries. But the next morning, when the clerk knocked on her door, he had no news. And he said, "You can't check out until your bill is paid. Stay in there."

Pinky was crying and watching television an hour later when the clerk knocked again. She had locked the door, but he had a key. He saw her cowering against the wall. He demanded that she take her clothes off, and when she did, he went nearer. He said, "You know all about it," and slapped her head and pushed it down.

When he was finished, Pinky said, "Now can I go?"

"You owe me," the man said in a fierce voice. "You owe me."

The man took all her clothes and left her in the room naked.

Later that day he knocked again on Pinky's door. A man was with him. "This is my friend." He left the man with Pinky.

"I was in the service in the Philippines," the man said. "Where are you from?"

"Cebu City."

He knew the place.

"Help me," Pinky said.

"First you help me," the man said, and steered her to the bed, holding her arm tightly.

When he was done, he left without another word. Pinky wrapped herself in a towel and looked out the window and saw him get into a truck. The big truck swayed and bounced onto the road. Still looking at the truck, she saw the motel clerk walking toward her room with another man, and then she heard the knock, and "You know what to do."

After that man she saw three or four others, and more the next day. She was awakened in the dark with the knocking. She felt sick. One morning she went into her bathroom to vomit and saw, written on the wall with her lipstick, *Truck Whore*.

Each time the door opened she hoped it would be Skip and that he would take her away on his motorcycle. Sitting on the bike, holding him, deafened by the blatting of the engine noise, she had been happy. But it was never Skip. The clerk who had taken her clothes away brought her food. How much time had gone by at this motel? A week or more. Pinky was hopeful when she saw that the clerk had brought her a Filipina and an older man. Pinky wore a bath towel that was folded and tucked like a costume from Palawan. The Filipina said in Tagalog, "I am Joey and this is my husband. I am from Ilocos Norte. Where are you from?"

As though nothing had happened in the meantime, and in her mind she wanted to believe that nothing had, Pinky told her the name of her district outside Cebu City.

"My husband wants to take pictures of us."

"That's it, get acquainted," the old man said. He took his video camera out of a suitcase.

"Please help me," Pinky said. "I want to leave this place."

While they were touching, Joey whispered her own story: the old man had married her but refused to help her family, would not bring her mother to the States and would not send money. Joey was an older woman, not pretty, but she knew how to speak to the man.

"I will see you tomorrow," Joey said. "Bring your passport and papers and a warm sweater."

The next day, the motel clerk said, "You're going with him." He gave her clothes to wear, then said to the old man, "I want her back here at eight. That's my busiest time."

At the house, which was a lovely place a half hour from the motel, on a street with other, similar houses, Joey welcomed Pinky. She gave her a drink of juice and showed her the bedroom. It was beautiful. The old man had set up a camera near the bed. Pinky turned away to take her clothes off. Hearing a crash, she turned and saw that the man had fallen over and dragged his camera with him. He lay on the floor with his mouth wide open.

Taking all the money from the man's wallet, Joey said, "He is asleep. I gave him something. Hurry, they will start looking for us when he wakes up."

Joey drove Pinky in the man's car and left it in a parking lot in a city. They walked to a bus station and bought tickets to Los Angeles. In the back of the bus, Pinky slept with her head resting against the warm woman, feeling grateful.

In Los Angeles they got jobs as cleaners in a hotel near the airport. The supervisor taught them to make beds and clean bathrooms. One morning a man entering the room Pinky was cleaning said to her, "Don't go." She knew that smell. She said softly, "I need money." The man locked the door and gave her twenty dollars, and she went to him, seeing him smile.

After that, whenever she saw a man alone in a room, she took her time cleaning or sweeping or polishing the mirror, and the man sometimes spoke to her. She said, "I need some money. Can you help me?" and almost always the man would lock the door and give her money and touch her or tell her to kneel. Forty dollars and sometimes more.

One day in one of the corridors a black woman ran toward her, and as Pinky smiled the woman slapped her face. That night, Pinky cried when she told Joey the story.

Joey said, "You deserved it. You're like her."

"I need the money. I am saving to go home."

"I am never going home," Joey said. "I am bringing my mother here."

Pinky was more fearful after the slap in the face, though she still lingered in the rooms. She could not understand why one man she smiled at got so angry that he reported her to the manager.

"She's a little whore! She propositioned me!" the man said when Pinky was brought to the manager's office. The manager said that he would deal with her. After the man had gone the manager called her a whore, and then he touched her and said, "Take your uniform off. It doesn't belong to you anymore." Pinky did as she was told. The manager then pushed her to the floor and sat on her. When he was finished, he said, "You're fired. Get out. Take this, too." Seeing that it was her uniform, she thanked him.

She had enough money for her ticket to the Philippines. Joey said goodbye. Pinky's mother, who was still in Manila, cried when she saw her daughter. Pinky's father had died. Her mother said, "Why aren't you crying?" Pinky didn't know. She never cried anymore. She didn't tell her mother that she had been to the United States. She applied for jobs. She said, "I have worked in hotels."

She became a maid in a hotel in Manila. The job was low paying and hard work. Her mother quit: she was very sick, too weak to work. Her Aunt Mariel said, "You are twenty — find a husband." Pinky put an ad in the paper, written by Aunt Mariel.

An American man answered the ad. She said to herself, I would marry him. But the man said, "I will make a video of you for my agency. It is the new way to find a husband. Maybe a foreigner."

He showed her one of the videos. It was an interview with a young Filipina.

"It costs two thousand, but if you have no money we can make other arrangements," the man said.

He photographed her naked on the bed. Then he said, "Put your clothes on," and he interviewed her.

She did not hear again from him. She turned twenty-one, still working at the hotel. Although Philippine hotels were dirtier than American ones and the work was harder, anything was better than being bitten by a man or trapped in a motel room and hearing a man's knock. For a year she sat and watched her mother die. Uncle Tony showed up and began visiting her at night. One of those nights, her mother died.

The week she started at Reception, with the Trainee badge, she got a letter from America — Buddy Hamstra, Hotel Honolulu notepaper. He said that he had seen her video. She had forgotten about the video. He would meet her in Manila.

Uncle Tony and Aunt Mariel went with her to Buddy's room. They slept on the floor, but she woke them at midnight, gave them some pesos, and sent them away. Buddy embraced her.

In the morning she begged Buddy to marry her.

He did, on the fourth floor of the Hotel Rizal, panting from the climb, complaining that the elevators weren't working. Aunt Mariel's friend had made all the arrangements. It took two months for Pinky to get her United States visa.

"Look," Buddy said to me. "An angel."

40

Hearts of Palm

THE CHRISTMAS CAROLS in Waikiki were being sung in Japanese. On the second-floor lanai, which contained the overspill from Paradise Lost, Buddy was comparing our Christmas decorations with those of the other hotels. I knew what was coming: the reminiscence of Santa Claus nailed to a cross, Mickey in a manger (a plastic saucer) surrounded by the Seven Dwarfs, Jesus wearing a Santa hood. "And last year — great!" The Japanese man next door in the Kodama had signed all the company Christmas cards and then jumped out the window, landing messily at the edge of the swimming pool.

"He thought he was being a good owner. Funny thing is, they had to send new cards."

"Holiday depression — I get it sometimes," Peewee said.

"Yeah, Christmas is always a ratfuck," Buddy said. "God, I hate those carols."

"I don't mind that one." Even sung in Japanese, it was clearly "Rudolph the Red-Nosed Reindeer." I said, "Something like 'In the Bleak Mid-Winter' never fails to undo me."

We could see the tops of the palm trees that fringed the beach, two streets and a row of hotels away. No Old Masters existed in our museums, but we had Turner sunsets and Titian heavens, and I remarked that at least the world's clouds have not changed in the planet's history — sometimes I imagined our skies as Renaissance ceilings.

When I pointed to the sky, Buddy muttered something about a new Ramada hotel going up near Fort DeRussy. He was a big bulky man who whenever he was idle was always leaning on something. His elbows rested on the railing and his hands cradled his cheeks.

"I love looking at the sultry fulguration of these skies," I said, just to try out the sound. But it didn't register with him. Just a noise I was making.

Keola said, "You so hybolic."

"Oh, yeah," Buddy said. "Hey, look at them palms."

I often stared at them too, thinking: South Seas dream, where the golden apples grow, balmy Paradiso, under the hula moon.

"Some good eating there."

I thought Buddy meant the tall sign on Kalakaua Avenue advertising the sushi bar, but no, he was still talking about the palm trees. Having seen them yanked down and their feathery fronds battered by hurricane winds — never uprooted but set gracefully upright again as soon as the wind eased — I came to regard palm trees as indestructible.

"You basically lop off the trunk and tear open the core. Chop it up. Pickle it in brine. It's awesome in salad. I had palms in my yard in Waimanalo. It looked clear-cut when I moved. I basically ate the whole yard."

To this fat man with lovely teeth, the memory of feasting on these tasty trees made his mouth juicy with saliva.

"Any palms in England?"

"No palms. Just qualms."

He queried me by squinting and opening his mouth. "What's the book?"

"This is Céline. *Journey to the End of the Night.*"

I read: *The human race is never free from worry, and since the last judgment will take place in the street, it's obvious that in a hotel you won't have so far to go. Let the trumpeting angels come, we hotel dwellers will be the first to get there.*

"That babe knows what she's talking about. I love to read," Buddy said. "Maybe I should read one of your books one of these days."

"Not necessary."

I was a little sensitive on this point. The week before, Sweetie had told one of the hotel guests I was a writer. I had specifically warned her about this. "Say 'hotel manager.'" It had the virtue of being true and was less of a mine field.

"Your wife tells me you're a writer," the guest said.

I smiled, dreading what was to come.

"Do you write under your own name?"

"Yes."

My name rang no bells, and yet, keen to demonstrate his love of reading, he recommended several books I saw in the hands of sunbathers whenever I strolled along the beach. My anonymity made me happy here, and I reflected on how in a touristy place, as one of the herd, no one ever gets to know your name, no one ever questions why you're there.

Some guests, seeing posters for the *Nutcracker,* said to me, "There's ballet here?"

"Indeed there is. Also opera and the Honolulu Symphony."

"We love shit like that," one guest declared.

I said, "Just because you see palm trees and barefoot residents tossing beer cans out of their car windows doesn't mean there's no cultural life."

But going to the ballet in Hawaii seemed to me ostentatious and vulgar, the height of philistinism, the very opposite of refinement. Give me barefoot beer drinkers and brainless surf bunnies any day. I hated talk of books. It embarrassed me when Buddy, who boasted of his barbarism, mentioned books in his unconvincing voice. I needed to talk to Peewee about his bread recipes. I liked hearing Buddy tell me something I didn't know about hearts of palm and how he ate his way through a half acre of them.

Sweetie considered herself an intellectual because she listened to the audio book of *Cujo* while she Rollerbladed.

Peewee said, "You must miss the big city."

I said no, truthfully. That I hated the foul air. That I was just one of the big mob, in my little slot, feeling tiny and hemmed in by huge buildings. That in big cities it was never dark and never silent.

"But the culture," he said. "Shows and concerts, like we only have at Christmas, and not even the real thing."

"You can carry it with you. Your recipes are culture, Peewee," I said. "And you know language is culture."

Peewee's girlfriend, Nani, said, "I got my own language. Pidgin."

Nani said, "More betta . . . talfone . . . bumbye . . . I never wen learn English." Keola, washing windows, smiled in comprehension, as heartily as if he were hearing music. But it was a sort of fractured birdsong, a debased and highly colloquial form of English composed of moody-sounding grunts and utterances and willful approximations. Everyone called it "Pidgin," and they said it was a separate language, like Portuguese or Greek — it wasn't English, they said. But it was, just a slovenly and ungrammatical version, never written down, without the verb "to be," and mostly used in the present tense. This helped, though, for they spoke nothing else but listened all the time, and in their squinting attention were used to translating what someone said on the basis of sound alone.

Nani said, "Why howlie heah. He *huhu?* Assa madda you — pickin' pines. No more nuttin' fo' do. Or udda ting. Dis howlie *lolo* he stay *kolohe.* But he *keiki* more bettah." She gasped. "Like dat."

I said, "Would you say there are any verbs in this language?"

She looked insulted. "You fucking with me?"

"In that sentence, 'fucking' is a verb. In this one, 'is' is a verb."

"Peewee, man, this howlie fucking with me," she said. "So you pretty hybolical."

Peewee said, "Try wait, Nani."

She said, "Why he went for see you, was."

I said, "A linguist would say there is no overt verb "to be." That's a type of defocused sentence with a postposed 'was.'"

"Hybolical," Nani said again.

Peewee said, "I told some people I knew you. They were like, 'Hey, he's famous.' They want to meet you."

But I declined. So, on Christmas Eve, I was left with Buddy, Peewee, Nani, my pretty wife and daughter, and several guests at our annual party, on the second-floor lanai outside Paradise Lost.

I said, "I'm through with books. Some are just junk and I get sad when I see them."

"Books are good," Peewee said.

"It's Christmas," I said. "I'd rather talk about birds. Or turtles. Or the sea. I saw a whale last year from the roof."

Peewee said, "Nani saw some dolphins yesterday."

Nani heard her name and said, "We got so many frikken birds we no know their name. But like in Whyan a turkey no gobble-gobble. He *kolo-kolo.* And Whyan Santa Claus is Kana Kaloka."

I smiled and told myself that an ignoramus was preferable to a pseudointellectual. Some hotel guests spent hours telling me the plots of books they liked. Others, returning overdressed from a local production of the *Nutcracker,* lorded it over the tourists gaping at our Happy Hour hula.

"I wanted to call her Taylor, but my husband said no," Sweetie was telling one of the Christmas party guests.

"Taylor means tailor," I said. "It seems inauspicious. Like calling her Cobbler."

"That's a kind of drink," Nani said.

"Logan is a real nice name," Sweetie said. "Or Shannon. Next kid maybe."

"Shannon is Irish," I said.

"I got some Irish in me," Buddy said. He was peeling the foil from a platter of salad. "The crazy side. Also the strong side. Go ahead, have some."

"You know what's really incredulous?" Peewee said, picking up a white disk from the salad and eating it. "The way they treat prisoners. Hey, they should put them destructive guys in mailbags and line them up in Aloha Stadium one morning and get big fat Samoan women to beat the bags with baseball bats. If a guy woulda lost his life, they'd take it more serious."

"Them trees are making him hungry and driving him nuts," Buddy said.

"Don't laugh, you'll be joining me." Sniffing the pine boughs, Peewee burst into tears. "That's the smell of my childhood," he said. "We were real poor."

No one was listening. I was murmuring, "Shtrong. Morneen. Makeen. Driveen. Joineen. Dee-shtructive. If he woulda lost his life."

Laughing, Sweetie said, "Sometimes I see him writing. I go, 'What you doing?' He goes, 'Nothing.'"

She had not said this to me before in the almost seven years I had been married to her. She could only say it in front of other people; she felt protected by them. They were witnesses, and her people. Unlike our daughter, Sweetie was afraid of me.

"I never know what's going on in his head. He real high maintenance."

I was looking west, toward the beach. I said, "I bought some Christmas lights for the palm tree out front."

Buddy said, "I put that palm tree in this salad."

41

Mr. and Mrs. Sun

EOPLE IN THE HOTEL said, "They hold hands," and always smiled because Mr. and Mrs. Sun were in their late forties and rather plain and well past the hand-holding stage of marriage. Even some of our honeymooners didn't do it. The Suns had chubby hands like gloves, which made the hand-holding noticeable. I liked saying, "So what?" The hugging and clasping was less interesting to me than the Irish names of their children, Kevin and Ryan, very skinny kids, a different physical type altogether. Plump parents usually had plump kids. This seemed to be breaking some fundamental family rule. The other thing was, their kids were famous brats.

The first year — my first year, their fifth or more — the Suns came without their children. After that, they brought them. While the parents were model guests, the two boys had a reputation for trouble. One was destructive, the other a thief. "Attention seeking" was one of the kinder explanations for their behavior. I liked the hand-holding Suns without in the least understanding their children. They were from San Francisco, Chinese Americans.

Soon after I arrived in Hawaii, I had reflected on how the sunlight here was so dazzling, it gave us the conceit that we were virtuous and pure and better than other people. Everywhere else on earth was worse — people got sick and cold on the mainland and had to wear socks, Africa was poor, China was overcrowded, Europe was senile, and the rest of the world was dark. We took personal credit for our sunshine and expected gratitude from strangers for sharing it with them. This Hawaiian heresy was dangerous, for it made us complacent about the damage we did to these little crumbly islands. We were so smug about our sunshine, we were blind to everything else, as if we had been staring at the sun too long.

Nevertheless, I found Sun a lovely, bright, open-faced name. More American than Chinese, Calvin and Amelia were quiet people, and I had not paid much attention my first year because I had mistaken them for middle-aged lovers, for whom no one else existed. On their visit my second year, I still saw them as distant, inward, happy, compliant, practically magnetized lovers, but also realized they were the parents of two disruptive teenage boys.

In spite of the staff's warning the boys for a week about various infractions, one night they had thrown furniture into the hotel pool.

I was checking to see that the chairs and tables had been fished out when I found a soggy book lying on the tiles. It had been badly splashed, an early edition of Michener's *Hawaii,* and although the inked inscription was blotchy with water, the handwriting was so upright and enthusiastic I could easily read it: *To my dear husband, to commemorate ten years of the greatest happiness I have ever known. May the future shine as brightly upon us and let our joy be endless! Your adoring wife, A.* And a date.

Apart from the old-fashioned and impossible-to-mock romantic gusto, and the date — five years before — I was struck by the joyous penmanship, the exclamation mark as bold and expressive as a Chinese brushstroke. The book was nothing special, but the inscription made it a trophy.

"That thing down there with legs is one table," Keola said to me. "Something like one occasional table."

He meant the dark object at the deep end that the young fools had thrown in with the chairs and ashtrays and cushions.

"What did you say, Keola?"

I loved hearing him repeat it, the unexpected precision of "occasional." The wooden table, now split and ruined, was from a guest room.

"Them Sun kids again," Peewee said. "I know what I'd do with them."

We had the weird vitality of spectators at a disaster, and stood marveling at the wreckage, watching the junk being hoisted, hoping there were no corpses.

"Burlap sacks," Peewee said. "Samoan women. Baseball bats."

I went upstairs to the Suns' room and knocked. I heard a soft voice: "I'll get it, darling."

Mrs. Sun answered the door. Her husband was in a chair across the room, holding a book. Another chair had been drawn up next to it. It was lovers, mostly, who pushed chairs together like this, or (also like the Suns) who moved the nightstand and pushed the twin beds cheek to cheek. Lovers were habitual rearrangers of furniture.

"Yes?"

I never spoke to the Suns without feeling I was intruding on their intimacy and perfect peace.

"We've had another complaint about your boys."

Mrs. Sun looked so sorrowful I found myself apologizing and eager to get away, suddenly finding the vandalism trivial compared to my disturbing the happiness of this wonderful couple. Mr. Sun set his book down. They both looked abject. How many times had they been put in the position of having to be sorry and make amends?

Mrs. Sun said, "I'll ask my husband to speak to them. Of course we will pay for any damage."

"The patio furniture isn't a problem. There was some breakage, though," I said. "And a guest room table will have to be replaced or refinished. It ties up Maintenance when these things happen."

"I know it has happened before because of our boys," Mrs. Sun said — something I had planned to say.

"Are they around?"

"Across the hall."

She knocked. No answer. I knocked, then used my master key. But by then Mr. Sun had called to her with affection and concern, and she was now back in their room with the door shut.

The boys were out, but judging from the condition of the room, Maintenance and Housekeeping would have some work to do: broken mirror, broken blinds, spills on the carpet, footprints on the wall (*on the wall?*), and that was only what I saw from the doorway, peering in.

"That's nothing," Trey said later. "A few years ago they trashed the bar. Buddy went ballistic."

One boy was a drunk, the other smoked dope, Trey said, but admitted he did not know which was which. It didn't matter. They were a year apart, fourteen and fifteen. In the second week of their vacation the older one was caught stealing from a convenience store, and the younger one was picked up for vandalizing a public telephone. Because of their ages, no charges were filed. The boys were left in the custody of their parents, which was meaningless because I never saw the four Suns together. The children were seldom around.

One day the Suns volunteered the information that they were just returning from St. Andrew's, the church in which they had been married. Their visits to Hawaii were always planned around their wedding anniversary.

They were, as always, holding hands. Mr. Sun tugged his wife's hand with such affection that I was moved.

"I can see that the romance hasn't gone out of your marriage," I said.

"It never will," Mr. Sun said.

Is a marriage a family? Mr. and Mrs. Sun were inseparable, utterly devoted to each other, quiet, and kind, their love creating a magnetic field of orderly flowing energy between them. The flow neither attracted nor repelled anyone else. No one else was magnetized, no one else mattered.

They left, all of them. The following Christmas, on a sunny afternoon, one boy shot himself in a motel in Great Falls, Montana. The other boy moved to Seattle. I didn't know which boy did which.

42

Henry James in Honolulu

IT WAS ONE OF the many moments in my life when I whispered to myself, "Where am I?" — in the larger sense. In the smaller sense, I knew I was smiling in impatience at my two symmetrical scoops of macaroni salad on King Kalakaua Night at the Honolulu Elks Lodge in Waikiki with my wife, Sweetie, as a guest of Lester Chen, my number-two man, and his new wife, Winona. "My kine no go shtrait," I heard. They were discussing in-line skates — were they bad for your ankles? I was also thinking how the plain truth like a sentence about this setting resembled the first line of a poem to which there is seldom a second line.

The boast of the Honolulu Elks was that they were next door to the much classier Outrigger Canoe Club. An Elk could walk out to the beach and bump into an Outrigger. There was just such an Outrigger in a blazer and a Panama hat standing on this shared margin of beach, staring at the sunset. I envied that dapper man for his belonging to this beach and not thinking, Where am I? Or so I presumed.

For myself, I was somewhere I had never been before, nor ever read about, nor knew anything of.

"There was an Elks Lodge next to the Washington School in Medford, Massachusetts, when I was growing up," I said. "I never saw a single *Homo sapiens* enter or leave. Beautiful building, though, and a profound mystery to me."

One of those perplexed silences ensued, of the sort created by someone in a chatty group suddenly lapsing into echolalia or the gabble of a foreign language. The others looked away from me. Sweetie left for the buffet. Was it "*Homo sapiens*"?

"Everything kind of one mystery when you one *keiki,* yah?" Lester said. He was at his most banal when he attempted to be aphoristic in order to shut down a conversation. He had the Chinese hatred of direct questions, seeing them as a personal challenge, fearful of the conflict they might create. "This club also mysterious, okay?"

Who am I? was my next question, but also in a larger sense.

"You Sweetie husband!" Winona said to me, like someone just waking up. "I hear about you." She turned to a purple shrunken woman seated behind her. "He Sweetie husband!"

We were all badly dressed and barefoot in loose loud shirts and shorts like big misshapen children. Yet the meal was strangely formal and adult, even ceremonial, with two long speeches in the middle of it, and loyal toasts, and a strict order of courses — dinner at half past five, the setting sun glaring into my translucent macaroni salad, making it glow.

The grotesque novelty of the situation baffled me and made me suspect it might be significant. What was new to me always seemed important. If this scene had been written, I had not read it. But how could it have been written in this green illiterate world, and by whom?

In the unreality of being a solitary witness are intimations of dementia. You wonder where to begin. Maybe it is a fever? I had believed that writing hallowed a place, established the setting as solid, palpable, credible. The place bulked, it had color, you believed it. An unwritten-about place seemed invisible until it was described by someone made confident by imagination. People grew up on a little island or in a small town and felt they had to leave home to find a place to write about, a "real" place, Chicago or New York or Paris, because their little home didn't exist or wasn't visible to the naked eye. Other writers had made the great cities real.

Yet long after I left Medford, I was encouraged to believe in the existence of my hometown when I read Henry James's story "A Ghostly Rental." The haunted house was located in a part of Medford not far from the Elks Lodge. I was reminded of what Lester Chen had just said.

"This club was mysterious in what way?"

"Exclusive," Chen said. "Okay?"

"You mean expensive?"

"Not expensive but strick," he said. "We could not join, okay?"

I took the "we" to mean Chinese. He hated these questions.

"When did the Elks allow you to join?"

"Not for a long time. Okay?"

"Statehood?"

"After that." He shook his head and said peevishly to Winona, "Okay, when that old lady try get take the bus?"

"Which old lady? Which bus?" I asked.

"In Alabama," Winona said. "Yah?"

I said, "Rosa Parks?"

"Yah."

"She was already on the bus. She wouldn't change her seat."

Rosa Parks helped integrate the Honolulu Elks? In the course of this halting revelation, Sweetie had come back from the buffet with a full plate — a scoop of sticky rice, two slabs of Spam looking like a pair of pink epaulettes, a dill pickle, cold clotted potato salad, a dish of gluey poi, a broken and buttered muffin, a glass of fruit punch, a bowl of Jell-O with fruit chunks suspended in it.

Winona said, "She eating ethnic."

Sweetie had heard the end of the conversation. She said, "The people in a club don't want you for join, and you want join? How that make sense, yah?"

Sick of the subject, Chen turned his back on us and said, "The sunset. Like for make a picture."

The western sky was like an amateur painting, one of those behind-the-sofa pictures on black velvet — garish and overly simple, fatuous, too much of it all at once, the sun too round, the ocean too wide, too yellow. Most clouds become two-dimensional at sunset. All this sunset lacked were dancing dolphins and a three-masted schooner, I was thinking, and just then I *saw* a three-masted schooner, a dinner cruise, sailing into the liquefied light of the bright brimming ocean, preceded by dolphins spinning and flopping like badly behaved kids in a pool.

Stifled by the unreality of this, too, like a florid dream brought on by indigestion, I went outside and joined the man in the Panama hat. He was mustached, small, precise, smiling slightly at this hundred-egg omelet of nature being beaten into the sea.

"The red light breaking at the close from under a low somber sky, reached out in a long shaft," the man said, seeming to quote, and gesturing at the shaft, "and played over old wainscots, old tapestry, old gold, old color."

"I was thinking how the sunset is sort of liquefied on the sea and dissolving into the chop of the waves."

"Tessellated, more like," he said, nodding. "Rubious. Effulgent. And the languid lisp of the Pacific."

I stared at him as though at a brave brother voyager from our old planet. He still wore his half-smile. I liked the neatness of his appearance and imagined him wearing a monocle.

"There you are," Sweetie said, walking from the Elks' lanai, raising her knees and having to take dance steps because of the deep beach sand. "Time for the prizes, Dad."

She looked very pretty, her hair blown by the sea breeze, giggling as she balanced in the sand. Part Chinese, part Irish, and part Hawaiian, she had big dark staring eyes and the smooth chinless face of a seal pup.

"I'm like a basket case," Sweetie said, and laughed. "Ate too much!"

"It's King Kalakaua Night," I said.

The man looked seaward again. "The honest, dusky unsophisticating night."

"Good grinds," Sweetie said. "Kinda hard for me. These grinds made by my peers. They got expertise!"

"We're guests of the Chens," I said. "Lester's an Elk."

"Now he's on skateboards," Sweetie said.

"My wife, Ku'uipo," I said to the man, who gallantly touched his hat brim.

"May I see your watch?" the man asked.

Sweetie's watch, a gift from Buddy, showed a hula dancer, her arms the watch's hands.

"One has a dilettante's interest in horology," the man said.

"Everyone says that about the hula, but it's not true — this is *pono*, this is righteous," Sweetie said.

The man turned to me and said, "We must meet for luncheon."

"Luncheon" clinched for me what "tessellated" and "rubious" had clinched for him: he was certainly a fellow inhabitant from our distant galaxy. Among these islander earthlings, we were two travelers who had met by accident, and in spite of looking like everyone else, we were unquestionably extraterrestrials. No one else knew this, yet instantly we recognized the nuances and were able to communicate in our old, strange multisyllabic tongue, a secret and subtle language spoken by no one under the palm trees here.

We exchanged our full names — another habit from the old planet — and I realized I was talking with Leon Edel, the biographer of Henry James. Edel, whom I had heard about, had been living in relative obscurity in Hawaii for many years. He said he knew my name.

"And I know yours."

"My friends on the mainland all think I'm crazy," he said.

"Mine think I'm dead," I said. "Have no idea where I am. If they knew, they'd say I'm crazy."

"They don't know what they're talking about." He touched his hat brim in farewell.

"We're not crazy. This is the place."

I resumed my seat in the Elks and whispered my question again, for the pleasure of knowing the answer.

43

Rocket Men

"I HAD NO IDEA you were here too," Leon Edel said. That "too" was nice and made me feel I mattered. I volunteered that I was here as a hotel manager. He was tactful enough not to inquire further, and when he pointedly asked whether I happened to be working on anything, I just smiled. Not wishing to talk about writing is easy for another writer to understand, and a writer's not writing is more natural to another writer than writing is.

"I'm thinking of a book, titled *Who I Was*," I said.

"Yes, yes, yes."

I met him at the Outrigger for lunch, so as to keep our friendship secret from my hotel people. Even his calling this meal "luncheon" would have made them squint in suspicion.

"Call it work in stoppage."

Because we met as two people who felt a little strange and hidden here, we found it natural to confide in each other. We sat by the sea, eating salad, sipping iced tea. Leon was eighty-seven, my father's age, though my father was gone. One of those rare men who could be a stand-in for my father, Leon was precious for his age and his kindness. He was also wise. And it was a pleasure just to sit with him and talk about our wonderful old planet.

"Your wife is lovely," Leon said, interrupting himself.

"Yes, a coconut princess. Maybe a little provincial."

"She's a provincial of genius. She's life itself," Leon said. "She's for the bright rich world of bribes and rewards."

After that, we changed the subject to Hawaii, but in effect it was the same subject, for Hawaii, like Sweetie, was beautiful and healthy and fresh. You could be so happy in Hawaii's embrace you did not notice what was missing.

"James once spoke of a void furnished with 'velvet air.'"

"Did he know anything of the tropics?"

"Florida," Leon said. He raised a finger to make a Jamesian point. "You could live in Florida with an idea, he said, 'if you are content that your idea shall consist of grapefruits and oranges.'" Leon let this sink in. I could see the named fruit in a cut-glass bowl. "Also he was in San Diego. Coronado Beach. That's where 'lisp of the Pacific' comes from."

"Would he like it here?"

"We like it here," Leon said with assurance, a perfect way of saying yes: Henry James would love Hawaii, because we did.

"He'd dine out more than we do."

"Probably every night. He would see into every corner. He would use the pulses of the air. He would know people we don't. Doris Duke, the Hawaiian royalty, the way Stevenson did. Stevenson drank champagne with King Kalakaua. James would have found his way. Hobnobbed a little, cultivated the right people, and perhaps some of the wrong people too."

Henry James in a billowing aloha shirt approached us as Leon spoke, seeming to conspire, speculating about another inhabitant of our world. I listened closely because I wondered how much of this description fitted me and my living here. James with plump sunburned jowls, in island attire, his stout Johnsonian shape, short pale legs, round belly, big busy bum and fluttering hands, breathlessly stammering one of his inimitable voice-overs in Waikiki, indicating the throngs of tourists and the effulgent clouds, followed by his panting dog, Tosca.

That day I went back to the Hotel Honolulu and found Keola on the front steps, stabbing an ice pick into a block of blue ice.

I said, "Shouldn't you be doing that in the kitchen?"

"Bull-liar bitches talk stink about me."

"Do it later, then."

"Later I go for lawnmower da grass."

The next time I saw Leon I said, "What would James have made of the locals?"

"He would have been attentive to them, as he was attentive to everyone. Some of them he would have called 'ragged and rudimentary.' Maybe he would have mentioned their 'robust odor . . . thick and resisting.'"

He might have said that of many of my employees. So, strange as it was, I began to see my life in this way, as an alien in an aloha shirt, looking at Hawaii through dark glasses, measuring my impressions against James's. Leon helped me understand it. Worthy of James in every way, he had immersed himself in the master's life like a monk in the steps of a lama on the path to enlightenment.

Once a week, "luncheon" in our old language, we talked about our former lives. We mused without regret, knowing that we really belonged back there but had succeeded in slipping away. Leon was a whole happy person, with a power to evoke our old home. I got sentimental being with him, discussing things the hotel knew nothing of.

He said, "New York was so busy, so crowded."

I said, "I love looking at the empty sea. The echolalia of the waves."

He didn't wince at the word. He said, "This is a fresh little Eden. Rather new and enigmatic, perhaps, but that's the price."

He might have been describing Sweetie.

"I came to see London as clammy and ugly. All those bomb sites. Budget-conscious buildings. Twice-breathed air. I hated having to wait a whole year for spring to return."

"I used to go back to New York several times a year," Leon said. "Then it was once a year. Now I've stopped going. I don't envision ever going back."

His saying that encouraged me to think that we could stay for good on this green island. Hawaii was at the center of our friendship, and Henry James in it — Henry in a hibiscus-print shirt from Hilo Hattie's. Hawaii was beautiful, and its genius lay in its look, like a new flower opening, like a starfish cluster of fragile fluttering petals, whose bright primary colors gave it an air of unselfconsciousness and false innocence.

We admitted that New York and London, ugly and crowded and clammy as they might be, were full of life. They were home, they were human, everyone spoke our language there.

"Nudda drink, uncle?"

"I believe I have had a sufficiency," Leon said.

"Nuh?"

One luncheon day Buddy Hamstra saw us. He was with Pinky, who had become famous for always biting him on the forearm while he drove to town. The scars were as purple and permanent as tattoos. Now he called attention to them and used them as a boast to introduce his wife. See this?, he'd say.

"Getting any mud for your turtle?" Buddy tapped me on the shoulder and shouted at Leon, "He wrote a book!"

"He wrote a book too," I said, indicating Leon.

"Two of them!" Buddy said to Pinky, who giggled into her cupped hand. "Two whole books!"

After they left, I said, "Maybe Hawaii is now what London and Paris were for Americans in the late nineteenth century. A place to vanish in and become corrupted."

"Not here — not corrupted here."

"Become idle, maybe. Eating grapefruits and oranges."

He laughed and quoted Thoreau, another of his biographical subjects. The reach of Leon's knowledge amazed me — the books he had read, the writers he had known, snaking deep into the past. Many of those writers lived at the height of the nineteenth century and were acquaintances of James, including Edith Wharton, whom Leon had known a little, and her lover Morton Fullerton, whom he had known well. He had been a student in Paris in the late twenties. He had returned as a soldier in newly liberated Paris, had met Hemingway, whom he had not liked, and had been on the best of terms with Edmund Wilson, whose diaries he'd edited. He knew Bloomsbury and had written about it. With all this erudition there was a sweetness in the man, and even at his most intellectually severe you could see his sentiment and the depth of his love — loved his wife, loved books, loved Hawaii, loved life. Leon was the happy man I hoped to be at his age, sitting in the sunshine at the Outrigger Canoe Club.

Familial rivalry was a constant subject with us, because he had a twin and I had many siblings, and Henry had William. "My younger and shallower and vainer brother," William had written confidentially to the secretary of the American Academy of Arts and Letters, declining to be a member.

James was the third person at our table or on the lanai, but he was not always a whole, round, upright man, smiling between puffs on a cigarette. He was kindly and wounded. Sometimes he was supine, a patient undergoing an operation, half his skull drilled out and removed, his belly cut open, the contents of his stomach — all those rich dinners — in a big enamel hospital bowl, his "obscure hurt" visible as a scrotal bruise, his mouth gaping. His bowels were a wreck. He was now and then on a couch, as Leon recalled his breakdowns, his sadness, his panic attacks, how he could not bear to be alone.

Leon could quote the sad paragraph James had written to Morton Fullerton, who had asked blandly, in the French manner, how he had begun — from what port.

"The port from which I set out was, I think, that of the essential loneliness of my life — and it seems to be the port also, in sooth, to which my course again finally directs itself!"

And Leon could go on to the end, in the piteous description of the man from our homeland.

"He knew what it was like to feel unwanted," Leon said.

James's story "The Beast in the Jungle" — Leon had quoted the sunset sentence from the beginning of it the evening we met on the beach — said almost everything about his disappointment and the way he had yearned for a great passion. Yet passion had eluded him. He had mistimed it, as Marcher does in the story. His advice to "live all you can" Leon and I had heeded. Leon, in a sense Henry James's valet — forever sorting and seeing to his things — was a man without regret. He had fallen in love in Hawaii, married a woman he loved, found happiness here. I had done the same. Hadn't we lived all we could? Being in Hawaii had so far taken me from my writing, yet I was living in a way I never had, in a green world, far from home.

"I like it here, but I don't write much," I said to Leon on one of those Outrigger days.

"As you get older you write less. Look at me. I write an hour a day. Sometimes half an hour."

"I don't write at all," I said, breathless from the sudden confession, and at once felt like someone disclosing the symptom of an illness.

He smiled at me like a doctor with a patient who was ill but not seriously so. And in the manner of a doctor suggesting exercise and a change of diet, Leon prescribed for me a regimen of James stories: "The Altar of the Dead," "The Lesson of the Master," "The Middle Years," "The Death of the Lion," "The Figure in the Carpet," "The Real Thing."

"Read the work that James wrote when he was your age, a hundred years ago."

Locked in my office in the Hotel Honolulu, hidden from my staff, I read the stories. They helped, but still I didn't write. Maybe once you stopped, you dried up and there was nothing more.

We still met regularly for lunch, Leon and I, above the hot beach, under the blue sky that made the sea so blue, for the pleasure of speaking in our own language of the beauty of this island.

"For years I thought about James's stories," Leon said. "Then one day it came to me. His stories were his fantasies. Each of them a separate one. Read them all and you have the man's inner life. Perhaps all short stories are fantasies."

"I used to write them," I said.

Under a sky of Mediterranean azure, shot through with the shafts of dusty gold you see in Renaissance paintings, everything imaginable in the huge sky, even cherubic clouds, everything but a risen Savior; within earshot of the lisp of the sea, the slosh of little waves brimming at the beach, we sat in the watery light, in the velvet air, feasting on grapefruits and oranges. With Leon I was happier than I had ever been, but away from him I felt a new sadness, and now my nonwriting life at the hotel was almost unbearable.

44

The Real Thing

She had descended upon us and made us conscious of our frailty, I wrote, but before I could put a title over this first line of my story, I was called to Reception for the awkward ritual of a celebrity check-in: Jesse Shavers, the actor, very tall, very bald, very black, his monosyllabic responses giving him a dignified hauteur.

Presiding over this time-wasting ceremony, I remembered how the day before, facing just this way, I had seen a woman — the subject of my proposed story — plodding through the lobby with her head down. This woman, who had sadly turned to Rose and snatched her up, was perfect. "Your daughter's got conjunctivitis!" she had said, a sudden and precise diagnosis. I had gotten used to hotel guests making demands, but here was one who offered some shrewd medical advice. She said she knew what she was talking about. Her name was Monica Thrall, and she looked unwell herself. Under the influence of a Henry James story I had just read, I decided to write a short story based on her and, I suppose, the fear of my daughter's falling ill. After the Jesse Shavers interruption I returned to my office and wrote "The Real Thing" in block letters at the top of the page.

Monica Thrall had been furious with me. "How can you treat your daughter this way? If she thinks you don't care about her health, she might do something really terrible. Don't you see that?"

She was so passionate and sad, and her abuse of me so urgent and emotional, I ordered flowers for her. But her anger was the point. The woman with the Jamesian name had descended upon us and made us conscious of our frailty. And she had been right. I got the eye drops and soon Rose stopped rubbing her eyes and smiled more.

"I try deliver the flowers again?" Marlene asked — no knock. I looked up from my blank pad. "Could not deliver yesterday. Was a Do Not Disturb sign on her door."

I nodded for her to complete the errand and thought how I should have just such a warning sign on my door, so I could write my short story about a middle-aged woman from Gary, Indiana, who casually diagnoses a rare illness in another hotel guest and thus saves his life. Had these two strangers not been in the same hotel, the man would have died. Never mind the Do Not Disturb sign — I couldn't even close my office door. I was on duty. Someone might need me.

One of the contradictions of writing a short story in Hawaii — something I had never before attempted — was that I could do it only when I was working. Writing was impossible in the cramped two-room suite I shared upstairs with my wife and child. It annoyed me that while my six-year-old daughter had a desk there, I did not.

The nurse in my story needed a new name and a new hometown. I was so out of practice in writing stories that I could not imagine improving on her reality. There was no better name for her than Monica Thrall, no better hometown than Gary, Indiana. The alternatives I thought of sounded false and fabricated. So I began writing, describing the woman who had seen Rose's eye problem, but in this story I imagined that she would be sitting by the pool and watching a woman in a bikini, and from years of observation would detect on the woman's almost naked body the symptoms of a rare form of melanoma. Or was she in an elevator, diagnosing the other riders?

Seeing Trey approach my office door, looking grim, I slid a sheet of paper over the first sentence of "The Real Thing," as though concealing a love letter to my mistress.

"Boss, we got a problem poolside," Trey said, walking into my office without any hesitation. "A guest upstairs just phoned down that he could see there's some people balling in the pool. They seen his peepee."

"Tell the fornicators in question to stop it."

"I did. They just give me stink-eye."

Sometimes at night there were such complaints, but this was a first for me — a couple screwing in the hotel swimming pool at five-thirty in the afternoon, in broad daylight, in full view of the Happy Hour customers, who seemed to be enjoying the wet spectacle from the Paradise Lost lanai. I recognized the couple, because at check-in they had asked about renting a motorcycle in Honolulu. While Chen made the phone call, the man had shown me some snapshots of his Harley, the way other people flashed pictures of their children. The woman seemed equally proud of the bike. One of *those* couples, with unimaginative tattoos, eager for attention, now locked together at the deep end, the woman's back against the far corner of the pool, her white legs encircling him in an animal grip, her heels pressing his hairy back. The man's submerged and rotating buttocks glowed plum blue in the cloud-filled water like a monkey's bum.

"I'm afraid I'm going to have to ask you to go inside," I said.

"You got a problem, pal?" The man was obviously drunk. "Stink-eye" said it all.

"Not me. Blame the Board of Health. You're not in compliance with the guidelines. I have to cite you for health code violations." And before he could interrupt me, I said, "Glass beverage containers are forbidden poolside" — a dozen scattered bottles of Corona beer, most of them empty — "and you're not suitably attired. You need bathing suits."

Disconcerted by my obliqueness, the man said, "How can I do this in a bathing suit?"

"Try it upstairs in your room."

My standing there whistling, fully clothed, with my back turned, supervising Trey as he collected the clinking beer bottles, seemed to make the couple self-conscious. They swore and splashed and went away, wrapped in towels, as the Happy Hour customers hooted and whistled.

Back in my office, I resumed my story. The woman, Monica Thrall, came from Gary, where — maybe she was a nurse? — on buses and commuter trains she had developed the habit of diagnosing the other passengers — observing their eyes, the texture of their skin, their tremulous fingers. As this paragraph took shape, the phone rang.

"Doesn't anyone speak English in this hotel?"

"Thanks for your inquiry. I'll have someone in Hospitality help you."

"Hey, I just got a hand job from them and now I'm getting a hand job from you."

The guest, a Mr. Gordie Steen from Orange County, California, was elderly, cranky, and like many other complainers merely wanted a listener to his grievances, which I took to be racist. The ignorant obsession with foreign accents is nearly always racist.

Miss Thrall swept into the hotel elevator and swiftly assessed the other occupants, all of them wearing bathing suits. Because people in elevators do not look each other in the eye, she was able to size them up. One had conjunctivitis, another arthritic hands and deep facial creases from years of smoking. This one panted — terrible circulation. One man's eyes had gone yellow.

"Man want to see you," Marlene said, waving a bouquet of flowers. Before she could finish, the man barged past her, gabbling in fury.

"My fiancée's just been abducted," he said. He was stout, about forty, big and pale, but misshapen, almost lopsided, in a way that suggested weakness in spite of his large size.

"The sign's still up," Marlene said. My head was so full it took me a moment to understand that they were Miss Thrall's flowers, the real Miss T. in the hotel, and the Do Not Disturb sign was still on her doorknob.

Filling my doorway, the big agitated man said, "We're in the bar and she starts talking to this black guy. He's an actor. She's seen him on *Oprah*. Very articulate. Next thing I know she's gone, and so is he."

"How is that possible?"

"I didn't see them. I was looking at those two bozos fucking in the pool." He chewed his lips, suddenly embarrassed by this crass admission. "I thought you handled the situation very well. Now will you please get my fiancée out of this guy's room?"

"You could knock."

"There's a sign. Do Not Disturb."

The man was afraid, and who wouldn't be? Jesse Shavers was known for his violent roles. "I'll pinch your fucking head off" was one of his better-known lines. If the man had truly thought his wife was in danger, he would have knocked or called the police. His fear was, of course, that his fiancée was enjoying herself.

"I can't help you," I said. "Marlene here will tell you that we never enter a room where there's a sign up. She's been trying to deliver some flowers for two days to just such a room."

"I gave her a ten-thousand-dollar engagement ring! Tell her I want it back!"

"I'll put Mr. Shavers's message light on," I said. "We can't intrude unless it's an emergency."

"What do you call this?"

"Your fiancée is in another guest's room, probably in bed, probably naked. What do you suppose we call it?"

Perhaps I had gone too far. Squinting with his grief-swollen eyes was the man's way of stopping his tears. He left my office as lopsidedly as he had entered.

Marlene said, "So, what about the flowers?"

"Try again later."

I resumed my story. I wrote four lines: Miss Thrall was still in the elevator, peering at the strange color of the guest's eyes, seeing jaundice, perhaps kidney failure. How I hated to invent.

I got no further. The stink-eye couple I had banished from the pool were now making so much noise in their room that guests down the hall from them were complaining. I put my story away — the two paragraphs, the borrowed title; hardly a story — and went upstairs. There was no sign on the doorknob of the noisy motorcyclists' room, but something else caught my eye. They were next door to Miss Thrall's room. She had not complained of the noise. Her sign was still hung as Marlene had said, but there was a more telling sign of trouble: two newspapers lay stacked in front of the door. That meant she had not left the room for two days. This, in sunny Honolulu, was unthinkable.

I used my master key and saw her motionless in bed as soon as I entered. She was dead, already ripe. There seemed to be drug paraphernalia on her bedside table. There was no note. Dr. Miyazawa, Buddy's doctor, said she had given herself an overdose of insulin. It was the most efficient way of taking your life. She had to have been a doctor or nurse herself, Doctor Kim was saying in my office, as I put my tiny fragment of a story aside and wrote my shocking statement for the police.

45

Camera Obscura

THE ONLY PORTRAIT OF Wayne Godbolt that was ever painted by his brother, Will, hung in the Honolulu Academy of Arts for a week before it was removed one morning without explanation. At about the same time, Will flew to Honolulu from his Big Island home and quietly checked into my hotel under an assumed name — strangely enough, his brother's name. I had no idea who these brothers were, but Buddy happened to see Will, and it was he who told me all about them. Their family history was part of the oral tradition of Hawaii.

The sighting of Will at the hotel made me want to see the painting, and it was on that visit to the museum that I discovered it had been removed. A security guard told me that it was being held in a dark room somewhere downtown. "That's appropriate," I said. This man, with the name Balabag on his ID badge, opened his mouth wide, just dropped his jaw, his way of showing incomprehension, something Buddy did all the time. The portrait was called *Camera Obscura*.

What made the removal shocking was that Wayne had died so recently, and that he and his brother, the photographer and the painter, were so loving toward each other, like twins on a mission. Will's paintings had a fanatical exactitude that was photographic; Wayne's photographs were impressionistic — cloudy, airbrushed, meddled with in the darkroom, with a ghostly and abstract liquefaction.

The painting that had been on view in Honolulu showed Wayne in a darkroom holding his old-fashioned camera. The composition had a scumbled background of glossy maroon-dark paint that was so blistered it made you think of dead beetles and brittle wings. Wayne's eye, just a brush stroke, stared like a camera's lens. An unmade bed, stark as a sacrificial altar, was part of the foreground, but the glossy blistered color dominated. On the Academy wall one day, gone the next. What had happened?

"I'm a vegetarian, he's a cannibal," Will had said of Wayne, the painter brother of the photographer brother. "It's why we're able to love each other."

Will was known on the mainland, and his work sold there; Wayne was not, so his work didn't. That was Hawaii's test of artistic talent and success, though the distance was merciful: because we were in the middle of the ocean, we were unaware of the further fortunes of anyone enjoying celebrity on the mainland. Local people seemed to disappear when they went there, even when they were enjoying great success. Hawaii residents with great reputations on the mainland — W. S. Merwin, Leon Edel — were mostly faceless and unspoken of here. Will Godbolt's paintings were better known in New York than in Honolulu.

The wordy label stuck to the Academy wall explained that a camera was a room as well as a photographer's instrument, and a camera obscura was a simple device for viewing. The label also mentioned the closeness of the two artistic brothers, how they had been raised by their mother in the most fertile part of the Big Island, the slopes of Kamuela. The Godbolts were an old *kama'aina* missionary family. The mother, Lydia, was a Daughter of Hawaii; the father, Simon, had been killed in the Solomon Islands during World War Two.

The rest I knew. Lydia Godbolt had not remarried. She had raised her children and they had remained her children, had not married, saw her all the time, did portraits of her. Each son's portrait of her was distinctly different, two women entirely. Will used Lydia's own cosmetics on the canvas, lipstick and powder to heighten the facial features, making the portrait an amazing likeness. Wayne's photograph would have been shocking except that the image was almost indistinguishable as a woman and looked like a shattered meringue — just as well, for it depicted his mother in the nude.

The Godbolt brothers still each kept a bedroom in the family house, though for the first twenty years of their lives, until they left home, they shared the same room, on the north side of the house. In that dark room they developed and came of age.

They made many portraits of Lydia, but they boasted of never having portrayed each other.

"No competition!" Will declared. Wayne agreed.

Wayne, the wilder of the two, was a tormentor. When Will had a girlfriend whom he began to call his fiancée, Wayne teased her, teased Will, cried out, "She's hairy! You're a fairy!" Her name was Laura. She winced, anticipating mockery, whenever Wayne opened his mouth. And Wayne mocked. Laura had been in the Peace Corps in the Philippines. "Say 'Rice-a-Roni' in Tagalog!" Then he jeered at her for acting insulted and criticized her for being thin-skinned. "Look at me — I'm harmless!" He so frightened Laura into silence that she stopped making eye contact. Wayne said, "Why are you mute? Being mute is a form of nagging. Silence is aggressive." He kept at her until she cried, and then Will pleaded with him to stop. That night in the dark room, in a knifelike voice, Wayne said, "If you could get rid of her by pulling a plug, would you pull it?"

A luminous life study of the young woman and Will, one of his many self-portraits, hung in Will's studio. *Caine and Mabel,* Wayne called it. He ridiculed her skinny thighs, his beaky penis. "The bugfucker! Spiderwoman with webbed feet!" Wayne seemed to flap around the studio, his stiff coat flying like big articulated wings. What was most remarkable in this painting was the clotted shade of yellow that made the bodies glow.

The dense sunny color, Will explained, was the sort obtained in India by feeding mangoes to sacred cows and then collecting and evaporating their urine until only a residue like pollen dust remained. This yellow "cow cake" was used for the rich pigment in the holiest temple paintings.

"You've been feeding mangoes to a cow and saving its shee-shee?" Wayne said.

Even in their forties the brothers frequently used baby talk, Wayne more than Will.

"Laura has been eating our mangoes" was all Wayne said.

Wayne was just finding out that fact, yet the technical details that lay behind that painting were described in the gallery's press kit and contributed to the popularity of the traveling exhibition. It was a sellout on the mainland and made Will's name.

Wayne usually ignored Laura, though he invented clownish names for her mother, Carol-Ann (a divorcée who lived in a condo in Aina Haina), for presuming to write poetry, saying it was a sign of approaching senility, calling her Anna Banana, reciting her poems in a screechy voice and English accent, beginning, "Welcome to *Masterpiece Theatre*." He was rude about the mother's boyfriends, her passion for cats, her clothes, her attempts to get parts at the Manoa Valley Theater. "She's shapeless! She's shameless! She's a thespian!"

This cruelty toward her mother isolated and demoralized Laura. Yet Laura went on cooking for the brothers, and sometimes the ailing Lydia, in the family house. Sometimes, pushing his plate aside, Wayne said, "Yup, I think I'll just open a can of Alpo." He seemed to dance around his brother and Laura, pestering, satirizing, making funny faces, talking baby talk. He borrowed money from Will. He often showed up at Will's openings in old clothes, wearing them like a taunt, and if anyone remarked on them, he screamed, "Snob!"

Wayne's pleas for money were like a reproach to Will's success. Will handed over the cash, but when he mentioned that he needed it repaid, Wayne howled, "I can't believe what a cheapskate you are!" and said he was hurt, all the while demanding more, which Will gave him. Laura said, "What about our future?" Long, horrible nights. Wayne's weird vitality. Will was finally so worn down he wanted to pull the plug.

He didn't have to. Laura, the only woman he had ever loved, left him after weeks of tears, and Wayne, relieved, was gentle and consoled his brother. Not long after that, Lydia died and the brothers were alone. Once, Wayne said, "I owe you so much. Please forgive me." But when Will reminded him of it, Wayne said, "How many times do you want me to say it," speaking with such surprising anger that Will stopped using the word "loan." He said, "This is a gift."

Although Wayne called himself a portrait photographer, and cursed the big businesses in Hawaii for not hiring him to make expensive boardroom portraits, his specialty was abstract pictures of cluttered interiors. He claimed they were aspects of his melancholy — attics, cellars, rooms piled high with junk: musical instruments such as hautboys and sackbuts, printed sheets, fever charts, musical scores for unusual duos, brass fittings, stacks of magazines, stuffed toys, tools such as spokeshaves and plumb bobs, wooden printing type, stenciled crates, a cider press, an oryx skull, closely scratched whale teeth, Shaker baskets, smeared palettes, hand looms, elephant bells. The assortment defied interpretation. Baroque conglomerations, the images were allegories, he said, for the room that framed them was the brothers' dark childhood room.

Wayne screamed like a parrot when sarcastic critics listed the objects, cramming them into a mocking paragraph like the one above instead of — as Wayne demanded — interpreting their harmony and significance.

A pitchfork, a cigar box, a cranberry scoop, a stack of cups and saucers, a flintlock, a gramophone, a dagger, a pair of women's riding boots, a Coca-Cola sign, a mildewed book of piano duets, and two leathery balls that might be mummified heads in an anonymous room.

"The heads and the music were the whole point," Wayne said, and, furious, he never exhibited his photographs again. He had piles of photographs. "I am withholding them!" He put away his old plate camera and hardly worked. He grew scruffy and cross. He began to say, "I like the way I smell."

He knew his brother had become, if not famous, then well known outside Hawaii, which was a great and enviable thing. Will was loved for his vivid colors, the creation colors of the Edenlike islands, including the urinous mango-juice yellow, green from crushed hibiscus leaves, dusty purple from wild plum trees on Java, and a peculiar russet in his *Country Road, Kamuela* was a pigment of red clay he had scraped from the very earth he had depicted.

"Stop brooding, Willy."

"I never brood."

The brothers were truthful in using their lives in their work, never allowing Hawaii to stand for paradise. Hawaii was a real, flawed place, with melted mountains, fallen trees, iron in the soil, crumbled coral. Full of aliens and transplants, the islands were choked with vines and pests, which had destroyed the old native growth. That clutter had been the point of Wayne's photos. There were angry children in Will's paintings, and on Will's fruit there were always teeth marks.

"We are witnesses!" Wayne said.

The mainland exhibit traveled to Honolulu. After Buddy told me about the brothers, I went to the show and saw that the portrait of Wayne was missing. Buddy had no explanation, though he said he had known the brothers as crazy teenagers when they stayed at the hotel with their mother. It seemed that the portrait had been hurriedly removed by the police. After it was examined, the blistery paint was identified as Wayne's blood. The Honolulu papers reported that Will was wanted for questioning in connection with his brother's murder. Among Will's possessions was a photograph that Wayne had taken of him and cruelly retouched. Will was arrested in his room at the hotel and led through the lobby, Buddy said, "laughing like a naughty boy."

46

Domination

OUR NEAR NEIGHBOR, Dickstein, manager of the Waikiki Pearl, seemed boringly faithful to his mistress. One of the conventional paradoxes of marital infidelity is this absurd loyalty to the one you're cheating with. How could it be love?

Daniel (but this was Hawaii; he dubbed himself "Kaniela") Dickstein was a monster for the way he screamed at his staff. "Verbal abuse" didn't begin to describe it. Dickstein's other habit was spending afternoons upstairs at my hotel with one of his employees. Kendra was her name, a tall, olive-skinned, part-Hawaiian beach queen — gray eyes, small breasts, a surfer's sinewy legs and muscly bum. She carried a gym bag to these weekly assignations. Naturally you'd want to know what was in such a bag. Compared to Dickstein I was passive, yet I felt I had power.

Having a wife and children on the mainland, living at the hotel he'd previously managed, where his wife still worked, did not justify his sleeping with the staff. It was wrong to become involved with employees — not only morally wrong but imprudent, bad for discipline, unfair to the others. And when the affair ended and the rejected sex partner was still on the payroll, what then?

Yet somehow Dickstein managed. I could not bring myself to call him "Dick." Nicknames seemed misleading and overly familiar to me, though Honolulu was full of them — "Buck" Buchwach, "Gus" Guslander, "Sam" Sandford, "Link" Lindquist. "Kaniela" Dickstein had a big irregular head, a jaw like a backhoe, and the lumpy defiant face of a general in a war movie. He was a screamer, a swearer, and he threw things, anything he happened to be holding. He flung pencils at Kendra and once a coffee cup, which smashed against the door she was closing as she fled. He demanded that she return to clean up the mess. This was her lover.

Dickstein never raised his voice to me. He always greeted me with "Shaloha," his own cross-cultural coinage. He was grateful to me for allowing him to use the employees' entrance and the service elevator so he could slip up to room 710 for three hours every Wednesday afternoon. Scheduling a midweek tryst made it seem unsentimental; there would have been something sweet about their meeting on a Friday, and weekends were romantic. Wednesday was like work, more like an appointment, because they never skipped a week and were seldom late. Nevertheless, something in me said, Lucky dog.

As the manager of the Hotel Honolulu, I had employees for the first time. I was struck by how they made me feel powerful, and the less I confided in them, the more power I had. I had not asked for it. I did not pursue it. I needed only for them to do their jobs, because I was so helpless myself, in fact not powerful at all, no more so than a superior-looking puppet. That was how it seemed to me.

Everyone except my wife and child credited me with powers I didn't have. My employees said I was farsighted in my approving orders. They praised my judgment. Even the strongest ones remarked on my strength. I was skeptical. Beware of anyone who praises your intelligence, for nearly always in saying so they are complimenting themselves.

Flattery always sounds like mockery to me. I suspected my employees of being scornful this way. Keeping their praise vague was also a cute way of not having to be answerable for it. And usually I hated the excuses they invented for me. "How were you to know she was cockroaching the money?" Or "I wish I could do this half as good as you." Or the too frequent "Man, you've been around, yah?" if I showed the slenderest acquaintance with a fact of world geography.

Fortunately I didn't have to live up to this inflated image of myself, nor did any of my employees believe it for a second. Their task was to prevent me from being a failure. They did all the work. All I had to do was let them continue. I could only fail by firing them. They were fully in charge.

Aware of this inverted power structure in my hotel, I was curious to know how Kaniela Dickstein succeeded. He was famous for his tantrums and fired employees all the time, even his head chef, forcing Dickstein to take over the supervision of the kitchen himself. His "You're outta here!" was a well-known catch phrase.

"Firing people keeps the others on their toes," he said to me one day when I asked him how he managed. "Think of it as a reign of terror." He set his jaw and said, "I am very angry when I wake up in the morning."

The Waikiki Pearl was no more successful than the Hotel Honolulu. In terms of rates, occupancy, and quality of service, they were pretty much the same, except that the Pearl got Japanese guests from a Tokyo travel agent and we got none. We had more local business, since we were associated with scandals, of which Madam Ma and Chip and Puamana were just a few, not to mention Buddy Hamstra's excesses.

But I saw Dickstein's hotel as being run by him alone, and mine run by my employees. I would have been lost without my people. His workers were expendable. I gave my employees second chances — third, even. A single mistake meant a Dickstein employee took a hike.

"Doesn't it make the others nervous?" I asked him.

"Exactly," he said. "Fear is the whole point."

"When someone is afraid of me, I'm uncomfortable."

"Then you're a fool," Dickstein said. "Mine are yellow in every respect. That's the only kind of person I would ever allow to work for me. The quality I value most in an employee is fear."

"Frightened people drop things."

"Or they learn how to hold on," he said.

We talked this way on Wednesdays after his time with Kendra, and I wondered how frightened she was. She was punctual, but they arrived and left separately, for the sake of appearances. Having finished with her boss, Kendra had to go immediately back to work. Dickstein was paler afterward, puffy-faced, weary-looking, and satiated, I supposed. His hair, a bit too well combed, flat and still wet from the shower, stuck to his scalp and made him look older.

Although he tried to pay me for the room, I refused his money. This dispensing of a favor gave me the illusion of power, so one day he would have to give me what I asked. The hotel business was nicely reciprocal. Dickstein's parent company owned hotels on the mainland. I had no parent company. Sweetie and I might want a hotel room in Florida someday.

One week the whole thing ended, and from the fuss it caused, Dickstein's affairs were better known than I had thought. Dickstein stopped coming to my hotel. Kendra had resigned. She had not been forced to; she quit. This was unprecedented at the Waikiki Pearl under Dickstein, who controlled everything. Dickstein dropped from view. I guessed that it disturbed him, for Kendra was not just an employee who quit suddenly, but his mistress.

Buddy called me that same day. The news had reached the North Shore that quickly. "What was that man thinking? Doesn't he know this is a small town?"

"What have you heard?"

"Dickstein in a dress. People talking story."

What followed became that island recreation, a scandal in installments. Gossip is always steamy in a place too small and semiliterate to support sleazy tabloids. I had heard a little, but in time the whole story came out. Kendra got her revenge by blabbing. For weeks Dickstein was infamous in Honolulu, and my hotel was talked about for being associated with his disgrace.

The part about Dickstein's being a brute was apparently true. Kendra said he was a nightmare to work for — hypercritical, bullying, impatient, loud, demanding, foul-mouthed. But there was a side of him that no one had guessed at (there can be such simplicity in small towns and tiny islands), and this was exhibited to Kendra on Wednesday afternoons.

Dickstein was tied up, forcibly cross-dressed, and spanked, not with the flat of Kendra's hand but with a wooden hairbrush. He was sat upon. He was insulted by Kendra, who called him foul names, after which she relieved herself, emptied her bladder, on his sputtering lips.

Everyone in Honolulu who knew Dickstein learned these details, and some people discovered who he was through the vividness of them. The cross-dressing involved more than just Kendra's putting women's clothes on him. Dickstein was in his fifties. The women's clothes he wore were the high heels and tight dresses of his high school pinups. He was transformed into a big square-jawed calendar girl.

Dressed this way, a clown's version of Marilyn Monroe, he was forced to lie face down on the bed. Wearing thigh-high leather boots and surgical gloves, Kendra manipulated him, then sodomized him with her strap-on dildo. She was so ferocious that, though Dickstein moaned and protested, he was hardly able to form a whole word.

Room 710 of the Hotel Honolulu was transformed into a mistress's dungeon in which Kaniela Dickstein in a prom gown was spanked, humiliated, pissed on, and sodomized. "You slut," Kendra would say as she slipped the panties on him, and she repeated the insult with the long stockings, the high heels, the ridiculous brassiere. She made him kneel. Some of the names she called him were words she hardly knew, or ones she had never before uttered.

Though he was greedy for it, the sessions so exhausted her she could not face him afterward. She always left my hotel feeling wrecked. That part of it was not gossiped about, and no one talked about what lay behind it. Dickstein was a sissy — a pantie, in the local slang.

No one understood that this was just another example of his bullying. The script was Dickstein's; everything that happened in the room was done at his command. Kendra had to learn precisely what to do, and if she failed in any detail, Dickstein was furious. He dominated her by forcing this pretty and submissive island girl to be his dominatrix.

"I couldn't take it anymore," Kendra said. "I thought maybe I could just do it the way you do stuff in hotels, like clean guests' bathrooms, but it just got worse."

No one would listen to Kendra's accusation of sexual harassment. She tried to get Dickstein into court. Her argument was "He made me hit him." Her case went nowhere, nor was she able to prove her claim for workers' comp, for her sore arm that developed bursitis, her insomnia, and her panic attacks. And Kendra was still in counseling in a clinic in Mapunapuna when Dickstein got his promotion.

47

The Dream House in Kahala

OVERHEARING a request for monthly rates, I knew it was either a Canadian escaping the winter or a local man who had been thrown out of his house, his marriage gone bad. The man, Alex Holt, who was local, winced at the rate, but after I heard his story, I lowered it and was tempted to give him a free room. It was that sad. In his soft voice, he had an oblique and apologetic way of describing the reverses in his life: "I'm pretty much broke," and "She kind of destroyed me," and "It was pretty much kind of a disaster-type thing."

"My wife's quite a bit older than me," he had said.

Why did that sort of admission always sharpen my curiosity?

"Ex-wife, I mean," he added, and I thought, Of course.

Becky, the ex-wife, had a troubled ten-year-old girl, Kristen. The child had liked Alex Holt, and the promise of a bond had been part of the reason Becky had married him. She wanted security for the child, she wanted to stay in Hawaii, and she wanted a house in Kahala. She was a dental hygienist.

"Becky kind of dreamed of living in Kahala," Alex said.

Of the high-priced Honolulu suburb of Kahala, Buddy always said, "Kahala is a pig farm. I know it's full of millionaires, but as far as I'm concerned it's still a pig farm. It's flat and uninteresting."

Alex Holt was in advertising at a time when the agencies in Hawaii were going broke, the 1980s slump. And yet by getting some mainland clients, he had managed to find the money for a corner lot, three streets off Kahala Avenue. Becky was successful in her work, and she had contributed to the down payment. The idea was that they would knock down the existing house and build a new one in stages — prepare the lot, draw up the plans, complete the building. It might take five years or more. As Becky said, "That's what marriage is all about, building for the future. Having a time line that's also a dream."

Alex felt that way about the child, too. Kristen needed a good education. He enrolled her in Iolani and paid half her fees. Kristen joined the volleyball team and the drama club — one year she had a small part in *Our Town*. She said she wanted to write poetry, and wrote a poem that Alex printed, making it into a greeting card with the office copier. It was called "A Love Letter to My New Dad." Alex legally adopted her and took full responsibility for her tuition. He sometimes drove her and Becky to Kahala and parked near the teardown house on the corner lot. Together they tried to imagine how their dream house might look.

An architect was found. He was one of Becky's patients. She asked Alex, "Are you comfortable with that?" This was the way she talked. Alex said he needed to meet with the architect first to see if he was right for them.

When Alex was satisfied, he hired the man. The architect entered completely into the spirit of the dream house. He said, "You can save money by getting generic windows, but remember, you're near the ocean. If this were my house, I would get Wadsworth's Weatherproofs — they're vinyl-clad, double-glazed, hurricane-proof . . ." The tile roof with a wide hip for the rain and sun, the screened lanai, the extra bedroom, the track lighting, the Sub-Zero refrigerator, the Viking range and dishwasher, the Mission furniture — all of it, he said, was the sort he would buy if it were his home.

"Home" was the word he always used, never "house."

"Don't think of this home in terms of time," the architect said. "Just think quality. Think permanence. A home has a soul."

Such quality implied the high six figures. More clients had to be found on the mainland. Alex was away a great deal, traveling constantly. He saw himself as a modern version of a hunter-gatherer. The value of his sacrifice was apparent each time he returned home: the sketches became plans, the plans became blueprints, and soon they were deep into what the architect referred to as the "permitting process."

"He's good," Alex said. He did not comment on the architect's youth — how he was uneasy hiring someone younger than he was.

Becky said, "A person's teeth say an awful lot. I've worked on his teeth for years."

Alex was also delighted by the eagerness Kristen showed on his return. Kristen's reaction wasn't faked: Becky had the whole family she had always sought. He had shown Becky that in becoming a faithful husband, attentive to Kristen, he had become the girl's father. What worried him were Kristen's early-teen spasms of rebellion, like a child sticking a finger in a flame. Kristen tried smoking, stole a book from school, put up lurid posters of tongue-wagging men in evil makeup in her room. "It's a rock group, Alex!" Kristen loved horseplay, especially liked to wrestle on the floor with Alex, or sometimes at the beach he would fling her onto the sand and she shrieked as though she were being tickled. And sometimes she sneaked a cigarette.

Alex was happiest when they all sat around the kitchen table in the rented apartment in Kaimuki studying the floor plans of the dream house. They mentally moved into the flat white spaces.

The architect said, "Let's work through this," and praised their vision — the contours of the double-pitched roof, the proportions of the lanai, the privacy fences, the way each room was self-contained, the kitchen as a family focal point. Alex had an office; Becky had the dressing room and closet space she had always wanted; Kristen's room was to be soundproof.

"I got the big family room idea from the Dillingham House in Mokuleia," Becky said. "That's where we had our wedding reception."

"Your house will have your look," the architect said. "Very unique."

Hearing the architect say "very unique," Alex wanted to correct him, as when he said "home." But Alex knew that as an advertising man he was more word-conscious than the architect, who thought in pictures, using the left side of his brain.

To save them money, the architect said that he would supervise the construction, and he hired his own subcontractors. Often, calling from the mainland, Alex was surprised when the architect picked up the telephone, or Kristen did and handed it to the architect. He told the man he was grateful for his close attention and long hours. As for Kristen, the man said, "She likes being on-site. She's getting involved." Alex heard the girl giggle.

"When they saw the wood it smells like popcorn!" he heard Kristen say.

"Isn't that special! It's what I would want if someone were designing a home for me," the architect said. "I know the pitfalls — you don't. And even if you did, you'd probably be risk averse."

Instead of commenting on "risk averse," another turn of speech that drew his attention, Alex asked the architect where he was from. The man's answer, "The Bay Area," told him nothing.

Alex returned one weekend to find four enormous Tongans building a wall of lava rock in front: the architect's idea, Kristen's design — she'd sketched it herself — which Becky approved. The man also urged them to get their furniture custom made in Hawaii: "No veneer. Solid koa. Why not? The koa forests in Hawaii are nearly depleted. The wood will be unobtainable in a few years."

Agreeing to this meant more visits to the mainland, and setting up a mainland office, just a fax machine and a telephone in a small rented cubicle in Los Angeles, which Alex hated yet endured: the dream house was taking shape.

"I notice you usually relax like me in a chair after work," the architect said, tapping his head in a knowing way and then sketching on his pad. He had decided to design the furniture that would be custom made. Scraping with his pencil, he said, "I'm going to rough out a chair with a real high back and lumbar support." Scrape, scrape. "Nice wide arms. Tiny little details matter the most."

There was no point in letting a harmless expression like "tiny little details" bother you, and yet it did bother Alex. He made the mistake of mentioning it to Becky that evening in the stifling apartment in Kaimuki, and she turned on him.

"You're never satisfied! Here he is, designing a chair for your own butt, and you criticize the way he talks."

She was angry because he had also mentioned the architect's harping on "home" and repeating "very unique." Under this onslaught Alex was embarrassed ever to have thought of himself as a hunter-gatherer.

Not long after that, he was in Los Angeles and eager for news of the house, which was nearly finished. He called Becky. She surprised him by saying, in a telephone voice she kept for strangers, "Yes, what is it?"

He had heard her say that into a phone to telemarketers.

"It's me," Alex said, hoping that she was speaking this way because the line was bad.

"I know it's you."

Then he knew something was wrong.

"What is it?" he said. "Is Kristen smoking again?"

Becky said, "We have to talk," and hung up.

The headwinds that impede a plane flying from Los Angeles to Honolulu most winter days can add as much as an hour to the normal five-hour flight. That happened the morning in January Alex Holt flew home, knowing that something was seriously wrong but not sure what. He was heartsick. Becky met him at the gate at Honolulu Airport among the people offering leis and shouting in glee and carrying signs saying *Paradise Tours Meeting Point,* or uniformed drivers with placards reading *Dr. Kawabata* or *Mr. Dickstein.* And when he greeted her, he found himself too weepy and inarticulate to speak. Becky hurried on ahead while Alex found a skycap to help him with his bag. Driving from the airport down the H-1 Freeway, she glanced at him in the passenger seat, saw his tears, and said, "Listen carefully. I have something to tell you. I've been seeing Ray." Ray, of course, was the architect, whom Alex had never thought of as having a name you needed to know, any more than the skycap who had jogged his bag on the luggage cart.

"Seeing Ray" was supposed to mean everything. In the silence that followed Becky's saying this, Alex imagined some of the implications. Seeing the man naked was mainly what he imagined. Seeing him laugh, seeing him talk, seeing him make promises, not seeing anyone else.

At the Kaimuki apartment, also in silence, he said, "Where's Kristen?"

"She's staying with friends. She doesn't want to see you."

The apartment seemed more spacious, but that was because it had been emptied of most of the furniture.

Becky said, "I've moved my things."

"Where to?"

She seemed genuinely amused. "Where to!"

"Kahala?" He saw the house in his mind as Becky began to leave. He said, "You said we needed to talk."

"We just talked." Again she turned to go.

Alex said in a pleading voice, "Can't we talk about our marriage?"

"Don't do that to me," Becky said. "You're trying to bring me down."

"What was wrong?" Alex was in tears again.

"It doesn't matter," she said. "I've already processed it."

"Processed" was one of his words — had to be.

Becky filed for divorce. She asked for child support. Kristen stayed with her. "She needs a stable home." They were by then living in the house in Kahala, and Alex suspected but could not prove that the child support was going toward the mortgage. Alex challenged her on this, lawyers were hired, a suit filed, and in her deposition Becky said that Alex had been neglectful, constantly away on the mainland, and verbally abusive. She said that she suspected him of child abuse, "inappropriate touching and fondling" and spending much more time than was normal with her teenage daughter.

"She hit me with a pretty good lawsuit," Alex told me.

Without money for a lawyer to contest her claims, Alex dropped the suit. At that point he checked into the Hotel Honolulu and, after telling me his story, got very depressed. "Kind of suicidal, but it wore off." Then, some months later, he heard that Becky, calling it "tough love," had thrown Kristen out of the house for smoking *pakalolo*, and that Kristen was living with her Samoan boyfriend somewhere in Nanakuli. Alex said he was sorry about it, but "I pretty much try not to let it bother me."

I said, "I want to know a bit more about Kristen."

But he wouldn't tell me more. He said that talking about this whole thing, and especially about her, had only made him feel kind of worse.

48

The Happiest Man in Hawaii

O NCE, AFTER AN excellent bottle of wine in the hotel, Royce Lionberg fixed his lawyer's lie-detector eyes on me and said, "I know you're going to write about me." I had first met him at the "service" for Buddy's wife Stella, the happy funeral. Apart from Leon Edel, he was the only person in Hawaii I had met who had read my books. He expressed genuine shock that I now managed a hotel. The statement about using him in my writing was intended to take me by surprise. I told him what was in my heart, "Never," and he believed me.

I did not tell him the reason I said it. I would not have attempted to deceive him. He lived on the North Shore, up the hill from Buddy, a mansion on a cliff. He visited the hotel once or twice a month and indulged himself in a Buddy Burger (Peewee spiked the ground beef with vermouth) and a bottle of Merlot. He had retired early because of his brilliant instincts and his sense of timing. He was a man without any regrets. He also used to say, "People come into my house and think, What can he do for me? What can I get out of him?" He smiled when he said it, knowing that he was way ahead of these people.

But I wanted nothing from him — that was why we became friends. I said "never" because he was impossible to write about, though I could not explain this without offending him.

I could have told him, as I had once tried to tell Sweetie about Stephen King, that it takes only a modest talent to write about misery — and misery is a more congenial subject than happiness. Most of us have known some suffering and can understand and respond by filling in the gaps. But great happiness is almost incomprehensible, and conveying it in print requires genius. The thankless result for such luminous prose is a character so happy he can seem undeserving, like those skillful boardroom portraits of smug company presidents that make you want to spew. Gloom finds kindred spirits, but write about pleasure and readers feel mocked and excluded. Happiness is almost repellent in black and white — even in life: apart from Buddy, Lionberg had few close friends. He was the happiest man I had ever met.

Craving anonymity, Lionberg gave his mansion a street number but no name. He lived alone, on the highest part of the bluff, facing west over Sharks Cove. A dense, blossomy hibiscus hedge around his property camouflaged a thick steel fence and security cameras. Visitors to the North Shore sometimes detoured to look at the high gates, but not because of Lionberg. He was a recluse, whose justified paranoia was summed up in his attributed question "What can he do for me?" A rumor that Elvis had lived briefly in Lionberg's mansion in 1968, when he was here making *Blue Hawaii,* brought out the gawkers.

"If I had known about that Elvis connection, I wouldn't have bought the place," Lionberg said.

Yet he was so happy that he hardly left the property. At first I had taken Lionberg to be one of those Hawaiian millionaires who was secretly snooty, always measuring himself against his competitors. His dismissiveness about Elvis seemed like the proof. A rich recluse is usually someone who craves the right company, an intensely social but fussy snob. But after I got to know him better I understood that when Lionberg said he wanted to be left alone, and not written about, he meant it.

Buddy Hamstra had introduced us with the usual "He wrote a book!"

Lionberg said he knew my work. I recognized him as a conventional American millionaire in being mean with his money and rather a know-it-all, a terrible listener, somewhat defensive in his manner, especially in his never discussing the source of his wealth. I took this to indicate that he was superstitious and self-conscious about it, but hearing that he had been a lawyer, I also had the impression he was a little ashamed of how he had made his money. Buddy, a gossip, mentioned that it was a huge settlement Lionberg had won — "The largest sum ever awarded in a personal injury suit in" . . . was it California? Lionberg had one of those California accents that always shows the speaker's fine California teeth.

"I'm a knucklehead," Buddy said. "He's real smart." Buddy believed Lionberg and I were kindred souls.

"I'm surprised I know your work," Lionberg said. "I don't read many books." He was unapologetic.

"Books upset me," he said. "They take hold of my mind. When I'm reading one I can't think of anything else."

I said that seemed to me a sign that he was perhaps a more dedicated reader than he realized.

"That I take books too seriously?" he said. "But it's such a commitment reading a novel. I'm not one of these people who read for enjoyment or to pass the time. Books tend to possess me. They get into my head. So I avoid them."

The act of writing was to him rather obscure — mingled with magic, touched with power. He was not used to associating with people who had more power than he. Anyway, few people did, and none of them was on the North Shore.

Lionberg never said to me, as others often did, "I wish I could write." He had everything, and he knew it. He even had me.

Instead of my tedious and unwelcome description of Lionberg's happiness, or my portrait of his beautiful house (whenever I hear, "They've got a lovely house," I think, Why should I care?), I would prefer to sort through some more telling incidents. They relate to Lionberg's being a do-it-yourselfer and a beekeeper. Though he had a handyman, Kekua, Lionberg did most of the chores on his property. He was so wealthy he could afford the time to carry out these menial jobs. He did them well, though his staff, Kekua especially, tended to applaud a bit too strenuously and nervously overpraised him. They knew he was dabbling and, worse, that he was trespassing on their turf. So Buddy said.

He was painting some beehives one day while I stood by; he was talking more than listening. He had a bucket of white paint — they were new hives, boxes that were put together by Kekua — and in the middle of a sentence, something about one of his visitors (someone with a "What can he do for me?" attitude), Lionberg spat into the bucket. He had been smoking a big cigar, and his spittle was dark brown, and it looped like caramel on the glossy white surface of the paint. He stirred this gob into the paint

— three twists of the mixing stick — and there was no trace of it. He went on applying the pure white paint with his brush.

He smiled at me. This for him was like a whole signifying speech, and yet he had not said a word. If this was a reply to something I had said, I could not remember what had provoked it.

I knew what I had been thinking, though — that in the middle of my life I found myself alone, and so I latched on to people, thinking they were strong; but they were alone too, or else they wouldn't have let me. Whatever inconsequential thing I had said — for it was relaxing to be with Lionberg — that thought was going through my mind. I was drifting and clinging like everyone else, except him.

Being happy, he did not draw off my energy, and I always left his house feeling revitalized. His calmness calmed me. He had no envy, none of the needy attention-seeking that could be so tiring. And his happiness did not mean high spirits and hilarity. Quite the opposite. It made him meditative and thoughtful. He was serene, fulfilled, the real thing, the person no one wants to hear about, a happy man.

Somewhere in his past there was a wife — wives, maybe — and children. He mentioned them as you might allude to old friends, without any rancor, always with generosity and affection.

"I was talking to Didi yesterday," he said. "She grows orchids. Doing very well with them."

"Was that the woman I saw in the garden?"

"No. Didi's in Mexico," he said. "My first wife. We were married thirty years ago. She was just a kid in her mid-twenties."

Working the paint into the grooves of the beehive, he went on talking.

"That woman in the garden is a psychic. She's a funny person. She was a truck driver somewhere on the mainland. She realized she had a gift and has been doing it full time. She's very colorful. For a while she was a prostitute. She predicted a change in my life."

"How do you feel about that?"

"Frankly, I'm happy with the way things are," he said. "Like a lot of prostitutes, she is also a lesbian. She came highly recommended by Buddy, who swears by her."

Lionberg might have been in his sixties, but he looked forty-five. He was a small man and had the appearance some small men have — perfectly proportioned, very fit but quietly so. You never saw him exercising; perhaps the chores kept him in shape. I believed him when he said that books upset him, yet he had an extensive library. He also had a collection of telescopes and chronometers, ships' compasses and clocks. He was a cultured soul. He saw films and listened to music. He was a patron of the Honolulu Symphony, the Hawaii Film Festival, and various charities. He was generous and undemanding; everything he attempted seemed to succeed. His flowers bloomed, his mango trees were heavy with fruit, his hives were full of honey. He experimented with coffee bushes on one slope — he had twenty acres altogether — and I knew they would flourish. I assumed that his whole life had been like that. It was how he had become wealthy — quietly, without fuss. He took no special credit. "Ram a broomstick in this soil and it will grow. Everything grows here."

I am giving the impression that he was aloof, and I suppose he was where most people were concerned. But preoccupied would be a truer word. He had a passionate interest in details — the life cycle of the bee, the medicinal properties of shrubs on his land, the traditional uses for blossoms, the hallmarks of antique silver, the accuracy of certain timepieces. He had time for everything, and in that respect he was rich. He said, "Time is wealth."

Buddy Hamstra was in most respects Lionberg's opposite, but he was useful for comparison. Like other disturbed and excitable people, Buddy was unhealthy and accident-prone. Lionberg was an example of someone whose health and contentment seemed like radiant consequences of his clear mental state.

He lived, embowered, behind hedges, in the fragrance of his bushes and flowers and his buzzing bees, bathed in the light of the Pacific, facing west. Now and then, people came to consult him as though he were an oracle. They had problems and they were convinced — his house and his life were the proof — that he had solutions. His reluctance to encourage anyone to believe in him made people more credulous and persistent. He also knew how, smilingly, to turn them away.

It was hard to imagine anyone so serene and satisfied that he looked at the world and, possessing such experience of immense pleasure, saw nothing he wanted. It was like achieving an ideal state of being, for there was something godlike in having conquered all desire.

He had a few eccentricities. One was his general refusal to eat anything but his own food. He did make exceptions (the Buddy Burger was one), but his fastidiousness kept him from going to dinner parties — not that he was interested. It also kept him from traveling. He said he didn't mind: "I've done my traveling." Another oddity of his was his thoroughness in removing the brand names from everything he owned. His car, his microwave, his toaster, his oven, his telescopes. Even from something as insignificant as a watch dial he effaced the brand name. He hated logos. "I detest advertising. It makes the thing look as though it's on loan."

Besides the bees, the painting, the carpentry, and his accomplishments as a handyman — he made birdhouses, he kept tropical fish — he had a great assortment of simple weapons: air guns, slingshots, crossbows, throwing knives. And much more: a suit of armor, a blunderbuss, a working cannon, shields, spears, a collection of war clubs from various Pacific islands. In the room that served as his arsenal, he also had a wind-up phonograph and a jukebox.

"What do you want to hear?"

"What have you got?"

Pressing buttons, he said, "Here's a favorite of mine."

It was Frank Sinatra singing "Blue Moon."

"That was very popular when I was at school."

That was how I got an idea of his age.

"Did you grow up with guns like this?"

"Oh, no," he said. "My mother hated guns." He paused, smiling at the music or a memory. "Hated rock-and-roll too." He looked around the room and said with pleasure, "This would have appalled her."

I understood him better then. These were things he had always wanted, that he had finally attained. It was really very simple. He didn't yearn for "Rosebud" — he possessed it and had all the time in the world to enjoy it.

I never saw him angry or drunk or depressed. He had the patience of a Buddhist monk. He was modest; I never heard him boast. He was compassionate and kind, and he yearned for nothing. His staff loved him. I liked being with him — and, as I say, I always felt better afterward. He gave me confidence and energy. I saw him as one of the lucky few.

But he confounded me. A happy man cannot be the subject of a story. You never saw his sort in a story. Happiness is hardly a subject — Tolstoy said as much in the opening sentence of his hybolic masterpiece. It amazes me that I have written this much about Lionberg, the happiest man in Hawaii.

49

aloha.net

THEY HAD AGREED that he would be in the Hotel Honolulu lobby holding a copy of *Honolulu Weekly,* and so
would she, but coming up behind the man reading the
personals and chewing his knuckles, she hoped he was the wrong
one. Her eyes racing, she took him in all at once in desperate scrutiny, looking for something positive, any feature, as if she were
trapped in a strange room and searching for an exit. He had not
noticed her yet, still he was reading, and she was short of breath
seeing the page headed *Women Seeking Women.*

Perhaps he seemed uglier than he really was because she was so
afraid of him. Certainly the instant she saw him sitting there,
gnawing the back of his hand, she forgot that she had ever spoken
to him. He might well have been a reasonable-looking person, but
the moment made him hideous and she could not recapture any of
the innocence of her first glimpse. Had her mood, her distorting
memory, made him into a monster?

He might have looked like a nice guy — she would not have
approached him otherwise — but later, all she could remember
was that she had feared him from the first — his size most of all,
for he was big, sacklike, with small shoulders, sprawling pillowy
hips, weighty legs that seemed even wider because of his baggy
shorts, the sort of tightly laced sneakers that made your feet
sweat. His head was tiny and two-sided, exaggerated by a cheap
haircut.

His earrings worried her more than almost anything else: he

wore one in each ear. Two earrings — what's the deal? was a question she tried to improvise. She wanted him to be the wrong man, not "larc22" from aloha.net but just a fat guy with the *Weekly* where "larc22" should have been.

His narrow shoulders twitched in premonition, then twisted, and he squinted at her and smiled. Had he just eaten a candy bar? He had parentheses of chocolate scum at the corners of his mouth.

"Aloha, Saddy."

Her heart pinched. She said, "Sadie."

The e-mail name was "Saidy," but she could not blame him for getting it wrong — she had never spoken the word before.

"Daisy, actually," she said. "Are you 'larc twenty-two'?"

Only now did she remember his mentioning the Milky Way candy bar he usually ate when watching *The Tonight Show.* Yet he had also claimed to like scuba diving and said something about riding around the island on his motorcycle. It was easier to imagine him in his room, eating candy and watching TV, and on his shelf the first catcher's mitt he had ever owned and the scattered parts of a turntable he was fixing so that he could listen to his collection of old Hawaiian 78s. She knew everything about him.

"Or should I call you Carl?"

As he had come toward her, walking flatfooted as though tramping through sand, she had stepped backward. She registered that he was heavy but not tall and that he had a hungry smile.

"I spend so much time online, I don't even think of myself as Carl anymore."

Another scary factoid, she thought, that he regarded himself as "larc22," like one of those bulgy-faced robots on *Star Trek,* the reruns of a show he never missed. He had warned her, *I'm a Trekkie.*

So that he would not come any closer, she sat down, and he sat too, heaving himself into a nearby chair, seeming like an obstacle.

"Did you come here on your motorcycle?" she asked.

One of his habits — in this minute or so she had established this, had seen him do it twice — was knuckle-chewing. He did it again.

"Sold it," he said. His gnawing made him scowl. "So you want to go somewhere?"

She wanted to go home. But she was fearful of upsetting him by rejecting him so fast. She was already afraid of him and wishing to placate him, so that she could leave and never see him again.

"How about right here?" she said. "There's a bar and a lanai."

Something in his manner made her want to stay in the open with him. She went ahead into Paradise Lost, imagining she could feel his breath on her neck. She hurried past the booths and made for the outside tables, sitting quickly so he would not touch her.

"I know you don't drink," she said. "But this is a nice place."

"I'm a cheap date." He had made that comment every time he mentioned how he didn't drink alcohol. "But go ahead, have your frozen margarita."

She almost did not order one, to spite him, but the waiter was hovering and listening, and she thought the drink might help her get through this. After a sip of it — he was drinking Diet Pepsi — she said, "Isn't there anything you can do? I mean, is your liver permanently damaged?"

"Stays fried," he said, and explained his hepatitis once more, how he had contracted it on Maui one New Year's.

I cannot believe I'm having a conversation with this strange man about his liver, she thought. In her mind she saw a purplish piece of raw liver on a white dish.

"So are you still getting those dizzy spells?"

"I just told you I am," he said.

She hadn't been listening. He had been describing his ailments while she had been abstracted thinking of them. To hide her face, she lifted the wide margarita glass and sipped.

"I really hate him."

"Who?"

"Jimmy Buffett."

She knew that. She just hadn't made the connection. He hated the Grateful Dead, too. He liked Hawaiian music and Philip Glass. So did she. He liked scuba diving. She was certified. And motorcycles. She had imagined herself a passenger on his. *But I hate these macho bikers,* he had once said to her. From that remark she took him to be small, perhaps delicate, slender anyway, and saw him somehow in light slacks and sandals and a fluttery aloha shirt. But no, you could hate machismo and still be a big soft spud with two earrings.

"So how's the diving?"

"I haven't been lately. We usually go to the North Shore."

She knew that, too — Haleiwa Beach Park, with his friend Mickey.

"Wetsuit's shredded. Have to get them specially made. Credit card's maxed out."

His manner of speaking was so like one of his e-mails that she smiled and absent-mindedly touched her forearm.

"You got this habit of touching your arm," he said, which made her look at his bitten knuckles. "So that must be from the accident, huh?"

Before he could touch her arm, she pulled it away and sat back in her chair. He knew all about her scooter crash on Beretania Street. As he lowered his head to see the burn scar on her calf from the exhaust pipe, she turned aside.

She could have done the same to him, talked about the finger he had smashed in a door. He said it "twinged" when he typed too long. Sometimes it was his sign-off. *Finger's throbbing.* Or his feet — the "cookies" he put in his shoes for arch support. She understood his bad feet now. He was allergic to shellfish, too. He complained of carpal tunnel.

"So how's your mother?" he asked.

This was painful, such a question from a stranger.

"She's okay."

"I go past there almost every day."

Why had she told him about Arcadia, where her mother lived among old folks because of her stroke? As the youngest of the four children, but the only one still on the island, Daisy had been unable to care for her mother, and so Arcadia was the expensive answer — they all chipped in. He knew about that, this big strange man who went down Punahou Street and thought of her mother. It was a terrible mistake to log on late at night and lonely.

"I have to go," she said.

"We just got here!"

She had suspected that it would be hard to get away. He had hope. She had none.

"Hey, my father's not doing too good," he said.

Months before, on one of those late nights, when she had mentioned how badly she missed her father, he had commiserated, had quoted a poem he'd learned at school to her: *my father moved through dooms of love.* How could she cut him short now?

"It's the chemo," he said, making it into a Hawaiian name.

She didn't want to know more. She said, "They have these online support groups. I really have to go."

"There's about two hours before the news," he said.

Saying that was like a chess move. He was a chess player: he played against his computer and sometimes won. He knew how to be obstructive with a single move. He was reminding her that she watched the ten o'clock news every night.

"I figured we could watch the news together at my place."

The very idea of his thinking that terrified her so much she could not reply to it.

"What about your workout?" *Hand weights,* he had said. *Treadmill. The Cardio Club.*

"I'm taking a night off."

That was a lie. He had pretended to care about fitness, because she had. She had not expected muscles, but how about health? She didn't believe he scuba-dived at all.

He noisily suck-vacuumed the bottom of his glass with his straw and then tipped an ice cube into his mouth, cracking it like a nut, working it around his teeth.

She could not dislike him. He reminded her that messages were typed by people who had fat fingers, who were big and clumsy and hungry and lonely. She felt sorry for his failed first marriage, how he had caught his wife in bed with his best friend; sorry for the death of his brother, for his father's prostate cancer, the chemo. He treasured a memory of fishing with his father. His mother had sold advertising. She was German, sensitive about the war, but she had been a little kid then. *Whenever I think about her death I can't stop crying.* And more, much more. She knew everything about him.

All this was for someone else to care about, not her, and she regretted everything she had ever said to him. When he touched her with the hand he had been gnawing, she almost screamed. She wanted to leave before he touched her again with his bitten hand. Just his staring at her made her feel naked.

Not speaking — she couldn't — she got up and stiffly tried to go. But he stuck out his leg to block her.

"I know you think I'm a loser, but you're wrong. And you'll never get away."

She had started to cry. His voice caused it, the way he spoke. She had never imagined that his voice would sound like that, human and horrible. She thought, I know nothing about him. She was afraid.

"I'll find you." His knee against her made this emphatic, and all the chewing of his knuckles made the threat much worse. "I can find anyone on the Net."

When she finally got free of him she hurried to my office so I could sneak her out and make sure she was not followed. She told me the whole story, but that was only the beginning. He found her, found out where she worked, her telephone numbers. He called repeatedly. A temporary restraining order did no good.

He stalked her single-mindedly, as though she were the only woman in the world, and he loomed larger and uglier than any other man on earth.

A threat of legal action made him threaten to countersue for defamation. He harassed her for a full year, until she went to the mainland. Even then, with a new e-mail address, selecting *Get Mail*, she saw his ridiculous name attached to shrill disgusting messages to her, which she was obliged to download for the police, who did nothing about these foul things because she was on the mainland.

He attended her mother's funeral; she did not. But I was there, at her request, and saw him for the first time. He was tall and muscular and quite young, one of the handsomest men I had ever seen in my life.

50

Rain

IN THE WAY THAT Buddy had introduced me, he introduced Rain Conroy, a cousin from the mainland, to Royce Lionberg. "It's an emergency, Roy-boy."

A relative back in Sweetwater, hearing that Rain was going to Hawaii, said, "You've got to look up Buddy," and sent the girl on, knowing that Buddy would be amused. But Buddy's new wife, Pinky, became jealous. At first she refused to eat. She said, "I'm not hungry." Then she bit him on the arm, one of many such bites.

He said, "Hey, I thought you said you weren't hungry."

When he said that Rain was his cousin, Pinky became even more suspicious, and it seemed like further proof to Buddy that Filipinos were the incestuous bunch he often accused them of being.

Lionberg knew that Buddy was also a wealthy man and wanted nothing from him, and so he was a sympathetic listener to Buddy's woes — always unusual problems. On the telephone to Lionberg, Buddy said that in her fury, Pinky had locked herself in a closet and wouldn't come out.

"Did you say a closet?" Lionberg asked.

"Right. A clothes closet. Full of mothballs."

"How long has she been in it?"

"Day and a half."

"That's amazing," Lionberg said. He had an innocent fascination for that sort of chaos, because his own life was so orderly. "I wonder how long a person could stay in a closet?"

"I don't want to find out," Buddy said.

He said he would lose face with his Nevada relatives if he turned Rain away. Yet Pinky was becoming hysterical, whimpering in the darkness of the closet — or worse, keeping silent — with the door locked.

"I forced the door open this morning," Buddy said.

"Probably a good idea."

"She bit me again."

All this time Lionberg was laughing silently, glad that he was on the telephone and could hide his reaction.

"It's just for the weekend," Buddy said. "On Monday I'll pick her up and put her on the plane to the mainland."

Lionberg agreed, swallowing his laughter, because he was secure, happy, occupied with his bees and his garden and the huge house and walled compound that was his world.

He also knew when someone wanted to take advantage of him. Not Buddy — after all, this was a simple favor — but the girl, Rain. When he saw her he was certain that he would have to be careful.

She was in her early twenties, tall, slender, very pretty and self-possessed. For all her delicacy she seemed strong — something about the way she hurried toward the ocean-facing hedge and looked down at the cove.

Buddy was saying, "She won't be a problem. When a woman has a body like that, you know she's got nothing between her ears. She's real simple."

Lionberg was looking at the girl, whose back was turned to them.

"They either have looks or brains. I've never found one with both. Anyway, even if I did, I wouldn't know what to do with her."

Buddy honked his horn and prepared to leave. Rain did not look back. She hardly seemed to care that he was leaving her with this stranger, at this enormous empty house. Then Buddy shouted, and Rain turned and waved, and it struck Lionberg that she was either supremely confident or foolishly naïve. But when she saw the house, she would be thrown. Then she would not want to leave — they never did. She would see it all with a hopeful hungry gaze.

"Shall I send someone for the rest of your things?"

"These are my things." She picked up her small bag.

Lionberg was trying to imagine what essentials were in the bag.

"It's real warm here," Rain said. "You don't need many clothes."

"It's not that warm."

"I've learned to do without," she said.

She seemed to be reproaching him — that was how Lionberg felt. But that was typical: most people tried to remind him that they had nothing, which was usually the prelude to their asking for something. "I'd kill to own something like that," a woman had once said to him, of an Annamese celadon bowl.

"Buddy's from the rich side of the family," Rain said. "His side's got everything."

"Lucky them."

"They've got the problems, too," Rain said. "Like I say, they've got everything."

Was she cleverer than she seemed? This was concisely subtle. Lionberg wanted to tell her that some people had managed to succeed without becoming dysfunctional. But the conversation was making him feel uncomfortable, because with all this talk about money — Rain saying frankly that she had none — they were walking off the terrace and into the house through the thrust-apart sliders, and Rain had turned and was looking at either the Hockney or the telescope.

Lionberg said, "It's a Celestron, the best one they make. I took the labels off. I don't see the point of brand names."

"Right. But you just told me what it was."

He hated to be contradicted, and he found himself counting before he replied.

"It's got wonderful optics. I photographed that comet last April."

Rain said, "Actually, I was looking at that bird."

"It's a white-rumped shama thrush," Lionberg said. "Yes. It's lovely. Listen."

The shama was warbling and whistling, a tumbling sweetness that was polyphonic, like falling water made into sparkling lozenges of pure sound.

"Much nicer than a lark or a nightingale," Lionberg said.

Rain smiled. How could she have heard those songs?

"It's a native of South Asia. They've only been in Hawaii since the 1930s. It's not a shy bird."

"It's real pretty," the girl said.

"Like your name."

"It means queen in French, except my parents couldn't spell."

She was standing in the living room next to the sunken sofa and the wall of African masks, a rack of Fijian war clubs, the large rock-crystal fish, the celadon, the paintings, the aquatints, the fine mats and baskets, the koa bowls, the Tunisian carpet, the Ming dragon of glazed porcelain. The plain black stereo played a Vivaldi cello concerto.

"I like your hat," she said as she walked off the veranda.

It was a baseball hat with a mass of torn stitching where it had once been lettered *The Plaza*. He said, "I'll turn the music down."

"Whatever," she said. She seemed not to have noticed the music. She was still listening to the song of the shama thrush perched in the hibiscus hedge.

The bird flew boldly to the lawn, nearer her, and pecked at an insect, then returned to its perch in the hedge.

"I'm kind of hungry too," she said.

"What would you like?" Lionberg said.

But the girl was reaching into her bag. "I've got a sandwich. Buddy made it. Look, it's huge."

Eating is one of the pleasures of life, Lionberg was thinking as he watched her eat the sandwich. Standing up, in the middle of the lawn, it was all hurry and denial — she wolfed it down, cramming it into her mouth and nodding as she chewed. The very idea of this made him smile.

All this time chewing, her mouth full, she was apologizing with her eyes and her pretty fingers.

She was licking her fingers when she said, "Mind if I go for a swim?"

For an instant he thought how clever she was to have noticed the pool when she had noticed so little else of the house.

"Go ahead. It's not ornamental — it's a real lap pool."

"I meant the beach."

"I'll give you a lift."

"I need the walk," she said, and waved with her back turned as she left.

He was surprised by how lightly she had come and gone. But he did not feel rejected, for she would never understand why he could not go with her, that he never walked down that busy road. For him it was unsafe — so he had been told — and it was not a risk he wished to take or a question that ever arose these days. He couldn't remember when he had last left his compound.

From an upper window he watched her on the road and then walking down the hill. Fifteen minutes later he watched her through binoculars as she swam off the rocks at Sharks Cove.

Usually visitors said, "How about a tour?" and he reluctantly took them through the ground floor of the house, showing the less valuable items. He kept all visitors from his study and his bedroom, and he had stopped showing his library — people had picked up books, opened them and saw his underlining and notes, and he felt as violated as if they had read his mail or his diary. Some books had gone missing. He believed they had been stolen.

Lionberg did not want anyone to know him. Everyone made an attempt. It seemed odd that Rain had not tried. Yet he had expected it and prepared himself for it.

Carrying Rain's bag into the guest house, he was amazed by its lightness, yet apparently everything she needed for her days in Hawaii was in it. He thought of looking, just to see what the girl regarded as necessities, but he resisted, slightly disgusted by his impulse.

After lunch he worked among his flowers, feeding his gardenias and washing the leaves with a soap mixture where they were covered in smut from the aphids and ants. It was strange the way the ants kept the aphids as domestic animals on the shrub, but this ant-farm arrangement, fascinating though it was, crudded and killed the leaves. And this year the flowers were beautiful, with a piercingly sweet fragrance.

As he washed the leaves, bringing the green back, he looked out for Rain. To hear her approach better, he turned the Vivaldi off.

It was rare for him to know a day without music. But he had a reason today — he did not want Rain to be locked out. The security system had been designed to exclude anyone from casually entering. So there was no music. He needed to hear the bell or she would be left standing in the street, perhaps for hours.

There was no music, but there was no silence either, for silence was unknown on a hot afternoon on the North Shore of Oahu. A thousand birds loudly contended, in addition to the whine of insects and the distant growl of a descending plane. He heard doves cooing, the whistling of bulbuls, and the complex song of the shama, which Rain had commented on. Most people were deaf to birdsong.

"Hello."

How had she gotten in?

She seemed to understand that he was flustered, even to divining the reason. "I came through the side gate."

"That's the service entrance. It was locked."

"I guess it wasn't."

"It's supposed to be locked . And there are motion sensors."

Rain was smiling. "Well, here I am!"

Lionberg felt insecure and outwitted, but the girl was looking around once again.

"What do you call those trees?"

They were tall and weedy-looking, with slender trunks that popped up everywhere, and especially flourished in the gully that lay between the hedge around Lionberg's garden and the perimeter fence.

He said, "To tell you the truth, they're a nuisance. Christmasberry. Brazilian pepper. Schefflera. Gunpowder trees."

"They're so green."

He was holding a newly washed gardenia bough in his hands, but she said nothing about that.

"I've put your bag in the guest house. I think you'll be comfortable there."

"Hey, thanks." She started away.

She was graceful-looking yet had no grace. The young could be so abrupt.

"Dinner's at eight."

"That's okay, I won't be eating," she said. "I got some bananas at Foodland and ate them coming up the hill."

Lionberg said, "We were expecting you to have dinner, I'm afraid. I think the chef made something special for you."

Had she seen a look of disappointment on his face? He hoped not, because he knew that he was not disappointed. It was simply that the guest, like the host, had certain obligations.

"Okay, I'll come. Hey, that's real sweet of the chef."

He repeated the time. He said there was no dress code. But he thought: Why did I insist on her coming? Why did I mention the chef? He had never done that before. He had always been happiest eating alone. And by the time dinner was ready, he had stopped being annoyed with himself and begun to resent the girl for making him feel so ill at ease in his own house.

51

Dinnertime

"HERE I AM AGAIN," Rain Conroy said, sounding so willing, though he knew she was there because he had insisted. Yet she seemed convincingly enthusiastic, and as always her voice sounded cheery. There was something whole-hearted and uncomplaining about her, and even the way she looked tonight reassured him. She wore a simple black dress that showed off her long legs, which were beautiful. The dress was so small and insubstantial Lionberg imagined plucking it off her by its spaghetti straps and cramming it into his pocket.

The skirt was riding up her thigh — she was leaning, peering into the side room, Lionberg's study. "Calla lilies," she said eagerly, and looking closer, she walked into the room.

Who had ever before entered Lionberg's study? The maid, a carpet layer, a cable installer. They had no idea where they were. It was a source of pride to Lionberg that no one other than a handful of employees or laborers had ever seen the room in which he worked, had ever seen the place in which he used his mind, had ever seen his desk, his scattered papers, the books that mattered most to him, his favorite paintings, everything he regarded as revelation. Even his handwriting, which he was sensitive, even a bit vain, about — he wanted no one to see it, no one to know him through it, did not want to hear any comments about it. He sensed that if someone saw it, he would be exposed and would lose something of himself.

And here was Rain Conroy with her hands on his desk, smiling at the painting.

"Georgia O'Keeffe. An amazingly introspective image, I always think."

"I used to grow them," she said. She wasn't listening.

"I can't tell you the number of museums that have pestered me for it. I wouldn't part with it. I never get tired of looking at it."

"They love fish fertilizer, nitrogen especially," she said. "You can tell when they're happy. They get very white. And when they're not looked after, they get all limp and sort of rot."

"'Lilies that fester smell far worse than weeds,'" Lionberg said.

"That's really true, you know."

"Shakespeare. Sonnet Ninety-four." She didn't hear that, either.

Lionberg turned some papers over. Not that the girl was looking at them, but seeing his handwriting made him self-conscious.

"This is my study," he said. "I do my work here."

"What kind of thing do you do?"

"I am a man of leisure," Lionberg said. "A little writing. Some gardening. Some beekeeping."

She was in his room; he had revealed what he did there. She could see his papers, the pictures — not just the O'Keeffe but the Matisse sketch of a footbridge and the photograph of himself at age ten, posed on the porch of his parents' house. Anyone could see that he had been a deeply unhappy child; he had sorrowful eyes. Lionberg pitied the child when he looked at it. She was unimpressed by everything except the flower — not the painting but the species.

"Isn't this sketch incredible?" He decided not to say it was Matisse. "Pencil."

"Anyone could erase it," she said.

He decided to surprise her by switching on the old jukebox, which had been in shadow in a corner of the room. She laughed at the red and blue and yellow lights, the flashing lights inside its fishbowl top, where the black plastic records shimmered. The light was on her face.

"We've got one just like that at the diner where I work," she said.

Lionberg switched off the lights.

Rain was still smiling, moving forward. The study led to a lanai, which was attached to his bedroom. She commented on the palms in the colorful Sicilian vases, the plants — strawberries in terra-cotta pots, herbs in a planter. At the edge of the lanai sat several large Chinese water jars, glazed red, that held fish and water lilies and greens mats of hyacinth.

"Those are nice."

"When I can't sleep, which is often, I come out here and shine a flashlight in and look at the fish."

"I have the opposite problem. I have trouble waking up."

He realized that she had seen nearly everything on this floor of the house. Walking back to the dining room, she glanced to the side and said, "That's the second-biggest TV screen I've ever seen."

She meant the television set in his bedroom, which she had glimpsed through the lanai window. It was his secret that he often lay in bed and watched old movies on the screen that took up most of one wall. No one had seen it because no one had been on his private lanai, which was accessible only from his study.

Lionberg asked, "I'm curious. Which TV screen was the biggest?"

"Pigskin Lounge in Sweetwater," she said. "It's a sports bar. Buddy's cousin owns it. You never want to go there alone if you're a woman, my father used to say."

Lionberg's only thought was that he had never been in such a place.

"This is great," Rain said, seating herself at the elaborately set table — all the silver, four glasses each, the stacked plates, the napkin rings. "My father was always so big on mealtimes."

"And you're not?"

"I don't think about it much."

"One of the pleasures of life."

"I usually eat standing up," Rain said.

Lionberg said, "If I had a daughter, I would never say, 'Don't go there, don't do this or that.' I'd tell her to go anywhere she wanted. Complete freedom."

"Excuse me, but if you lived in Sweetwater, you sure as heck wouldn't. You'd be warning her and worrying, just like my daddy did."

Lionberg realized that in trying to please her by seeming open-minded, he had made himself look naïve. He even wondered whether he believed what he had just said to her. But then, what did it matter? He had never been in such a bar. He was bored by sports, by the noise and the frantic spectacle. The sight of big men competing seemed to him gladiatorial and frightening and sometimes sissified.

"Bars like that are dangerous," she was saying, sure of herself, seeming to know how ignorant he was of such places. "If a single woman goes in, the men figure she's looking for trouble. And she usually is, or why else would she be there? It's a man's place."

He was smiling, as though she were not being logical.

"Just a joint," she said.

"Did your father tell you that?"

"He didn't need to," she said.

Then she fell silent and began on the soup, eating slowly, using her spoon a bit too carefully, as if this were not a meal but a sort of laboratory procedure. She looked uncomfortable while Lionberg watched.

"My daddy died two years ago," she said.

"I'm so sorry," Lionberg said.

"It was very —" She didn't finish the sentence. She had stopped eating, too. Her silence and immobility gave this unfinished sentence a significance that was obscure but suggestive — a pause hanging over them, the thought of the dead man, bereavement, sorrow.

Lionberg said, "When my father passed away the world looked different."

"Smaller," Rain said. "And old people look so fragile. I see them and I just want to protect them." She was staring at the tablecloth. "I'm so happy when they let me help them. When they sort of admit they're frail and accept the attention."

"Do you get much chance to help old people?" Lionberg asked. "I would have thought they weren't your speed."

Put on the defensive, she framed her answer as earnest questions, saying, "That diner I told you about? Where I work? In Sweetwater? There's always these little guys there, looking like kids, and helpless and all bowlegged?"

Her eyes were shining as though she wished she could be bolder, because those old people sometimes made her fiercely maternal. But she was a guest here and had to be grateful to this man who, so far, had only listened in a silence that seemed reproachful.

"When they leave the diner they wobble on their crooked legs like they're going to fall over and break," she said, and twisted her mouth in regret.

"The world is full of little old guys," Lionberg said.

"But they're all different," Rain said. "Like some of them have osteoporosis."

The word made Lionberg smile again. Simple afflicted folks who couldn't spell knew such terms as "carpal tunnel syndrome," "peripheral vascular disease," and "angioplasty," not because they could read but because they suffered.

"They make me think of my father," Rain said.

She had not noticed Lionberg's silence, she seemed hardly to notice anything, and when she commented on one of his treasures it was the most trivial aspect of it — ignoring Georgia O'Keeffe and chattering about the flower. She had no attachment to anything here, and that would have made her seem frivolous except that she was still talking, still going on about her father.

"He had a heart condition," Rain said. "He was sixty-two."

"God, that's not old!"

Seeing he had startled the girl, Lionberg then touched his face with his napkin in a self-conscious gesture, cramming it against his mouth as though dabbing it. He wondered what he had revealed in having protested so strongly.

"I was kind of an afterthought," she said. "I'm twenty-six."

And that's not so young, he told himself. It was the same age his wife had been when he had met her. But he did not see his ex-wife's face on Rain's — he saw someone else, different features, other details, another sensibility. Rain, who came from somewhere else, was another shape and size, leading another life, one he had not led. Just the fleeting thought of it gave him the sort of pang he felt when he saw something that was out of his reach, not fame but peculiar forms of contentment — the solitary explorer or single-handed yachtsman, the expatriate in a hammock attended by his islander wife, the prospector who had staked all his savings on a risky claim and found gold.

"'Time heals everything,'" she said.

"My ex-wife and I are the best of friends," Lionberg said.

Rain looked up, querying this unexpected statement. What had she said to provoke it? She frowned, thinking of lapsed time and her dead father.

"Only it doesn't," she said.

"Of course not," Lionberg said.

"'It all happens for the best,'" she said.

Lionberg stared at her. She was still talking, but in quotation marks, in another person's voice, being ironic.

"'Everything works out in the end,'" she said. Now concentrating, she was holding her knife and fork like weapons, their handles jammed against the white tablecloth, and she wasn't eating. "'You get what you pay for.'"

"It sounds as though you don't agree," Lionberg said.

"They're all lies. Time heals nothing. Nothing happens for the best. Nothing works out. I just shut my eyes and miss my father more. And it's harder for me. My mom started dating."

"'Dating' is a word I have never really understood," Lionberg said. "I suppose that dates me."

"Dating is what me and my boyfriend do."

She had not heard his play on words. The girl was grim, gripping the knife and fork in her fists. Now she put them down and frowned at them.

"All this, um, flatware," she said.

"It's nothing special," he said insincerely. "People say you should never own anything you can't afford to lose."

"People say," Rain said, and just repeating it she ridiculed it.

Lionberg smirked to mask what he felt. He had not thought it would be this hard. He was unprepared, on the verge of exasperation.

"I don't own anything," Rain said.

He surrendered to that, and it ended the meal.

On the moonlit lanai Lionberg offered her a drink, suggested sauterne, and she accepted. He took the lens caps off the telescope, intending to show her the Pleiades for their exquisite drama and their lovely name in Hawaiian, Mak'a'li'i, the Eyes of the King. It was the sort of thing that would please her.

He saw that she was still holding the full glass of wine and that she had apparently agreed to accept it only to please him. Positioning the telescope, twisting knobs to adjust it to the correct azimuth, he heard her cough and begin to speak.

"I'm really tired," she said.

Her tallness now made her seem gauche rather than graceful. She put her glass down, and wine slopped onto the tabletop. She hesitated, did not know how to excuse herself and say good night.

He helped her with those few words, just the sort of formula that she had made such an issue of over dinner.

"See you in the morning."

He could not say whether he liked her or disliked her. No, he told himself, I don't resent her for being young. The oddity was that in spite of his wide experience, she was new to him, but perhaps her whole generation was the same. What did he know? He had no children, no grandchildren. Rain was a child.

52

Visiting Darkness

IN HIS BEDROOM Lionberg turned on the movie that had put him to sleep the night before, *The Barefoot Contessa,* with Bogart and Ava Gardner, but he became self-conscious again. It was his memory of what Rain had said about the large screen, and he did resent her for this, for keeping him from enjoying the movie.

When he put the light out and lay in the darkness, he knew he was too wakeful to sleep. The floor plan of his house was in his head, so perfectly etched he was able to get up and walk through two rooms and a corridor without a light.

He went to the guest house using the covered walkway. Though the fluorescence of moonlight gave a blue-white, almost snowy gleam to the lawn and the paving, there was only darkness in the guest house itself. He did not hesitate. This was his world, and he kept on, treading lightly, barefoot, rotating his hands in front of him to feel his way forward, like a confident blind man.

Entering the room, his footfalls were soundless on the cool hardwood floor. He stood over her and watched her sleep.

She lay in the bed like a treasure in a Chinese box, sunken in silk. She was canted sideways, one arm flung out, the other across her bare breasts, her legs apart, the sheet tangled around one of her legs, her hair spread on the twisted pillow. The rarest and most fragile Chinese jades, many of them as asymmetrical as Rain in this posture of sleep, came to him in specially constructed boxes, fitted into a silk cushion, the beautiful thing presented just like this slender sleeping woman.

He lingered, listening to her breathe and liking the way the moonlight made white jade of her skin. He guessed that she was naked. He considered lifting a corner of the sheet.

Then he became self-conscious again, as he had at dinner and in his room, feeling awkward and confused, wondering what to do next. He stepped back noiselessly into a shadow just outside the doorway and paused. There he remained, and watched, studying the way the woman's body was configured, each detail, and then simplifying it and seeing it whole, as a finely carved jade with an entire story in bas-relief, or seeing it as a familiar shape, like a shell. But there was also something plantlike in the way Rain lay.

She got up and groped to the bathroom. Lionberg held his breath. He did not move. The silence hummed for a moment, and then from the far doorway there was an interval of dribbling, the bright sound of a small bottle emptying into a still pool, the last trickle and the high notes of the drops made echoey by the blue tiles. Finally the suck and splash of pipes, followed by a hiss and sigh, and by that time she was in bed again, in the same posture, her body pressed into silk.

The rapture that Lionberg felt just then immobilized him, and yet he had never felt more alive. He was aroused. He touched his useless erection in a gesture of restraint, and it was as though his fingertips grazed solid bone. He could not move, had no wish to, and watching her claw at her beautiful hair and stretch and thrash in sleep — a slow supine ballet in the bed that batted the coverlet lower on her naked body — he felt like a bird on a branch, steadied by his toes, neck extended, beak forward.

With her fingertips against her head, Rain arched her back. She lay like that for a long time and then rolled onto her side, freeing herself from the sheet, and finally came to rest on her stomach. Her buttocks upraised, her feet parted and slightly pigeon-toed, she seemed to be lamenting in a posture of submission. Time did not exist for Lionberg then. He heard the girl's long fingernails gently clawing her pale skin with a lovely sound of chafing as she patiently scratched her smoothness. Lionberg had risen in a levitation that was opportune — silent, invisible — and he hovered just above the ground, not breathing, listening to her sigh as she stroked herself between her legs for the longest time, finishing with a sob of relief.

The night was not long enough. The moon sank and the shadows were being rinsed from the eastern sky by dawn as Lionberg stepped back without any sound, seeking darkness, to the main house and his room at the far side. In the blinking light of the video machine he saw that he had spent three hours in his vigil.

He was at breakfast first, and to make his hands busy, because he was unaccountably anxious, he deliberately cracked an egg as she entered the room.

"Did you sleep all right?" he asked.

She shook her head. "Hardly at all."

He said, "But you're the one who sleeps like a log."

"Not last night." She sipped a glass of mango juice. She said, "And you had a little trouble too."

"How did you guess?"

She smiled at him. He began to groan, and he looked away, because there was power in her smile.

"Paying me a visit like that," she said.

Lionberg blushed, his ears reddened. He had never blushed in his own house. But she had seen him by the bed. She knew that he was lurking while she was in the bathroom, that he had heard, and seen.

"I'm so sorry," he said.

"It's all right." The way she ate made her seem confident and unconcerned. "I pretended I was asleep. And then, I —" She laughed as a way of finishing the sentence.

"Were you afraid?"

She hesitated and then said, "I liked it. Couldn't you tell?"

Even in her most awkward moments she did not lie. Her truthfulness fascinated him — this revelation, for example.

"I just didn't know what to say. And I guess you didn't either."

In the way she spoke to him, she made him into a boy, and now it seemed she was the mistress of the house and he the clumsy guest.

The white-rumped shama began singing again, its whistling warbling song, and this helped him change the subject. She asked him to remind her of the name of the bird.

Soon after breakfast she said she was going to the beach. Lionberg gave her some bottled water and said, "Drink when you're not thirsty and you'll avoid dehydration." As she walked down the hill to the beach the sunshine followed her, increasing as she

268

descended, until she was walking in a deepness of heat and light. Lionberg could see her bright shape through one of his low-powered telescopes. He spent all day watching her. She swam, she lay on the beach, she seemed to sleep.

He did nothing else that day except watch her and wait for her to return to the house. When she did finally come back, at five, and she saw that he was waiting, standing with his arms at his sides, mute, eager to hear her say something, she became tentative.

"Drink?" he said at last.

"I am so tired." She looked sunstruck, her skin glowed, her fatigue showed in her smile.

Lionberg watched helplessly as she went to her room. It was still light. He drank alone, and he felt his routine had been disturbed. He had started drinking too early, so it tasted different and wrong.

He ate dinner alone, conscious of being alone, that very word in his mind. The book propped open next to his plate was *Dongxuan Zi — The Thirty Methods*. Though the paintings were good enough, Lionberg found the text poorly written and bloodless. He murmured the captions aloud, as though rehearsing them to amuse someone at dinner: "Wiggling Dragon . . . The Great Peng Bird Soaring over the Dark Ocean . . . Cat and Mouse Share the Same Hole . . . The Mule of Three Springs . . . Autumn Dogs . . ."

He stopped, shutting the big expensive book. He had lost his appetite. He caught himself staring at the empty chair and thought that perhaps Rain had had too much sun. *Drink when you're not thirsty and you'll avoid dehydration.* Hadn't he told her that?

Her room was in darkness. She had apparently drawn the curtains to shut out the sunlight, and now the moonbeams were blocked. It took Lionberg minutes of standing there in the dark, holding a glass of water, to make out her form on the bed — for the longest time he could not even see the glass of water in his hand. The sheet was tossed over her. If that small crumpled shadow on the floor was her bathing suit, she was perhaps naked.

He stood over her, feeling happy once again, and happier still when he realized that it was a recaptured feeling, inspired by her, belonging to him.

"What's that in your hand?"

Her voice was sudden and very clear and awake. Had her eyes been open all this time?

"Brought a glass of water for you."

"You read my mind."

She sat up, drawing the sheet over her shoulder like a toga. Yes, she had to be naked.

She drank quickly. Between her thirsty gasps the odd gulps stroked her throat like sobs. She put the glass down on the marble side table with such directness it was as though she could also see in the dark.

"Sit here."

He laughed with relief and went to her. It was what, in his mind, he had been imploring her to say.

"What time is it?"

"Maybe ten."

"Gosh."

"Not late."

"No."

Beneath this simple talk he slid nearer to her and touched her, moved his hand along the warm skin of her thigh. He was so close to her, his arm was pressed against hers and he felt her fingers creeping across his own thigh. He was thinking how the most primitive reassurance in a person's life was the offering of warm skin, and the thought made him feel less like a man at the moment of conquest than an imploring child yearning to put his mouth on her.

The suddenness of her fingers reaching him where he was most tender made him sigh, but she drew back, startled by its bigness, as though it were an accident. He took her hand and clutched it, pleading, hand to hand.

He leaned forward to beg her, and kissed her instead in a begging way. Her lips tasted grapy, from the flavored water.

"No," she was saying into his mouth.

She moved away from him on the bed, so that there was now a shadow between them.

"Not now," she said.

There was desire in her voice. Lionberg knew that she wanted it as much as he did, but that she was being wise, because there was something all wrong about this, the timing especially, and he loved her for that.

She touched him where he was hard and raw and said, "I can't let you go like that."

Twisting herself in an unhesitating motion, she moved her head down his chest while gripping the raw stick of his penis with her hand. When she licked it and put her mouth on it, it was as if she were medicating it, coating it with warm ointment, a kind of salve she was administering with her tongue and lips, soothing it softly as she moved her head, her long hair tumbled over Lionberg's thighs. She seemed to concentrate more and held him harder as he let out a small cry, and then she used her hands, pumping the last of him into her mouth.

"I've dreamed of sex like that," he said in a voice he hardly recognized as his own.

From the way she moved against him, he could tell she was laughing. She said, "That's not sex."

He drew her up, kissed her smeared lips, and said, "I like you, honey," and left the room, striding into the darkness without looking back.

53

Departure Gate

"ROY-BOY, where's my gal?" Buddy Hamstra was roaring into the phone. "I'll bet you'll be glad to see me!"

From the peculiar crackle Lionberg knew that he was using his cellular phone, in his car, driving up the steep hill on the switchback, where the reception was always bad.

Lionberg shook his head. Soon after that — sooner than Lionberg wanted — Buddy was at the gate in his BMW, honking in mock impatience. He kept honking gleefully even after Lionberg had opened the gate.

A stuffed animal, bigger than life size, a dog as big as a man, sat upright in the back seat, grinning foolishly.

Seeing Lionberg's glance, Buddy said, "Wile E. Coyote."

"That's right," Lionberg said, though he had no idea.

"So where is she?"

Buddy still sat in the car. He wore a gold chain around his neck with a shark's tooth and Stella's wedding ring on it, aviator sunglasses, and a T-shirt lettered *Life Guard*. He seemed fatter each time Lionberg saw him. He was holding his cellular phone in one hand and a Mars bar in the other. He fooled, talked into the Mars bar, pretended to bite the phone, made a face, and shoved half the candy bar into his mouth. With his mouth full, he shouted incoherently.

"I haven't seen her this morning," Lionberg said, speaking so faintly that he heard in his own voice something worse than mere reluctance. He had been dreading this moment like an amputation.

Buddy swallowed the mouthful of chocolate and yelled, "Hurry up, Rain!"

Howling like that was something Lionberg would never have done — he winced at the sound of it — but the girl responded with a howl of her own. "Coming!" She appeared a moment later, breathless, smiling, carrying her small bag, looking beautiful. She is twenty-six years old, Lionberg said to himself, yet that explained nothing.

"Hi, uncle."

"You've got a plane to catch, toots."

Lionberg said, "Don't be late."

"It's not till tonight, one of these redeyes," Rain said. "But I want to buy some presents."

"We're having a plate lunch in town," Buddy said. Whenever he mentioned food, he sounded hungry.

"Thanks for everything," Rain said, and got into the car.

Buddy said, "Hey, Roy-boy, don't look so relieved to be alone." He laughed and eased the car through the gate in reverse, backing onto the road.

Lionberg was dumb, too stunned to speak. He wanted to leave the girl with a thought, with a gift, with a kiss anyway — he had not imagined it happening this quickly. He smiled until the car was out of sight, then listened hard. The sound of the receding car was the last live sound of the girl, like a sigh that becomes silence, a last expiring breath.

He closed the gate, feeling faint, and sensed that all his happiness had fled. A large cloud passed overhead. As always, the sunshine seemed to follow her. He went to his small telescope and caught them as they made the turn into Waimea Bay. He was briefly revitalized by the dazzle of sunlight on the car's windshield.

He stood alone in the empty house, listening for her, and was disturbed to hear nothing. He went to the guest house and sniffed impatiently in her room, trying to discern her odor. "That's not sex," he said in her voice, and was aroused again. The bathroom was still humid with her and held her presence. He pulled back the sheets as though unwrapping a ghost. The bedclothes were warm enough to retain her smell. He followed these fugitive scraps of her from object to object — the pillow, the towels, a long strand of hair in the sink — sniffing like a dog. Then he lay on the bed where she had lain and told himself that he was a savage, that he needed a fetish from her, hair and feathers, a rag of her underwear. He wanted her back. He asked himself, Is love a girl?

That night he ate alone, turning the pages of a rare book that had always pleased him when he dipped into it, *In the Sargasso Sea,* by Thomas Janvier. Tonight it bored him and seemed false, and he disliked himself for having been duped by it in the past.

After dinner he fell asleep in a chair, but when he went to bed he could not sleep. He knew why. The lighted clock on his side table told him that her flight was about to leave.

He called the airline, wishing to hear anything related to her, even flight information. "That flight has been delayed," a man said, striving to sound efficient. The new flight time was after midnight.

Dressing hurriedly, Lionberg was so desperate to be on the road that he set only one burglar alarm. He grazed the hedge at the gate — there would almost certainly be a scratch on the fender of his black car, from which the insignia and the Lexus name had been removed. Never mind the scratch on the paintwork. He saw it as a sacrifice and was proud to have a visible scar.

Outside his house he always felt he was on another planet. Tonight he thought, What is happening to me? The damp shoreline, the darkness of the pineapple fields, the lights and fences at Schofield Barracks, the empty freeway, then green lighted signs saying *Airport* and the clock on the airport tower, which told him he had time.

The delayed flight had been a reprieve. He simply wanted to give her the kiss he had been denied in the driveway that morning, to see her again. He wanted her to see him, too — to show her that he had driven the forty miles in the dark.

Buddy was at the gate, sitting with his feet out, his hands on his big belly. He was drinking a Diet Coke.

"What are you doing here, you crazy bastard?" he said when he saw Lionberg.

"She forgot her hat."

It was the baseball cap he had worn when she first saw him, which had once been lettered *The Plaza.*

"Where is she?"

"On line. She's boarding."

Rain smiled with unmistakable gratitude when she saw Lionberg approach. She stepped out of line, stumbling against the boarding passengers.

Lionberg took her hand with desperate confidence and said, "I'm going to miss you, honey."

It was what he had wanted to say this morning, what he had come forty miles to say. He badly wanted to impress her.

"I'll miss you too."

He looked for meaning in her eyes and thought he saw what he wanted.

"Why are you leaving?"

"I'm going home," she said. She touched his hand softly like a reminder. "Back to my life."

That made him sad, that she had a life he knew nothing about.

He said, "This is for you, honey," and gave her the baseball cap.

She laughed and put it on. When she kissed him this time the visor poked his head.

"Gotta go," she said.

"Crazy kid," Buddy said, standing with Lionberg. They looked like an older couple seeing off their daughter — that same admiration and forgiveness, that same love. Buddy, fleshy, even bosomy in his T-shirt, was the gruff and bossy mother; Lionberg — small, leaner, forgiving, infatuated — was the tender father. They stood with the others saying goodbye at the departure gate as Rain entered the tunnel. When she was gone, Lionberg felt sick, and he wanted to get away from Buddy.

"Funny seeing you here," Buddy said, panting to keep up with him. "I haven't seen you out of your Bat Cave in ages." He poked his finger at Lionberg. "You're a very mysterious guy! You've got secrets." He called out to a man mopping the airport floor, "This is Royce Lionberg! He's got secrets!"

Lionberg drove slowly back to the North Shore on the empty roads, thinking how he had no secrets now. He wanted to be on that plane with Rain, to be going home with her. What she had said of Sweetwater had moved him in its simple solidity. It was home in a sense that he had never known the word. He had made a home, but she had been born in one and still lived there. That was so different. It was permanent, it was safe and secure. Why would you ever leave?

Reentering his house that night, he was angry. He saw it with Rain's eyes and disliked it for being cluttered and airless. It was wrong, it was selfish. He couldn't remember a time when he had felt so dissatisfied. His collections, his treasures, seemed merely pretentious, just decorative, without significance, worthless.

The expensive humidor disgusted him. He took out a cigar and, in his reading chair, cut and lit it. A cigar always calmed him, even gave him moments of great happiness. Puffing smoke, he remembered how, long ago, in the days when he gave parties, he had been infuriated by seeing that someone had stubbed out a cigar in a carved jade saucer.

The moment enlightened him. The things people accumulated — old pictures and pewter, jade and carved ivory and ugly-faced masks and books and tapestries and large yellow sperm-whale teeth scored with scrimshaw, silver platters and spoons and sugar tongs, the incidental and ill-assorted objects that were supposed to have value — all of it was merely borrowed from the vast store of the world's artifacts and ultimately returned to it, sold, bequeathed, lost, stolen. These objects were protected, and found another home, another thief or borrower, but in any case just an overburdened custodian, until they were returned again or destroyed. They had no meaning or use beyond their being handled or looked at.

Had he been a writer, he would have written that, and he wished he could write it, to rid himself of the sadness of its truth: nothing was owned. He was merely a watchman, a menial, with illusions, buffing things, polishing, dusting, being careful not to break them.

He had made a provision for everything as a legacy, but people did what they wanted. In time, it would all be sold or deaccessioned or snatched in spite of his wishes.

It was worth no more than a glance, which was what she had given it.

His cigar splintered and sparked and came apart as he dug it into the white jade saucer, laughing angrily, pushing it against the fine carving. While the smoke rose like bitter incense he took down his Matisse footbridge, knifed open the taped back of the frame, and slid out the sketch. Holding it down with the flat of his left hand, he worked a cheap pencil eraser on the lines at the center of the bridge, leaving his mark, making it uncrossable. He felt savagely happy, with an intimation of insanity, desperate for his happiness to last and fearing that it would end at any moment, leaving him bereft.

54

Triple Word Score

HIS HEAD LOWERED in reverence, the dark islander put out a set of fetish objects, like a shaman engrossed in a ritual for telling the future or interpreting the past. He crouched beneath the ragged wind-shredded fronds of the leaning palms, in the mossy corner of the shadiest part of the property, an islander at a jungle pool, the water's reflection spangling his belly and making it gleam. His face was close to a painted square that was blocked with the sort of mystical patterns you find in the boldest mandalas of Oceania.

I went nearer, feeling intrusive and awkward, until I saw it was Keola with his shirt off, bent over a board game. Peewee hurried behind me and said, "You want to play?"

It was Scrabble. They had started playing it between shifts at the far corner of the hotel swimming pool, after it closed for the evening. Everywhere I had lived, Scrabble was played differently, the game adapted to the culture and the lingo, certain words allowed and not others, challenges restricted, one society making a noisy free-for-all of it, another an intellectual exercise. The game of Scrabble reflected the people who played it, as when Trobriand Islanders made the game of cricket into something riotous, a reconciling adaptation known to anthropologists as syncretism, as valid with Scrabble as with cricket or Christianity.

"Only problem — Peewee take hours to choose a word," Keola said, which alarmed me, because Keola was the slowest worker in the hotel.

While he was talking, Marlene joined us, shaking her head. She had heard Keola and obviously agreed with him.

"Let's do rapid transit," I said. I explained how each player would have just two minutes to choose a word; if time ran out, the player's turn was forfeited. This way the game would be shorter and more exciting.

They liked this idea. They passed me the sock that served as a bag for the letters and told me to choose one, to determine who would start. I got an "M," which I was sure was no good, and handed the sock to Peewee, and smiled at the thought they were letting me join them. They knew that in a former life I had been a writer, Buddy Hamstra still introduced me by saying, "He wrote a book!" but they were not in the least put off by the prospect of my playing.

"Maybe I should have a handicap."

"You got a handicap," Keola said. "You one *malihini*."

It meant newcomer, but was I that new? More than seven years had passed since I had come to Hawaii and taken over as hotel manager. But the longer I stayed, the deeper my understanding of the paradox that the people with the lowest status had the greatest seniority. Like Mohawks in Manhattan, Hawaiians in Hawaii had no wealth and were almost placeless, yet they could pull rank even on the missionary families. Hawaiians were like impoverished aristocrats who had sold the castle, the land, and the family silver, and yet, battered and threadbare, they still kept the family name. This also meant that every human encounter involved a tricky negotiation, because pride was involved.

"I'll do my best."

Marlene went first and put down "ped" at the center of the board.

"You allow abbreviations?" I asked.

"The sign say 'Ped Crossing.' Is a howlie sign," Marlene said, and chose three more letters from the sock to indicate that the discussion was over.

Peewee used the "p" to make "zap." Keola made "moped," which I put into the plural with the vertical word "same." Telling me I was wasting vowels, Marlene used my "a" to make "ama," and before I could question the word, she said, "Means outrigger in Whyan."

"Hawaiian words okay?"

"Dis Whyee."

"But they aren't in the dictionary."

"Try look in one Whyan dictionary," Keola said, and used his full two minutes to make "lua," which he declared meant toilet in Hawaiian, as well as the number two. One entire side of the Scrabble board began to bulk with Hawaiian words: "lolo," "manao," "puna," and "kumu." And then, after Marlene made the word "hi," Keola added two more letters and created "shim."

"Dis a word, brah," he said before I could question it.

"Pidgin," Marlene said, and defied me to challenge her. "Dis a language. If you know it, maybe you make more better words."

"'Shim,' it English," Keola said. "Use in construction."

Something in the way he pronounced it, *conshruction,* made me doubtful, so I challenged the word. Because it wasn't Pidgin, neither Peewee nor Marlene backed him. "Too bad we don't have a dictionary," I said. Keola lost a turn.

Peewee put down "less," and for his turn Keola put "fut" in front of it. *Futless?*

"It mean confused," Marlene said, speaking for Keola. "In Whyee."

I said, "You're peeing on my leg and telling me it's raining."

Futless was how I felt when the game ended and Marlene sulked as she was declared the winner. I came in last, behind Keola, who had always seemed to me a borderline moron. But I wasn't discouraged, just fascinated, for in my office I looked up the word "shim" and saw that I had been mistaken. It was a tapered piece of wood used as a brace or a filler, as Keola had said, in construction.

The next evening, when the shift changed, I was eager to play again. Trey took Peewee's place. Marlene was still gloomy-looking. They challenged me on "kerb," I challenged them on "laff," and let the other words pass: "owch," "dri," "gaz," "yo," and "dis." Keola was way ahead of everyone. Trey put down "toni" and glared at me.

Instead of challenging "toni," I took my turn and converted this worthless fragment into "ultonian."

Marlene grunted, shaking her head.

"It's an adjective. Relating to Ulster."

Marlene was already flipping through the *American Heritage Dictionary* — she had brought it in a plastic shopping bag because of my previous day's challenge of "shim" — and she triumphantly told me, holding the fat volume in my face, that no such word was listed in it.

Losing this challenge, I lost my turn. On my next turn I used the word "ergo." "Sound like a funny kind of word," Keola said, and challenged it. I confidently looked it up and showed it. "It's Latin for therefore."

"Latin! That hybolic!" Marlene said, and put down "pau."

"I know it means end in Hawaiian," I said. "But I guarantee you it's not in that dictionary."

"Because of it one frikken racist dictionary," Marlene said. "We used to get licks from the teacher in school for using Whyan words."

"Maybe she wanted you to learn English."

"Maybe she was a stupid howlie like you," Marlene said, her eyes shining in anger.

Trey put down "Dion" and explained, "Celine."

Marlene, still furious, said, "Howlie bitch. Got a face like a horse."

"But da kine horse I would fuck," Keola said.

Trey declared the game over, rubbing it in by saying, "This game is *pau*." Each player's points were added, and Trey came in first, Marlene second, Keola next. I came in last again.

On the third night, Marlene refused to play, but Sweetie said — it was news to me — that she loved playing Scrabble, and so with Peewee and Keola we resumed, passing the sock, selecting letters, making words that were not words — "jin," "hink," "dred," "carni." I didn't care. I loved witnessing the creation of a whole new lexicon. Peewee challenged me when I put down "quod," and he was annoyed to find it in the dictionary. In spite of missing a turn, he was still ahead, for he knew (and I did not) that an ern was a sea eagle, an ai was a three-toed sloth, and a zho was a sort of yak.

Using the "a" in "ai" to make "figa," Sweetie said, "It's a real word, promise to God," and slipped her thumb between her fingers, thrusting upward with this fist, a gesture I now recognized, but how did she?

"Some surfer dudes do that," Keola said. "The ones from Brazil."

Keola made "roop," Peewee made "fi" ("like 'hi-fi'"), and I tried to use my "x." Only after I made "axe" did Keola point out that I could have made "axle" on the other side of the board. Peewee put down "casa." I gave it to him because it was one letter short of the corner, which would have given him a triple word score.

Adding an "l" to the corner square to make "casal," Sweetie collected the triple word score and said, "I'm out. I win."

"Wait a minute," I said.

Sweetie giggled and said, "'Casal' means double bed. Like queen size. The big beds."

While I stared at Sweetie, Keola said, "The ones you do boom-boom on."

Sweetie said, "It's Brazilian. Like 'figa.'"

"How do you know that?" I asked.

"Just smart, I guess."

The sense of blood rising through my body, heating me, making me short of breath, kept me from asking more questions about the Brazilian surfer who had taught my wife those words. And anyway, much to the delight of the others, Peewee, who had been placidly paging through the dictionary, found my name in it.

"Usage Panel!" he crowed, and pointed at me. He showed the page: there was my name. "He on the dictionary Usage Panel, and the bugga come last!"

I never played again. It was not only that, playing Scrabble, I realized that my workers didn't like me very much, and that my wife had a past; it was perhaps the truth of Keola's saying, when he consoled me, "You know, brah, not all the words you say are in the dictionary."

55

Love Is a Girl

WEEKS AFTER Rain Conroy's visit, Buddy called, apologizing to Lionberg for imposing the girl on him and inviting him for a drink.

"I've got my hands full at the moment," Lionberg said.

That was pride and humiliation. He was paralyzed, could not move, hated his thoughts. Superstition kept him around the house, trying to complete just one task in the routines he had set for himself. But he was stuck in a chair, frowning at the lawn. He did not want to develop new habits — meeting Buddy down on the beach or going into Honolulu to eat one of Peewee's hamburgers at the hotel. He had never been idle before, but now he was worse than idle. He seemed to be suffering massive trauma to his brain, the words doctors used to describe a serious head injury. He had heartache, too, for which any thought on his part would cause him more pain.

He hesitated to ask the question in his mind, but he risked it anyway. He said, "What do you hear from Rain?"

"Oh, she's back in her box," Buddy said. "Probably at the diner, and doing her volunteer work."

"Is she still working at the diner?"

Lionberg had said too much. Buddy didn't know anything. He was careless, he was free.

Never before had Lionberg been restless in his house. He was not miserable but discontented. The feeling helped him recall times when, very young, promises were made but were not kept. His uncle saying, "We'll have to get you over on the boat sometime," but it never happened. His mother saying, "If you're good, maybe you'll get binoculars for your birthday." But there were no binoculars. Times of impatience, of being kept waiting, of longing — most of all knowing that no one would give him anything, that he would have to make his own life and fend for himself in this vast, mobbed, indifferent world.

This affair was out of his hands. So he took another look at his possessions and was consoled by them once more. He resented Rain for making him doubt their value. They were his achievement. The Matisse could be restored.

For some days he disliked Rain for making him feel vulnerable and full of doubt. He saw her as shallow, casual, breezy, presumptuous — just young. She had stayed and patronized him. And she was the worst kind of coquette — teasing him, arousing him, putting her mouth on him, sucking him off, saying, "That's not sex," then going away.

Yet he never reflected this way without concluding that she was a perfect flower, that there was nothing to dislike, that all the flaws were his. She was innocent and, even out of her depth, she was buoyant. He longed to see her again. He thought, Yes, love is a girl.

It must have been about this time that he called me. His calling me was such a rare event that I suspected a problem. When he suggested meeting at the hotel bar for a drink, I was sure that something was wrong.

He was early that night at Paradise Lost. He looked as conspicuous to me as he probably had at the airport when Buddy saw him.

"You left a house and a wife and a whole life in London," he said. Not waiting for me to say anything, he went on, "And you started all over again here."

"That's the short version," I said.

"All I mean to say is, it can be done."

"Didn't you know that?"

"I've had a bit of a shock," Lionberg said.

"What kind?"

"I've discovered I'm human."

"Good for you."

He didn't smile. He said, "I mean, I'm not happy."

I wondered then whether this was his way of expressing despair, yet I laughed at him without realizing how wounded he was. But how was I to know?

Lionberg said, "In the months before I left my wife, we still slept together. I mean that — slept, body to body. I would wake up in the middle of the night and think, I am leaving you, and I would feel her body against mine."

There was no possible reply to this. I wanted him to get off this sorrowful subject.

"Flesh can feel so sad, so mute and helpless. It is so fragile. Flesh can feel like clay. You can sense death in it."

"But Royce, that was years ago."

It was as though I were talking someone suicidal off a high ledge.

"Those nights were unbearably sad," he said.

Feeling sad now, he looked back and saw his past as a succession of failures.

I said, "This isn't like you."

"When someone says, 'If I had my life to live over again,' people laugh. It sounds ridiculous. But I've just realized that I want to live my life over. That's what love is. The vital force that gives you the strength and optimism to do it over again."

"So you've found someone," I said.

"I hate writers," he said.

"Is that your way of saying yes?"

"I saw a very plain couple last night on television," he said. "They were holding hands, two chubby people who probably had nothing but debts. They were so happy I started to cry. I envied them."

"So why don't you get it together?"

"Maybe I will."

Touched by a transforming power, he looked haunted and hopeless. He wanted to believe that he had touched her, whoever it was (I was new to this story), and that it meant something.

I was no help to him, and I was uncomfortable with the painful way he enjoyed his irrationality. He was very specific, like a man hurting himself with a fetish. I said I could not bear to see the Matisse sketch he had partly erased. He abandoned me for a while. He called Buddy and paid him a visit at the big disorderly house on the beach. Pinky was sulking, thinner and stranger than ever. She reminded Lionberg of a feral cat, forever twitchy and watchful, possessed by hunger, with feverish eyes.

"Look what she did to my arm," Buddy said. "Bit me again!"

Lionberg instinctively glanced over at Pinky's teeth, which she flashed, reacting to his glance. The teeth seemed large and blunt in her thin face. Then he stared at Buddy's discolored flesh and saw a crescent row of bite marks in the mottled patch.

"Difference of opinion," Buddy said.

They went out to the lanai and sat, watching the sunset. Pinky retreated to her room, somehow squatting in the shadows, still sulking. Sunset was the occasion for Buddy's ritual, a drink in one hand, the heart-shaped container of Stella's ashes in the other.

Buddy took off his sunglasses and squinted at the setting sun.

Pinky began to howl softly from her room.

Lionberg wanted to talk about Rain. He began by saying, "What sort of — ?"

"Wait," Buddy said. He raised his arm, and without removing his gaze from the setting sun, he took a drink.

The distant ocean shimmered, the water's surface glazed with fiery light. The sun grew small, it was halved, then it was a drop-ping dome, and at last it winked and was gone.

"Yes!" Buddy cried out. "A green flash! Did you see it?"

Lionberg said yes, though he had seen nothing.

"That's Stella," he said. "She's talking to me."

Was he drunk? He had finished that glass, whatever was in it. He clutched the container of ashes.

Lionberg said, "Time for me to go."

"Did you want something?"

"No," Lionberg said. He had felt that being near Buddy would bring the thought of Rain near. But it hadn't, and she was even more distant. He left envying Buddy.

After another day of futility, he called her in Sweetwater.

"Hello," she said brightly, and then she told someone — who was it? — "I'll take it upstairs."

A moment later, upstairs, her voice was different.

"Who were you talking to, honey?"

"My mother," she said.

Why did this simple detail cheer him up?

"I'm so glad you called."

286

"I've been resisting," he said. He had interrupted her. He was confused — wanting to hear her voice, wanting to talk.

"I was going to call you, to thank you," she said.

He said, "I miss you, honey."

"I've been missing you," she said. "It seems crazy. I've been so unhappy. I'm not needy. I'm a strong person. I've never been this way."

Hearing her say that was a consolation, because it was how he felt. In gratitude he wanted to tell her his secret, that he loved her.

He stammered and finally said, "I really like you, honey."

"I really like you, too."

A tremulous silence swelled in the wire that connected them.

"You once mentioned that you had a boyfriend."

"I still have one," she said. "He thinks I should see a shrink."

"I'd like to be your shrink."

"I'd like you for something else."

That meant so much to him that he didn't say anything more. He only wished to hold that thought.

"He wants to marry me," she said. "He gave me an ultimatum."

Lionberg sighed and looked around his room and was reproached by every object he saw.

"Hey, I have to go to work," she said. "I'm on nights. Gotta go."

"I love you, honey," he said in a terrified voice, but there was no reply. She had not heard it.

In bed that night, after the first brief wave of sleep had curled over him and he woke again, he thought: Marriage? She has her whole life ahead of her. That was part of his desire, that she had so much life in her. It also appalled him — the very thought of her setting off down the long road. *Love is a girl.*

Lionberg's sense of peace, formerly unshakable, standing like a bronze on a plinth, had been whipped from him, and the world that had seemed so manageable before was now vast and shadowy and without symmetry. He was lost in his house amid the jumble of everything he owned. He thought of going to Nevada. It was not a long trip from Hawaii; planes left for Las Vegas all the time. He devised an itinerary, he went through each stage of the journey, but he could not get beyond seeing her. And what of the boyfriend?

The damage was done. Lionberg had never been discontented before. She had created that — or had he? She had touched him and unwittingly made a promise that could never be kept. She had shown him what he would never again see. Though she had been innocent the whole time, she had destroyed him.

He called his ex-wife in Mexico at an ungodly hour, waking her, confusing her. The line was bad, adding to the confusion, for everything he said had to be repeated. And he frightened her by begging her, saying "Please forgive me" in a voice of such sad atonement the poor woman began to cry.

He knew he would see Rain, but what was in his heart would probably horrify her and speak to him of death, for she was no cure for his sickness. There was no cure at all, but only a ruinous knowledge of what he wanted, and that it was impossible, and the denial that he would taste for the rest of his life. What appalled him was not the thought that he would never possess her but that he would have to live with what she had rearranged in his past, for what was worse than the uncertain future was the realization that his previous life was blighted. He had once believed that he had been happy, but he had lost even the memory of his happiness. Though it seemed that nothing had changed, that his life was sweeter than ever, he was drowning in misery — suffocating, so he told me.

56

Drop-In

A WILD-HAIRED MAN, thirty or so, entered the hotel sideways one blustery afternoon like another feature of the bad weather, blown there by the gusting trade winds. I was at Reception, filling in for Lester Chen. The drop-in looked local but was paler than he should have been, and vague: he seemed like someone from much farther away. He claw-combed his hair with his dirty fingers. He rocked a little in his rubber sandals, as though trying to form a sentence with his feet. He finally asked, "Sweetie 'round?"

It was plain he didn't know we were married. Sweetie was out picking up Rose at school, stopping at Costco on her way back, though I didn't say so. He was too fidgety and furtive a man to trust with any personal information.

"Maybe I can help you?"

"Looking for a room. Except for I gotta get a discount."

You gotta get? No, it was wrong to reply sharply to this drop-in. I could not read anything behind his smirk. He was muscular, in a T-shirt and shorts, waxen rather than the hue of fruitwood he should have been. He had that Aztec look of a part-Filipino, bright eyes, bony face, but too twitchy to be handsome.

"If you've got a valid Hawaii license, I can give you the *kama'aina* rate."

"I don't have no license."

Never mind the grammar, that was a fact to remember.

"Maybe some kind of ID?"

"What would that get me?"

I told him the rate for a single.

"Then we got a problem."

I smiled, not amused but swelling with the urge to say *We?* Yet in literal-minded Hawaii, sarcasm was not useful on inarticulate people. Many slow-speaking and stammering islanders were aggressive out of pure frustration. They squinted instead of replying, or grunted, or gaped like fish — all threats. Wordless people can be dangerous, for no other reason than that they are wordless. Chatter to them and they are provoked.

He darkened, rocking in his rubber sandals again, and said, "Maybe I come back a little later."

"The rate will be the same when you come back."

I was pushing my luck saying this, but I could see he was a dim prospect. Anyone asking for such a discount at the outset is unlikely to be a lavish spender later on.

"We see."

It was a hopeless moment in which I knew I was being perceived as an undifferentiated howlie, and now I just wanted this babooze to leave my hotel.

A screech of greeting made me look up. Puamana was rushing toward him, and his face had been transformed into a smile. I had never before seen Puamana look so bright or greet a guest in this effusive way. They must be related, I thought, for relatives have the ability to stimulate expressions like no one else.

"Kalani! How's it? You come back, yah? Sweetie at the school, picking up her *keiki*. She be here soon, yah?"

They embraced, groaning with affection, a sound like hunger, my mother-in-law and this scruffy stranger patting each other on the back while I stood by clicking my ballpoint pen.

"Puamana, you look so great, seesta."

Just an expression — she was certainly not his sister.

Sweetie returned as they were complimenting each other. Rose ran past me to the back of the lobby where she saw Puamana's cat sleeping on the rattan sofa. Sweetie visibly hesitated before going forward, as though trying to determine in those seconds how I figured in this. But Puamana snatched at her.

"Here she come! Sweetie, look at dis!"

Another hug, more grateful groans. They all kissed once more, then smiled and just laughed instead of speaking.

"I see you already met the family," Sweetie said.

The three of them stared at me, the ineffectual alien.

"And that's Rose," Sweetie said, nodding at Rose, who was tormenting the cat.

"Hey, brah!" Now the man was friendly, more than friendly, greeting me with a handshake and a hug, as though I had just been joyously inducted into the family.

"You related?" I asked.

"Yeah, I wish." Kalani turned to Sweetie. "I was asking you husband for a rate."

Turning to me, Sweetie creased her face in an imploring way.

"Coupla-three nights. I'm on my way to Hilo."

He stood very close to Sweetie. Puamana was still beaming proudly at him. When had she ever beamed at me?

I gave him the rate. He thanked me without turning to face me. Sweetie looked happy, embarrassed, awkward, but she and her mother were clearly pleased to see this man.

"Maybe Keola can help you with your luggage?"

"I got nothing!" he said, which caused Sweetie to smile and Puamana to scream with delight.

"What about dinner?" Puamana said.

I interrupted, saying there was a movie I wanted to see. Sweetie hesitated, then agreed to go with me. It was *Howards End,* at the Varsity Theater. She hated it, and as soon as she finished her box of mochi crunch and popcorn, she fell asleep, and she cursed when I woke her. Back at the hotel, though it was late and we both had an early shift, I made love to her suddenly, subduing her, possessing her, like a slaver with a whip. My abruptness alarmed her. She resisted, but that provoked me by making me desperate. I still was not finished. I turned her over onto her stomach, and when I held her down I could feel her whole body trembling.

"Go easy." She whimpered like a child about to cry.

"Tell me you love me," I said fiercely.

57

Waterspout

THE SUGGESTION WAS that we would have dinner, my wife, my mother-in-law, and this stranger — stranger to me, not to them, which was why I had put it off. Who was he? What I had seen of him so far had not convinced me that I should spend an evening with him. I couldn't refuse to be pleasant to him, or any other hotel guest, but sitting down at the same table was another matter. A big meal was a contract in which you agreed to get along. I had come to understand that a whole lifetime could be squandered like that.

To prevent such waste, to preserve my happiness, I had a mental list (perhaps everyone has one) of people I would never eat with again. In any new place, and especially in the hotel business, it was an ever-lengthening list. In fact, with these thoughts in mind, the people I was speaking to right now were on it: Floyd and Claudine Zinda, and Ed and Pearl Gerbig, bridge-club friends from Michigan who, late in life, discovered (so they had told me) that they suffered from seasonal affective disorder. Hawaii was the preferred destination for many such victims of winter darkness: there was no cure but our sunshine.

But that was not the topic today. On their way back from a Thai restaurant in Aina Haina, they had seen a waterspout.

"We also saw Debbie Reynolds — at the restaurant."

"I will always think of her as Tammy," Pearl Gerbig said, and began to sing the lilting song in a small girl's voice.

"It came right off the ocean," Floyd Zinda said, referring to the waterspout, "and whipped around and tore the blame roof off of a little shack by the beach. There were people inside!"

"Laughing — because what else could they do?" Claudine Zinda said.

"Ed said they were naked."

"They looked naked to me. They were sopping wet."

I said, "How did you know it was a waterspout?"

"Driver said so. He slowed down for it. He told us the Whyan word for it."

"What did it look like?" I asked.

"Real amazing."

"Like nothing you ever seen in your life."

This vagueness made me impatient. I saw Rose sucking her thumb and said, "You haven't met my daughter."

As I introduced her, Rose said, "Can I have a motorcycle?"

"Little girls don't ride motorcycles," Claudine said.

"It's a dirt bike. Anyone can ride them. You don't even need a license."

"We'll see," I said.

"I'm stoked," Rose said.

"But you've got a three-wheeler and a skateboard."

"They suck," Rose said, and flounced off.

"That was my daughter."

"Kids today want everything," Ed said.

Upstairs, Sweetie was dressing for dinner — her red dress, her Tahitian necklace, her heels. The necklace she had tightened around her neck like an elegant dog collar.

"What's that?"

"It's a choker."

"For dinner at the Pearl?"

"I want to look nice." She smoothed her dress. She angled her body and looked critically at her legs. Women dressing up seem to scrutinize themselves with other people's eyes, with new expressions. I had never seen this expression on my wife's face before, these eyes.

"Where were you this afternoon?"

"Took Rose to the zoo."

Downstairs, Puamana was at the bar with Kalani. She, too, was dressed up. I had seldom seen her so fashionable, the dress and high heels that made her look like Sweetie's sister, a yellow silk scarf flung around her neck. Mother and daughter looked at each other with a sort of incestuous approval.

Kalani wore an aloha shirt patterned with pineapples. "I just bought it," he said. He fingered Puamana's scarf. "Like that movie *Basic Instinct,* where the guy gets tied to the bed with it. Like, don't get any ideas, yah."

"Like, you just gave me one," Puamana said.

From this exchange and their laughter I concluded that they had been in the bar a while. We walked to the Waikiki Pearl. The manager, Kaniela Dickstein, owed me.

"I'm stoked," Kalani said.

Sweetie said, "That movie was awesome."

I glanced away so I wouldn't see my wife saying this.

"You still sit there eating mochi crunch with popcorn and a big root beer?" Kalani asked.

That was an accurate depiction of my wife at a movie.

"And you with a six-pack."

"You see that *Titanic?*" Puamana said.

"They didn't show it where I was," Kalani said.

I said — my first offering — "They showed it everywhere on the planet."

Puamana glanced sourly at me and Sweetie frowned.

"I know some places they didn't show it," Kalani said. "Anyway, I heard it sucked."

There was silence after this, and it continued after we were seated at the Pearl's restaurant.

"I'm Shayna. I'll be your server. Can I get any of you guys a cocktail?" She was a young, sturdy mainlander with a mainlander's direct gaze.

However marginal my hotel was in the world of hospitality, however thin my managerial experience, still "Aloha" was our greeting — on Buddy's instructions — and no one on my wait staff would ever have introduced himself in this way. Only I seemed to notice.

Kalani said, "Like, I've already had about ten!"

Sweetie ordered a margarita. Puamana giggled with Kalani, who ordered a vodka tonic. I studied the menu.

Kalani said, "I love seeing people eat — just grinding. And laughing. The louder the better. And fighting, that's great. Especially women fighting. That's awesome. Like those women mud wrestlers at Gussie L'Amour's over on Nimitz. The place still there?"

Reflecting on how I disliked seeing people stuffing their mouths, and laughing, and fighting, seeing only open mouths and rows of teeth, I heard Puamana say, "Oh yeah, Gussie still over there."

"When they quarrel, most people turn into monkeys," I said.

Kalani clawed his hair. "That's what I like about it."

That set Puamana laughing again, and my wife too.

"Now what can I get you?" Shayna the waitress said, setting down the drinks and wagging her pad and pencil.

"I would like for lick you leg, starting down here and ending up here," Kalani said, and then indicated those places with his scummy tongue.

I feared legal action — Dickstein would blame me — and was surprised to see Shayna laugh. She said, "You're terrible!"

"That what Buddy's always saying," Puamana said.

Kalani was still showing his tongue. "Like Buddy say, 'If you tongue ain't green, you gal ain't clean.'"

I said to Shayna, "Please ignore him."

"He's kind of cute," Shayna said.

"I'm a real bad influence," Kalani said. "Ask them."

I alone did not find anything humorous in this.

We ordered our meal, and after Shayna had gone, to fill the silence, I said, "There was apparently a waterspout off Aina Haina today. Some guests reported seeing it."

"That's, like, real exciting," Kalani said. It was impossible to tell from anything he said whether he was mocking me.

"What's the Hawaiian word for waterspout?"

Puamana shook her head. "I'm too drunk to remember."

Until the food was served there was silence at the table. They started talking as soon as they began to eat, mumbling with their mouths full: movies, meals, the deaths of mutual friends — some of them extremely violent. One had burned to death in a car, another was found with his throat slashed in a cane field, a third had been thrown from his motorcycle into the path of an oncoming dump truck in Nanakuli.

"He was, like, in a million pieces," my wife said as she chewed her meat. It was as if she were chewing one of them.

I stared at her.

"That sucks," Kalani said. "But we been on that road a few times, yah?"

I stared at him.

"I seen some scars on people you wouldn't believe already," Puamana said.

I stared at her and concluded that it was not them. It was me. They belonged; they were content. I was the freak. Knowing Leon Edel had reminded me of how out of place I had felt here, but I had never imagined that I could be so ignorant.

What I missed most was solitude. I had not minded being cut off from my past — in fact, one of my first pleasures in Hawaii was that my past did not matter. But somehow I had taken hold and become involved with these strangers, who seemed as ferocious and simple and unreadable as savages, and in time I had learned that they had unguessable, improbable histories. I had attached myself to them, attached myself to another past. So their history mattered, and I had to listen to its details, even if it was not mine.

"After you had a kid, it's real important for meet your fitness goals," Sweetie was saying.

"You got one awesome little cakey," Kalani said.

Thinking about my history, I heard this on a low frequency. From the silence, which seemed to oppress me like an airless hole I wore like a hat over my ears, I realized that Kalani had spoken to me.

"Thanks very much," I said.

The table had gone quiet and was part of that airlessness, until Puamana said, "The word is *waipuhilani*. Waterspout."

Now I had an image for my wordless feeling. It was as though a tall column of energy had passed over the table, scoured it of every sound, turned it over, and dropped it. Something within me had been stirred. I gave it the name jealousy, but it wasn't really that. It was a more complex emotion, the feeling of having looked into the window of a house I would never be able to enter. And looking through the window was no good. I had to wait until a waterspout tore the roof off to see the naked people inside.

After Kalani checked out of the Hotel Honolulu, I felt subdued, and Sweetie was quiet too. The wind had dropped. Rose kept begging me for a motorcycle, my seven-year-old crying, "I want a dirt bike!"

Once when I mentioned Kalani, Sweetie said, "I think he's funny."

"I don't," I said, with a "Take that" tone.

"Then you got a problem."

And another time, out of the blue, she said, "What was I doing before I met you?" But I hadn't asked. "I was in a room. Alone. Just watching TV. Reruns of *Gilligan's Island*. Waiting for you to show up, yah?"

58

First Love

SOMETIMES THIS WOMAN, my wife, surprised me with flashes of intelligence, appraising me like an unsentimental stranger, reminding me that I had to be careful of what I said. It made being married to her difficult at times, as though she weren't deaf but just hard of hearing, not blind but nearsighted. In other places I had lived, people had just enough language to make demands on me but not enough to comprehend when I told them why their demands were unreasonable.

Sweetie and Puamana said I had offended Kalani, so they were hosting a makeup meal. Their suspicion that I disliked him made them think I disliked them, too. Their identification with this oaf made me uneasy. I could not make them understand my objections to him, and so I was in the wrong. I had to appease them, pay for the meal as a sort of *ho'o ponopono,* a peacemaking ritual.

"Kalani was poor. We was stay poor" Sweetie said. "If you poor, with clothes all broke, sometimes you don't know what happening to youself in the world. And you go make mistakes."

What was this goddamned woman talking about?

"How you know — you never went poor."

"That's crap. I've been in hell. Have you ever been in hell?" I told her that I had known hard times in strange countries that would have terrified her. The worst fate was that of being miserable and distant, and not just distant but out of the known world, which was like being buried alive. She had never left home, where there was always someone to help.

"I don't mean helpless, I mean misunderstood."

This fine distinction, in her uneducated voice, threw me, like the sight of a dog walking on its hind legs. But she could not explain further.

"Or maybe I could talk story."

There was a young girl in Honolulu who wanted to look older, Sweetie said. She thought she might succeed at it by dressing up. All she had was the little money her mother gave her, so she went to thrift shops and picked through clothes racks, looking for stylish clothes that had been expensive when new. Some places sold secondhand designer clothes — wealthy women in Honolulu brought their dresses and shoes for the store to sell on consignment, at a fraction of what they had originally cost.

From this scavenging the young girl put together a lovely combination: a short skirt, a silk blouse and patent leather shoes with chunky heels and a buckle. It had taken weeks to find the right clothes at these prices. The shoes alone would have cost several hundred dollars. They made her taller, and she looked much older than she was.

"How old was she?"

"Say, fifteen."

Dressed this way and wishing to be seen, she sat at a bus stop one afternoon near Ward Warehouse, legs crossed, kicking her foot up and down, listening to her Walkman. She realized that the man next to her was talking to her. He touched her shoe to get her attention. She plucked off her earphones and smoothed her skirt.

He was about twenty-two or a little more, a "howlie." He worked at a car dealership, Hoku Honda, on Ala Moana. She was flattered when he said that he wasn't waiting for a bus but had stopped because he had seen her and wanted to talk to her. She hadn't been waiting for a bus either, but she didn't tell him that. He invited her to the Starbuck's around the corner, where — she didn't drink coffee but had a guava-honey smoothie — th' man suggested they go to a movie the next day.

There was nothing safer than a movie — all those other peo' around. She even told her mother that she was going "wi' friend." Friend meant boy, though she didn't mention his ag'

She wore her special outfit. In the theater, the Cinera' King Street, across from Gas N Go (the movie was *Seven,* ' Brad Pitt), the *haole* guy did a nice thing. He said, "Put ' here." He lifted them to his lap, making her squirm sideways, and he clasped her shoes. He didn't kiss her, or touch her in any private places. All he did was hold her shoes, his fingers around them, stroking the shiny patent leather. He did not touch her feet. They sat that way through the scary movie for two hours. She was happy; it was a real date. She liked this man and he seemed to like her. Most of all, she thought, *He's a gentleman.*

Walking her back to the bus stop where they had met — she didn't want to tell him where she lived — he asked whether he could see her again. She said yes. *I got a friend, this howlie guy,* she said to herself, smiling in the darkness of her bedroom just before she went to sleep.

The next time, he picked her up in a car he had borrowed from the dealership. "I told my boss I'm taking it to Lex Brodie's for a wheel alignment." But even saying this, something plaintive in his voice expressed disappointment.

"You're wearing slippers," he said, frowning at her rubber sandals. She was also wearing shorts and a T-shirt.

"I thought maybe we go to the beach, yah?"

He wasn't *huhu,* angry; he seemed frustrated and moody. So she hurried home and dressed up, and because she wasn't able to run in them, she put on the shoes in his car. The man was happy — more than happy. He agreed to take her to Hanauma Bay. She agreed to stop at Zippy's for a shake on the way. "You look nicer like that," he said in a grateful voice. She felt for the first time in her girlhood that she could ask anything of him, that she had power over him.

They sat on the grassy edge of the bay, under the palms, and he held her feet in his lap. She wanted to take off her shoes to walk on the sand.

"Don't bother. We'll be going soon."

He drove her to a place that sold shave ice. When they finished eating the ices he seemed surprised, saying he lived right nearby.

"Want to see my place?"

She knew there was no greater risk than going alone with a man to his room. But older women did it, and she had started to love him. He was older than any boy she knew, and because of that she trusted him. Besides, she knew where he worked, Hoku Honda. She had begun to understand, from something as ordinary as the pressure of his hands on her feet, that she was his secret friend.

"Promise not to hurt me?"

"I would never hurt you."

The room was on the ground floor of a house just off Kapahulu, behind the shave ice place and across the street from an elementary school. She could hear the small children playing. So recently she had been that age and playing! She thought, But I am not a schoolgirl anymore.

The *haole* guy was happy again. He sat across the room so that she would not be frightened. Then he rolled up the narrow carpet and asked her to walk up and down the wood floor as hard as she could, stamping her heels. In his chair, moving his lips, he seemed to be praying.

That day, leaving the house, he said, "I want to buy you something nice. What do you want?"

She said, "I'm saving up for something special."

He folded a twenty-dollar bill in half and put it into her hand. He did the same the next time, after the movie (*Lethal Weapon*), where he had held her feet again; and after the beach, where he had taken pleasure in gripping her feet and hoisting her to a tree branch in the park; and after parking awhile to watch the Honolulu lights from the road on Tantalus. It was not always a twenty he gave her; sometimes it was a ten or a five. The only request he made was "Please wear your shoes."

Those secondhand shoes! She was self-conscious about them; she wanted to tell him where she had bought them. She was worried he might have minded, because wearing someone else's shoes was like a trick. Sometimes she wished he would kiss her lips instead of her shoes, stroke her nipples the way he stroked the shoe buckles. And she wanted to touch him. She had feared that he would want more; now it was she who wanted more.

He was still her secret friend, but there wasn't much to keep secret: his mouth on her shoes and the Polaroids he took of them, and the time he said, "Step on my face," but playfully, ir Kapiolani Park, lots of people around, many flying kites. Once ' cleaned the shoes, "my secret way," by licking them.

It was not enough. She thought that he might please her m' she pleased him more. She took all the money he had give borrowed some, stole a little from her mother's purse, and bought the best pair of shoes she could find at a consignment shop, swapping her own for ten dollars (she had paid twenty-five for them, but it had been worth it). "Manolo Blahnik. Killer spikes," the salesgirl said. And then she called him at Hoku Honda, something she had never done before. But she was confident now. His helpless staring and his secrets had made her feel powerful.

The shoes were red, sexy, with steeper heels than the old pair.

"Manolo Blahnik. Killer spikes, yah?"

The *haole* guy was polite. He smiled. But he closed his eyes and murmured when she said she had swapped the other shoes. He did not touch her, did not even touch her new shoes. He said he had to meet a customer about a leasing agreement. She never saw him again.

"First love," the girl said, though she felt that way only after it was over. And that was how my wife became worldly.

59

The Private Party
on Mauna Kea Street

"I COULD WRITE one great story," Puamana said. "Except I went never learn write."

I got that all the time, because of Buddy's "He wrote a book!" But as my mother-in-law, Puamana commanded my attention. I listened politely. She said nothing more.

"Just tell me the story," I said.

"You won't believe."

"Those are the ones I usually believe."

This woman, she said — speaking quickly, nervously, as though she had thought about the woman in the story a great deal but had never uttered these things aloud — this woman was married to a man who was so lazy he hated owning shoes with shoelaces. The woman bought him all his best clothes, the silk shirts, white pants, a plantation hat with a feather band. He liked Oakley sunglasses. He had three pairs.

But he so seldom went out of the house, he hardly wore his beautiful clothes. Most of the day he stayed home watching television, a large-screen model his wife had also bought him. They lived on Nuuanu, near the corner of Beretania, in a new apartment block that had a wall around it and a doorman. When he was bored with TV the man stared out the window at Chinatown, at nothing in particular. The wife paid the rent. She paid everything. It had never been necessary for the man to work.

Most women would have killed him, or left him for another man, or told him to get a job. But his wife loved him. She was grateful that he accepted her, delighted when her gifts pleased him. She was like a slave, like a child, like a possession. She adored him and became terrified when she thought that, should she ever lose him, she would be lost herself. He was her husband, her father, her boss, her master, her lover. Her own father had been abusive to her, and she had been rescued by her mother and raised in the *hanai* system by a foster family, a friendly couple. Her own daughter, conceived accidentally one night in Kahala with a stranger, was being raised in this way too.

These days she worked on Mauna Kea Street, returning with her salary and tips in cash. You would be amazed at what waitresses could earn in Waikiki. Hostesses made much more. She was a hostess.

The house rule was that relatives must not show up on the premises. There wasn't even a question of her husband's agreeing to this: he didn't care, didn't even ask about the job. The woman's support and generosity had made the man indifferent to her work and her odd hours — she set off in the middle of the afternoon and returned home well after midnight, sometimes at two A.M. She always found her husband at home, usually asleep after an evening of drinking beer, watching TV, and the Honolulu habit of low-stakes gambling. They both slept late, then they had sex — his rolling on top of her, that fumbling, was her reward.

"He got real heavy," Puamana said, giving the words weight.

Most people would have said that this arrangement was doomed to fail, but the truth was that it worked very well. The woman did not complain. Far from it, she was grateful for her life and the passive fidelity of her husband. She worked even longer hours, so she had more money to give him. Eventually, pocketing the money, it was the man who complained, in this way: "You're out all night. You have no time for me."

Because she was working! Buying him clothes! And recently a PlayStation with lots of games! Anything he wanted!

In a meek voice, stroking his hand, she told him that. Still, he grumbled, but unconvincingly. He knew how dependent he was on her money. He had begun to gamble more recklessly. She barely remarked on that. She even encouraged him a bit, seeing his gambling as something that would make him more dependent on her. He stopped complaining, though she could tell from the way he ate — working through his heaped plate but with almost no appetite, just a habit of stuffing himself — he was discontented.

A video camera, a CD player, a La-Z-Boy recliner, a waterbed — she bought him these and more, and more clothes. He seemed to cheer up. He must have liked the clothes, because he wore them and went out more, to the bookie's or to game rooms. Sometimes the woman returned home and found he wasn't there. She'd wait anxiously until he showed up, smiling.

"I worry that you'll leave me for another woman."

"Never. There's no one like you."

It was what she wanted him to say, so, naturally, she doubted him. But she also allowed herself to think that, by working very hard and giving him everything, she had managed to please him. Married life was strange and a struggle. Had she succeeded? Had her sacrifice been rewarded?

One night while she was working, she looked up and saw her husband among the guests.

The place on Mauna Kea Street was not a restaurant, nor even a bar. She worked in a large tenth-floor apartment, as a hostess at a private party that went on every day. "Hostess" was the only word she dared to use when thinking about her work. The party, to which there was an admission charge, collected by the Korean owner, catered mostly to male Japanese tourists. When they arrived, they were offered drinks by the hostesses, with whom they chatted a little. At a certain point the hostess would say, "Would you like to go inside?"

The important thing was to get the man to leave without his thinking he had been hurried.

"We do volume, no outcalls," the Korean owner, a woman who was all business, brisk and precise, had told the woman on the first day.

The sex must be perfunctory, clean, and safe. You had to be fast or you were let go. The pay was excellent. It was the reason the wife brought her husband all that money, but for the same reason, especially lately, she had sometimes been too tired to have sex with him.

Was this why he had come here? He stood in his beautiful clothes among all the shuffling, muttering Japanese men.

"What are you doing here?" the wife asked.

"Yah, me awready!" the husband said.

Instead of being angry, he laughed. Seeing this, the woman laughed too. It was a great moment, one of the best of their marriage. He bought an expensive drink, sat with her, and they went to one of the rooms and made love — passionately, as they had never done before. Back home the man shouted, "They make me for pay! Two hundred!"

He watched his wife leave the next afternoon and, now that he knew where she was going, he was amused and excited — this was better than any present she had given him. A vivid recollection of her in the place aroused him. He dressed and went to Mauna Kea Street that night, and found her, drank with her, insisted on her pleasing him in a way he had only fantasized about previously. This involved a mirror, a blindfold, her own lingerie, and her saying certain demanding words over and over. He was exhausted and gabbling like a drunk when she woke him.

She said, "Be careful. If they find out who you are, I'll get fired."

But he returned again. They made love. He paid, but he protested loudly, crudely, and he was overheard.

The Korean woman said, "That's the price. If you can't afford it, don't waste our time."

That woman is my wife! the man wanted to say.

He kept visiting the apartment on Mauna Kea Street — visiting his wife, for the other hostesses did not interest him. He was like a fanatic, a desperate addict, and he lost all inhibition. His former gambling now seemed to him childish. This was what true gambling was, and he was winning. In the smoky, seedy apartment his marriage was complete. Sex there left him in a gratified rapture that he savored in a way that he had never felt before. He loved his wife, could not imagine loving her more. He now went to the private party on Mauna Kea Street every day. He was the slave now.

This was a wonderful reversal of roles. But there was more, for time passed and one day he didn't pay, absolutely didn't have the money. So his wife paid. The next day the same thing happened. Denying her the money meant that she had to pay twice and had less to bring home. The man could not afford to pay, and yet he had never needed his wife more.

Put in this unusual position, the woman was accused of stealing, of conspiring with a client (it often happened with Japanese men in search of Honolulu mistresses), who she could not admit was her husband. She lost her job at the private party.

The Korean owner said, "You're lucky I'm just letting you go. I could pay someone to hurt you."

But the woman was already hurt, as much as if she had been physically injured. With a reputation for stealing, she could only work as a streetwalker, which was unsafe and poorly paid and despised by her husband.

She became a hostess in a restaurant and didn't earn enough to pay for the apartment. Her husband lost interest in her and they split up, though she said she still loved him. Eventually, she reclaimed her daughter and raised her in a hotel, working at odd jobs for friends, and sometimes it was hula lessons, and sometimes sex for money.

60

Dog Lovers

VISITING JOURNALISTS, brazenly demanding a week of freebies in exchange for a few paragraphs in a colorful puff piece, were unknown to me until I began managing the Hotel Honolulu. Stephen Palfrey had asked for a free week, comp room (nonsmoking), meals included, and did we have an in-house masseuse, and could I get him a deal on a rental car? These potential guests always asked to see me, and they'd announce, "I'm a travel writer." I associated this term with the people who recounted their experiences in knowing articles in the glossy in-flight magazines found in the seat pocket next to the barf bag. They always enjoyed themselves hugely, and product placement was their specialty. Palfrey's promise, one that I had heard from others, was that he would write a glowing review of the hotel.

"Why do I find that prospect so difficult to imagine?"

He missed my irony and said that travelers would flock to us. Even "a mention" mattered, so he patronizingly indicated. Subtlety was never a strong point with these travel people, either in person or in print. And although they had the frowny faces and short attention spans of toddlers, and complained when they weren't being cosseted, the travel pieces they wrote about having a marvelous time seemed absurd as well as dishonest.

"Travel at its best," one of them wrote about the Hotel Honolulu.

Travel at its best, in my experience, was often a horror and always a nuisance, but that was not the writer's point.

I would have slung Palfrey out, except that Buddy insisted we needed the publicity — we never bought ads and we had no public relations. And Buddy, claiming to be ill, seemed needy, and believed he was colorful. He wanted to be known to the wider world.

For this one week, Palfrey said bluntly that he was willing to feature us in his column and would write about our food. "I've done lots on food and beverage. I could cover your brunches." We had miserable brunches. Peewee's loco mocos, Spam musubis, and Serious Flu Symptoms Chili. There was hardly a sandwich served in our coffee shop that did not have the imprints of the server's thumbs.

Palfrey also added, in an enigmatic aside, as a further inducement, that if anyone in the hotel had a dog that needed attention — "And the key to a dog's nature is that they require constant attention" — he would provide it: would walk the dog, feed it, primp it, deflea it, whatever. "I'm kind of lonely," he said. He badly missed his own dog, a Labrador retriever, which he had had to leave at home on the mainland because of Hawaii's strict quarantine laws.

"And I know Queenie's miserable, too."

Left-at-home pets were a frequent topic among the guests: I miss my pet, my pet misses me, want to see a picture? People at the hotel moaned in soppy self-pity, and I just wanted to howl at them for their pathetic fatuity. Filipinos here eat dogs, I wanted to say. On Buddy's advice, I agreed to Palfrey's staying for a week, though I said we had no dogs. When I suggested he could busy himself with Puamana's Popoki, he winced, as dog lovers do at any mention of cats. I requested his credit card imprint as a deposit.

"What would that be for?"

"Breakage, pilferage, minibar, and miscellaneous charges, let's say."

He sighed in a defeated way and handed over his credit card as well as his business card, on which he was listed as *Stephen Palfrey, B.A.,* and under his name, *Adventure Travel, Society of American Travel Writers, American Society of Media Photographers,* and *American Kennel Association.*

"Not just Queenie. I also breed Labs," he explained. "Can I have your business card?" He winked at me. There was something unnatural in the way he did it, contorting his face. "I might want to mention you in my piece."

I wondered what he would make of my card.

"Your name rings a bell," Palfrey said.

"I can't imagine why," I said, defying him to produce more evidence.

My certainty made him waver. "I think there's a fairly well-known writer by that name."

"But you see I'm the manager of this hotel," I said. "What did this namesake of mine write?"

Palfrey admitted he had read nothing. Mine was just a hard-to-pronounce name on the cover of a book he had once seen somewhere. Unfortified, he caved in and smiled wanly, sorry he had raised the matter.

That was the beginning, but days before his free week was out, Palfrey had packed his bags and signaled to me that he was leaving.

"I don't have enough to write about."

He was booked on a midnight flight to the mainland, and so between his checking out and the arrival of his taxi I heard his story.

A woman in Paradise Lost had sat on a stool next to him and said, "Boxers or briefs?" Then another one, at a bar on Kalakaua, had sidled up to him and asked if he wanted a date. He said no. She repeated it, seeming to corner him, but he finally got away.

That had been his first night. I wondered whether I should tell him this was nothing unusual. The next day, at Irma's Diner, having eaten a plate lunch, and killing time over his coffee, Palfrey looked up and a woman said, "Hi." When he smiled and returned her greeting, she sat down across from him and began talking about herself. A radiologist, she had come here from a suburb of Pittsburgh. The money was good, but housing and food were expensive and it was really hard to meet new people, and she said, "What are you doing tonight?"

"I'm pretty busy," Palfrey said, startled into a transparent lie by the sudden question. He was not busy at all. ("The funny thing was that I was lonely," he told me. "Ever had a crying jag?") But the woman radiologist was panting, sucking lemonade through a straw, wearing green scrubs. She was bigger than he was, and distinctly mustached and chubby. When she finished her drink, she sat with her mouth open, looking hungry, as though he were a piece of meat. Palfrey left Irma's in a hurry.

"You felt like a piece of meat?" I asked.

"Just listen," he said.

He had wanted to use Irma's men's room, but the radiologist was so intrusive he hurried out. On his way into the one at the International Marketplace, he felt a hard, hot pinch on his bottom, a sharp pain that made him squawk. He turned to see a woman laughing at him, holding her mouth wide open, showing the shiny gray fillings in her teeth, like metallic dentures. She had big beefy arms and broken nails. She mocked him with the fingers she had used to pinch him, holding them like a pair of pliers.

He was fearful inside the men's room. He was fearful leaving it. But even when he was free of the place, he noticed that nearly all the women prowling the Waikiki sidewalks were staring at him.

Nestled behind its signature monkeypod tree just two blocks from the beach, Palfrey wrote in his room at the Hotel Honolulu, *one of the last family-owned hotels, where brunch is a Honolulu tradition, the Hotel Honolulu is one of Waikiki's best kept secrets.*

A secret kept from Palfrey himself, perhaps, for he could go no further. Oppressed by his hotel room, he walked to Ala Moana Beach and felt calm again. His folding chair seemed jammed — sand in the joints of the legs — and as he jerked at it, a woman came over, snatched it, and said, "Let me do that," and popped it open.

"*Mahalo,*" Palfrey said.

The woman said, "Now, how about you do something for me." She touched herself on a lower panel of her bathing suit and licked her lips.

This was down near the orange lifeguard chair at the Magic Island end of the beach. The woman was lined and leathery, purplish from the sun, with salt-stiff hair and salt rime on her too loose bathing suit. Patches of coarse sand clung to her calves and elbows.

When Palfrey said no, the woman swore at him ("It was gross") and swaggered away. At this point, out of desperation, but also thinking it might be a good story idea, Palfrey went to the Hawaii Humane Society at the south end of King Street and announced himself as a member of the American Kennel Association. The lobby reeked of the burning hum of cat shit and the eye-stinging tang of cat piss. Taking a shallow breath, Palfrey asked whether any of their dogs needed walking.

"You know about our Canine Caregivers Outreach Program?" the woman at the counter asked. She had the patient, long-suffering look of a foster mother, and Palfrey was encouraged.

Shortly afterward, a man in overalls brought out a large jittery dog that began barking pointlessly and stumbling with excitement.

"This is Soldier," the man said.

"He's definitely got some Lab in him!" Palfrey cried. He made faces at the excited dog and was thankful for the dog's attention. Palfrey was happy, he felt purposeful. This was something real he could write about: the Canine Outreach Program and also the theme that when he was with a dog, he felt content. He left the building with Soldier, a big black creature with the snout and some of the contours of a Lab's solid head, the big soft nose, the grateful eyes and busy tail. Soldier had a slack tongue and thirsty-looking jaws. The dog shook himself on the sidewalk and strained at his leash, glad to be outside and wanting more. Palfrey talked to the dog in the sort of continual flow of affectionate banter that other people might use on a mildly backward and much-loved child who had not yet learned to talk.

Comforted by Soldier, feeling protected, Palfrey returned to Ala Moana. After the dog had had a good run near the tennis courts, Palfrey sat on the sea wall, the dog's snout resting against his knee. He took out his notebook and looked at his opening: *Nestled behind its signature monkeypod tree just two blocks from the beach, one of the last family-owned hotels, where brunch is a Honolulu tradition, the Hotel Honolulu is one of Waikiki's best kept secrets.* He doodled and tried to resume, attempting to marry factuality with gaiety. Hearing a burst of human squawking, he looked down the beach and saw some local youths, two boys and a girl, spitting water and yelling "Fuck you, Buddha-head!" at a Japanese man and his small daughter — tourists, probably. Palfrey scratched the dog's belly, watching its eyes grow contented. He was safe with this animal.

Four women passed by that morning, each asking Palfrey the name of the dog and had he taken it through quarantine here? Three of them he ignored. The fourth was prettier than the rest, very pretty in fact. She, too, had a dog in tow, a yellow Lab. Soldier raised his head, and his tongue, which was thick and purple, tumbled out, trailing a string of elongated drool. The woman's dog gave a low growl and got to its feet.

"Miranda," the woman said, cautioning the yellow Lab.

Palfrey smiled at Miranda. The woman reached down to stroke Soldier, though Soldier, too, had his eye on Miranda. His muscly tongue lifted and curled, as though a sign he was taking an interest in the woman.

"Doing some writing?" the woman said.

Palfrey saw the line *Nestled behind its signature monkeypod tree just two blocks from the beach* and covered the page. "I'm a travel writer," he said, and casually mentioned his name and the title of his monthly column, "A Little Latitude."

"That rings a bell," the woman said. She didn't specify whether she meant his name or the column title. "I'm Dahlia."

Her hand was hard and damp, and white streaks stood out on her forearm. She was fattish, with big soft cheeks and kindly eyes. Her shoulders were freckled from the sun, and her hair was sunstreaked. She wore a loose flower-print dress, open-toed sandals, rings on some of her toes, a tattoo on one knuckle. Free spirit, Palfrey thought.

As Soldier began to poke his snout at Miranda's tail, Miranda crouched slightly and glanced around at the seemingly single-minded animal.

"You're so lucky to be able to write for a living," the woman said.

They were now both looking at the dogs.

Palfrey said, "It's not a job. It's my life."

"I feel that way about my ceramics."

Now he understood her rough hands and the powdery streaks on her arms. Clay, obviously.

"You could write a *Travels with Charley*–type book."

"My favorite book." He took out his wallet and showed her a snapshot of Queenie.

Now Soldier and Miranda were romping in the grass, chasing each other around the banyan trees. Palfrey recognized the barks: not warnings or fear but yelps of pure excitement. He explained that he had taken Soldier for the day as part of the Canine Caregivers Outreach Program. He could see on her face that Dahlia was moved by his saying this. Perhaps it was her plumpness that caused her to exaggerate her facial expressions? She touched his hand, and he could not keep his own hand still, for her fingertips were coarse and heavy. She believed he was strong. Palfrey didn't say he had felt afraid and lonely and put upon, that he needed the dog for reassurance, that the dog's leash was preventing him, Palfrey, from straying.

Dahlia said that she never went anywhere in Honolulu without Miranda. She said, "I'm fearless when I'm with my dog, because my dog is fearless."

In gratitude, Palfrey extended his hand and touched Dahlia's arm, and when he did so, she reached over and snagged his fingers, saying nothing, for the gesture was unambiguous.

"Almost time for Miranda's supper."

"I wish I had something for Soldier."

The dogs were now rolling in the grass, gnawing at each other.

"I've got something for your dog," the woman said. When she smiled Palfrey could see that she took good care of her teeth, so he knew that health maintenance was a priority for her. "Well groomed" was an expression he did not care for, yet it described an essential habit of sanity and cleanliness. Something grubby in a person, a certain smell, ugly clothes, even something as simple as a salt-crusted bathing suit, indicated to him an unsoundness of mind.

Now he was following Dahlia, and both of them were following their dogs.

To get to her apartment, they detoured down a side street, past an optical shop, a Korean restaurant, a sushi bar, an adult video store, a pharmacy advertising beta carotene in both English and Japanese, a lingerie shop, and a strip club. Neither Palfrey nor Dahlia remarked on the storefronts, yet their silent acknowledgment of these wayward businesses was like a form of preparation, as if this detour had been signposted, *This is the world*.

At the apartment, Dahlia said, "These dogs are thirsty!" She put out a bowl for each dog.

Palfrey recognized a dog lover's household — comfortable but nothing fancy, nothing delicate to break, a certain hairy odor in the air. He walked to the window.

"I wonder if I can see my hotel?"

When he told her he was at the Hotel Honolulu, she laughed so hard he decided not to reveal the fact that he was staying for free, writing a travel piece about it. *Nestled behind its signature monkeypod tree just two blocks from the beach, one of the last family-owned hotels,* he was thinking, as Dahlia stepped behind him, her laughter still present in her body as motion rather than sound. Palfrey could feel the mirth on her flesh when she embraced him from behind and pressed her face against his neck.

Receiving her embrace, Palfrey was keenly aware of the contentment of the dogs, their tongues in their bowls, their jaws masticating their lumps of food, and finally — satiated — the compulsive grooming, licking food flecks from each other's splashed face, snuffling and nipping, playing still.

"Getting personal," Dahlia said.

Did she mean the dogs? He didn't ask. In any case, they closed the door to the bedroom to keep the dogs out. But even here Palfrey recognized a dog lover's bedroom: a dog bed, chewed pillows and chair legs, teeth marks on the rubber toys, dog pictures in frames, a thick aroma of dog sweat and dog hair.

Dahlia took off her clothes, but her size, her very flesh, so much of it, swags and bags, made her seem less naked.

Palfrey was obliquely remarking on this when he said to her, "You never think of dogs as naked. And yet they are."

Dahlia said, "There's a Chinese lovemaking position called Autumn Dogs."

"Next time," Palfrey said, grateful for an exit line.

In the elevator, a woman said to Soldier, "So where are you off to, darling?" and Palfrey began to cry.

I asked Palfrey the same question. He said, "Home," and looked a little tearful. He actually did write a piece in "A Little Latitude," which he sent to me, a box drawn around it. Using Hawaiian superlatives, he praised the rainbows and the sunsets, the convenient location of the Hotel Honolulu, and the great taste of Peewee's chili. Nothing about Dahlia, nothing about the dog.

61

A Chinese Story

TRAN, ONE OF the bartenders, was looking past Pinky, through the lounge, at the next building, but he saw hot blue ocean and, without a horizontal seam, hot blue sky. He, too, was thinking of death. But he could hold two whole ideas in his head, and said, "Freshen your drink?"

Pinky's head possessed one crowding idea. In a hissing voice she had told Buddy that she planned to kill him with a razor some night when he was asleep. ("It gave me insomnia," Buddy explained to me.) But after issuing the threat, Pinky spent five days at the hotel, in the Owner's Suite, hiding from him. Glad for the break, Buddy pretended he couldn't find her. She had succeeded in terrifying him — not only the threat, but something in her smile.

"After I kill you they never catch me."

"In your dreams, baby."

This was when she had smiled her wicked, toothy smile.

Speaking like a troubled child to whom everything is logical, she had said, "Because after I kill you, I kill myself."

"Keep an eye on her," Buddy said to me. "She's figured out the perfect crime."

Downstairs, she kept to the bar, always at odd hours. Even when she was doing something as simple as drinking root beer, she stared bug-eyed over the rim of the glass, looking for Buddy; or eating pretzels, she chewed and scanned the doorway; sometimes smiling — though it was never a smile — she was swivel-headed like a feral cat.

Tran had an eye for upset people. He said, "So, you come from the Philippines?"

Skinny and uncertain, she bent over, got smaller on the bar stool, her knobby elbows and knees making her seem suspicious, and even her big teeth were like protruding yellow bones. She had death in her face — murder, suicide, illness, mayhem. She was capable of anything, Tran knew.

"Me, I was on Palawan Island," Tran said.

This fact from the Chinese man made no sense to her. She squinted at her empty glass and went back to her suite. Buddy picked her up. She sobbed, not in sorrow but in confusion, as though her head were full of violent plans. Her fingernails were bitten, her hair clawed into strings. Her small body and loose clothes showed how reckless, how dangerous she might be.

Tran had mentioned the Philippines because Pinky looked so desperate and unhappy. He was sympathetic, moved by misfortune, upset by misery in a way that made him compassionate. He was a good listener, quick with his hands, unflappable — the perfect barman.

Even an expression of slight inconvenience could rouse his pity.

"So did they care that my cable was down for two hours and I missed my soaps?" one bar patron groused.

"So sorry," Tran said.

Another drinker, a local woman who had dropped in, complained that because her daughter's social worker had been late, she had had to spend the night, and "Try sleeping without an air conditioner sometime."

Not having an air conditioner himself made Tran more sympathetic, not less. He lived alone in one room in McCully, behind a Korean bar, with music, screaming, the whine of industrial air conditioners, and foul-smelling noise until two every morning.

"So I'm at the beach," a man said in a suffering voice. "The whole entire afternoon without a drink. The sun's brutal here. Any idea what that's like?"

"Very hard!" Tran said. The man smirked, doubting his sincerity. Tran added, "I once didn't drink for eleven days."

"That's hysterical. How come?"

"Long story." Tran made a face to indicate *too long*.

"*Un cuento Chino,* the Spanish say. A Chinese story." The man sipped his drink. "It means a long story."

"Thank you," Tran said. He murmured the expression in order to remember it.

On the King Street bus a man complained to the other passengers, Tran among them, that it was his first time and why was the goddamned bus always stopping? His car was in the garage, he said, having the windows tinted.

Tran offered to change seats with him.

"What good would that do?"

Tran felt that the man who had never taken the bus before was uncomfortable in that seat, and as a regular bus passenger it was his duty to be accommodating.

Another day on the bus, a woman said, "Want to know something? They don't take food stamps for cat food. They could care less if your cat starves."

Tran did not say that he had once eagerly eaten cats. He fumbled in his brown bag and said the woman could have a slice of Spam out of his sandwich for her cat.

"Trixie would just spit that out!"

Tran smiled in confusion.

The woman chanted, "Trixie wants her fish! She's going hungry! You know what that's like?"

"Oh, yes," Tran said, which made the woman snort.

On his shift at the bar one afternoon, he was wiping an outside table at which a man was watching a football game on a small portable television set. The man's wife sat nearby.

"Please?" Tran said, asking permission to wipe around the set.

"Can't you see I'm busy?" the man said, misunderstanding Tran's intention. "Patience is a virtue — anyone ever tell you that?"

Tran smiled. The man was right. Patience was necessary.

The man's wife said, "Move the umbrella, okay? I'm boiling in all this sun." As Tran adjusted the umbrella, putting the woman in the shade, she said, "Listen, too much sun can make you real sick."

"Yes, yes," Tran said, returning to wiping the tables. "That is right."

An African American at the bar, drinking Wild Turkey, confided in Tran, saying, "People think that things have changed, but I'm here to tell you that nothing has changed. We seek empowerment. But this is two countries. White and black."

"Yes," Tran said as the man signaled for a new drink with one hand while tipping his glass back to finish it.

"What I want to know is, when are you going to give me my rightful share?"

Tran said, "Anytime."

"You're blowing sunshine up my ass."

Keola heard this. After the man left, he said, "What's he complaining about? We Whyans went cheated out for our land. We worship the Eye-nah. But we got none. That no fair."

"Not fair," Tran said.

"You're standing on my land. Dis my Eye-nah."

Even I complained. "My wife is late again. Is your wife ever late like that?"

Tran laughed in a miserable sympathizing way. "Got no wife!"

A big friendly Chicagoan sat at the bar one night and said to Tran, "I'm a sightseer, but not the usual kind. I want to see something special. Wherever I go — islands, foreign countries, France, Cancun — people say to me, 'You want to see the ruins? You want to see the museum?'"

Tran was smiling, saying yes, as he mixed the man's third mai tai.

"I say the hell with the museum. Take me to your house. I want to see where you live."

"Pow-hanna at five," Tran said, and they went in a taxi to McCully after Tran finished his shift, *pau hana*.

The man kicked the weeds growing through the cracks in the sidewalk and narrowed his eyes at the *Club Lucky Lips* sign and said, "I was fifteen when I saw my mother for the first time. Never saw my father. People were paid money to raise me."

"Too bad," Tran said. "I'm sorry."

"My father was a bum. My mother was institutionalized. I went to night school. I own my own company now."

"This is where I live," Tran said, indicating the flat-faced building, the alley, the stairs to his room.

Inside, the man said, "You have no idea how fortunate you are."

"I know. Very lucky."

"Don't let success spoil you." He picked up a coconut shell ashtray and turned it over as if looking for a brand name. "I've never told that story to my children. Who's that of?"

It was a family photo, water-stained, faded, seven people standing and sitting stiffly, taken one day in a studio in Saigon, in 1962.

Tran was a boy. The man had mistaken his father for Tran, his mother for Tran's wife.

"My family."

"Lovely family," the man said. "You're lucky. I never had a family."

Except for Tran, all the people in the picture were dead, though Tran didn't say so.

Just married, Tran had left the Mekong Delta in 1978 with his wife and his parents, his two younger brothers and two younger sisters. The boat, not more than forty feet long, held 550 people, all Chinese from Vietnam. It was a five-day trip to Malaysia, where they were turned away by soldiers with rifles. "Guam is America," the captain said, and headed there. After three days at sea there was a terrible noise as the boat hit a reef and stopped. There was no sign of land, nor even of birds. Eleven days passed, and in that time forty-five people died and their bodies were thrown overboard. The people prayed, they wept, some drank urine. On the twelfth day clouds appeared, rain came down, and a swell lifted the boat. But even under way more people died, thirty-seven more, the rest of Tran's family, and lastly his wife, before they sighted land — an outlying island of the Philippines. The survivors were taken to Palawan, and after three years in a camp, Tran was given permission to enter the United States. Now he was glad to have a phrase for what had happened to him.

"Long story — Chinese story," Tran wanted to say. He said to me, "I can write a book."

62

The Sexual Life of Savages

"**A**ND NEVER PLUMP your foot straight into your shoe in the morning," Earl Willis said. Anyone could tell from the way he parted his lips and leered that he knew he had a meaningful gap between his two front teeth.

We waited for more, the five of us, the *hui* — Sandford, Pee-wee, Buddy, Lemmo, me — but I was on duty. Saturday night, quieter than usual in Paradise Lost, and Sweetie was bowling with her team in Pearl City. At the other end of the bar, men whispered to their wives or girlfriends, romance on the lanai under the hula moon.

"I did it once in the Philippines," Willis went on. He sipped his drink, sucking it through the gap.

Drunks can be smilingly patient. Everyone was drunk but me. This was one of those evenings, like islanders meeting on a beach, Buddy and his pals, not listening, just taking turns to talk. Tran kept the glasses filled.

"There was a centipede inside," Willis said at last. "That cured me."

"That's in the book," Buddy said.

The book was *The Sexual Life of Savages,* by Bronislaw Malinowski. Buddy had bought it for the title alone, believing it was racy. Discovering that it was anthropology, describing village life in the Trobriand Islands, he boasted that it proved he was an intellectual, and flashed it like a badge, saying, "I'm real area-dite." He said he had plenty he could tell Malinowski, but when I mentioned that the man was dead, he shouted, "I want to finish my fucking book! You'll help me, won't you, like you did with my Fritzie story?"

"Sure."

Buddy's favorite section of Malinowski's book described the island of Kaytalugi, populated entirely by man-hungry women who went about naked. The island was to the north of the Trobriands, two days' rough sailing, but it was worth it: the women were voracious and insatiable. They waited on the beach, and when men arrived the women pounced, ravishing them. Buddy loved the part about the women using the men's fingers and toes when their penises went limp. Boys were sometimes born to the women of Kaytalugi, but they were fucked to death before they grew old. As intensely as the chest-thumping men of the Trobriands, Buddy dreamed of going to Kaytalugi.

"I am in the Philippines once. Nice place, but plenty of bugs," Tran said, pouring gin, jerking caps off beer bottles, and no one heard what he said for his being an employee.

"I've seen spiders like this," Peewee said. He made a fist and hefted it bravely, lifting it to his eyes, seeing a dangerous hairy creature. "In Tahiti."

"That's small for a spider in the Trobriands," Buddy said.

Sandford said, "Who hasn't had spiders in his boots?"

"The most poisonous spider in Australia is no bigger than your fingernail," Lemmo said, beckoning with his finger, displaying his bitten nail. "If you're stung, you die. Nerve toxin. You're fried in five minutes."

"Goddamn rat curled up and died in my shoe in Samoa," Buddy said. "I wore the shoe all day without even noticing. It was a very small rat."

"Fungus is worse than any animal. I went green between my toes from some crud I picked up in Tahiti," Peewee said.

"Ever get ookoos in your crotch?" Buddy said. "I had them in Fakareva."

"Buddy loves saying Fakareva," Sandford explained to me.

Hearing that, I was reminded that they were not really talking to each other; they were talking to me, as other people did, with deadly insistence, knowing that I had once been a writer. I thought: If they had read anything I had written, they would never tell me stories.

Willis filled his cheeks with beer, but before he could swallow, he sneezed and spewed a mouthful, as mist, as droplets, as foam, as specks of surf, and everyone laughed at the coarseness of it, and his dripping chin.

"He's locked and loaded," Sandford said.

"You once asked me what a ratfuck is," Buddy said to me. "This is a ratfuck."

He was drunk, with a sense of relief — relieved to know that the others were too, and safe because of it, so it was like a brotherhood. When had I ever asked him what a ratfuck was?

All their slurred and lispy talk of foreign places suggested bed, implied sex, and the word "woman" was unspoken so far, yet conspicuous. There was a woman in each man's story, in the boots, in the bedroom, in the jungle hut. Each spider was a woman, each leggy centipede, the small rat was a woman, the fungus a woman, the "ookoos" in your crotch, the mentions of poison and bites — women.

"This girl in Pukapuka," Lemmo said. What girl in Pukapuka? "She scratched and cut me until I was bleeding. "She had these sharp little teeth. You wouldn't believe the things she did to my body."

"Yes, I would," Buddy said. "It's in the book."

"I had one of them little Negritos in my room one morning," Willis said.

He was going to say more, only then an older woman walked by, a hotel guest I recognized as Mrs. Bailey Nivens from Tucson. She moved in that fastidious and balancing manner of a top heavy woman, her hands slightly raised like an overweight acrobat treading a tightrope, the hands giving a stateliness to her toppling gait. Buddy and his friends fell silent, like bad boys caught boasting. She was about their age, mid-sixties, yet they looked utterly unlike her, furtive, conspiratorial, shamed by her motherly nearness. Willis blew out his cheeks and held his words until she went by.

"She must've come through the floor, this Negrito woman, oiled her body and squeezed through. She was naked and greasy. She looked like a dead monkey in the moonlight. I says, 'Get over here,' and she climbs into my rack and starts giggling."

"Amazing little people," Lemmo said. "And they fight like terriers."

"Reason she was there was we were having trouble with the

locals. This was in Mindanao," Willis said. "They were stealing parts off our vehicles and hoisting our dogs. Then we sent word to the Negritos."

"Negrito women look like cute little girls with huge knockers," Buddy said.

"You can buy them — their families sell them. I knew a guy who outright owned one," Willis said. "Anyway, these Negritos went into the jungle and killed some monkeys and cut off their heads, about ten of them. They stuck the monkey heads on posts around the camp. We never had any trouble from the locals after that."

"Hoisted your dogs so they could eat them," Peewee said. "They marinate the dead dog in Seven-Up to get the smell off, and then stew it with potatoes and pineapple chunks."

"I've eaten that," Buddy said. He laughed in a chewing way. "I've eaten pretty much everything."

"Know how we used to catch monkeys when we were in New Guinea?" Sandford said. "We used to get 'em drunk."

Peewee said, "How'd you get 'em to drink?"

"We'd go buy a big bottle of the cheapest wine we could find. Then we'd go to where there were a bunch of 'em in the trees and pour it in a big flat bowl, put it on the ground, move off a little, and just sit there and watch. Sooner or later one would come down and taste it, splashing some into his mouth with his hand. Then he'd go back up into the trees. After a while, he'd come back and splash some more. There'd be others, too. Pretty soon one of them would be jumping back and forth in the branches, and he'd miss and fall to the ground. Then we'd run in and grab him and put him in a sack and run like hell. All the others would start throwing sticks and stones at us. If we got a real young one, the mother could be real tough. She'd hit you with a stick and knock you down."

Willis said, "I saw a woman in the Philippines giving a monkey a bath. I don't know why, but it made me real horny."

Lemmo said, "I once saw a woman breastfeeding a dog in Tonga. A little puppy."

"Most of the things you see in the Pacific were done in Whyee once," Buddy said. "Probably right here where we're standing."

The five of them straightened their backs and blinked through the entrance of Paradise Lost into the lobby.

"I wonder if that's in the book," Buddy said, and leaned over the counter, grunting at Tran to pass him the thick book, which was well thumbed enough to be a Bible.

"Lots of times I've seen women getting it on with dogs in Olongapo," Willis said. "In bars. That used to be the big thing. 'Hey, Joe, you wanna see girl and dog?'"

Buddy opened the Malinowski. He moved his lips, looking prayerful as he read. "It mentions a guy who was caught sodomizing a dog. He was a laughingstock."

"Speaking of tattoos," Peewee said — who had said anything about tattoos? — "that Marquesan woman I lived with in Tahiti was covered in tattoos. She used to cheat at cards. I brought her here once. She wanted a guitar. We visited my ex-wife and my mother. They couldn't believe I was with a sixteen-year-old. She waited on me like I was a king. I said, 'She's not my girlfriend. She's my pet.'"

"I had one of them in Zamboanga," Willis said. "She was just a kid. We used to fight and pretty soon we'd be in bed."

"That's in the book," Buddy said. "I remember one ratfuck we had in Waimanalo. I was completely shitfaced. Momi was away. I woke up with a little *wahine*. She says, '*Mahalo*. That was nice.' I didn't remember a thing! I says, 'Hey, how old are you?' She says, 'Fifteen next birthday.'"

"That's in the ballpark," Sandford said.

Willis said, "I knew this guy in the Philippines who had three girls living with him, none of them older than sixteen. His rule was that one of them had to be naked all the time. They took turns. It was kind of a harem-type thing."

Sandford said, "We had a welder in our crew in Bangkok who used to pay a hooker to go with him to restaurants and bars. He'd get her to jerk him off under the table while he looked out the window making faces at the people going by."

"Like these massage parlors in Whyee," Peewee said. "Places to get hand jobs from Flips for thirty-five bucks."

"Peewee knows the exact price!"

"Lap dancing costs twenty. It's just kids."

"Lots of the hookers in Fiji were schoolkids making a few extra bucks," Lemmo said. "Wherever there's Christians, there's hookers."

"I don't blame them. If I was a sixteen-year-old girl, do you think I'd be working at McDonald's? I'd be selling my ass," Buddy said.

"And you'd starve," Sandford said.

Peewee said, "Friend of mine meets a girl in Aina Haina once a week. She's part Whyan. They have sex and then he takes her grocery shopping."

"I know islands where having sex is like shaking hands," Willis said, and showed the gap in his teeth.

"'Me want mary,' we'd say in New Guinea," Sandford said. "Meaning a woman."

Buddy said, "When I was on Kauai in the sixties there was a hippie commune. I went over there whenever I was horny. They called me Pop. I used to nail the hippie girls in the back of my van."

"I once knew a woman who had five vibrators," Lemmo said.

"It's funny about Pinky. It's the best sex I've ever had in my life."

"She's crazy," Willis said.

"See, that's the reason."

"Just after the war, the best place to be was Japan," Sandford said. "They were defeated, humiliated, their currency was in the toilet. The country was practically destroyed. Everyone was looking for a dollar."

"Korea was like that," Peewee said. "Korean women . . ."

"You could get a Japanese woman to do anything! It was normal for them to be submissive, but after the war they were willing to be slaves. I had one that used to feed me with chopsticks. She gave me baths. She did it naked and then I realized I wanted her to be dressed. She put on a kimono and that did it for me. I was just a kid!"

"This guy I knew in the Philippines with the harem. Ever see a naked woman cooking? A naked woman ironing clothes? A naked woman scrubbing the floor?"

"A naked woman polishing a big mirror. That would be nice," Buddy said. "That's not in the book."

"The thing about Tahiti," Peewee said, "was that there were always girls available. They loved going off with older men. She looked after you, and you looked after her whole family."

"Samoa's the same," Buddy said.

"I once had a mother and daughter," Willis said. "Not at the same time, though."

"There'll never be anything like Japan after the war," Sandford said.

"Look at the time," Buddy said. "Pinky's probably going nuts. Tough luck."

At that moment, Rose entered the bar in her pajamas, carrying her teddy bear.

Buddy hid his face in the Malinowski book. Willis looked ashamed. The others slouched like bad boys, as they had when the older woman, Mrs. Bailey Nevins, had walked past. But this was worse.

Rose ignored them and came to me, and when Willis cleared his throat she looked at him in annoyance.

Willis's wife had left him years before and now lived in Nevada. Sandford's third wife had recently left him and was living in his Manoa house with a younger man. Peewee's wife had run off with another woman. Lemmo was a diabetic who had not enjoyed a functional erection for ten years. Buddy and Pinky slept apart. She claimed he snored. Buddy had found a method for divorcing her that would not cost him much money, but she wouldn't sign the paper. As for me, Sweetie was bowling.

Rose said, "I can't sleep, Daddy."

Buddy and his friends looked ruined and old, like drunks who glimpse their faces in a mirror and are shocked by the corpse staring back — mirrors late at night are like a reminder of death. Just then, with a shout of vitality Buddy said that instead of going home we should head right then to Gussie L'Amour's out by the airport to watch women mud wrestle. On the way, he told us again about the island of Kaytalugi, and the women of his dreams.

"It must be true," he said. "It's in the book."

63

Family Affairs

ONE NIGHT, without warning, Pinky crept into Buddy's bed fully clothed, moving against him so hard he could feel her sharp bones poking him like the edges of a broken basket. She smelled of onions, and gleaming on her teeth was a sourness, probably chewed fruit. The very pressure of her body was an imploring question.

"So what do you want?" Buddy said, gasping because only one lung was working well.

Her breath was damp, and her tongue teased his ear. "Take my cloves off, Daddy."

Buddy loved smutty innuendo in her gluey accent. He knew her so well. It aroused him to pluck off her warm clothes, though he insisted she wear her high-heeled shoes. Then she did the rest, crawling over him. He listened with delight to the sighing sounds she made, a greedy woman at a great meal — he told himself — though perhaps overdoing the noise in order to impress him or to prove something.

When she was finished and wiping her sticky lips, making a smeary snail trail across her cheek with the back of her hand, she said, "I miss my sister."

So that was what she wanted. All along, the understanding had been that she would see him through his forthcoming operation — crank up his bed, bring him donuts, push his wheelchair. "I trust her because she's afraid of me," he had told me. He was convinced of that when she stopped mentioning her crazy murder-suicide plan for the perfect crime. She must have been afraid. She had slept on her own until the night of her sexual invitation when she said she missed her sister.

Buddy stalled until he saw a recent picture of her sister, quite a different face from the one in the picture-bride video two years before. She had been a gaunt doll-like girl with staring eyes. She was fuller-faced now, smiling, twinkly-eyed, about twenty or so, plump-breasted, with delicate fingers propping up her chin. Her name was Evie.

"I miss her night and day," Pinky said.

Song lyrics often accounted for her way of speaking.

Buddy laughed. "Hey, I want you to be happy. If you want to see your sister, get naked." He encouraged Pinky in this taunting way for several days, using her eagerness, liking the fact that he had something she wanted, the means to fly her sister to Hawaii. In the past she had been stoical and self-denying, and that irritated him. At last he said, "Okay, I'll send her a ticket."

But he said to me, "All air tickets are like lottery tickets. Anything can happen. I need hope — my surgery is coming up. And I'm jazzed by the idea of two pretty sisters in the house. Maybe nail them both."

I wondered politely whether Pinky would go along with something like that.

"She's so kinky she doesn't even know she's kinky."

How kinky was it that she was keeping Buddy at arm's length most of the time? She knew he was depending on her to get him through his operation. But his plan was to pension her off afterward — give her some money and send her back to Manila. "Then I'll have Evie," he told me.

Evie showed up a month later at the airport, Buddy and Pinky watching from among the families and tour greeters holding leis and signs.

"Who's that man with her?"

"Uncle Tony. He very nice man. Can wash you car."

Then Buddy remembered him from the ridiculous wedding, but the man had somehow grown much older and uglier. The long plane journey had turned him into a tramp, with a broken suitcase, a cardboard box, and two days' growth of beard. He saw Buddy and held his mouth open. Uncle Tony had paid his own fare, which made him freer and less controllable. Buddy reasoned that a man was much worse than a woman, for a man was naturally suspicious. This one seemed in just one toothy glance to know Buddy well. A woman, an auntie, would have been greedier, dependent, and so more pliable. On the way to the North Shore, Buddy sized the man up as incurious, stupid, selfish, hungry.

"You got any plans?" Buddy asked Uncle Tony.

"Maybe I wash you car." After that, speeding through Hele-mano, Uncle Tony squinted at the fields and said, "Fine-apples. Fine-apples. Fine-apples."

Seeing Buddy's house made Uncle Tony hungrier. He touched the furniture, he tapped the walls, he sniffed Buddy's leather armchair. Evie was plainly fearful, but she was joyful, seeing Pinky, and she brought out a new Pinky, the one Buddy had first met and married — smiling, girlish, bright-faced, willing. Evie, being younger, was more active, worked hard, talked less. She was so shy she ate with her head down — the sort of timidity that roused Buddy, filling him with desire.

Half promising, half threatening, Buddy managed to get Evie into his bedroom alone with surprising smoothness. And he understood her: for her, silence meant yes. He gave her money, told her he loved her. She was his. After Pinky had persuaded Buddy to pay for Evie's ticket, she stayed away from his bed, so Evie was all the more necessary. But there wasn't much to it, and anyway the sex was brief, and then she was back in her own room. She seemed invisible to Pinky and Uncle Tony.

Uncle Tony was small, knobby-faced, incomprehensible, furtive. He smiled far too much, but he was helpful, absurdly so, not to the others but to Buddy — opened doors for him, fetched the newspaper, brought him the ice bucket and tongs, even had a way of saluting, as though he might once have been a civilian worker at a military base in the Philippines. After meals, he carried Buddy's plate to the sink, but no one else's. Buddy was uncomfortable with this attention, and at last became suspicious and wanted him to go. He suggested the man might leave.

"Evie like it here, but if you want we go, okay," Uncle Tony said.

It was a small price to pay for Evie, who now made regular visits to Buddy's room. She lost all her shyness and became nimble and sniffly and pliant when Buddy turned off the light. He soon stopped hinting at Tony's return.

Buddy's children and their families started dropping in, always asking Buddy about his health. They seemed puzzled, if not disappointed, when he said, "I feel like a kid again." They had heard about Uncle Tony and Evie, and they discovered that Pinky had taken over the big downstairs bedroom (once Melveen's), where she now slept. Bula urged Buddy to get rid of them. Whatever his children wanted, Buddy suspected the opposite had to be preferable. To make his point, he crammed a twist of dog shit in Bula's hair dryer again. It stank like a rude reply when it was switched on.

Pinky ignored them. She was happier, less moody, less demanding; the arrival of her sister had changed her disposition. Pinky and Buddy had been sleeping apart for some time. "Him snore." "She farts." Neither was true. Buddy brooded over his impending surgery, hating the thought that everyone assumed the operation would be a failure. Evie's visits cheered him up. Almost every night she knocked. "No can sleep, meesta."

Buddy was always reminded of a small animal — desperate, devious, watchful, wild, pretending to be tame because the thing was so hungry — the impression he had once had of Pinky, in Manila, when Uncle Tony and Auntie Mariel had chaperoned her. Eager to please, crouching over him, Evie was smooth, ratlike in a nice way, Buddy thought, a nibbling rodent. Afterward, as Buddy lay smiling, she pleaded with him to let Uncle Tony stay. Instead of saying yes outright, he took pleasure in tormenting her with his apparent indecision.

Was Pinky aware of Evie's nighttime comings and goings? If she knew anything, she did not show it. She was indulgent with the girl, more like an aunt than a sister.

Uncle Tony washed Buddy's car and swept the driveway. He had a love of objects he could oil or polish. He rearranged the garden tools in the garage, hanging them on hooks. He sorted screws and nails in old coffee cans. Sometimes he raked the portion of beach that fronted Buddy's house.

Buddy's children hated Uncle Tony for his tidy habits and his having become a self-appointed odd-job man whose fussing gave him access to the house that bordered on ownership. You had to ask him where anything was these days. "I get for you," the man said, as a caretaker might. A change came over the household, as when the Malanut family had moved in, over the period when

Buddy had pretended to be dead. The big table was set differently: Buddy in his usual seat at the head of it, with Pinky and Evie on either side of him, so he looked like a polygamous island chieftain, rich in wives, fat and fortunate, presiding over his board, holding his belly. Uncle Tony was nearby. When they were at the house, Bula, Melveen, and the others sat at the far end of the table, farther from Buddy than they wished to be, displaced by Pinky and her family.

Now and then, Buddy invited me to witness this spectacle.

"No can sleep, meesta," Evie murmured at Buddy's door not long after that, but instead of crawling into bed with him, she stayed fully clothed, upright in a chair, next to the narrow table.

"Want a massage? That there is my massage table."

Evie said, "I want to find my father."

"Your father is dead, honey. Pinky said so."

"No. Father of Pinky dead. Same mother, different father."

Did that explain Pinky's seeming like an auntie? "Where is he?"

"In America somewhere," Evie said, and pointed vaguely with her finger, as though America were a distant fabled land. "Please, you help me."

A woman who pleaded for help could make herself useful in her desperation, but why was Evie so unwilling? They were a demanding family. And within days Pinky was asking for a ticket so her brother Bing could come from Manila.

"What if I don't give him a ticket?" Buddy asked.

"Evie den go back."

That proved Pinky knew that he was sleeping with Evie. But Buddy did not feel pressured. This was all a cynical arrangement. Just as cynically, he gave Pinky the ticket — and Pinky was happy, and Evie more affectionate. Uncle Tony continued to be intrusively helpful.

Now there was only Evie's father to find. Buddy repeated his promise to assist Evie in her search, for now she was an eager student in bed, open to any suggestion; just a hint from Buddy and she was at work on him. No longer was Buddy anxious about Pinky's jealousy or her threats.

Although she still nagged him about finding her father, Buddy was so happy with Evie he did not wonder why. Had he wondered, he would have found the answer downstairs, where every night Uncle Tony slept with Pinky and sometimes sneaked down the hall to tutor Evie. And when the brother Bing arrived, he was accompanied by Auntie Mariel. "Uncle Tony wife" was what she claimed. But Auntie Mariel and Bing were lovers, though Bing had his eye on Evie.

Buddy had no idea. He sat at the head of the table, smiling, with the five new members of his household on his left and right. Often when he was asleep he heard the rub of muffled footsteps on the floorboards and imagined busy mice, the sort that chewed holes in the screens.

64

The Hook

"THERE WAS ONCE this young girl named Mahina — after the moon — about your age, who hated her stepfather," Buddy said, in just that storytelling way, after a meal one night. He was seated, as usual, at the head of the table, Pinky and her relations on either side. I was at the far end, marveling at Buddy's poise — and taking courage from him, too, for here was a man, a multimillionaire ("multi-eye"), sixty-seven years old, who recklessly surrounded himself with strangers. But, then, he had always appeared to me like a rock, a slippery rock in the sea, to which many people were trying to cling, the very embodiment of this Hawaiian island.

"The stepfather gave Mahina love, but not enough," Buddy said. "He gave her money, but not enough. He gave her clothes, but not all of them fit the girl. She wanted more, and she wanted the truth — to find her real father."

The stepfather often told how he had received a pair of expensive gloves one Christmas, and how the sight of the gloves made him laugh. Here Buddy paused, waiting for someone at the table to ask, "Why did the man laugh?" When the question came, Buddy explained that the man had a hook where his right hand should have been, and only two fingers on his left hand.

"What was left of the man trembled like jelly at the sound of a lawnmower," Buddy said.

The tip of the man's hook was so sharp he called it "my nail." He gaffed fish with it; he poked holes in the wall; he sank it into an overhead beam and hung on it; he stabbed papers with it; sometimes he accidentally snagged it on a cushion, or someone's pants, and tore through the fabric with a vicious swipe. The hook replaced his hand, but it was also a weapon. Little did the girl realize the man was her dearest friend.

Mahina's natural mother, a tall watchful woman, designed her own shapeless clothes and wrote poems. She had run off with an Episcopal priest, who in marrying her had lost his congregation. He sold insurance now. Mahina had traced her, found her mother's house, and was admitted by the hunted-looking former priest. Her mother acted intruded upon. She scowled and said, "Sometimes it's better not to look," and sent Mahina a poem about a nosy little girl in which this statement was repeated. Although she refused to reveal the name of Mahina's birth father, Mahina discovered what it was.

Her birth father was just a name, but a nice name. Her stepfather was a damaged man, and the sharp silver hook stuck on his arm stump frightened her, trapped her, and made her think her stepfather was cruel. How she hated the man's gloating over his handicap, brandishing the dangerous hook beak.

I have a real father, Mahina thought, and sometimes said it. And, My real father is just like me.

Her stepfather pondered whether he could ever love her enough. Could he satisfy her desire for money and clothes? He had adopted her, given her everything she had asked for. After his wife had left him, he had raised the girl in the helpless, adoring way of a man abandoned with his little daughter. What sort of a job had he done? Obviously not good enough, for the girl was dissatisfied.

She was unlike him physically, and it wasn't just the hook. She was tall, slender, Asiatic-looking. People said she appeared exotic. She was dark, her fox face hinting of nomads and wanderers, like someone from far away, not American at all but a foreigner with a secret. My father looks like me, she thought. Her stepfather had built up her confidence by teaching her to demand, when she was afraid of someone, What is your name? A stranger, a bully at school, a policeman, an abuser: What is your name?

At this point, Pinky interrupted, saying, "I no understand the story. She got one problem?"

Buddy leaned over and said, "She wasn't satisfied with her stepfather. She wanted to find her real father."

"So, what — she find him?"

"How she found him is the story," Buddy said. "What happened after is also the story. Everything I am saying is the story. So shut up."

"But thing wen go wrong, or else it no be story."

This, from the illiterate Uncle Tony, I found to be an astute insight into the art of fiction.

"Shut the fuck up," Buddy said to Uncle Tony, and he resumed his story of the hook.

The stepfather with the hook loved the girl so much that he finally offered to help her find her real father. Why did he agree? Because he loved her. He would have done anything for her. "When you do something so unselfish for someone," Buddy said, "that is the deepest love."

Pinky said, "So, the girl — she find her father?"

Evie was listening closely, hollow-eyed. She winced at every mention of the hook, every mention of the father, and whenever Buddy paused, Evie seemed impatient and tearful, searching Buddy's face for a clue as to what might come next.

"The stepfather had many friends," Buddy said, and Evie nodded slowly. One of the friends found out where the girl's real father was living. His address was distant, but near a big city and an airport. So that she would look respectable for the meeting, the stepfather borrowed money and bought the girl new clothes. He gave her some cash in a purse, bought her a ticket, and drove her to the airport, steering the car with his hook. He kissed her sweetly and put her on a plane.

Mahina hated that kiss. She did not think much of the stepfather's sacrifice. He was just a hook to her. At last I'm going to meet my real father, who is like me — this was the thought in her mind, and when the plane landed she rushed to the nearest telephone.

"Hello?"

"It her real father," Uncle Tony said, breathing hard.

"Who is this?" Buddy said in the suspicious father's voice.

"Me — your little girl daughter," Pinky said.

The man was happy when he heard this, and his voice became kind and gentle — kinder than her stepfather, and generous, as though he would give her anything. He sounded sorrowful, too. He explained that he had to go to work, but that he would meet her at his trailer after he knocked off. The girl waited at the airport, and nearer the time, using the money her stepfather had given her, she took a taxi to her real father's address, which was a trailer park, and found his trailer.

The taxi ride cost eighty-seven dollars, but it was worth it, for her real father was much younger than her stepfather. He was a handsome man, but his worn-weary face said that his life had not been easy. Mahina saw her face in his — the eyes, the nose, the chin. He was tall, he held her shoulders in his two strong hands, and when he kissed her she started to cry, she was so joyful.

"That good story, happy story. Family story more better," Uncle Tony said.

"There's more," Buddy said. He smiled, teasing them with his silence, and then did the real father's voice: "We could go out to eat, okay? I haven't got a lot to eat in the trailer. Just some cans of stuff. How's that?"

"That okay," Pinky said, and glanced at Evie, who had cheered up.

At the diner, the real father said that payday was not until next week, so could he borrow some money? He wanted to pay for the meal — it was not right that his daughter should pick up the check. She gave him two twenties and she ordered the chili. "I'm not too hungry," her real father said. He drank a bottle of beer, then another bottle, and then a glass of whiskey, which he said was much too small, so he had another ("Too much," Uncle Tony said). While he was drinking, he told her how unhappy he had been. He was happy now, but why had she run off like that with that rotten priest?

"How could you do that to me?" he asked, not looking up and almost without opening his mouth.

He seemed to mistake his daughter for her mother, and he repeated himself. He growled and grew unhappy and sick-looking.

"Why she no run way?" Pinky asked.

"Her real father held a glass of whiskey in one hand," Buddy said, "and in his other hand he held the girl's fingers and was squeezing them so hard she couldn't get away. She said, 'Please can we leave?'"

In the parking lot her real father put his hands to his face and began to cry. He said he was sorry. He begged his daughter's forgiveness and said that he was ashamed of himself. He held her by the shoulders again and looked sorrowful. Then he led her by the hand to his trailer, and when they were inside he grabbed her roughly and got his fingers into her clothes. When Mahina tried to get away, the man pulled the trailer door shut and shoved the bolt across to lock it. Seeing she was trapped, Mahina begged him to let her go. Now, looking back, she realized how happy and safe she had been before. She wished she had never left her stepfather.

"Please don't," she said, because the man was putting his hands on her. Fighting him off would only make him angry and more dangerous.

"I'm your father," the man said. "You belong to me!"

Though this was unfair, it was logical in a horrible way — the man put on earth to protect you was the one who could do you the most harm, because you trusted him. In this terrible moment she realized why her mother had rejected her, and why her father was hitting on her. She was a child of rape.

Mahina could not cry out, because her father's stinking hand was pressed against her mouth. His other hand was tearing at her clothes. These whole usable hands and all his fingers seemed wicked, like two evil creatures clawing at her body.

Just as Mahina's father had toppled her to the floor and was kneeling between her legs, there was a clattering noise — not a knock at the door, but the metal door itself warping as it was wrenched from its hinges. The whole trailer shook. Mahina could not see past her father's head, but never mind. A silver hook encircled the throat of Mahina's father and lifted his bug-eyed head, choking him. He was jerked like a doll and flung aside, his skull cracking as he crumpled in a corner.

And now the stepfather towered in the real father's place, gazing on Mahina, who was naked and helpless.

"There he stood, looking down."

Buddy let this sink in, another spell of stifled, vibrant silence.

Turning to Evie, Buddy said, "And what do you suppose she did then?"

Evie stared wordlessly at him, her mouth gaping, her fingers on her throat.

"She say 'Thank you'?" Pinky said.

The gravel in his voice made Buddy's words seem dramatic and inevitable: "She got to her knees and put her lips to the hook and kissed it."

65

Invasive Procedure

BUDDY'S DOCTOR, Miyazawa, was explaining the risks, the pain, the discomfort, the infection, the trauma, and "opportunistic germs" when Buddy said (his worst jokes being the key to his personality), "Maybe you can detach this parasite from my body," and reached around to squeeze-honk Pinky's breast. "Momi was built for distance. Stella was built for comfort," he said, now gripping Pinky's skinny arm. "Pinky's built for speed."

Pinky closed her eyes and opened her mouth as if to howl, but no sound came out. What did this mean? It was seldom possible to know how much English she understood, though she claimed to speak six languages, Japanese among them, from her days as a dancer in Tokyo.

"She's sucking out my strength, doc." Was she the problem or the cure? Buddy never knew with women. He had been wrong so often.

"Being as this is an invasive procedure," Dr. Miyazawa was saying slowly. It was elective surgery, he went on, and he needed backup, so he would operate at Straub Hospital.

"I want new lungs," Buddy said to Pinky.

The doctor's office was in a second-floor suite in a strip mall off Kapiolani Boulevard, between a sushi bar and a video store. The procedure was still somewhat experimental, the doctor said, but Buddy was willing — more than willing. He loved the idea of innovation, saying, "I'm a guinea pig!" He liked ambitious doctors who were eager to tinker with his body. His ailments were not new, but they were, so he claimed gleefully, "state of the art." He had gummed up his lungs with a two-pack-a-day cigarette habit and too much *pakalolo*. He had dropped acid and tried cocaine, and though he had given up drugs he drank more than ever. He was a big, badly behaved boy with lots of money. Greed and recklessness had turned him into a breathless popeyed man who couldn't laugh without gasping for air and pleading for more time.

"Think of an old sponge — what they look like," the doctor said. "That's your lungs. You can go on, but you'll need an oxygen bottle."

"At least I've got someone to carry it," Buddy said, but turning to Pinky he thought, I need her to help me, because I need to be free of her.

Pinky had opened her eyes but had not shut her mouth. Sitting in the doctor's office with her jaw hanging, she could not have seemed more mute — nothing dumber than a gaping mouth with no sound issuing from it. Yet it was her lizardlike way of listening, something Buddy did too when he was thoughtful, as though you received vibrations on your tongue.

"He one bad man," she finally said.

"We know Buddy here," Dr. Miyazawa said.

Pinky turned to Buddy and said, "I take care for you."

That promise alarmed him. Pinky was tapping her foot. He had no one else — no one who was fearful enough. Her sister Evie was no use — too young, too simple. Pinky needed him alive, but what incentive was there for his own family to keep him alive? He was worth no more than his assets, and his living longer only diminished his wealth. His spending alarmed his children. None of them would have dared to say what they felt — that they hated Pinky and her creepy relatives.

"Invasive procedure," Buddy said, repeating it so as to remember it, for it suggested going into battle.

The next time he was at the hotel, he used the phrase on me. I could see he liked its neatness, the implication of hot lights and sharp knives. He thought of himself as a bull staring down a matador's glittering sword.

His health was a subject Buddy usually avoided, not out of superstition, but because once he had strayed onto the topic, he was unstoppable and tended to disclose more about himself than he wanted. Talk of illnesses is often confessional, greatly revealing of a person's life and bad habits. It is impossible to discuss an operation without indicating what made it necessary.

The nose job had been first. "Deviated septum" was how he referred to it, but he had hated his nose. It was his father's, and he wanted a new one. His beak was anesthetized, smashed with a mallet, softened, and reshaped into something more acceptable. After that, fat and incapable of dieting, he had an intestinal bypass, twenty feet of gut removed by an invasive procedure. As a consequence he farted more, for the remaining intestines were less efficient in dealing with food. Farting was less dire than the fate his cousin Charlie had suffered: after Buddy bullied him into getting the same operation, Charlie died of kidney failure.

Since he'd had laser surgery, Buddy no longer had to wear the horn-rims he had grown to loathe. The bags under his eyes were removed. Who would have guessed Buddy to be so vain? He liked making improvements to his body, providing they didn't require physical exercise. He would pinch his cheeks or a swag of flesh on his arm and say, "I want to get rid of this." The procedures had all been cosmetic, and there was more: hair implants — a patch of plugs; liposuction — "just a few quarts" from his thighs; and the injections he got to rid himself of crow's-feet. When he was told the syringe was full of botulism, he said, "Why didn't you say so? I could have brought my own from the hotel kitchen!"

"I'm having a flare-up," Buddy might say out of the blue, by which he meant herpes. Something that had endeared Pinky to him was her indifference to his herpes. He loved her for shrugging when he raised the subject, and then he suspected that she might have been afflicted with it too, from her years as a dancer.

Lazy and gluttonous still, Buddy ignored the doctor's advice to cut down on food and booze, and was as fat as ever. All the intestinal bypass had done was made him gaseous. He had not kept up the Botox injections, so his crow's-feet returned much deeper. Open-heart surgery wasn't far off.

His breathing was so stertorous we had a standing joke. Gasping for air and gagging on his tongue, he would say, "Don't make me laugh."

"Are you choking?"

"No, I'm serious!"

The invasive procedure proposed for Buddy's lungs, a surgical technique for which Dr. Miyazawa was becoming well known, meant a morning in the operating room: the first lung gutted like a fish and drained, the spongy material removed, the remaining sponge holes opened, the tissue renewed. After a spell in the hospital, Buddy would be discharged. If Buddy exercised and avoided alcohol, he would breathe better. In time, the second lung would be renovated.

Pinky was part of the procedure. She would accompany him to the operation, then join him as a roommate in his hospital room, where she would assist him, bring him Peewee's food from the hotel, protect him from his children, and make sure he got through. Buddy didn't trust anyone in his family. He had no one but Pinky. Still, when she said, as she did often, "I take care for you," he replied, "That's what I'm afraid of!"

In the way that medical emergencies tended to redistribute the power in relationships — made a child of the person operated on, made an authority figure of the companion, and clouded the future — Buddy's life was turned upside down. Now he was captive and helpless. Pinky became his nurse, his mother, his jailer.

Over drinks at the hotel, Buddy talked about all the things he would do with his new lungs — visit the Grand Canyon, fly to Rio for the Carnival, spend Christmas in San Francisco. Pinky wasn't part of these plans, for he intended to return to Manila and find a new wife. He needed the lung operation to free himself of Pinky. When he was back on his feet he could pension her off. He never said he hated her, only "It's not working out," as if he had made a bad choice at a pet shop.

Late on the day of the operation, I drove over to the hospital. The woman at the reception desk said, "No visitors allowed."

"It's that bad?"

She was tapping on computer keys. She said, "No. It says here he's doing fine, but family says no visits."

"I'm family."

"Family is in the room."

"Family" meant Pinky. I imagined Buddy after his experience of sedation, the surgeon's mutters, the bright lights, and Pinky bossing him as he lay strapped to his bed. Now he was the fearful one, fearing that she would fly into a rage.

I wasn't sorry to be turned away. Something about a hospital, the human smell of illness and decay, is a reminder of mortality that stays in your nostrils. I was sure that Buddy had experienced that same whiff of extinction, and that he wanted to live. I knew he could not bear the thought that Pinky might abandon him, though he longed to abandon her. She didn't know that the invasive procedure was Buddy's way of ridding himself of her.

Dr. Miyazawa pronounced the operation a success, but before Buddy was sent home, the doctor sat with him and Pinky in the hospital room and gave them instructions.

"I must tell you that this procedure will not be a complete success until you strengthen your lungs." The doctor gave Pinky the diet Buddy had to follow and described the exercises. "Use the treadmill. Deep breathing. Get your heart rate up. And especially no drinking."

Buddy nodded solemnly, so did Pinky, and with the doctor lecturing them, they were exactly what they had seemed — children, with the same faces that children put on when they are being scolded by an adult. Hearing "no drinking," Buddy immediately wanted to sneak a drink, and this made Pinky conspiratorial.

"Only one, to celebrate," Buddy said when he got home. Already Pinky was pouring it, because she was afraid of him, Buddy told himself. The vodka tasted as sharp and beneficial as medicine.

She was afraid — of course she was. He knew that. But he wished to be rid of her anyway, because he needed her so badly. As long as she was needed, the operation was a failure. And still she sat by him, frowning each time he said, "Give me another one, just a little one this time."

66

Aftercare

"I CAN BREATHE," Buddy said, though he was so overwhelmed by the drama of the operation he could not manage
anything else. He looked in wonderment upon a world that
seemed new to him. Now he dared to hope for more, because he
felt he was going to live. His boozing proved it.

Pinky repeated her ambiguous promise: "I take care for you."

Buddy filled his lungs again without much effort. The air was
like hope entering his body. He said, "I'm going to be all right."

His hospital stay had been misery. His other operations had not
prepared him for this ordeal. To get at his chest cavity, four of his
ribs had to be sawed through. The incision was a vicious cut,
chest to back and under his arm, like a gory sash. As soon as the
anesthesia wore off, he began coughing, and he thought the cut
would burst. He was fussed over by masked white-capped aliens.
One gave him his stuffed Wile E. Coyote to cling to. When he was
able to sit up, he was told to blow into a plastic tube that had a
ball inside. Blowing hard, he got the little plastic ball to rise to the
top of the tube. The aliens praised him for this, but then he
coughed even more, bringing up from his lungs flotsam of evil-
looking dried blood and dead tissue. But he had survived. He was
a new man, and he wanted his world renewed, to reflect this re-
birth. No sooner was he home than he began talking of buying a
fancier house. He boasted openly, in front of Pinky, of divorcing
her and sending her back to Manila with her relations, of finding
a surf bunny, a coconut princess. He bought a new BMW. And: "I
should put the hotel on the market. That land's worth a fortune."

"Do you think you'll do it?" I asked, fearing for my job.

"I haven't currently made a determination."

That way of speaking was also a weird novelty, something to do with Buddy's operation and aftercare — his Latinate vocabulary another sign that he was throwing his weight around.

"But in my judgment it's worth contemplating," he said.

Anyone listening to him now was uncomfortably aware of being dispensable. Even I felt it, and was surprised and ashamed of my insecurity. The prospect of my having to prove myself made me face the fact that I had no practical skills. In Pinky's eyes, bloodshot with sleeplessness, I saw a greater fear. Her ruthless tenacity, her eagerness to prove her worth to Buddy, made her my rival. She quarreled with me and tried to put me in the wrong.

The lung operation had first frightened Buddy, and then had made him fearless. The invasive procedure had changed him, cut fear out of him, introduced hope and sewed it up. He was surprised and relieved; he was saved. Though he had always been sentimental, he had no natural piety, so his survival made him arrogant and more obnoxious. From being a boisterously contented man, counting his blessings in a shouting voice, he now spoke of radical changes. His operation had been like a near-death experience. He had seen the truth of the world; he said he now knew what mattered. "Rejuvenated" was a word he used. He became pompous and wordy, with at times an incomprehensible garrulity.

"At this juncture, I want everyone out of my face."

"Dad hybolic," his son Bula said. "That no good fo us."

"Currently, I require personal space. Elbow room, if you will."

The only hint of indecision in this new, robust Buddy with puffing lungs was his choosing which changes to make first. Pinky took comfort from that. So did everyone who knew him, including me. "Don't be rash," I said, fearing that I might lose my job. I resolved to become a better hotel manager. Pinky sidelined Evie, who had not visited Buddy's bedroom ("No can sleep, meesta") since before the operation. Pinky made the visits now, rekindling Buddy's sexual interest. Her job, her future, depended on it.

Buddy felt so energetic that he put off his exercise, avoided the treadmill, drank much more, and puffed a cigarette now and then. He was indignant when anyone called attention to his habits.

"Do you realize what I've endured?" he said. "I've been through hell, for want of a better word."

That also, his expression "for want of a better word," was new. Like "if you will," it made me smile, but still I was worried about my job.

To help Buddy regain full use of his lungs, the doctor had given him an oxygen bottle. Pinky lugged it around, and every so often Buddy would say, "I need another hit."

"Are you doing your exercises?" Dr. Miyazawa asked at Buddy's first post-op checkup, and Buddy said, "At this juncture, yes," because he felt so much better than before.

The doctor examined him, tapped his chest, slid the smooth cold medallion of the stethoscope across his back, cueing him to breathe; yanked a rubber tube around his arm, cinching it until Buddy's hand was numb, and took his blood pressure; looked down his throat and shone a light into his ears.

"No drinking? No smoking?" the doctor asked in a cautioning tone, delicately broaching the subject. "You sure?"

"Nothing!" Buddy said, much too loudly, showing his tongue, like a child protesting because he is in the wrong.

"This true?" the doctor asked Pinky.

She who poured the double vodkas, she who lit the cigarettes said, "True."

"Remember, this operation only works if you do exactly as you're told," the doctor said. "The exercises. No alcohol or tobacco. Or else catastrophic obliteration of lung."

Tinkering with his body was Buddy's pleasure and preoccupation. Like the best hobbies, the pastime educated him, made him bold, and gave him something to talk about. The doctor said that he might feel a little weak at the outset, so Buddy bought a wheelchair, which he pushed himself, manipulating the wheels, Pinky following behind with the oxygen tank. Not long afterward, Buddy demanded that Pinky push him. She obliged and steered him briskly through the hotel, seeming to enjoy seeing Buddy's employees, me especially, jump out of the path of Buddy's oncoming chair, his big feet splayed like a cowcatcher.

On that first occasion, in town for the checkup, Buddy had Pinky wheel him into Paradise Lost, where he sat with a drink in one hand and a cigarette in the other, shaking his head. He coughed, his eyes were bleary, his skin was blotchy from vodka. He was mystified by Miyazawa's insight: "How do you suppose he knew?"

Buddy's confidence grew even as his strength seemed to slacken. The operation had made him tyrannical and short-tempered. "In my judgment, your time is up!" he said to Keola because a leaky showerhead had not been promptly repaired — fired, just like that. Keola blinked, smiled, and said, "Sorry, boss." Though Buddy allowed me to rehire him, Keola was a different and much warier man from then on.

Too impatient to argue or explain, Buddy simply issued orders. He warned Tran, his longtime bartender: "I'm recommending you for probation." Even his old friend Peewee he scolded. I assumed I would be next. I hated Buddy's dropping in, because for the time he was at the hotel, he was the boss and I the underling. The way Buddy bellowed reminded me that his lungs were rotting, and that was all I thought about, Buddy's lungs, their frailty, and how they somehow gave him the coarse, commanding voice of a chain-smoking hag.

With Pinky's skinny fingers on the handles of his chair, pushing him forward like a bulldozer, Buddy terrorized his family, threatening them, sending them on pointless errands, seeming to test their loyalty. "You owe me in a major way!" he roared to Bula. In between sucks on his oxygen, he wheezed, he gagged, he choked, making his scoldings sound more severe. No foolery, no laughter. He had become a survivor, the operation a close call, and like a man yanked back from the brink, he was frantic and incoherent. In his convalescence, this spell of drunken shouting, he was impossible.

"I want everyone in compliance, for want of a better word, at this juncture."

The muddle of his first weeks was over. Buddy continued to be assertive, but his physical condition had not improved. Indeed, for all his conviction, he appeared much weaker than before. He had monkey breath and boiled eyes, yet believed the doctor to be clairvoyant for suspecting he was covertly smoking and drinking.

"I can't understand what I'm hearing," Dr. Miyazawa said, coiling his stethoscope on his hand. "Are you sure you're doing your exercises?"

It was too late for Buddy to begin. He was too weak, and just thinking of the effort demoralized him. So he lied — lied with such indignation that the doctor doubted himself, mistaking Buddy's assertiveness for good health, even for strength.

"This is a new procedure," the doctor said. "We've had all sorts of results and we've got to watch for septicemia."

I had never witnessed such a thing. Now I knew what it meant to be reprieved. Buddy was saved, his life had a sequel. He was transformed from an ailing and uncertain man into an angry and impulsive one. He talked about marrying again, raising a new family. "Little kids everywhere you look! I got the money, I got new lungs — what's the problem?"

"What about me?" Pinky said.

"Get your sister."

Keeping everyone in suspense was more brutal than disposing of them. He behaved like a man with secrets. The boyish side of Buddy was absent, yet there was something childlike in his tyrannizing, and at his most demanding he was like a kid bellowing for candy. He was selfish, greedy, overeating again; he made no pretense of pleasing anyone but himself. I was reminded of his practical jokes, how I had concluded that such a joker is at heart a sadist.

Once Buddy saw a stripper at Foodland and invited her back to the house. Indifferent to Pinky's rage, he offered to swap sex for room and board. But he could not perform and, breathless, rang for Pinky to bring the oxygen tank. The stripper, still naked as Pinky entered Buddy's room, hurriedly dressed and left.

With a crumpled smeary face, Pinky wept as she handed over the oxygen mask, which made Buddy look like a porpoise. What could she do? By becoming a big, strange, disaffected man, whom she feared, he had broken her. He was capable of anything — and she was someone who knew the deranged possibilities of the word "anything."

Hearing him breathe, I was warned of Buddy's condition, but I did not seriously worry about his health. He would not just pull through. He would be a giant again — someone so loud, who so dominated a room, he would inevitably get his strength back. He had never stopped shouting.

He hired a driver, Chubby, and gave him Bula's bedroom. During the job interview, to Buddy's pestering questions the man had said he did not believe in God or an afterlife. "That's the best qualification for a safe driver," Buddy said. He sat beside the man in the new BMW, Pinky in the back, the oxygen tank on her lap.

He banished Pinky's uncle and aunt to the tiny room under the stairs.

"I'll marry your sister!" he taunted Pinky.

His eyes bulged, he grew fatter, he began wheezing badly. And as the weeks passed the conviction in his voice was like a form of despair. The staff at the hotel worried about their jobs, but Buddy was more desperate and driven than any of the employees or any of his family. His desperation made him a terrifying visitor to the hotel.

In the past he had been predictable, as healthy people are, but now we had no idea what he would do next. I had thought that his operation, meant as a cure, had made him ill, and now it seemed to me that the operation had very nearly destroyed him.

67

Full House

HEARING THAT Buddy had recovered, his children appeared again, and now they stayed at his North Shore house for days at a time. And not just Buddy's family but Pinky's too, the odd assortment: Uncle Tony and Auntie Mariel moved from under the stairs to the garage, where they made the workbench into bunk beds; her friends the Malanuts, from way back, turned up with hammocks. Evie and Pinky's brother Bing were now cohabiting. Pinky was glad, because it removed Evie as a sexual threat, and she admitted, "He not my real brother." All of them wandered around the house, listening and gaping.

The whispers were that the operation had been a failure, but that Buddy somehow managed to remain upright. He used his wheelchair less, and he had a narrow elevator installed. As it was big enough for only two people, he enjoyed trapping someone in it with him and farting in sharp trumpet blats as he ascended three floors.

Buddy was a spectacle, his illness a subject of gossip: the weakness, the medical details ("lungs fill up with water," "lungs like a sponge," "lungs leak"), the hospital visits and post-ops. The house was crowded with starers and mutterers. At first Buddy had been like someone back from a distant journey that people gaped at, but after they took a good look, he was like someone back from the dead.

He was haggard, slack-jawed, slow, with vacant watery eyes. He was often drunk. People said, "You look good," because he looked terrible, much older, more breathless. He had choking fits, during which he turned purple and put his hands up, as if to say "I surrender." Seeing him gag, Bula looked at his father's bright bulging face and said, "At least you got good color."

"You need round-the-clock nursing care," Melveen said.

"I take care for him," Pinky said.

"Yah. Is the problem."

For it was known that Pinky had threatened to burn the house down, to kill Buddy. Her bite marks were still visible on his arm, bluer, inkier, darker than his tattoo. She had made a serious suicide attempt, overdosing with pills — it must have been serious, because everyone in the house had been inconvenienced, which it seemed was one of the intentions of suicide. Her stomach had been successfully pumped, though afterward she spoke (perhaps to spite me, perhaps to ruin business) of drowning herself in the Hotel Honolulu swimming pool.

Bula moved into the house with his three children. "My wife stay in rehab," he explained. Pinky's brother shared the downstairs room with Evie, Uncle Tony moved from the garage to the garden shed, and low froggy noises suggested he, too, had taken a new lover. Buddy knew what was happening, but it was a sign of his feebleness that he didn't care. More quarrels erupted than usual, and at some point he was always asked to intervene — Buddy blow-sucking on his oxygen mask, a big man struggling simply to breathe.

Because there was more of him, it was worse than seeing a small man fading away. He looked like a wounded bear, roaring and smashing his giant paw against his head.

There had always been some shouting and banging in the house, but now the place seemed violent and disorderly. Buddy shouted back, to assert himself over the nine adults, five small children, and their many pets. The worst sort of illness was the one that made a man visibly a spectacle, helplessly suffocating. Often the oxygen bottle did no good, and Buddy was left snorting at the plastic tube or blow-sucking into the face mask. All the relatives, his and Pinky's, stood by, watching with their mouths open as he fought for air.

When we were alone Buddy said to me, "They're waiting for me to die."

Desperate to be included in his will because he looked doomed, they lacked the subtlety that might have strengthened their case. They were worse than obvious and kept appealing to him, demanding that he referee their grievances. When Bing put a nick in one of the doors of Bula's pickup truck, Buddy had to rule on the liability. When Uncle Tony left dirty dishes in the sink, Melveen said, "If you no talk to him, then I talk, and he no like it."

"They're my dishes!" Buddy said. "It's my kitchen!"

"What I say?" Melveen said, squinting, her tongue clamped in her teeth.

Evie played loud music, but it wasn't the noise that was objectionable but the reason for it — to cover the sound of her lovemaking with Bing. The music was silenced. Evie said, "He not my brother." Before, when Evie had been discovered in bed with Uncle Tony, she had said, "He not really my uncle." And for all this sexual rotation, Pinky's family showed scabby symptoms of herpes and spoke, as Buddy did, of "flare-ups."

Buddy was asked to calm Pinky's family, but instead of sorting them out, he saw that he could promote greater uncertainty by doing nothing. He allowed the chaos to continue, and it gave him more power.

For her supposedly wayward behavior, Buddy's family sniped at Pinky. "She after his money." "She bite him again." "She cuckaroach Stella jewelry." "She try kill herself." "She one *lolo*."

"Tony drank all the beer from the cooler, Dad," Bula said.

"It's my beer," Buddy said. He was annoyed that Tony drank it, but when had Bula bought any? Reflecting on this, Buddy concluded that he hated them both.

Finding Evie alone on the lanai one night, Buddy said, "How about you and me going upstairs?"

"Pinky you wife, not me."

"Pinky's in town tonight. You got no aloha for me?"

The sister refused. Buddy guessed that he seemed so feeble to her that she didn't feel she needed even to attempt the pretense of pleasing him. As was the case with many sick men he had known, he was already dead, as far as his household was concerned.

"We out for rice," Melveen said. Or it might be flour, sugar, cream crackers, potato chips, soda, Spam, corned beef, cookies, macaroni, tubs of poi, bundles of laulau — the staples. In the past, when Buddy had been well, and with a robust man's appetite, he had kept the kitchen well stocked. Now he ceased to care.

The quarrels continued, all of them petty, over sheets that were washed but not dried, leaky pipes, loud radios, mouse holes in the screens, sand tracked in from the beach, gecko turds which had the look of two-toned exclamation marks. "Someone stole my Boogie board." Bula's kids claimed that Uncle Tony swore at them. Aunt Mariel borrowed Melveen's house key and lost it. The house needed painting. There were never enough towels. "Who use all the t.p.?"

Uncle Tony said, "What we gonna do about the revetment?"

The rocks on the beach below the house had been tumbled apart by recent storms, and the house was in danger of being undermined by the tides. It was worth my driving the forty miles from Waikiki to hear the man utter that word.

Receiving no reply, Uncle Tony said, "How about the TV?"

Apparently the TV in the family room was broken, or perhaps the cable bill had not been paid.

"This Evie, she a slut like her sister Pinky," Melveen said.

"Pinky's your mother," Buddy said, to annoy her. Sometimes he stood in the doorway and watched them eating at the long dining table, gobbling their plates, their snouts in the trough, and he thought, Porkers!

Buddy realized that he had the answer to all this. He didn't bother to make an announcement or post one of his usual notices, signed "Da Boss." He just roused Pinky and his driver, Chubby, packed a bag and his oxygen tank.

One of Bula's children was playing in the driveway the day Buddy left.

"Where you going, Gampy?"

"Into town."

"When you coming back, Gampy?"

"Never."

You had a problem, you disappeared. So did the problem. It was perfect, really. His whole life he had lived that way.

68

Owner's Suite

O N THE WAY TO Honolulu, after abandoning his North Shore house, ditching his family like a crab shucking its shell and all its barnacles, Buddy had an explosive urge to push Pinky out of the car. "Or else swerve and heave my *okole* into the breakdown lane." On long rides he found Pinky unbearable for her silences and her sniffing. Was it a deviated septum that made her snuffle and blink like a rat?

"Does your wife ever just go quiet and not answer your questions?" he asked me.

"All the time," I said. I had never met anyone so antagonized by talk as Sweetie. "Hey, I'm just making conversation," I'd say, making me sound stupid. My questions annoyed her. My saying nothing soothed her. Was this her upbringing? Hawaii was a culture of grunts and mutters. Perhaps she didn't have the answers. Her manner of conversing was to turn away from me and read signs out of the side window: "Zippy's. Office Max. Taco Bell. Big Burger. Dragon Tattoo. Absolutely No Parking."

"What's the longest you've gone without talking?" Buddy asked.

"Couple of days."

"Would you believe two weeks for me and Pinky? And she's sitting in the same house the whole time."

Sitting in that enormous house was different from her sitting next to him in the car. She had her own room, her own bathroom; she often ate alone, hunched over her plate with her face down and her elbows sticking out. Riding in the car with her was torture, Buddy said. He wanted to scream at her. He knew she wanted to bite him again.

And so they moved into the Owner's Suite of the Hotel Honolulu, and it was worse than the car. Buddy wondered whether he had made a tactical mistake in abandoning the house to his quarreling family. Even though it was large for a hotel suite — bedroom, sitting room, kitchenette, foyer, double lanai — it seemed to Buddy like a cage. After a few days he said, "I have never spent so much time with Pinky."

"How does it feel?"

"Like I was ate by a dog and shit off a cliff."

He had been sick and supine in his big house. His operation had failed — made him weak and dependent, impatient and pompous. He had fled the house, and now, in the Owner's Suite, he felt that he would die unless he got away from Pinky. He could see in the dark iridescence of her eyes, could hear in her cold disgusted silence that she wanted him dead.

"Find me a single room with a sea view," he said to me.

I put him in 509, the room Miranda the carpenter had occupied and decorated, where the noise of his carpentry, the care he took in making his own coffin, had sounded like lovemaking in the room below it. That memory was now a hotel legend. The room had a glimpse of the sea.

Buddy was in the room less than an hour when he phoned me.

"Tell Pinky to bring down my oxygen."

He sounded as though someone had him by the throat, thumbs pressed against his neck. Pinky joined him, lugging the tank. Buddy sent her away when he was breathing better.

"I can't stand to be in the same room with her."

In his whole life, he told me, he had never lived in so small a space. On the North Shore he was renowned for the length of his dining table, the breadth of his bedroom, his king-size bed, his wide-screen television, his big armchair. His favorite glass held a pint of vodka tonic; his ashtray was a Fijian kava bowl. He said that he had not realized the Hotel Honolulu was so small.

"Open up this room," he said, and gave me orders to have a contractor knock down a wall and make an Owner's Floor, so he could spread out and isolate himself from Pinky. The builder's estimate was fifty thousand dollars. Furnishing the space and decorating it would be another twenty. He authorized me to supervise the work, which would be a drain on my time as well as a down-sizing of the fifth floor. It meant deleting three of the best rooms in the hotel.

"Are you sure you want to do this?"

"What's the alternative?" he asked.

"Sending Pinky home? Hiring a nurse? Hanging out."

"Why didn't I think of that?"

He delegated his lawyer, Jimmerson, to talk to Pinky. Jimmerson appeared, big and busy, and closeted himself with Pinky in the suite she had ceased to share with Buddy. The papers had already been drawn up.

"I want for take care my husband," she said. In defiance, her head jammed against her shoulders, grinding her teeth, she became smaller, more compact.

"He wants a divorce," Jimmerson said.

"Never."

"He's willing to offer you a cash settlement."

"How much?"

"Ten thousand dollars."

Pinky made no reply. The amount was more than she had expected, and convinced her that she had no idea of Buddy's wealth. She had lived in a hut, had worked in a bar — until she had met Buddy, her life had been unlucky and dangerous. She had so much to hide from him that she could never remember what she had told him and what she had concealed — and much of what she had told him was untrue. She had imagined a future here, but it was sometimes simpler to take the money and go.

"I want for be American."

"That can be arranged."

"And twenty," she said.

"Ten here, ten when you get back to Manila."

She closed and opened her eyes in agreement.

Buddy was elated when Jimmerson gave him the news. The money was less than he had expected, and much less than it would have cost him to renovate the fifth floor.

Whether she was soothed because of the finality of the agreement or calmed by another of her many moods, Pinky was quieted. She sat so peaceably in the Owner's Suite that Buddy moved back in. He said that most of the time he was hardly aware she was there. Without being summoned, she could tell from the tiny variation in the sound of his breathing when his oxygen was needed. Buddy would be laboring to inhale and on the point of blacking out, so stifled he was unable to speak, when he would see Pinky at his side holding the oxygen, which was life to him.

Helpless in his wheelchair, which he preferred to his bed, he raised his face to her. She sat by him and held the rubber face mask to his nose and mouth and watched him blow-suck and recover. He swelled a little and his face lost its pallor. When he could speak he batted the face mask away and said, "Get me a drink."

The doctor had told him: no alcohol. His children had nagged and warned him. Even I questioned his drinking. But Pinky got up without a sound, went to the wet bar in the suite, mixed a large vodka tonic, filled the glass with ice, and brought it to him, saying, "For Daddy."

"Don't go away," Buddy said. He was stronger with air in his lungs and booze in his veins. He shoved at his wheels, going closer to her.

Watching him, Pinky stood in her shorts and a T-shirt that said *Local Motion Hawaii*, like a small girl, his daughter, with her skinny face, buck teeth and big dark eyes, and bony feet.

"Take your clothes off," Buddy said.

Pinky did as she was told, but slowly.

"All of them," Buddy said.

She picked up her panties with her toes and dropped them onto the chair with her shorts.

This little woman was his wife. He had gotten her to agree to go away for twenty grand. When she was gone he would be alone, womanless in the Owner's Suite.

"Dance for Daddy."

She did so, flexing her arms and legs, a stick figure, all hollows in the half-light of the afternoon, until Buddy was asthmatic with lust. She saw this clearly and, still dancing, brought him his oxygen.

And so she danced naked as he watched, and watching made him breathless. She danced forward with his oxygen again.

"We're back to basics," he told me, blow-sucking like an aquatic mammal. "This is my . . . ."

"Marriage?"

"For want of a better word."

69

Human Remains

FOR YEARS, Royce Lionberg had driven from the North Shore once or twice a month to the Hotel Honolulu to dine on one of Peewee's Buddy Burgers. Then he began to visit almost every night, to drink instead of to eat, so it was obviously that something had changed. He always asked to see me. The man who had been so secretive and subtle was now expansive and blunt. He would turn to a woman wearing heavy mascara at the bar and say, "You look like a raccoon!" And not in jest but angrily, as if — even if it were true — she had no right.

In the way a domineering drinker at a bar becomes chairman of the board, Lionberg engaged in lengthy monologues instead of conversing — monologues that with modest elaboration could have been worked into short stories. I was tempted but had abandoned the business, and anyway, I liked the bare bones of his stories and the telegraphic way he told them: "The Shutter sisters. Famous twins. All sorts of celebrity as a double act. Merle died, and so Beryl could not be famous anymore. She kills herself."

In another, a man named Cyril Dunklin — they always had names — indulged himself in sexual fantasies on the phone with his high school sweetheart, Lamia, whom he had not seen for years. It went beyond phone sex. It was a phone relationship, which included the wildest sex. Unable to stand it any longer, they met, had a solemn, awkward cup of coffee, and parted. After that, there were no more calls. The relationship was over; they had met.

"Andy Vukovitch was a very good friend of mine," Lionberg said.

Whenever a speaker prefaces a story by mentioning how close the friend is, you prepare yourself for the worst.

This Andy loved his wife, Lynette, but was at his most passionate and demonstrative when he was being unfaithful to her and feeling guilty. In the course of a long affair with his mistress, Nina, he was glimpsed by her being tender toward his wife. Nina dumped him and, without a secret life, Andy became demanding and hypercritical. He seldom went out — why should he? He was doggedly faithful to Lynette, who eventually could not stand his constant scrutiny, and left him.

"Maybe it was doomed to happen," Lionberg said. "There's a point in life, if you live long enough, when everything that happens is just repetition. You have done this before in precisely the same way. You have met this person already. You already own one of these contraptions. You've seen it, you've heard it. It's the nightmare of the eternal return — nothing is new. You are not hungry. You don't want any more of anything. You see in life's repetition that your life is over — nothing to look forward to. You are able to anticipate what the man or woman will say, and you want to yawn or scream, because you know how everything ends."

Lionberg himself was full of plans. "I bought myself a treadmill," he said.

I said, "A treadmill is somehow not a declaration that you are going places."

He didn't laugh. He probably hadn't even heard me Anyway, humor for a monologuist is an unwelcome interruption. He was smaller, paler, more persuasive and talkative as a drinker than he had been as an eater, with the face and posture of a compact burrowing animal. He announced his plans: cruising the inside passage off the Alaskan coast, his great seats at the Elton John Millennium Concert in Honolulu one year hence, a slot in a timeshare in St. Barts, a backroads trip in a limited-edition battery-operated electric car. All his plans involved considerable expense.

The socialite Mrs. Bunny Arkle stopped at the hotel one night asking for Buddy.

Lionberg said, "She's a fine woman. I knew two of her husbands. I should marry her, I really should."

Mrs. Bunny Arkle heard this through Buddy and began showing up when Lionberg was around, the smiling suggestion of appetite on her lips.

Lionberg ignored her, yet he said to me, "We'd make a great couple. What does it matter that I have no sex drive? She's probably past it too, though women of sixty think of nothing but sex."

Finally Mrs. Bunny Arkle gave up on him, saying that the worst of Lionberg was that these days she couldn't tell whether he was drunk or sober. Lionberg just shrugged. Out of the blue, he asked me whether I got sick of doing the same thing every goddamned day. I said I was too insulted to give him a reply, and I meant it.

"No more composing," he said. He knew that I had been a writer.

"Now I'm decomposing."

"Don't say that!" he said with his chairman's anger.

The saddest task for the ironist is having to tell the listener that it's a joke, because of course it is never a joke.

"I want to see the Taj Mahal. The pyramids. The Panama Canal. The Shwe Dagon Pagoda." He was off again, not listening, not even looking. "Make a great trip around the world, see everything at once. They have these tours. Cruise the southern ocean — Roaring Forties."

Even when Lionberg was not around he was in the hotel talk.

"You've been to Africa, right?" Buddy asked me.

"Yes. Lived there."

"Lionberg's going over there."

Keola told me that Lionberg had asked him to build an orchid house — very elaborate, with a triple-pitched roof, sprinklers, and its own climate control.

"I heard about your orchid house," I said the next time I saw Lionberg.

He didn't hear me. He stared, lifted his drink, and said, "You get these rich Japanese who kill themselves by slamming the door of their Mercedes on their silk Hermès tie and strangling by the side of the road."

I said nothing. His eyes stayed on me for a long time, as though to assess my reaction to this bizarre method of self-destruction. At last I shrugged and said quietly, "That's very sad."

It was odd and exhausting that he showed up so much, after

his quiet occasional visits of the past. "Kekua's doing the honey now," he would say, rambling on. He had the energy and that air of exclusion of a man possessed with plans. He was moving back to the mainland, buying a winery in Napa, investing in Intel processors, living on a yacht in Marina del Rey, ranching in Montana.

Maybe these were empty dreams, but his spending was a reality. He was so preoccupied with it that he could not do it on foot. He sat at his desk, and sometimes at the Paradise Lost bar, phoning his mail orders: Armani suits, Ferragamo shoes, shiny gizmos and trinkets from the Sharper Image. He developed a commitment to anything made of titanium. "It'll survive a nuclear winter. They use it on jet fighters." He bought a titanium Omega watch, titanium sunglasses, titanium golf clubs, a titanium bicycle. "They're indestructible."

Why tell me?

Perhaps he could read the question on my face, because as I was thinking this, Lionberg said, "I want to write a book. What's it like?"

"Awful when you're doing it. Worse when you're not."

"I'd do it in Mexico. Get a little place in San Miguel de Allende. Learn Spanish at the same time. Do some painting. Take my bike for exercise."

A gourmet cooking course in Italy was also on his agenda. A visit to the Hermitage Museum in St. Petersburg. Learning to tapdance and play the piano. Taking an astronomy course at Cal Tech. All these plans, and he always spoke with a smack.

"Do you see love in your future?" I asked.

He heard that. "I've known so many beautiful women. All my wives have been beautiful," he said. "But no one is uglier than a beautiful woman after she's hurt you or done something bad. Yes, she still has the right bones and contours, but there's a definite stink. Did you know that girl Rain?"

"Buddy mentioned her."

"She's getting married. I'm delighted. She's going to have a child." He sounded pleased and paternal. "I have a wonderful present for her."

Another plan, the wonderful wedding present, along with doing some skydiving, collecting Sepik River masks, adding to his collection of netsuke. Or learning to windsurf: "I'm not too old. Go to the Columbia River gorge — world's best windsurfing. Find a female partner."

"Sure, look at me," Buddy said. "Pinky's twenty-four. Best sex I've ever had. She's sick!"

Lionberg laughed at that, because Buddy was drunker than he was. It was tiring to be around Lionberg in his expansive mood, because of all the promises — the details required me to be attentive, to visualize him in Mexico riding a bike and learning Spanish, to imagine him harvesting grapes or hot-air ballooning. He gave the governor money for his next campaign and then prevailed on him to listen to his plans, some of which involved the state of Hawaii. He was at the bar almost every night, and we watched him closely, as you do someone who is mapping out a future and making predictions.

Then his chair was empty for two days straight. That seemed strange. We waited one more day, then reported him missing, as undoubtedly he suspected we would. He was found on a steep side road, off the Pali Highway, next to his expensive car. He had slammed the passenger-side door on his tie and strangled himself. No note.

70

Hawaiian Snow

O N ANOTHER BOYS' NIGHT (the gathering of Buddy's *hui* was a weekly event now that he had moved into the hotel), Buddy announced that he was cold — and not just cold but freezing. We were in Paradise Lost, Buddy and his friends. No one spoke, some of us hummed, we were so stumped for a reply. It was the hottest week of the year, Kona weather in mid-August, a humid southerly air flow without enough motion to lift the hotel's little flag. The whole of Waikiki howled with air conditioners that seemed to strain in first gear, pouring out mildew and noise. And our cooling system had blown. I was waiting for the man from Hawaiian Snow Climate Control to arrive, though I did not say so.

"My feet are like ice," Buddy said. "Go ahead, feel my hands."

No one dared. Buddy looked concussed. He had a dark, roasted-looking face; he had to be feverish. But cold? The temperature was in the nineties, the humidity just below that, giving the hot Honolulu streets the ripe stink of gasoline and garbage. The throb of overheated metal on car bodies made them look explosive. The sky was sealed, like the inside of a great sagging tent, low and gray with volcanic dust that had drifted in from the live craters of the Big Island. The air was sour with heat, the hotel door handles sticky from people clutching ice cream cones. Purple car fumes collected and thickened, as pretty as poison rising in the traffic. There was no surf. There seldom was on such days. Waves broke at the shore in low exhausted plops and were sieved by the hot sand on which barefoot tourists danced in pain. Offshore, the "vog" of the furry sky gave the motionless sea the overboiled appearance of reheated soup, and in places the ocean was as scummy and opaque as tepid bath water. Even the nonperspiring Japanese were glowing.

"Fucking freezing," Buddy said, angry because no one had spoken, nor had anyone taken up his challenge to feel his cold hands.

Just then I noticed Tran in front of the open refrigerator, pretending to be searching for a water jug but in fact snorting the cool air for relief.

Buddy hugged himself. He had to be feverish. He was gray, his eyes colorless.

"Look, I got chicken skin!"

His forearm, and even Pinky's bite marks that looked like tattoos, had the puckered texture of a cheese grater. Perhaps it was an effect of his drinking, for these days he was drunk well before noon.

To change the subject, I said, "Where's Pinky?"

"You tell me where she is," he said. "No, don't tell me. She makes me feel sick."

He had once told me that being with her or any woman for a long period killed his ardor. He needed to be away to stimulate his sex drive. That was one of his stories. Another was that he had no sex drive, and his saying he was cold reminded me of that.

Apparently he wasn't kidding. He wore a sweater and knee socks, and still he shivered, rattling the ice in his glass of vodka.

"Aren't any of you guys cold?"

Only Tran glanced up at him. The others — Sandford, Willis, Lemmo, and Peewee — looked at each other open-mouthed, gasping, haggard from the awful heat.

"The air con's down," Lemmo said.

"Good!"

Buddy looked pitiable, sallow, underdressed, and a bit waiflike in his little-boy clothes — shorts and socks and sandals. His blotchy hands reminded me of the word "extremities."

"Now that you mention it," Sandford said, "it is kind of cool, I guess."

"Not cool — cold!"

"Yah. What I meant."

But Sandford was perspiring and spoke through his doggy gaping mouth. He was hot, they all were, the whole island was complaining, the usual talk: it was global warming, the greenhouse effect, El Niño. Yet the boss said he was cold, so the rest of them conceded that they were, too, as a gesture of submission and friendship.

"My room's like an igloo," Buddy said.

"It's just that I've seen it so much worse than this," Sandford said, struggling to be reasonable. "Back home in Rochester in the winter of '78 the ground was frozen so hard they couldn't bury bodies for two months. Piles of corpses stacked up in warehouses."

"Don't mention corpses," Buddy said.

"Met this stewardess one time on the mainland," Peewee said. "She had this funny-shaped nose. I says, 'That's interesting,' and she says, 'Frostbite. Took off the tip of my nose. I was with Alaska Air then, based out of Anchorage.'"

"Some places have snow all the time — just winter," Tran said. "A Canadian guest told me that. 'Summer? Some years we don't have summer.' I thought it was funny."

He was digging ice in the ice cube bin with the big aluminum scoop when he said this, which made it a sharper and more somber allusion.

"It's not funny," Buddy said angrily.

The phone rang. Tran rushed for it to avoid having to face Buddy's wrath.

"It's for you." He handed me the receiver.

"Whyan Snow," I heard — the electrician, but I didn't say so. He had come to fix the air conditioner.

At first I was glad to leave the confusion upstairs, but then I was standing in the suffocating heat of the dark hotel basement with a man I didn't know, waiting for him to speak. Minutes ago I had said, "So what do you think?" and he had not replied.

He shone his flashlight, caught the yellow glint of rats' eyes, but the creatures were defiant. They squatted, sniffing, waiting for us to leave, thickening their bodies in protest: this was their home.

At last the electrician spoke. "This all there is?"

What he meant I had no idea.

"I can't see what you're shining your light at."

"That you panel," he said. "Junction box. Timers. Any other feeds?"

This talk made him seem intelligent. But then he went silent again. He resembled his own flickering flashlight — bright-dark, bright-dark.

"Maybe it's a fuse," I said.

"You mean circuit breaker?" He snapped a wired pair of metal clips onto two parts of the box. I braced myself for an explosion. "Nothing," he said in the manner of a pronouncement. "See, your voltage . . ."

His precise technical language was at odds with his clothes — *Ukulele Festival* T-shirt, grease-smeared pants riding low from the weight of his tool belt — and he didn't seem to know anything else. He was tapping a clutch of wires with a gauge.

"They bring these in from the mainland."

"Whereabouts?"

He just smiled. In his mind, the mainland was one simple place, not many different, highly complex ones, like the Hawaiian Islands — a notion I had almost begun to subscribe to myself after all these years.

"You Australian?"

"Do I sound Australian?" I said, controlling myself, out of the belief that you had to stay on the best of terms with noncommittal handymen and mechanics.

"Buddy said something about you being from off island. How's he doing?"

"Buddy?" *I'm fucking freezing.* "He's living in the hotel now with his wife."

"He's on his fourth wife now. Me, I'm on my second. What wife you on?"

"Second," I said, hating his question.

"I go fix this. Got a short in one breaker. Maybe bad wire. Got to look at the spec sheet, see the tolerances. Some of them are forgiving, some no. The power surges kill you."

I just stared at his chubby cheeks through his dim light.

A moment later he said, "Yah. I figure. Gecko. Buggers get inside and lay eggs."

A three-inch lizard and its pea-sized eggs had shut down the entire hotel air-conditioning system.

Upstairs, Buddy and his friends were still at it. As soon as I entered Paradise Lost I heard the ice rattling in glasses and Buddy saying, "Sure it is. Medical science will tell you that temperature going down is much worse than temperature going up."

"I could never take another winter like that," Sandford said.

"You can get snow in Nevada," Lemmo said. "I seen it one time when I was going to Vegas. Was a frost. I try open a gate lock with my mouth and the iron stick my lips. Was painful!"

"Nevada means snowy," I said. "In Spanish."

They looked at me sadly, as though they had just noticed there was something wrong with me.

Peewee said, "I read somewhere about a guy who had frostbite. Gangrene set in. Toes turned black. He had to snip off his own toes with scissors."

"I never see snow," Tran said. He still had the newcomer's manner of saying everything like a sigh, and for that reason no one paid any attention to him.

"I feel like I'm turning into a snowman," Buddy said.

He spoke with such certainty and self-pity that he made himself seem like a big, bulky, immobile zombie, simple and bloodless.

"Me too, sometimes," Willis said, to please him.

"Yeah," Peewee said, looking fearfully at Buddy's frosty eyes.

I thought, These men will do anything for Buddy. The temperature was ninety-two in the shade and they were complaining of the cold.

I said, "Eskimos prefer the cold and ice to a thaw. Their lives are designed for snow. They hate getting wet. They hate warm weather."

"You wonder how they take a bath," Peewee said.

"They bathe in their own pee, the Greenland Eskimos," Sandford said. "That's a fact."

"That's disgusting," Willis said.

"Depends on whose pee," Buddy said. It was like a sign of health for him to attempt a joke.

Keola, sweeping the floor of Paradise Lost, said, "They say Eskimos same like Whyans. Except they stay up in Alaska. Eh, but Whyans not American Indians. Whyans not Native Americans. We da kine —"

"That's bullshit," Buddy said.

"We *kanaka maoli*," Keola said. "It so frikken hot I no can splain it." He kept sweeping, sweeping his way out of the bar. His mention of the heat confirmed, as if we needed confirmation, that it was indeed stifling, yet Buddy sneered as if to show that Keola had blasphemed.

"Sometimes you don't feel your hands or feet," Peewee said.

Buddy said, "That's right," as though he were experiencing the phenomenon at that very moment.

"Was this guy," Peewee said, "in one of these freezing cold places with two dogs. He was starving. He wanted to eat one of the dogs, but he had no knife. The dogs — that's all he had. So what you think he done?"

Buddy said, "I know how he feels."

"He took a shit and made the shit into a knife shape, and when it froze rock hard he used it to cut one dog's throat. He skin the dog and eat the meat. Then he make the dog's bones into a sled and strip the skin into belts and harness the second dog and get pull back to his camp."

Breathing hard in the heat, we stared at Peewee.

"I read in a book," Peewee said.

"Never mind," Buddy said. "Whyans aren't Eskimos or anything like them. They need blankets at night in Wahiawa! They'd never make it in a cold place like the mainland."

"What about the snow on Mauna Kea?" Lemmo asked.

"Get plenty snow over there," Keola said.

"I've seen that snow. It's not real snow. It's Whyan snow."

Buddy had gone gray. His skin was paler, his lips blue, ashen at the edges, like the ghost of someone we used to know.

Even the absurd agreement, all the cold stories told in sympathy, did no good. But what worried me about the cold stories on this hot day was their absurdity. They did not matter, because Buddy was gone already, dead but still standing, and we were speaking to someone we had given up for lost, being kind to him out of superstition, because everyone on earth treated the dead with reverence, and we were no different.

No one contradicted him. You never contradict the dead, because the dead and dying — the condemned, like Buddy — know much more than you do.

71

Brudda Iz

WHAT SET HIM OFF was the remark "Whyans not Native Americans. We da kine — *kanaka maoli*." And a few days after that, the visit from the man known as Brudda Iz, a popular Hawaiian singer who sometimes traveled with a forklift, to hoist him onstage, because stairs were impossible for him. Brudda Iz was a *kanaka maoli*. He weighed six hundred and fifty pounds.

Israel Kamakawiwoʻole — his proper name — was a distant relation of Keola, his so-called calabash cousin. Iz happened to be on his way from a concert at the Waikiki Shell and stopped in, steadied by his entourage of locals in T-shirts and sunglasses, baggy shorts and rubber sandals. Seeing the vast brown man enter the lobby, propped on two canes, Rose stepped away, retreating in fear, but when Brudda Iz said in his soft, appealing way, "How you gonna hide from dis guy?" Rose smiled and went closer to the Hawaiian giant.

Keola was granted a kind of celebrity through this visit. He had mentioned his kinship with Brudda Iz, but no one believed him. And now they were together, the big brown man who walked like a cripple on ruined knees because of his size, Hawaii's best-known singer, and his little cousin Keola.

They sat on the lanai — Iz on a stone bench; he didn't trust the chairs — and ordered loco mocos, a Hawaiian item that Buddy had put back on the menu under "House Specialties," for his own benefit after his lung surgery. Although Peewee had been making them in the staff canteen for years, Buddy took him aside and, in his new pedantic manner, described the perfect loco moco: "Pile up a mound of white rice in a bowl, lay a large medium-rare hamburger patty on top of the rice, slip a pair of fried eggs on top of the hamburger, with fried onions as garnish, and then, for want of a better word, ladle on enough brown gravy to cover the whole thing. Serve with soy sauce and ketchup."

Eyeing Brudda Iz, who ordered three of them, Buddy said, "He was nowhere until he got a howlie manager. Years ago I had some real big Whyan singers here at the hotel. I gave them their first break. This place was famous for their show, A Thousand Pounds of Melody."

"What happened to them?"

"We got closed down," he said. "But that was over another show, Tahitian Tita's Topless Hula."

He was so angry he didn't notice I was laughing. He raged over the visit from Brudda Iz, the sudden prominence and power of the janitor Keola, and that fact that he, the owner, was ignored.

"I knew the guy in Hilo that invented the loco moco," Buddy said. "They don't realize I go way back here."

I was only half listening. I couldn't take my eyes off Brudda Iz, who looked to me like a Polynesian monarch ("king of the cannibal isles," Buddy said when I mentioned it), sitting and eating, his big dimpled cheeks against his shoulders, his eyes squeezed deep into his face. People were reverential around him. They tiptoed, they sneaked looks, and when he uttered his high wheezy laugh, they stared.

Brudda Iz, too, had a tank of oxygen, because of his own overworked lungs. When Buddy was eyeing him, holding his mask against his face, they looked like a pair of astronauts, panting and suck-blowing at each other.

After Brudda Iz was gone and Keola returned to his mop, Buddy began to rant against Hawaiians, as though Iz and Keola stood for them all. His sick man's fear made him cynical and reckless.

They camped on the beach, Buddy said. They slept at the airport, they stole the avocados off your trees, they sat on your lawn and refused to go away until the police threatened them. And when at last they did go away, they left dirty diapers and plate-lunch wrappers behind. They were world-class litterers. Wherever there were Hawaiians, you saw billowing plastic bags, plastic cups, empty soda cans, and a trail of mashed Styrofoam.

I smiled hearing this from Buddy, because he had never been very tidy himself. But he was single-minded in this rant and as angry as any sick man can be. He had nothing else to do, and it was especially awful because he had nothing to lose in denouncing Hawaiians.

Sweetie said, "What's his beef?"

As the general manager, I had no choice but to listen to my owner.

He went on. These camped-out Hawaiians, eating Zippy's specials and saimin and Cheez Doodles, guzzling Big Gulps, said they worshiped the land. The land was sacred! So why did they leave their garbage behind, and all those Huggies and cups. Their beaches were fouled so badly with old refrigerators and rusty cans and human shit they had to be bulldozed and fumigated whenever the cops managed to evict them.

You saw them, Buddy said — "big shaven-headed fatsoes, bigger than me!" — flying the Hawaiian flag upside down from old pickup trucks in protest. They were angry, cranky troublemakers who knew no more than fifteen words of their own language. Even a mainland tourist knew ten after a week's vacation.

"I know about thirty myself," Buddy said.

Hawaiians sang hymns, made a fetish of churchgoing and a pious fuss of the family, unless there was trouble — like maybe spousal abuse — and then they demanded social workers. They used food stamps to buy Puppy Chow and tattoos. They said grace in Hawaiian before demolishing a pile of macaroni, a can of Spam, and a half gallon of Banana Karenina ice cream.

"But that's your favorite meal," I said to Buddy.

"This isn't about me," Buddy said. "Look at Keola. He's half Portugee and he blames Captain Cook for the hookers in Waikiki!"

But it was not unusual for Keola, and Buddy too, to be seen at the side entrance, leering at the hookers taking a shortcut through the alley when they started soliciting each night around ten. "There's a new one," Buddy would say. "Yo, mama!"

Although Buddy did not know the word "sententious," the people he described were the embodiment of it — licensed bores, as all aborigines seemed to be (so he implied), who had a proverb or a biblical passage for every reversal in life. Hearing that also made me smile, for Buddy himself often talked about Stella in heaven, and he believed that the green flash on the horizon at sunset was a coded message conveyed by almighty God to him from her.

"They hang around and pick fights with howlie guys and then try to fuck howlie women," Buddy said, adding that there was hardly a Hawaiian in the islands who didn't have some *haole* in his family tree.

Hawaiians distrusted each other, and at any one time there were sixty-odd groups saying they wanted the monarchy back and all trying in different ways to get land, because land meant money, and they wanted money to buy a new pickup truck and a TV and a loud radio. Having land meant they could sell it off to *haoles*, just as their ancestors had done, but these *haoles* would be casino people who would turn all the so-called holy places into gambling resorts.

Dark, moody, shiftless, ravenous, abusive — they were, most of them, the opposite of the popular stereotype: happy island folk, playing the ukulele, doing the hula, and singing off-key.

They were as puritanical, censorious, and hypocritical as any priest-ridden Third Worlders could be, and in private — because Buddy said he knew their most intimate thoughts — every last one of them was racist.

"Tourists say 'aloha'! Tourists wear leis! Tourists go topless!" Buddy said.

Local people feared the Hawaiians — the Chinese, the Japanese, the Koreans, anyone with an investment or money, the non-confrontational Asians who just hid when a Hawaiian blalah raised his voice.

"Hawaiians talk about culture — that's all they talk about," Buddy said, "which is funny, because I mean, what culture?"

The hula, hymn singing, high school football, and Spam.

"You once said that if you lose your language, you lose everything," Buddy said to me.

Had I said that?

"How can you have culture if you have no language?"

"I don't know."

"That's what you asked me once when we were talking story," Buddy said. "Talking story" made him sound so local. "If you don't speak Hawaiian, how can you be Hawaiian?"

"Some of them speak it."

"Maybe three. The rest of them just fiddle-fuck with a few words."

"Lost souls" just about summed them up, Buddy said. They had welcomed the missionaries — and they had swallowed them up. So blame the missionaries if you like — they had transformed the Hawaiians, taken everything away, even their memory. They could not remember a time when they were not Christians. Their history was the Bible, the language was Bible language, and even the ones who claimed they worshiped Pele the fire goddess sounded as sanctimonious and tiresome as Bible-thumping Baptists.

Topless hula was Buddy's obsession. When breasts were bared on the islands there might be hope, but until then Hawaii was just another place with a colorful minority, the least-educated state in the Union.

"What crap I've seen here," Buddy said. "Can you imagine all the Whyan nonsense I've had to listen to? It's worse than all the Paiute Indian crap I had to listen to growing up in Nevada."

Hawaiians were angry, and they were so tongue-tied they couldn't explain why they were angry, so they got angrier, Buddy said, sounding angry himself.

"They come to me for handouts. No one ever says, 'Give me money and I'll wash your car or work in your hotel.' It's just 'Hand it over.'"

The very people who were on welfare, got food stamps, and demanded handouts and government assistance were the ones who claimed they hated the government and wanted to be left alone. The reclaim-our-heritage fanatics wanted to open casinos on ancestral lands.

"They're more American than I am," Buddy said. They loved Twinkies and Christmas and beer and ball games and high school proms. The highlight of the year was the January Super Bowl, which Hawaiians watched at the beach, running an extension cord from the car. Virtually the only Hawaiian heroes were football players and entertainers like Brudda Iz.

Buddy raged on and on, and in describing the Hawaiian people, and especially Brudda Iz, he was of course describing himself.

72

Stand-In

BEING DEAF in one ear, Peewee walked slightly lop-sided, scuffing the sole of one foot, his head cocked to the side, his finger always at his bad ear. "Pacific" he said for "specific," and "pwitty good" and "pwoblem." And you had to shout. Even so, he heard everything Buddy had said about Brudda Iz. As though there were something moral in his hearing, he never missed anything that was unjust. Brudda Iz had the sweetest voice imaginable and could sing in the most plangent falsetto, Peewee said. He was the nearest thing there was to Hawaiian royalty; his size and his presence proved that.

"Don't talk to me about Whyan royalty," Buddy said as Pinky pushed him through the lobby in his wheelchair. "Most Hawaiian royals are gay or blond or howlie-looking or all three. They boast that they're *ali'i,* as though being a noble meant something."

"Don't it?" Peewee said.

"Only if you're Yerpeen," he said.

Peewee, a pacifist, just smiled and waited for Buddy to be rolled away on the rubber tires of his wheelchair. He reminded me of someone I knew well, but at first I could not make the connection. He was kind, generous, solicitous, most contented when he was pleasing someone. He seemed very familiar to me in this, and I liked to be with him for this reason.

His long residence in Hawaii and his travels in the Pacific had left him half deaf, blotchy and liver-spotted, blind in one eye, and he was small, not much taller than my eight-year-old Rose. As a chef and a habitual sampler of his own cooking, particularly his creamy coconut cake, he was plumper than he should have been. He had had a heart bypass, and because a vein had been torn out of his leg, he got calf cramps when he walked upstairs. He was about seventy-five and uncomplaining. Because of his sunny disposition, he seemed to me a healthy man. He said his afflictions were part of being old. He had adjusted to them. "Lots of people have it worse than me." He was always bright — up early, accommodating, helpful to me, praising me when I was least deserving of it, as though to buck me up with encouragement.

To be with him was always a pleasure and a relief, for like many other thoroughly sane and healthy people I had known, he made me feel stronger and gave me hope for myself.

After a few years of working with Peewee, I was able to make the connection. As with Leon Edel, he had many of my father's traits: upbeat, no grudges, an avoider of conflict, not a forced smiler but a naturally happy man. Being with him was like being with my father, whom I had loved. Treating him like my father, I was rewarded, for he became more like my father. "I'm a hollow oak," my father had said in his old age. After my father had been dead for some years, I began to see that many kind old men resembled him in the way he talked, deflecting hostility, offering generosity. In his apparent meekness there was such strength it helped me understand the Sermon on the Mount.

Peewee did not contradict Buddy to his face, nor even behind his back. In a casual way he said that even if some of what Buddy had said was true, it wasn't the whole story. Hawaiians could be just as lovely or mean as anyone else.

"Back in the days when Buddy was happy, he used to get along great with the locals, and he loved Whyan music," Peewee said. "We played it at night, at sunset, and Momi would do the hula for him. I never saw a happier guy than Buddy."

Peewee had once been married to an island woman. "I feel a lot of aloha for them," he said, using a characteristic turn of phrase. When he thought of Hawaiian history he got miserable.

"These people were here when we came. It's their land. They are *kanaka maoli*. If you don't know that, you don't know anything," Peewee said. "But that's why history is so sad."

Nothing on earth was more beautiful to him than a woman doing the hula at sunset — and all women were beautiful doing the hula, no matter what they looked like when they weren't doing it. The music was sweet, he said, and even the corny tunes, like "Lovely Hula Hands," were wonderful. As for the shouted chants, they gave him chicken skin.

Hawaiian-style objects — the calabashes, the wooden poi bowls, the old fish hooks — pleased him. They might look simple but thought had gone into them. What looked to us like a pile of stones might be an altar to a Hawaiian, and when you understood it was an altar, you saw how important it was and everything around it; you knew why it was there. Buddy had once known that. You had to be happy to understand, and understanding made you even happier.

Peewee believed that Keola had a sixth sense. It was true, as Buddy had said, that Keola cockroached articles from the hotel — soap, shampoo, once a broom, now and then an ashtray or glasses. But these were incidentals. The important thing was that Keola was truthful: if you asked him about cockroaching, he would say, "Okay, I busted."

"You can watch a thief," Pewee said. "You can't watch a liar."

How often had my father said those words? It seemed to me that Peewee was there to remind me that my father was not dead. Seeing my father in him, I grieved less, and I saw that even here in Hawaii — older and far from home — I was still part of some great cycle and my father was nearby. It helped me to see my father in him; it calmed me; it eased my pain.

Only if you were happy, Peewee said, could you see that what was best in Hawaii were Hawaiians — their lives and their history as warriors, navigators, fishermen, music makers, lovers. Their legends were as dazzling and grand as any from the classical world — they too had giants and demons and magicians and fabulous beasts.

Nowadays, Hawaii was like one of those beautiful broken bowls of koa wood: you could admire the beauty in the separate pieces, and you could also see how some people were trying with little success, to reassemble it. The effort was worthwhile, yet it was impossible to make it whole again — too many pieces had been splintered or lost. Even if it were possible, it would still be no more than a patched wooden bowl, a fragile antique.

Some nights after the dining room closed, I saw Peewee in the kitchen, bent over the butcher-block table, reading a book obliquely, looking sideways with his one good eye, and the book might be James Michener or Robert Louis Stevenson. One day it was one of mine.

"What are you doing with that thing?"

"It's pwitty good!"

I did not know what to say. My father also read my books obliquely, as though with one eye, not knowing what to think, not seeming to connect the author of that scabrous book with the young man he knew as his son. A similar confusion seemed to exist in Peewee's mind, yet after he finished the book he treated me the same, as fairly as always. He was kind to people. I had known he was considerate by the way he treated Hawaiians, always as friends, because in the same way I knew what a person was like when, seeing me as a stranger, they dealt fairly with me. I liked being a stranger for that reason.

Some time later, Peewee said to me, "If you can write like that, why are you working at this hotel?"

"I wrote that book long before I came here."

"So what?"

"I haven't written anything here. I don't know whether I can."

He would not be brushed off. He said, "You already proved you can write it."

Awweddy pwooved, he said, and *wite.* His speech impediment from his deafness made him sound wise.

"What would I write?"

"There's so much. Nobody writes about Hawaii really." *Weally.* "They don't see it. Buddy stopped seeing it — he's too worried about his health. It's not just the beach. It's the whole place, even the prostitutes." *Pwostitutes.*

I said, "You're so kind toward the local people."

"I'm local myself. I was married to that Tahitian girl with the tattoos. We were so happy. I was a chef at a restaurant in Kona. She introduced me to Whyans, and later I married one of them. We were all friends. They're good people. If you stay on the outside, you don't know them. If you get to know them, you understand."

"Everyone has something different to say about Hawaiians."

"Because they're anything you want them to be. If you see them as rascals, they'll hate you. If you like them, they will be your friend."

"So they're a reflection of your mood?"

"So to speak." He thought a moment. He went on, "I don't sentimentalize the Whyans. But I hate hearing Buddy badmouth them, because I know he doesn't really mean it. And it's somehow more cruel when you don't mean it."

"Maybe I should write about Buddy."

"People always say they're going to write about him, but they never do. They used to do interviews with him in the *Advertiser,* but they never sounded right."

"Buddy in paradise."

"This was paradise once. That was lovely — I remember it. Before Pearl Harbor. Before the war. I was just a kid. Of course, it's not paradise anymore. That's why I like the name you gave the bar — Paradise Lost — because the only place that can truly be hell is the one that was once paradise." He was silent and then said, "That's what makes Whyans so sad."

73

Hearsay

I WAS ALONE and at first glad of it, because I had secretly started to make notes for stories in these late-night hours: tentative, feeling foolish, even a bit shy, like a man reacquainting himself with an old love, fearing he might be rebuffed. The hotel was still, the bar shut at last, the music turned off, the pool closed, its greeny-blue blades of light sliding over the nearby walls. As soon as the last drunks had left the bar, I had sent Tran home. But afterward, I was sorry I was alone and had no witness to the persecution that then ensued.

The first voices I heard issued from the empty elevator. They were indistinct, probably mutterings of guests, but I heard my full name and mirthless, monotonous laughter like goose honks — nothing is less infectious. What was most irritating was that the remark preceding the laughter was inaudible.

Then, clearly, *Supposed to be a writer!*

Had I said something to a hotel guest? Had someone recognized my name?

Making a complete fool of himself, I heard in a different voice, though it was smothered by more laughter, a whole roomful of people. *And he thinks no one's looking!*

Perhaps it was not me at all. But then I heard a more particular accusation.

If it weren't for Buddy, he would never have gotten the job. And if he left, he'd never be missed.

Not only did this almost certainly refer to me, it was something I felt myself.

Another middle-aged howlie married to a local girl. The kid looks like his granddaughter.

At that I heard high-spirited giggling in the frantically hiccupping and unstoppable way of children. This mockery hurt most, because it was my worst fear.

I got into the elevator and pressed the button for the eighth floor, but when I was nearing six I heard the laughter, louder, so I stabbed at that button and got off there. It was impossible to find the precise source of the sound. It seemed to carry from one room, but when I went near, it echoed from another room. Finally I traced the laughter to an alcove, the end of a hallway where there was a cluster of three rooms, three differently numbered doors.

I heard the shouted remark, *It's easy to call yourself a writer when you're among people who don't read.* Causing the greatest giggling was the fragment of a remark: *That ridiculous bald spot he hides with a baseball cap!*

How could I intrude? What if it happened to be the wrong room? It might have been any of the three. I went into the emergency stairwell and climbed two floors, furious and ashamed, hearing muffled laughter from the concrete walls all the way back to my suite, where Sweetie and Rose lay sleeping.

The next day I tapped into the computer to get the names of the people in those three rooms: no one. The rooms were empty. What gave?

My complaint with the Hotel Honolulu had been that it was predictable and tedious, that the guests were intrusive and demanding. Paradise Lost was now dominated by Buddy and his boys' club. I had wanted security, a place to live, an easy job, sunshine, solitude. The price I paid was boredom of a kind I had never known before, something akin to being buried alive. Now I found the hotel so rich in piercing nighttime voices that I feared being alone, for it was only when I was alone that I heard them.

He's put on weight.

You can tell he doesn't belong here.

He is not a happy camper.

Oh, yes, he once wrote books!

Seeing how gloomy I was on waking up, Sweetie asked me what was wrong. I told her truthfully about these auditory hallucinations — or was it one of Buddy's bad jokes? She said I was making a fuss, that I was a big baby and a bad role model for Rose.

"But what if they're not real?"

"What they saying is true," Sweetie said, "so it don't matter whether they real."

Intimidated into silence by this logic, I simply stared at my literal-minded wife.

"You just sit and read books," she said. "Get a life."

I had not thought that anyone would notice something I was scarcely aware of myself: reading for me was like breathing.

"Like you could home in on your hotel skills," she said. "Get some expertise."

Fleeing to the beach did me no good. I had a book with me — Sweetie was right, that was all I did these days. I sat with the other idle people in the sun: the deeply tanned women and leathery men; the strippers — for young women with such bodies were usually free until early afternoon, and they nearly always had long hair; the little clustered families playing with food and toys. And the homeless man, the bum and his supermarket shopping cart, who actually looked at home on the beach — only there, with his back to a palm tree, for in his bulging plastic bags he had everything he needed.

For reassurance, to make myself feel better, I sought out Leon Edel. He invited me for lunch at the Outrigger Canoe Club. He listened carefully to my story of the disembodied voices.

"More M. R. James than Henry James," he said. "There's a splendid Edith Wharton story in which ghostly voices figure. And there's always Gilbert Pinfold, but his voices are almost comic."

I liked Leon for using books and writers to evaluate real life. It was what I had always done, what was never done in poor bookless Hawaii. The printed word was a source of energy to me, giving me hope and verifying what I felt. In fact, for long periods on this island over the past years I had felt that there was much more dreamed in literature than ever contemplated in heaven and earth.

"Ghastly comedy, the darkest kind," I said. "Waugh was having a breakdown."

I told Leon I wanted to write something. What had bothered me most as a preoccupied hotel manager was that, not writing, I lived an unsorted life. The disorder had begun to pain me, keep me from thinking clearly, make the time pass quickly, and leave me no clear impressions. Not writing gave me a bad memory and made me uncomprehending. I knew I would not understand the place, or the way I felt lost in it, until I wrote about it.

"You're a writer. Among other things, that's a pathological condition," Leon said. And then softly, turning aside, as though speaking to an invisible third person, "When the right moment comes, you'll do it well, precisely because of the difficulties you're describing."

"Short stories are hard. These are hearsay."

"Nothing is hearsay. What you're talking about will come straight out of your heart."

"Dozens of them, fifty or sixty, maybe more."

"All the better," Leon said. "That shouldn't worry you. You're lucky to have something to write. You have a loaf on the shelf, something new."

"I don't know whether I'm still in the writing business."

"You're in the lap of the actual!" And his laughter encouraged me. The man who knew James knew me. I felt lucky to have Leon as a friend, yet still I was oppressed by Hawaii, the tropical islands, their ghostliness, the way the beaches seemed just born, the mountains — those volcanoes — so ancient, the crags so spectral.

"We have celebrities here, both incipient and predominant," Leon used to say. Perhaps. But these were islands with no architecture, few ruins, fragments from the past, kitsch of the present, little worth preserving. That did not make it modern, only ghostlier. Being in such a sunny place did not make me afraid of shadows or darkness, but just convinced me that London fogs and shadows were predictable — you were forewarned, you expected accusatory murmurs and mocking voices. There was something much more frightening about such weirdness in broad daylight, and it could be absolutely spooky in sunshine.

Even at the beach I heard them, thin voices rising from the empty sand.

Who does he think he is?

He's supposed to be at work!

He'll probably be sitting here the rest of his life!

There's nothing left for him except death. He's waiting to die.

Should never have come here.
No one knows him but us!

They hurt me most, the way terrifying ghost stories did, because they were my own fears. Wherever I went I heard them. They came through the walls and closed doors of the hotel; I was never out of earshot. I understood how it was that people were driven mad: "The voices made me do it." And sometimes I could put names to the voices: Buddy's, my wife's, Madam Ma's, her imprisoned son, Chip, from years ago — even Rose's.

I don't want Daddy to come to the school play! He's too old.

Years before, Buddy had assured me that the hotel could run itself. My staff would do all the work. I was embarrassed by how little I knew of the hospitality business. I didn't like many of the guests, didn't feel particularly hospitable. My job seemed to lie in concealing my ignorance. Everyone was more experienced than I, who had no skills.

The day's figures, the week's figures, the projections for the month; occupancy, cancellations, maintenance, bar receipts, breakage, pilferage, the gross, the net — it all confused and angered me. When Keola said, "See this? Is one flange," I wanted to hit him for implying that I might not know this technical term.

More to my taste were the night staff's log books. I wanted them to be better than they were. Now and then I examined them.

1:22 A.M.   Kawika hear a noise in kitchen pantry.
1:40 A.M.   Was a rat. Catch with a sticky trap.
2:20 A.M.   Drunk man refuse to leave Paradise Lost bar. He say, "You know who I am?"
2:35 A.M.   Still explaining to Kawika. Was a former city councilor.
2:38 A.M.   Man escorted off property by Security (Kawika). Bar and pool area secured.

I wanted to read, "Voices from elevator, voices from walls, voices from empty rooms," but all I found were leaks, smells, floods, tripped circuit breakers, strangers, rowdy drunks, diners bolting from their tables to avoid paying the tab. The staff usually ran the place; sometimes the guests ran it; seldom did I.

After all his big plans, look where he's ended up.

I know exactly who he is. I just don't want to embarrass him by saying hello.

Something happens to people who come here, men especially.

They dress down, they pretend they're younger. The world has passed them by. All they have are fantasies.

"This island is not the world," I said to Leon Edel one day. Leon was my only witness.

"Not the world, no. But maybe it's your world."

"It appalls me to think that all I need in life is sunny days at the Hotel Honolulu."

He said, "At a certain time of your life you have less to write and you need sunshine. Every day is precious. You're taking James's advice to live all you can. And you strike me as someone on whom nothing is wasted."

Leon was amused and fascinated by Buddy Hamstra, "that poor peccable great man," he called him. And so we talked — about Edmund Wilson's diaries, and Bloomsbury, and Henry David Thoreau's narcissism, and Henry James. I could not rid myself of doubts about my choice of career as a hotel manager, but I still had Leon, my fellow rocketman from our distant planet.

Occasionally I had a message from that planet, in the form of letters forwarded by my former publishers, from readers: "There is a rumor that you are not dead but that you have just stopped writing and live in another country under a different name, like B. Traven."

One parcel I almost didn't open, because it was from a New York publisher. It contained the proof copy of a novel. The letter asked whether I would read the book, and if I liked it, would I kindly share my comments? At the bottom of this note, thanking me in advance, was a handwritten message and the overlarge signature of Jacqueline Onassis.

"That's Jackie Kennedy," I said to Sweetie.

"Right," she said.

"She wants me to read this book — she wants a favor, get it?"

"Jackie Kennedy wants a favor from you. Right."

"So she said."

Sweetie made a familiar face meaning, You got a problem. But Leon didn't laugh. He said, "She's a serious editor. She's very well thought of."

"So first it's voices and now it's famous people," Sweetie said. "Yeah, right."

I read the book and faxed my favorable comment. When she replied, Mrs. Onassis said how lucky I was to be living in Hawaii.

She mentioned that her son would be stopping off in Honolulu within a few weeks on his way to Palau, in the western Pacific, where he would be scuba diving.

The voices did not stop. To a nonreader, writing is a form of magic — unreliable, misleading; to an islander, everything beyond the shores of the island is unreal, dark, threatening, no matter how sunny the horizon looks. There is no memory of anything outside the island. What cannot be seen does not exist. And so I was alone with the voices, but that was not the only muttering. There were rumors that I might be crazy — not dangerous, but afflicted with island fever — rock happy. But that, too, was hearsay.

74

An Impossible Story

TWO YOUNG WOMEN JUMPED to their deaths, together and apparently at the same moment, off the fourteenth floor of the Outrigger Islander, four blocks away from the Hotel Honolulu. We knew of it within thirty seconds, from the screams. There was nowhere for a jumper to fall in Waikiki without horrifying pedestrians or tying up traffic.

"Maybe you write some kine story bout it," Keola said, which irritated me, because it was just what I had been thinking. But what did this smirking janitor know about writing anything?

I said, "Never," without meaning it. I was curious.

The next day Leon Edel was due for lunch. He had said he liked Peewee's Cobb salad and complimented me on the hotel's atmosphere — "It's the Hawaii I first encountered, years ago" — meaning, perhaps, that we were seedy and old-fashioned. He was too polite ever to be negative. We had no secrets now. He knew that it was painful to me that I no longer wrote anything. He praised me for my courage.

When I told Buddy that I needed a few extra hours for lunch with Leon, he said, "Try to get a column item in the *Star-Bulletin*. Something upbeat."

I did not see the connection. Buddy then went into his old rant about how it was really amazing how we had all these famous people in Hawaii — George Harrison, Willie Nelson, Jim Nabors, Kris Kristofferson, Richard Chamberlain, Sylvester Stallone, Mike Love (the Beach Boy), Boris Karloff's widow. Doris Duke, too, he said, though she had died.

"Take George Harrison. If we could say that one of the Beatles stopped by, can you imagine what it would do for business?"

"But why would George Harrison come here?"

"For a drink, one of Tran's mai tais, one of Peewee's burgers, the prize-winning chili," Buddy said, as if I had asked a dumb question. "And we could have a Wall of Fame like Keo's Thai Restaurant — signed pictures of all the stars who drank in Paradise Lost."

Buddy's inability to understand that it was unlikely that such celebrities would ever set foot in the hotel was, I felt, a sign of his failing health. Another sign was his blind rage at my disagreeing with him. His bad temper was almost certainly a result of his frailty and his heavy drinking.

"You're so negative," he said.

"What has that got to do with Leon Edel?"

"You told me he's a writer, didn't you?" Buddy glared at me. "He could do something."

Now I understood. The very idea that the eighty-nine-year-old biographer of Henry James and chronicler of Bloomsbury would write a squib for the local paper about his liking for the Hotel Honolulu was so innocent in its ignorance that I laughed out loud.

In his deteriorated state of mind, Buddy took my laughter for yes and cheered up.

"The Islander's going to be hurting for business," he said. "I'm thinking of getting that guy in, the fat Samoan guy who husks coconuts with his bare teeth."

He was trying to take advantage of the news story of the two women who had jumped from their room in the Outrigger Islander. Visitors who wished to avoid the scene of death and tragedy might be persuaded to stay with us if Leon provided a column item and placed it with one of the three-dot successors to Madam Ma in the evening paper.

Leon was dropped off by his wife, Marjorie, who withdrew, saying, "I'm having lunch with the *wahine*," meaning her women friends. Marjorie pronounced Hawaiian words correctly. She wrote poetry. The Edels adored each other in an admirable way, with the ageless self-sufficiency of lovers.

As a joke, I mentioned Buddy's column item idea to Leon.

"I was a journalist once, but not that kind," Leon said. "How is our poor peccable friend?"

He'd had to break two previous lunch dates, so it was good to see him. He appeared more frail, but he was so dignified that his frailty was like circumspection, another aspect of his courtesy.

"How are you feeling, Leon?"

"That depends. Some days like a weary, wasted, used-up animal. Other days, I'm tiptop." It was typical of him not to complain, though he seemed a bit flustered and unsteady until we were seated. "And you're flourishing."

After all these years I had come to see that he was the only person in Hawaii who knew me — and in the most profound and subtle way, through my books, the detailed autobiographical fantasies of my fiction. He had read a few of my books before we first met; since then, he had made a point of reading more of them. I had done the same with his books, and by now had read all his work, even *Writing Lives* and his pamphlet *Thoreau*. I reread the James biography. It was his great achievement, one of the greatest in biography.

With this knowledge and appreciation of each other's work, our friendship had deepened. His books were a postgraduate course on the man, as books often are — Leon as well as Henry James.

"Isn't the news terrible?" he said. "It must have happened right around here."

He meant the double suicide. I might scratch my head in disbelief at something I saw or heard in Honolulu, but Leon was there to verify it. How I loved these lunches, swapping stories. He was old enough to be my father, and was paternal. Yet as writers we talked as equals.

"They were military," I said.

He was sipping ice water, fastidious in his frail, elegant way. Always the Panama hat and the aloha shirt and the cane. Marjorie had been apologetic in the weeks before, calling me to say that Leon was unwell, just out of the hospital, and would not be able to make lunch. "Maybe next week." But there were more delays. I missed him, and I was glad when he turned up that day, and delighted to hear his reaction to the news story.

"I can't remember ever reading anything quite like it," he said.

There were certain unambiguous news stories that possessed and unified Honolulu — the all-day standoff, the missing hikers,

the hostage-taking, the child batterer's trial, the strangled trans-
vestite in the dumpster, the local Bishop Estate trustee's sex-in-
the-men's-room saga — the way dramatic happenings take hold
of a city, giving it something to talk about for a few days. Then
the drama passes, and the city returns to its divisive pettiness.
This was one of those stories. I wasn't surprised that Leon mentioned the suicide of the women soldiers.

Both young women (nineteen and twenty-four) had been injured in minor mishaps at their camp, Fort Leonard Wood, in
Missouri. On leave because of the injuries, they had left the camp,
gone AWOL, flown to Honolulu using one-way tickets, and
checked into the Islander, a double room on the fourteenth floor.
Here they became tourists, rented motor scooters, then a car, cir-
cled the island, took a helicopter tour, the submarine out of the
harbor, and had visited most of the hotels in Waikiki, eating and
drinking. They were remembered in several places for their boisterous good humor and their spending. Within two weeks they
had run up bills of eight thousand dollars on their credit cards.

I looked up their names on the credit card slips from our bar
and restaurant but could not find Brandy Rogers or Renate White
among them.

One evening at a nightclub, Renate, the older of the two, met a
Marine, a lance corporal from the Kaneohe base, and a week later
they became engaged. They exchanged rings, got Oriental love
tattoos, and made plans to marry soon — within a few weeks.
Still, the two women remained at the Islander. They bought swim-
suits, cosmetics, and a portable CD player.

Their families knew nothing of this, did not even know they
were in Hawaii. Both women had boyfriends on the mainland;
they too had no idea.

About three weeks after they arrived in Honolulu, Renate's
fiancé had visited as usual, but had left around one-thirty in the
morning. Back at the base, he had called Renate at five to tell her
he loved her. She said, "I love you." At seven-thirty the two
women were heard laughing and talking so loudly in their hotel
room that other guests on the floor complained. Hotel security
men knocked on their door and warned them to keep their laughter down.

Ten minutes later, they both jumped out the balcony, and four blocks away at the Hotel Honolulu, Keola paused in his sweeping, gripped his broom, and said, "Something happen. Something bad."

I asked him what.

"Someone *mucky*-die-dead."

At lunch, Leon said, "What details did you notice in the newspaper story?"

"That they each had slash marks on their wrists. They had tried to do it that way."

"'Superficial cuts,'" Leon said. "I believe that. What else?"

"The credit card bills — eight grand. Is that what you mean?"

Leon said, "What about their size? James would have noticed how diminutive they were. One was just five feet, the other only an inch taller, and both were young. Though the older one seemed to be paying most of the bills."

"It's still a mystery," I said.

"Of course, but that's not the point. The poignancy is that they did it together. In all the suicides that are committed on earth, it is hard to imagine that any are two women like this, jumping together into the morning sunshine off a hotel balcony. It was conjectured that they were holding hands when they did it. That's the detail you want."

"Such a sad story."

"Now it is our story. They dropped into our lives," Leon said.

"You remember more than I do."

"I had a lot of time to kill at the doctor's office — my weekly appointment. Normally I don't read the *Advertiser*, but there was one in the waiting room."

"It would make a great short story."

"Would it?" Leon looked doubtful. "An impossible story. We know too much. The art of fiction is all in the not knowing."

"Right. We don't know why they did it."

He smiled. "There's no art in guessing. Certainly no story."

Our meal was served — Leon's Cobb salad, my blackened ahi sandwich. We said nothing more about the suicides. Leon interrogated Fishlow, one of our seasonal hires: no salt, no dairy — they didn't agree with Leon's medication.

"Love," Leon said at last, after Fishlow had gone. "Why else do two people have the courage to do anything so rash — and not just the suicide but everything that came before."

"What about the Marine?"

"He has his own story to tell, but his story isn't theirs." Leon was too short of breath to continue. He coughed laboriously, apologizing by flapping his hand. When he recovered, he said, "Someone would be telling James a story and he'd say, 'No more. Don't tell me the rest.'"

"Because he needed to invent it."

"Yes. Look, 'The Author of Beltraffio' comes from one chance remark, that A. J. Symond's wife disliked his writing. And there's nothing to invent with those poor soldiers," Leon said. "There's more of a story in our talking here, now, in your hotel — more unspoken, more ambiguity, more layers of interest — than in that dramatic double suicide."

His laughter brought on another coughing spasm. I sat helplessly until it ended, and then, as always, we talked about how lucky we were to be here in such a balmy place.

As we left the dining room, I saw Marjorie was in the lobby waiting for us. She had never done that before — waited without telling us. I was touched by this patient expression of her love. I didn't realize that Marjorie had come, feeling protective, concerned because Leon was seriously ill.

"We can't pierce futurity," he had once said to me in a Jamesian way. He had deliberately not mentioned his condition. He canceled our next lunch, and the next. He died soon after that. He was cremated, and his ashes were scattered in a ceremony attended by many Honolulu people, some of them well known.

Buddy saw me leaving for the funeral. He could not possibly have understood my grief. He said, "Try to come back with a column item."

75

Sand

"WHY DO YOU CARE about that stupid howlie?" Sweetie said.

We were talking about a man on Maui, a visitor from the mainland, who had dug a deep hole in the sand at a Wailea resort to amuse his wife and daughter, and had climbed inside. The soft walls collapsed, a wave broke, burying him alive in the sand. He was rescued (shouts, screams, panic, plastic shovels) but was now in the intensive care unit at Kahului General Hospital.

"Such a howlie thing to do," Sweetie said.

"It's not funny," Rose said. About a week before, I had taken Rose to the beach. While we sat in the sunshine, she saw a small purple beetle struggle to get out of a depression in the sand, a deep footprint. It scuttled back and forth, dragging sand down as it tried to ascend, falling and tipping over, kicking its legs, beginning again. "Look, Daddy." I studied it for a while, the little creature trapped in a human footprint. I said, "That's the history of Hawaii."

"These people from the mainland!" Sweetie said.

"Speaking of which, guess which person from the mainland is coming to Honolulu?"

"John Kennedy Jr.?"

I was amazed. I had learned it only a few weeks before, by way of Jackie Onassis, who had asked me to give her a blurb for a Ruth Jabhvala novel. I had done so. How could I refuse? In her thank-you fax she had mentioned her son's stopover. This was not a suggestion for me to meet him, only an offering to me of the fact that John Junior would be passing through. I believed that I was one of the few people in Hawaii who had this information.

"How do you know?"

"He's staying at the Halekulani. He's getting certified for deep diving. I know the guy who's taking him out — Nainoa." Sweetie laughed. "It's a secret. So how you know?"

"His mother told me."

"Yeah, right."

My wife hardly knew me, even after eight years of marriage. Was it the hotel? You live in a hotel and every meal is either from Room Service or the coffee shop. Sweetie didn't cook and could never remember what I had ordered. She had no idea what clothes I owned, though Pacita, in the laundry, knew. Our suite was tidied by Housekeeping — Sweetie had long since quit her job. She was clueless about me. Did it matter? Maybe not — after all, I hardly knew her. When I tried drawing her out, I often got nowhere. The subject was usually old boyfriends, the key to understanding a woman's personality, or so I thought.

"He just went away," she might say.

"But why?"

"I don't know." Or, "I don't remember."

In almost anyone else this would have seemed evasive. "I don't remember" usually meant "I don't know how to explain." In her case I felt it was the truth: she had no memory. I had never spent so much time with someone whose most frequent reply was the conversation-killing "I don't know."

Sweetie's had seemingly been a life without logical transitions. Many months — years even — were missing from the chronology, and some of it had the irrational sequence of a dream. Yet the proof that she was full of surprises was her knowing the privileged information that John Junior was passing through town.

Rose, still fastened on the man on Maui, said, "If a man gets hurt in a sand hole, it's a tragedy. It's like the history of Hawaii, or maybe the world."

Sweetie smirked at me, a wordless reproach that I had influenced Rose in her saying this, for the word "tragedy" was not in Sweetie's vocabulary — nor, strangely, was "world." The daughter was smarter than her mother, as sometimes happens, and the new word was a novelty, like a toy. Sweetie was heedless and willful; Rose, like many eight-year-olds, was pedantic and sentimental.

"Sometimes you see these people on the sidewalk with winter coats in a pile and all their suitcases and bags, waiting for the van," Rose said. "It makes me sad the way they look, because that's a tragedy too."

"They going home," Sweetie said, "where they belong."

"Maybe they're not happy where they belong," Rose said.

Observation and memory were signs of intelligence. And I understood her point, which was vague, because she did not know the words "expulsion" and "dislocation."

My wife hardly knew me, but our daughter knew me well. Perhaps for the same reason, Rose was an enigma to Sweetie. So from her earliest years Rose and I had been confidants, spoke the same language. It was I who taught her the language, but the way she seized it and used it was a result of her intellect, which also isolated her and made her lonely.

Now and then my wife's old friends would show up. They played with Rose, who was susceptible to their careless exaggeration, their shouting, all their hollow promises. Promises were no more than penny candy, but the worst of it was that Rose believed them. Sweetie just laughed, seeing her child as a gullible stranger. But Sweetie was generous in her island way. She wearied of Rose's talkativeness, regarded the child's brightness as a kind of clowning, and in the way of a kind, unlettered, self-possessed mother, forgave her daughter for being intelligent.

I found Rose reading the *Advertiser*. She said, "He's still in the hospital."

"Having such a young kid at your age is like having a thirty-year mortgage," Buddy had said. How wrong he was.

I loved Sweetie because she was strong and good-hearted and beautiful — single men in restaurants looked up at her and swallowed when she walked by. I desired her, too. But I chose more often to be with our daughter, who knew me better.

A hotel is a hothouse. We were rooted there, always on view. Now and then I would come upon Sweetie in the lobby chatting with a man. I always knew when it was an old boyfriend, and it was always a shock. The look of them — the long hair, the tattoos, the T-shirt, the earring, their extreme youth, the way they talked — made me wince. But I was usually with Rose, and if Rose liked them for their friendliness, what could I say?

"Him," Sweetie said, laughing after one young man left the lobby and mounted his Yamaha. "All he did was ride down to the beach and drink beer on the sand."

That was my second shock: after almost nine years in Hawaii, I also had tattoos and an earring, and one of my pleasures was drinking beer on the beach. I headed for the beach because no one could find me there. The old boyfriend — his first name happened to be Ryan — knew that.

This was new to me, but appropriate. I had come to Hawaii as a refugee, building a new life on sand. But, married to a local woman, I somehow had come to resemble all her ex-boyfriends, and I wondered if I would become an ex-husband too.

Sweetie was apparently so simple, so unwilling to hold a conversation, it was impossible to know whether she had any secrets. It seemed to be true, as Buddy had said, that no one had secrets in a hotel. Sweetie was capable of great happiness. And she had learned, though I did not want to know how, that for a woman to keep a man's interest, she had to be sexually alert and willing. That counted for a great deal.

Rose said, "People are sending letters and cards to him. His daughter's name is Brittany. We had a Brittany in our class."

"What's she talking about?" Sweetie said.

At bedtime these days Rose asked me to tuck her in. We prayed for the man who had been buried in the sand.

Sweetie smiled without any interest. Rose bewildered her. She could handle the child, as a child, but whenever Rose showed a spark of intelligence or precocious insight, Sweetie laughed as though Rose had lapsed into another language.

The leaves on the lanai's poinsettias were looking crumpled, Sweetie said. They were pinched from an infestation of whitefly.

"They're suffering from rat bite," Rose said, wonderfully precise.

"Rats don't eat leaves," Sweetie said, missing the point.

What Sweetie called the banyan, Rose called the ficus, because I did.

"Ficus, ficus," Rose said, dancing. "Because I like us."

"I don't know what to do with her," Sweetie said.

That pleased me, because I knew just what to do with her. Send her early to Punahou School, make her happy with books and play, talk to her, listen to her.

Rose had an old hourglass egg timer I had bought for the pleasure of seeing her watch the sand drop into the lower half and turn it over and over.

"It's peeing sand," Rose said.

"Watch your language," Sweetie said. "The word is 'shee-shee.'"

But as with "rat bite," I loved it.

"Sand is time," Rose said.

Another day, Sweetie asked Rose, who seemed subdued and thoughtful, what was wrong.

"I'm in my blue period," Rose said, because we had been to the Academy of Arts the day before, looking at the Picasso.

Sweetie giggled. She had no idea. "Why doesn't she play in the sand like other kids?"

It seemed to me that was exactly what Rose was doing — a sort of sand, a sort of playing. Sweetie, so sure of herself, was a good example to her daughter in that respect.

I asked about John Kennedy Jr. — when was he due? Sweetie said, and in a voice of crisis, "Never mind him. What about Stephen King?"

"All these celebrities," I said.

"Was hit by a car. Was hurt real bad. He supposed to be a wreck."

These details were well known, even to me. I said, "What was that Stephen King story you were reading?"

"Listening to," she said, meaning an audio book. "I told you. Was about this supermarket. Like Foodland. Was these dinosaurs in it."

"Interesting," I said. "So, gross reality in the form of a careless driver on a country road in Maine now overwhelms his puerile and implausible fantasies."

"The fuck that supposed to mean."

Rose said, "It means his horror stories aren't as horrible as his car accident. Doesn't it, Daddy?"

We had already thrashed this out, Rose and I, over ice cream at the beach, the day we saw the beetle trapped in the footprint.

"I think you jealous of Steve," Sweetie said to me.

Perhaps I was. Certainly Sweetie had never gone Rollerblading listening to tapes of anything I had written.

"I'm not jealous. His work actually depresses me. And I just think it's salutary for a writer of horror stories to be reminded of what true horror is. It's not a dog that gets bitten by a diabolical bat and besieges a mother and son, or spooky ghosts that possess a writer in a haunted old hotel, or an arsonist who makes bonfires with psychic powers, or a creepy ten-year-old with clairvoyance who takes revenge on her schoolmates . . ."

"You finished?"

"No," I said. "Horror is a broken leg. A real novelist could have told him that."

"Like you?"

"Like I used to be."

"So what's 'salutary' supposed to mean?"

Rose said, "It teaches you a healthy lesson."

"Hybolic," Sweetie said. She remembered Rose's tone of voice — pedantic — without remembering the word or any of the pedantry. She wasn't annoyed; she was strangely fascinated, as though transfixed by a visible handicap. Sometimes people looking gouty limped across the lobby, and Sweetie followed them from the entrance to the elevator, frankly gaping.

"It's like the man at the beach. He was playing in the sand, but he almost died. That's worse than a horror story, because it's real," Rose said.

In time the man recovered from his injuries and went home. Rose said she was relieved. But a pattern had been established, and for weeks afterward Rose insisted that I put her to bed.

Tucking in this bright child was a lengthy business. And I was so preoccupied with Rose and my duties at the hotel that I was not aware of JFK Jr.'s visit until some days after he had left the island. Buddy told me, "Guess who was in town?"

I was wary of discussing this with Sweetie, but one day I raised the subject. It wasn't an idle question. After all, I knew, even if Sweetie didn't, that she was Kennedy's half-sister. Sweetie's friend Nainoa had given Kennedy his diving lessons. Had she met him?

She smiled, and color suffused her face, reddening her lips, lighting her eyes, making her even more beautiful, the coconut princess whom I had always found irresistible.

"What was he like?"

"I don't remember," she said.

76

Buddy's Big Night

WHEN OUR rich friend Royce Lionberg, after making
so many plans, buying a titanium watch and a new
car, and putting a down payment on an African safari
(gorillas in Uganda), saying how happy he was, how he loved life,
how he had the perfect present for that girl he loved, Buddy's
niece Rain in Nevada, then killing himself in the most deliberate
way — not much ambiguity in the death of a man who drives
himself to Pali lookout and hangs himself by slamming his tie in
the door of his Lexus — when all that sank in, Buddy stopped
talking about the future and was much happier. It was the past
that mattered.

"I want you to help me write my life story," Buddy said. I reminded him of the episode he had dictated to me, with the moral
"Never jack off a dog." But he said that was just the beginning.
There was so much more. This mood of reminiscence suited him.
He had chosen to be among people who could remind him of
witty remarks he had made or outrageous things he had done. He
stopped talking about his campaign to hold a topless hula competition, or start his own radio show, or open a gambling casino on
a ship anchored offshore or a revolving restaurant on top of Koko
Head crater.

"That's asking for it," he said. "Lionberg, when he made all
those plans. That was *bachi*."

The local word for a self-inflicted curse — asking for trouble.

Nowadays Buddy went to bed very late or sometimes not at all.
He was the worst guest I had known at the Hotel Honolulu: the

last one to leave the bar, the hardest to please at the coffee shop, the noisiest, the most demanding, and along with the departed Madam Ma, the most childish. But he owned the place, so what could I do?

Another thing about drunks is they repeat themselves, so for the third or fourth time Buddy was saying, "I want to go dancing."

Usually these nights he was too drunk to stand up straight, much less dance, but I stifled a yawn and humored him. It had been a long day, and I cringed whenever he spoke of his memories.

"With Stella," he said after a while.

Stella had been dead for years, but I took the remark to mean that he would dance holding the small heart-shaped jar that contained her ashes.

"Do you think dead people can see us?" he asked.

Like a child, he pleaded to be comforted at bedtime, though it was way past that. The Paradise Lost clock said two-fifteen.

"Maybe it's not a question of seeing. Maybe they know without looking. Kind of a consciousness thing."

What was I saying? Perhaps just hoping to soothe his troubled mind. He considered my explanation; I knew he was thinking of Stella. Alcoholic tears brimmed in his eyes.

He said, with a remembering whisper, "One time I was driving to town with Stella and she says, 'Let's stop and buy some mochi crunch.' I said no. We had an argument. Then it was over. We got to town on time."

I didn't understand it, yet I nodded as if I did.

"Why didn't I do what she wanted? Mochi crunch. It wasn't much." He heaved himself against the bar and tipped his glass with a sigh — adenoidal, rueful. "Now she's dead."

This night, like most nights lately, he was regretful. I could not see any memoir here, yet he insisted he needed me to tell his amazing life story.

I said, as though to a sleepy fretful child, "Why don't you think of the good times?"

"I could tell you a million stories!" Seeing Pinky entering the bar, his face fell. He said sourly, "Look, here she is, the wind beneath my wings."

Even I could see that Pinky was sulking. Scowling, her fists clenched, wearing a purple jogging suit that was shapeless on her small frame, she had one of those pinched shadowy faces that hid nothing — indeed, exaggerated the truth in shadows, especially when she was low. What was she doing up at this hour? Perhaps suspicious, wondering whether he was womanizing.

"Cannot find the clicker."

Buddy turned away from her. "Try using the buttons on the TV."

"Then I have to get up and get up and get up."

"So that's a big hardship," Buddy said.

Seeming to squint at the word "hardship" like an insect in the air, fluttering past her face — she twitched, didn't recognize it — she scowled again, and I knew a fight was starting.

"Find me the clicker."

Buddy said, "I wouldn't piss up your ass if your guts were on fire."

The time was now two forty-five, and I dreaded the long day that was about to dawn.

"I think the room girl lose it," Pinky said. "Give me Diet Coke."

Tran had long since gone home. It was for me to fetch the drink.

Buddy said, "Don't give it to her unless she says 'please.'"

I was so agitated and overtired the glass shook in my hand, the ice cubes clinking. Pinky extended her arm in silence.

"Don't give it to her!"

"Give me — now!"

This was one of those moments of dazzling clarity when I knew without having to remind myself that I was fifty-seven years old, a former writer and world traveler, a one-time literary success, who now lived on a small island with a simple wife and a small child, earning a low five-figure salary for managing one of the grubbier hotels in Waikiki, perhaps the only hotel manager in the world who was also a member of the American Academy of Arts and Letters, with the rosette in the lapel of my aloha shirt to prove it.

And I was holding a Diet Coke in my hand, standing between a quarreling couple, each of them nagging me, in a bar at almost three in the morning.

Buddy raised his hand to hit her. Pinky flinched, ducked, and muttered a word that sounded like "Freeze."

"She was brought up in a hovel in Cebu City, shitting in a bucket and eating woof-woof, running around barefoot. And now she can't live without TV and Room Service and, hey, pass the clicker."

"You make me so shame in front of peoples."

"He's family," Buddy said, meaning me.

Pinky pursed her lips and worked on the straw.

"Let me ask you something," Buddy said, and put his face near hers. "What was the best day of your life?"

"Don't know."

"Maybe when you married Mr. Meal Ticket?" It was his own self-mocking name.

"Nuh," Pinky said.

"Maybe when you were little?"

"Then I was a little animal."

That was the image I had always had. It was easy to see her crouched on her dirty knees, sniffing and blinking in a foul hut on a hillside.

"Maybe when you first came to the States?"

Pinky just held her glass in both skinny hands and glowered, saying nothing.

"The best day of my life started off like this," Buddy said. "Frustrating, things going wrong, guests on my case, the help going nuts, the plumber not showing up, checks bouncing. Everything sideways."

"What he saying?"

"Shut up. I want this in the book."

"What book?"

"Shut up."

Pinky sucked on her straw, silent but unafraid.

"But I was so used to it I didn't even realize how angry I was. You know me — I'm the one who doesn't take anything seriously. I'm the clown."

His attempt at making a funny face only made him look insane and possibly dangerous and more ill than ever.

"That night I discovered that the till was short about five hundred bucks. I figured the barman had stolen it, but how could I prove it? I was married to Momi then. She wasn't happy."

At the mention of Momi's name, Pinky became apprehensive. She was at her most animal in this mood, seeming to sense in advance when a threat was near, something upsetting about to be said or done — like a ground-feeding creature, spooked by instinct, a faint whir of peculiar molecules, a vagrant smell — and she made as though to flee. Buddy pushed her back on her bar stool.

"I was on Kalakaua, near the taxi stand. I had to get to the bank to drop the cash I had in the night deposit. Three thousand bucks in cash and traveler's checks."

He savored the moment, nodding at me, meaning, This goes into the book.

"Just then, two guys came over. One of them held the taxi, the other walked up to me. They were grinning — I knew exactly what was happening. They were going to rob me and take off in the taxi."

Hearing this ominous prologue, Pinky gathered herself compactly, like a monkey on a rock, moved her elbows against her sides, drew up her knees, shortened her neck. She seemed to know that a vicious blow was about to be struck.

"They didn't know that I'd had a bad day," Buddy said. "The guy next to me said 'Hand it over' while the other one opened the taxi door."

"So did you hand it over?" I asked.

Making me wait, calling attention to himself, Buddy gargled with his ice cubes, cracked them with his back teeth, spat them back into his glass, and gave me a taunting smile.

"I didn't know what got into me. I pulled back as if to run, kind of sucker-punched him, and then swung — a roundhouse — and connected with the side of his jaw. I felt his jaw crack, the bone under my fist. I loved the snapping noise. My fist felt like a rock. Every bad thing in my body shot up my arm and passed through my fist into that guy's jaw."

He weighed his fist as though he were measuring a handful of sand.

"It was the best feeling in the world. I had never punched anyone before. And not just the feeling but the sound of the crunch, like a basket breaking and seeing his eyes go dead and his legs wobble. He just crashed down. It was beautiful."

"Lucky punch," Pinky said, but she winced as she said it, for she had been startled by the story.

"Maybe. But it worked. I wanted to hit him again, but he was gone — on his back. He cracked his head open." Buddy sipped his drink, loving this. "The friend jumped over and helped him. I thought of hitting the friend too. My fist was a weapon of destruction. But then they both took a hike."

He swilled and swallowed the last of his drink with a satisfied gasp.

"That was the greatest day of my life. Nothing can compare with that. What did you think I would tell you? Something about sex or money? No, this was better than anything."

Now Pinky was fearful, looking at him in alarm, silent on her stool.

"That's for the book," Buddy said. "I'll tell you the rest later."

77

The Last Laugh

O N ANOTHER average day at the hotel, under the lovely sponged-looking skies of Honolulu, a young woman checking in asked for a discount because she was a travel writer. Guests could be ruthless, but ones claiming to be writers were the worst. I was summoned to the front desk to adjudicate.

"What's the most recent thing you published?"

She did not say, I did a think piece for *Forum* on penis size. But she might as well have.

At lunch I was told an elderly couple from Baltimore, the Bert Clambacks, had wet their king-size bed; another couple, the Wallace Caulkins from Missouri, a late check-out, had swiped the hotel's terry-cloth robes. Keola had put a bumper sticker on the staff bulletin board, *The Only Thing I'm Hooked On Is Jesus,* and Kawika countered with one of his own: *Hawaiian Sovereignty.* Rose said she wanted to change her name to Meredith. "Or Madison. Or Lacey. Or Brittany. But not Rose. And also I want a DVD player." Nigel Gupta, a guest from California, defying the rules (*No Glass Receptacles*), brought a jug of ice water, a bottle of whiskey, and a glass tumbler to the pool. He tipped over his table, resulting in so many scattered glass shards we had to close the pool. Among the guests who protested, Bill and Maureen Gregorian demanded a reduction in that day's rate and threatened a class-action lawsuit, since the pool was unusable. The elevator jammed; some guests were trapped for fifteen minutes; the thing itself was out of service for three hours. Guests had to be reminded not to hang wet bathing suits from the room lanais. A homeless man was reported wandering the corridors.

The homeless man was Buddy Hamstra. It was an example of how grim he had begun to look, how careless in his mode of dress, that the owner of the hotel, a multimillionaire in a dirty bathing suit and a Paradise Lost T-shirt, was mistaken for a tramp who had temporarily strayed from his shopping cart and his plastic bags.

Everyone found him funny; that became a theme. Without any effort on his part, he was rediscovered as a colorful character. This unasked-for comeback was so bewildering to him it made him furious, loudly so, resulting in more notoriety. "The old Buddy," people said, not realizing that his illness had made him seem clownish.

I waited for him to give me more material for his memoirs. "I'll tell you the rest later," he had promised. But there was no more. There was only pantomime, his blundering and shouting, and this unexpected excess energy made Buddy funnier than ever. He was angry at the world. Exasperated outrage is often the best comedy, for a protester's futile howls make him sound like a victim, the natural butt of a joke.

His cronies, constantly quoting him, attributed Buddy's new mood to the fact that he had found a method for getting rid of Pinky — to divorce her, give her some money, and send her away. The prospect of his new freedom, instead of concentrating his mind and making him lighthearted, confused him and made him explosive and forgetful. He had difficulty with names. He called Pinky, at various times, Stella and Momi. His friends found this hilarious.

Peewee said, "We're having dinner on the lanai. Someone asks Buddy to pass the salt. He just picks it up and drops it" — *dwops* it — "into the serving bowl of soup with a big splash."

"Is that funny?"

"We couldn't stop laughing."

To someone who asked for pepper, he made a big sprinkling gesture with the heart-shaped jar of Stella's ashes. "Just like the old days!" his friends said.

The mayor of Honolulu visited the hotel on a publicity tour of Waikiki, which was filmed for a promotion by the Hawaii Visitors Bureau. Buddy gave the mayor a lei, a raffia bag containing a jar of Peewee's salsa, some macadamia nuts, and a Paradise Lost T-shirt.

Buddy poked my arm and told the mayor, "He wrote a book!"

A microphone was brought over. Buddy said, "It's getting drunk outside," and farted. The mike picked it up and amplified it, making it sound like a car backfiring, so percussive that people jumped.

The mike also picked up Buddy's explaining to the mayor, "I had an intestinal bypass, your honor. My table muscle."

Buddy turned his big serious doggy-jowled face to the camera as the bystanders laughed.

On another public occasion, the Waikiki Hotel Association's Annual Prize-Giving, at the Hilton Hawaiian Village Coral Ballroom, Buddy stepped up to receive an award for the Hotel Honolulu: honorable mention for dessert, Peewee's coconut cake. He stumbled, took a fall, knocked over a tub of anthuriums, and landed near the first row. Snatching at the flowers for balance, he ended up on his back with fistfuls of blossoms. That was the memorable detail that made people laugh.

He became famous for his public stumbles. He fell at a Christmas party, collapsed on the beach at a surf-meet blessing ceremony, keeled over at the Merry Monarch Festival. He was not hurt, but in any case his new fame as a clown outweighed any of the injuries.

Our Aloha Chili Cook-Off entry was Peewee's Serious Flu Symptoms Chili. Buddy went up and down the street among the chili stalls, sampling the competition. When a camera crew from KITV asked him for his comments, he vomited on their hand-held microphone. Claiming to be dizzy, he sat down on a small girl's origami. Hearing that we lost, he screamed abuse at the judges, one of whom was the governor's new wife.

He gained more weight. He let children poke his arm to show how they left dents and finger marks in his puffy flesh. With children around him, prodding his body, he seemed dazed but happy, like a big hairy toy.

"Pinky's agreed," he said to me. I knew what he meant. He added that, apart from the money, her only stipulation was that she be granted United States citizenship. She had now satisfied the residence requirement.

When her citizenship application had been approved, and the

swearing-in day came, we all went to the federal building down-town, to make Pinky believe we were on her side, but in real-ity to support Buddy. Lester Chen, Kawika, Peewee, Tran, Trey, Wilnice, Fishlow, Keola, some of the girls from Housekeeping, Puamana, Sweetie, Bula and Melveen, his best friends Sandford, Willis, and Sparky Lemmo, and Rose and me — nearly the whole Hotel Honolulu family attended.

"Think of it as a farewell ceremony," Buddy said, helplessly farting, drowning out his own words with his backfiring.

We watched as Pinky, in a new dress and wearing a white hat and white gloves, took the oath and saluted the flag with a throng of others. She looked serious, no longer a young picture bride of long ago from the Great Expectations Agency video, but a grown woman, thin-faced, her big teeth bulging behind her lips like a mouthful of food.

Seeing Buddy staring, she turned away.

"Best sex I ever had," Buddy said. "Know why? 'Cause she's wacko." His eyes were glazed, perhaps with the memory of some-thing unspeakable. Then, seeming a little jarred by this, he said, "I'm not going to get married again. Just play the field."

Even haggard, he looked happier than I had ever seen him, beaming at the prospect of his new freedom.

The citizenship ceremony was much more heartfelt and solemn than I had expected. I was impressed by Pinky's upright posture, the tremulous way she held her head, her nervous clasped hands. There was pride, too, in the others, an assortment of people old and young, mostly Asian, with a sprinkling of Pacific islanders and a few grateful-looking Europeans. Their seriousness and close attention made the simple occasion into something momen-tous and gave allegiance — a word that was repeated — a power-ful meaning. New Americans — Pinky, of all people!

I prayed that Buddy would not pull one of his stunts, to upstage Pinky. I was so intent on this prayer and the progress of the cere-mony I did not hear him fall, though I heard the loud laughter and "It's Buddy!"

In the commotion I saw Pinky staring in fear. The citizenship candidates looked alarmed, as if a protester had invaded the cere-mony. I did nothing. I felt only annoyance, the sort a repeat of-fender inspires in his long-suffering friends. I raised my eyes and sighed.

But Buddy's closest friends were laughing hard. There was a variety of laughter peculiar to people who found Buddy's stunts funny — the rowdy hooting of oversize boys. The explosive, defiant sound of it was intended to irritate anyone not in sympathy, those who found Buddy childish.

Pinky bit her lip. She turned away from Buddy and toward the Stars and Stripes, her hand raised to complete the Pledge of Allegiance.

Buddy lay among the metal folding chairs he had brought down with him in his fall. He was vaguely smiling, as though in triumph: froth on his lips, his cheeks splashed with his own green slobber.

"Give him mouth-to-mouth," someone said.

"That's just what he wants you to say. Stop encouraging him."

"Cut it out, Buddy. It's not funny anymore."

78

Ashes

THE RISK TAKER, madly signaling for attention, is always preparing you for his death, and as time passes, this interminable anticlimax is more maddening than morbid. When death finally comes you just feel angry and want to blame the sadistic son of a bitch. That is what I had thought. It wasn't true. I wasn't prepared. It was worse than I had ever imagined, and I badly missed Buddy from the moment he was gone — missed him more because in his place was the strange, starved-looking, alien figure of his widow, Pinky.

Years before, Buddy had devised his own mendacious obituary. After his death, this was printed in the *Advertiser* exactly as he wrote it. *From the outside he seemed a clown, a fool, an incompetent, but deep down he was very serious, often weeping on the inside. He was proud of his ability to fix anything that was broken. He was proudest of being able to mend a broken heart . . .*

Pinky presided over the funeral, which was a mockery of the pointless pantomime we had rehearsed when Buddy had vanished for the sake of a practical joke. Bula pronounced a eulogy: "He a people person. He real nurturing. He like talk story. He a communicator. He a class act. He break down barriers. He so rich."

Hearing this, Peewee began to sob. His whole body shook. He covered his face and said sorrowfully, "Buddy go dancing."

As Buddy's friend and manager of his hotel I had been asked to say a few words. Peewee's sobbing embarrassed people, so I tried to strike a lighthearted note.

"Who was Buddy?" I said. "He was the man in the baseball hat who always sat in front of you in the movies, his head blocking the screen. The man who laughed out loud when an accident happened. The man who stopped to stare at horrible car crashes. Who spilled his drink in his lap and yelled, 'I'm not house-trained!' Who pushed the shopping cart too fast at Foodland, saying, 'Beep! Beep!' Who held up the line to tease the checkout clerk. Who shouted into his cell phone in the elevator. Who always wanted extra whipped cream and four sugars and extra cheese. Who argued with the man passing out leaflets. Who was the first to buy the newest gizmo, and the first to break it. Who hated the government and never voted, and maintained he was a good American. Who was always unconsciously auditioning for a part in a novel."

A stillness had settled over the ceremony. My eulogy had fallen flat. I sensed they felt I was being disrespectful, and yet that was what Buddy loved most — insult and anarchy.

Lamely, hoping to satisfy the mourners, I added, "Buddy was a man who never failed to pick up a hitchhiker, or loan money, or take in waifs and strays. I was one of those."

Buddy's ashes were scattered offshore, within sight of his beachfront estate. That same afternoon Pinky ordered everyone out of the house, for the day she became an American citizen, she had also become, as Buddy's widow, his heiress. In his fury, months before, when he moved into the Owner's Suite to escape his quarreling family, Buddy had cut everyone out of his will, leaving Pinky as his sole beneficiary. The sorry document was something even Jimmerson could not mend. Buddy had intended to rectify that, but he died before he could banish Pinky and make a new will. So Pinky had his millions; she had the Hotel Honolulu and the North Shore house; she had everything.

79

New Management

PINKY EVEN HAD ME — at least she thought she did. She believed that I came with the hotel. The day after Buddy died, she installed Uncle Tony on the North Shore with Evie and Bing and Auntie Mariel. And she took charge of the Hotel Honolulu, which meant she had charge of me.

"Peek thee rebbish," she said, snapping her skinny fingers. She meant the flowers, the leis and garlands and bouquets that had been strewn in the hotel lobby in Buddy's memory.

The finger-snapping was new to me. I hated it. She also rapped her knuckles on my desk. That was worse. The only pleasure I had these days was in hearing her call herself "Mrs. Hamster."

She ordered me to get the locks changed on the North Shore house. She demanded that I hand over all the keys. She opened a bank account in her own name, bought new clothes and shoes. She appointed Keola her driver, and since driving was easier than being a janitor, he transferred his loyalty from me to Pinky.

"She want see all the accounts," Keola said. He was her messenger, too. Her patronage gave him power.

"I see you got a promotion."

"I been kick upstairs. Next stop, Guess Services Associate."

She made me wait in the corridor outside her suite when I was summoned to discuss the accounts. And she received me seated, like an empress. Her orders were that I was to stop distributing the tips indicated on credit card receipts.

"There'll be trouble," I said.

"I give Christmas bonus."

The "I" was interesting. Overnight, she became the hotel, the house, the business, the bank account, everything Buddy had left. There was no "we."

Of course there was trouble. The waiters raged. Trey resigned, so did Wilnice and Fishlow. Before he left, Trey said to me, "Any time you need some stories to write, I could tell you billions, from the times I dropped acid." Tran threatened to go; as a poorly paid Vietnamese barman, he depended on his tips more than the others. But he hung on.

Pinky did not respond to any of the complaints. She said very little. I began to understand the nature of silence in the use of power. Instead of arguments and shouting there were various manifestations of silence, and a sort of subtle sulking, which had to be analyzed and interpreted, like the snapping of her fingers, or even the manner in which she walked away.

Sensing that I was being uncooperative, she sent for me again. She was propped on her bed, pillows at her back, stiffly dressed and imperious. She demanded that I rearrange her closet — all her newly bought shoes.

"Put them over here, all them."

I went to the closet, not to survey her footwear, but to reflect on my role here. This was not right. My lips were forming the words "I quit" when, behind me, I heard Pinky sob in her sinuses, like the whinnying of a little child.

"I no know what for do," she said, her eyes glistening.

This new American, a small, skinny, inarticulate woman, hardly thirty, with hairy arms and big teeth protruding in her narrow face, had the whole hotel in her bony fingers. Yet here she was, a millionairess looking like a waif, trembling at the edge of her big bed, her shoulders up around her ears.

"Please, you help me."

She looked so helpless I went over and, against all the rules, sat on her bed and tried to comfort her. Her hand was hard and scaly, like a chicken foot.

"Daddy," she said, beseeching me.

"What's wrong?"

She whispered, "I bad girl," sounding insane.

"I think you're unhappy because you miss Buddy," I said. "We all miss Buddy. He was a friend."

"He like spank me. He make me kneel down and eat him. Then he lock me in dark closet."

The look of shock on my face made her smile. She became playful and babyish again.

"I like too much," she said, curling her lips so I could see her purple gums.

I wasn't pure, yet I did not have it in me to engage in this game, which I could clearly envision, from the charade of my mistreating her and sexually abusing her, to locking her up somewhere in the Owner's Suite. If I treated her the way she demanded to be treated, however badly, it would be an enactment of her perverse power over me. She used her chicken-foot fingers to tug an answer from me.

"Sorry. You got the wrong guy," I said, standing up.

Her face tightened. Her eyes were scummy with hatred. "Get out for my suite."

She said *shweet*. The poor little thing was crazy. I knew my days were numbered. And after that she became an unambiguous tyrant. Tran resigned. Chen was miserable and so was Peewee. In their misery they became incompetent. The women in Housekeeping just wept. For the first time since being hired, I found the hotel impossible to manage, for I needed these people. I wanted to explain this to Pinky, but she kept to her room, the scene of her rejection. She was frightened, enigmatic, rude. Her new wealth had given her a sort of doom-laden quality, like a lottery winner trapped by the windfall and slowly self-destructing. And I was taken by surprise, too. Why had I not seen that all Buddy's foolery, his flatulence, his stumbles, his bad memory, and his popeyed look of suffocation signified that he had only days left?

One night around eleven, as I was locking my office, I saw Pinky in the lobby. She looked disheveled, uncertain, uncomfortable, limping in her new shoes, as though she had wandered in off the street. Yet I had also noticed a new Jaguar pulling out from under the monkeypod tree at the front door — Mrs. Bunny Arkle. The wealthy widow had begun to cultivate Pinky. This was in the nature of things. I was sure that, in time, Pinky would join the Outrigger Canoe Club, the Honolulu Women's Outdoor Circle, the Hawaii Opera Theater. She would attend the posh Annual Heart Ball, buy a table at the French Festival at the Hilton and the Christmas Silent Auction at the Honolulu Academy of Arts benefiting "at-risk teens" — would become a pillar of Honolulu society.

"What for you go home so early?" Pinky asked.

"This is my home," I said.

"What for you stop work?"

"I never stop. Say, is there something wrong with your fingers? They keep snapping for some reason," I said. "Why did you cancel the flowers?"

"I get cheaper in Waipahu."

Palama had been doing the flowers for five years, since Amo Ferretti's murder. And Palama was ill. He needed the money, and we were one of his last clients. I said, "Buddy liked him."

"Buddy dead." She walked away.

Small, dark-eyed, haunted-looking employees began to appear, scuttling: waiters, room girls, clerks, kitchen staff, moppers, scrubbers, mostly women — the Filipinos she had hired. They worked hard, they were answerable to her, and the hotel ran much as before. And as before, I had almost nothing to do with it. Pinky was impatient, mean with money, cruel to these newcomers, but the place was cleaner, better tended, more efficient. She had seemed a simple bewildered soul, yet she had a shrewd eye for cost cutting. Now there was a small vase of flowers in the lobby, but no flowers in the restaurant, none in the rooms. No one got a plumeria lei on arrival, or any lei. Bathroom amenities were discontinued — no shampoo, no bath gel, no plastic shower cap. Paradise Lost Happy Hour pupus were canceled, so were the bowls of mixed nuts. Buddy had insisted on bottles of Heinz ketchup and Tabasco sauce and a jar of honey at every table. The Tabasco was canceled, the ketchup was generic and, like the honey, it now came in a plastic squirt bottle.

Even though I had rebuffed her advances, Pinky kept at me. She insisted that I accompany her shopping, to carry her bags. She made me wait in the car with Keola, who took an uncouth pleasure in gawking at me as she gave me orders. In the stores at Ala Moana I would sometimes see her glaring at me, as though inviting me to turn on her.

"Put my shoes on."

I squatted and did so, marveling at the yellow bunions on her feet.

"You no like me," she said.

"I find you absolutely amazing."

My saying that just confused her, but it was true, she fascinated me, for the way she had worked her way up the food chain. The pathology of her story was the history of America — the twisted, tenacious little immigrant taking over from where the big, complacent Americans had left off. Pinky could not be faulted in her opportunism. She had saved herself and her family, while Buddy had allowed himself to degenerate and his family to slide into anarchy.

I had done little better with my own family. I had made no provisions, assuming, like an idiot, that I would continue to muddle along successfully. But my position was dire. I was fifty-seven. I had a small daughter and a poorly paying job. Living in the hotel, I had no need to buy a house. Now I could not afford one. I had come to Hawaii believing that I was in deep trouble; years later, it was much deeper.

Sweetie said, "Why you no say nothing?"

"Pinky's my boss. It's my job."

"So get a new job."

But since this hotel work had always been so easy, Buddy's favor to me, I was not qualified for any other job. As a young man I had always innocently believed that aging was progress. You lived and quietly flourished, as my father had done, and having reached late middle age you were settled and secure — comfortable, with your own chair and reading lamp and workshop, your own bed and books, your children bringing you news of the world. And you had no fear except the final one, of extinction. Yet I owned nothing. I was nowhere, living on a rock in the ocean.

"Why you no peek thee rebbish?"

My only satisfaction lay in smirking at her and pretending I could not understand what she was saying.

Within a month of Pinky's taking charge, the hotel, though it looked barer and more cheerless than ever, ran more efficiently than it ever had. I still checked the accounts before I passed them on to her, and I was astonished at our profits. Her cost cutting had worked. The new, smaller staff was mute — I hardly knew their names — yet they were desperately productive. Their motto seemed to be: Walk Fast and Look Worried. They scuttled from task to task. Their salaries were so low that we were making much more money. Without knowing the term "downsizing," but with a good grasp of the concept — probably from having been exploited herself — Pinky had streamlined the labor force and made the hotel cost-effective, running it along the lines of a sweatshop or a strip club. I knew that she would succeed — already Mrs. Bunny Arkle was her bosom friend. The time had come for me to leave, so I sent her my one-line note of resignation.

She didn't make me wait this time. She wore a white Chanel T-shirt with gold piping on the seams, gold slippers, and blue panties, looking like a spoiled child among all the pillows in Buddy's king-size bed. She was so small, so angular. She looked so unhappy.

Without my saying a word, she said, "I no want you leave."

"You don't need me."

"I need," she said. "Sit down — here," and she patted the edge of the bed. She pulled up her T-shirt, put her thumb in her mouth, parted her legs, and slipped her other hand into her blue panties.

"This isn't working," I said.

She went coy again, pulled out her thumb, yanked down her T-shirt. She said, "I need you listen, Daddy."

"Please don't call me Daddy."

She pouted, and then — perhaps to stir my sympathy, perhaps to shock me or impress me — she told me her story. Her childhood, the hut in Cebu City, Uncle Tony, the Japanese man, her trip to Guam, the visit to Hawaii as a dancer in a Korean bar, her flight to the mainland with Skip the motorcycle man, her days as a motel truck whore, her escape — all of it. It was a weird, upsetting tale, full of close calls, and it frightened me more than anything she had ever said or done before.

"Did Buddy know this?"

She shook her head sadly. "So now you know my story."

Not everything, but enough. Life is a series of decisions, people say. But it had not been that way with me. At crucial points in my life it was never a question of choosing but rather of having no choice except the obvious one, the only one. What looked like a radical decision was pure panic flight, when I had no choice but to jump.

"I no know what for do," she said. She plucked her T-shirt from the buds of her nipples. She looked hopefully at me again, her tongue against her teeth, as though mouthing the word "Daddy," and then her face fell. "What for you smiling?"

"Because I do."

80

Rock Happy

THE CLUSTERS of torch ginger, the heliconia and protea, and all the other flowers were gone from the lobby. Gone were Palama, Pacita and Marlene from Housekeeping, and Tran, who got a job at a Vietnamese restaurant and spoke of starting his own place, Apocalypse Now. Puamana fled to Puna District on the Big Island, where she had a calabash cousin. Buddy's topless hula posters, the freebies for Buddy's kids, the loaner beach umbrellas, the Nutty Nine-Grain Granola at the breakfast buffet — all of it was gone, and I was going, too.

At breakfast by the pool on one of our last days at the Hotel Honolulu, Rose said, "I want the other kind. This is yuck."

She dropped her piece of toast with sticky fingers, and instead of licking them, she wiped them on her napkin.

"What's wrong, baby?" Peewee asked. He was also on his way out, about to head for Maui to help at his son's bakery.

"I hate that honey."

When I tasted it I knew why. It had been another of Pinky's cost-cutting measures, her replacing the local honey with the Chinese honey that came in five-gallon pails and was poured into squirt bottles. This stuff was vile, with the dusty oversweet industrial taste of the Chinese corn syrup that had been used to adulterate it.

Peewee said, "We don't get Kekua honey no more."

Where had I heard that name?

"Lionberg's gardener," Peewee said. "Kekua's caretaker now. He took over the hives after Lionberg passed away."

So, even after Lionberg's suicide, we had still been buying his fragrant honey, which tasted of the North Shore, of eucalyptus and puakenikeni and ilima and gardenia, of red earth and big surf — Lionberg's bees toiling long after he had hanged himself. His name had not been on the label, so how was I to know?

The honey led me to visit Lionberg's house and Kekua. A drop in property prices meant that Lionberg's multimillion-dollar estate was unsalable in the late-nineties market. Kekua had stayed on as caretaker at the big rambling villa, with the impluvium, the lap pool, the orchid house, the rows of beehives, the Georgia O'Keeffe and the vandalized Matisse, the Fijian war clubs, Gilbertese daggers, Solomon Islands paddles, Hawaiian koa bowls, and dog-tooth leg rattles. Kekua did the dusting; the profit from the honey was extra.

The house and its contents had been kept intact, still in probate because of Lionberg's complex will and his contending children and several ex-wives. The rooms were full of his art collection, his gourmet kitchen gleamed, but the place was locked, empty of people, and looked forbidding in its neatness.

Was it a melancholy house, or was I projecting onto it my own yearning, for I owned nothing. But here, like a monument to irrelevance, was the Lionberg world of supreme luxury: Lionberg was dead. I knew more than I wanted to know of Lionberg's last year, his suffering over Rain Conroy, the young woman who was unattainable — too far, too young, too innocent, unwilling to be the captive wife of a man in his sixties on a remote hillside in the Pacific. The bees still buzzed, the predominant sound today in the late owner's garden.

"If the lawyer agree, you maybe go use the guest house," Kekua said.

Feeling superstitious I said no, and instead rented a place behind Lionberg's property, a small green bungalow, under a mango tree on a lovely sloping bluff of ironwoods. As at the Hotel Honolulu there was a monkeypod tree in front of the house, with clumps of tangled orchids clinging to its trunk.

"Them are hononos," Sweetie said. "Flowers come in March. Smell beautiful."

Though Sweetie was uneasy about the move — we were too far from town, she said — Rose was in her element. She delighted in the sound of roosters crowing. She wanted a dog. She found some friends and put herself in charge of them, telling them about the Waikiki hotel in which she had once lived, and enjoying the fact that they were impressed.

"Main thing about bees," Kekua said when I visited the estate. "The work easier for two people."

"You're in luck, Kekua."

I learned to harvest honey from Lionberg's hives. Kekua, a handyman, hammered together the shallow boxes, called supers, that we used for enlarging the hives, piling them like separate stories on the tenement of the hive. The towering arrangement reminded me of the Hotel Honolulu and how Buddy had referred to it as "multi-eye-story."

Kekua showed me how to split the hives. He identified the worker bees, explained how they created a new queen and how the drones went on a fertilizing flight. He smoked the hives and carefully lifted their lids ("Bees no like big noises . . . bees no like rain . . . bees no like cloud") and brushed the masses of smoke-drugged bees aside, exposing the racks of amber honeycomb. I poked my finger into the sun-heated comb and licked the warm honey.

"What you think? *Ono*, eh?"

"Yeah." And I thought, I am at last where I want to be.

In this lovely climate with long sunny seasons there were new blossoms every month, and never cold weather, much less a frost. So the bees flourished the whole year. With its long periods of idleness — and Kekua did the woodwork — this sort of boutique beekeeping was the perfect pastime, as well as a viable business.

"Like Sherlock Holmes," I said one day to Kekua.

But you had retired, Holmes. We heard of you as living the life of a hermit among your bees and your books in a small farm.

Exactly, Watson. Here is the fruit of my leisured ease . . .

Kekua smiled through his veil and kept chipping away at the accumulation of propolis on a hive.

"He's in a book," I said. "A detective."

Kekua shrugged inside his shapeless white beekeeper's suit. More than ever I was convinced that I was where I wanted to be, in a place where a good soul like Kekua knew propolis but not Sherlock Holmes, and as for books — as Buddy used to say, "We don't read 'em, we just chew on the covers."

In this gorgeous world, birds uttered long, meaningful phrases and people spoke in flat monosyllables. In the lunches I'd had with Leon Edel, we had told each other we were in the perfect place. And it seemed right somehow for Rose, too. I was happy to deliver her from Honolulu, and didn't have the heart to exile her to the mainland.

As for Sweetie, "This is the real country," she said. The woods frightened her, the wind in the ironwoods kept her from sleeping, the surf was far more powerful than in town, she got lost on the roads. She missed her friends, Puamana never called, there were no sidewalks she could skate on.

"What's that?" I asked her one day, seeing her on the sofa, bent over a thick book she held on her knees.

"*Anna Cara Neena*. Greatest book in the world," she said in a sad, cheated voice. "Supposedly."

"Who told you that?"

"Peewee."

She had bought it to please me, but she couldn't penetrate it. She sobbed with exasperation and said she was stupid. I took her in my arms and said, "Never mind."

"You're high maintenance," she said. "Tolstoy!"

"Tolstoys 'R' Us," Rose called out from the other room.

The smell of this big unread paperback moldering in the damp climate made the book unwelcome, but when at last I decided to toss it, to perform a kind of ritual purification, I could not find it.

There were feral pigs in the woods — hairy, black, tusky, wild-eyed. They made tunnels through the tall guinea grass. An owl, a local *pueo,* came out at dusk from the trees below the green bungalow as the neighbor's dogs began to bark. Roof rats nested in the eaves of the house — they got there by climbing up the mango tree, nibbling fruit on the way, and tottering along the branches, then dropping onto the roof. Wharf rats chewed holes in the walls. In Hawaii there were always rats, and always sharks just offshore, and cockroaches patterned like tortoiseshell, and geckos and moths and ten kinds of ants. These were the certain proof and reminder that Hawaii was paradise.

I did nothing for a while except work among the bees, straightening and tidying the hives, extracting the honey in the spinner, and sometimes driving with Kekua into town to sell it by the gallon at health food stores. I liked the simple-minded honey gathering — the bees did most of the work. Sometimes I was stung. The bee stings itched pleasantly afterward.

I remembered the day I had spent with Lionberg and the bees, having taken Sweetie along to meet him. He was harvesting honey. I helped him carry the boxes, which were the separate stories of the hive, filled with frames that contained the honeycomb. We took turns spinning the frames in the extractor. The honey whipped out of the cut combs and flowed smooth and syrupy out of the spigot at the base of the barrel. The honey gathered in the drooping drumhead of cheesecloth over a bucket and drained through in a steady stream, filling the bucket. There were always dead or dying bees in the heavy puddle of honey in the cheesecloth strainer.

Bees drown noiselessly in honey, without much of a fuss. It is almost as though they are enjoying it — they certainly seem so, in their drunken hesitation, their slow guzzling struggle, the brief flutter and then the stuck wings, the body mired, and at last, gorged on sweetness, they are motionless, dead and darker. It was the look of insects freshly caught in amber in the Paleozoic, all warmth and softness and smooth sap, and in time they became the black and broken bugs in the brittle fragments of resin. I used to watch the bees and think: This is the way a lush would drown in whiskey, sinking and smiling at the bottom of a still as the bubbles rose to the surface.

Lionberg must have known what I was thinking, because he made a point of marveling at the bees. He claimed he was an amateur beekeeper, but like everything else he did, he was careful and accomplished.

"That's you," Sweetie said, poking at a drowned bee in the depths of the honey puddle. It was understood that his life was perfect.

"No," Lionberg said. He smiled. "But I can imagine the feeling."

Now he was dead. Jogging along in sunshine in Kekua's pickup truck, I reflected on my life, beginning with my first misapprehensions. For years, especially your early years, you wonder how you're going to end up. Now I knew I had come to the end of something. Long ago, as a kid, I had seen myself as a fur trapper in the Canadian Arctic, and then as a doctor. In Africa I had imagined myself as an appointed official, or a chancellor of a university. Later, in England, my ambition had been to be lord of the manor — a particular manor in the Marshwood Vale of Dorsetshire. All this time I had been writing. Then my life was fractured. I fled and found myself with fragments of my life, and so swiftly had time passed that I had outstripped my ability to write any of it. And, having exiled myself to the Pacific, starting again with nothing, I suspected that there was no end for me but only a dying fall.

All those years running the Hotel Honolulu, and what had it come to? A rented bungalow in the woods of the North Shore. Rock happy.

"Write a horror book," Sweetie said. "Like Stephen King. He got bucks. And he hurt. You maybe take his place."

I just smiled at her and, as always, pondered her secret infidelities.

"Maybe they make it into one movie. Then you get more bucks."

"I've done that."

She had not known it. She was impressed.

"But I didn't keep the bucks."

"So what happen now?" Sweetie said.

"I'm waiting for a sign."

She understood that; it was how life was lived here. In Hawaii, we were small, like people on a raft. We lived on water, we watched the skies.

On that raft one day my daughter said, "Tell me a story, Daddy."

"I don't know any stories," I said. "Help me. Give me the first sentence."

"Once there was a man on an island," she began.

"He came from far away," I said.

"But what about the island?"

"It was a green island. He said, 'I want to stay here.' So he got a job at a hotel."

"What kind of hotel?"

"Very tall. Lots of stories."

"Tell me all of them," she said.

"Some of them are sad. Some are happy."

"All happy stories are the same," Rose said, wagging her head, pleased with herself. "But every unhappy story is different, unhappy in its own way."

I laughed and hugged her. "I wondered what happened to that book!"

With Rose's encouragement I renewed my old habit of seeing my life as something worth remembering and sharing. All the people I knew, their fortunes and their fate, were part of a bigger design, vivid and memorable because the hotel contained them — not specimens but souvenirs — part of my life.

When JFK Jr. got married, Sweetie had just laughed and said of his bride, "Such a howlie!" He died in a plane crash while I was writing my book — this book full of corpses — and Sweetie was inconsolable, like a sister, like a lover.

People elsewhere said how distant I was, and off the map, but no — they were far away, still groping onward. I was at last where I wanted to be. I had proved what I had always suspected, that even the crookedest journey is the way home.

FICTION

Blinding Light *"A bravura performance . . . enjoyable and worldly."*—*New York Times Book Review*
In this novel of manners and mind expansion, a writer sets out for Ecuador's jungle in search of a rare hallucinogenic drug and the cure for his writer's block.
ISBN-13: 978-0-618-71196-3 / ISBN-10: 0-618-71196-1

The Elephanta Suite: Three Novellas *"Stereotype-shattering."*—*Publishers Weekly*
The three intertwined novellas in this startling, far-reaching book capture the tumult, ambition, hardship, and serenity that mark today's India.
ISBN-13: 978-0-618-94332-6 / ISBN-10: 0-618-94332-3   HOUGHTON MIFFLIN HARDCOVER

Hotel Honolulu *"Extravagantly entertaining."*—*New York Times*
In this wickedly satiric novel, a down-on-his-luck writer escapes to Waikiki and finds himself managing a low-rent hotel. ISBN-13: 978-0-618-21915-5 / ISBN-10: 0-618-21915-3

Kowloon Tong: A Novel of Hong Kong
"A cleverly, tightly constructed, fast-paced book."—*New York Times Book Review*
One of many caught up in the hand-over of Hong Kong from Britain to China, Neville "Bunt" Mullard is forced finally to make decisions that matter.
ISBN-13: 978-0-395-90141-0 / ISBN-10: 0-395-90141-3

The Mosquito Coast *"A work of fiendish energy and ingenuity."*—*Newsweek*
In this magnificent novel, the paranoid, brilliant, and self-destructive Allie Fox takes his family to live in the Honduran jungle, determined to build a better civilization.
ISBN-13: 978-0-618-65896-1 / ISBN-10: 0-618-65896-3

My Other Life *"A seriously funny novel."*—*Time*
This wry, worldly, and deeply moving novel spans almost thirty years in the life of a fictional "Paul Theroux," who moves through Africa and between continents.
ISBN-13: 978-0-395-87752-4 / ISBN-10: 0-395-87752-0

The Stranger at the Palazzo d'Oro and Other Stories *"Masterly."*—*Vogue*
The intensely erotic story of an unlikely love affair leads Theroux's collection of compelling tales of memory and desire. ISBN-13: 978-0-618-48533-8 / ISBN-10: 0-618-48533-3

And don't miss Theroux's acclaimed nonfiction:

DARK STAR SAFARI: OVERLAND FROM CAIRO TO CAPE TOWN
ISBN-13: 978-0-618-44687-2 / ISBN-10: 0-618-44687-7

FRESH AIR FIEND: TRAVEL WRITINGS
ISBN-13: 978-0-618-12693-4 / ISBN-10: 0-618-12693-7

THE GREAT RAILWAY BAZAAR: BY TRAIN THROUGH ASIA
ISBN-13: 978-0-618-65894-7 / ISBN-10: 0-618-65894-7

THE HAPPY ISLES OF OCEANIA: PADDLING THE PACIFIC
ISBN-13: 978-0-618-65898-5 / ISBN-10: 0-618-65898-x

THE KINGDOM BY THE SEA: A JOURNEY AROUND THE COAST OF GREAT BRITAIN
ISBN-13: 978-0-618-65895-4 / ISBN-10: 0-618-65895-5

THE OLD PATAGONIAN EXPRESS: BY TRAIN THROUGH THE AMERICAS
ISBN-13: 978-0-395-52105-2 / ISBN-10: 0-395-52105-x

RIDING THE IRON ROOSTER: BY TRAIN THROUGH CHINA
ISBN-13: 978-0-618-65897-8 / ISBN-10: 0-618-65897-1

SIR VIDIA'S SHADOW: A FRIENDSHIP ACROSS FIVE CONTINENTS
ISBN-13: 978-0-618-00199-6 / ISBN-10: 0-618-00199-9

SUNRISE WITH SEAMONSTERS: A PAUL THEROUX READER
ISBN-13: 978-0-395-41501-6 / ISBN-10: 0-395-41501-2

www.marinerbooks.com